THE SPEECH

by Gabrielle Gouch

Publisher: Inspiring Publishers,
P.O. Box 159, Calwell, ACT Australia 2905
Email: publishaspg@gmail.com
http://www.inspiringpublishers.com

 A catalogue record for this
book is available from the
National Library of Australia

National Library of Australia The Prepublication Data Service

Author: Gabrielle Gouch
Title: The Speech
Genre: Fiction
ISBN: 978-0-6451228-6-2

Disclaimer

This is a work of **fiction**. Unless otherwise indicated, all the names, characters, organisations, places, events and incidents in this book are either the product of the author's imagination or used in a **fictitious** manner.

-1-

It's over. The best Christmas lunch they can remember. Juicy king prawns, citrus infused salmon with crisp peppered crust, grain-fed beef steak, chips and salad, garlic and herb breads oozing melted butter, red and white wine. Champagne bottles were popped, glasses clinked and over hissing and bubbling the staff has been thanked for their hard work of the past year. The tiramisu and the panna cotta with cherry sauce are gone too, and now the people are leaving, heading for the bar next door. All of them, except the two women still sitting at the table.

'You surprised me, Clara.'

'Surprised, why?'

'I thought you were an introvert. But you joined in, you even seemed to enjoy yourself.'

'I do like socialising now and then.'

'Now and then?' Marina asks, 'You have to socialise on every possible occasion.'

'I'm not that mad for company,' Clara says, smiling mischievously. 'Now only the best will do.'

'No sucking up, please. Seriously, good company, bad company, just socialise, go to every lunch, to every birthday celebration. Get involved, otherwise you'll end up friggin invisible.' *Friggin*, Marina rolls her Eastern European 'r', and Clara can hardly keep a straight face.

'Invisible, like me,' Marina adds.

'You invisible? Is that a joke?'

'It's not a joke. At work I am invisible.' She picks up the bottle of mineral water, pours herself a glass and drinks it in one go.

An airborne McDonalds bag whooshes past the window. On the street the tree branches are twisting furiously.

'Marina, look at that wind.'

'The southerly. At last. My body goes on strike whenever the temperature is above thirty. No wonder, I spent two thirds of my life in Europe.'

'And one third here. So, are you now settled?'

'More or less. My son was born here. He's fifteen years old and a real Aussie. He taught me English, swearwords and all.' Marina's face lights up with a loving, indulgent smile. 'Talking of Europe, are you planning to visit the Netherlands sometime?'

'No, not in the near future.'

'Don't you miss Amsterdam; don't you miss home?'

'I do miss Amsterdam, but my home is here now.

'You're lucky. I still don't know whether my home's here or where it should be,' Marina says.

The background music is petering out. A pause followed by the familiar voice of Elton John.

'Some people do,' Marina says.

'Do what?'

'Live like a candle in the wind.'

A fleeting cloud passes over Clara's face. 'I have to go,' she says.

Outside, the heat has broken. Shouting something, two boys skate past.

Marina smiles. 'Just like Alex.'

'Alex?'

'My son.'

'Oh.'

Clara looks at her watch: 'Marina, the next train is in six minutes. Do you think we'll make it?'

'Let's hurry.'

The train is in the station and they run to it. Two stops up the line, a noisy group of girls walk in and then a barefooted man with a beanie on his head descends the stairs of the carriage.

'Look at him,' Marina whispers, 'in a jumper in this heat.'

Tongue-tied, Clara shrinks into her seat, wishing to vanish. Vanish from the train, vanish from this world. The man is striding along, staring above commuters' heads as if he is just passing through. She is holding her breath. *He will go past. He will.* But just as her wish is about to come true, he trips.

'Bugger!' He kicks the guilty bag at the woman.

'Ouch!' the woman shouts and pulls her bag in.

Still trying to regain his balance, the man takes a couple of steps then looks up and as he does his gaze falls on Clara. 'Oh, it's you,' Peter says and sits down next to her. 'You finished work already?'

Clara is dumbstruck.

'We had the office Christmas party,' Marina bales her out.

'This is M-M-Marina, my colleague,' Clara mumbles.

Marina shakes his hand, her puzzled eyes on Clara. 'My ex, ex-husband,' she says.

'Yes, Clara is my wife.'

'Ex,' she hisses.

'There is no such thing as ex,' he says, puffs of acrid coffee smell accompanying his every word. 'You started your new job?'

'Yes,' she whispers.

'Doing what?'

But Clara is in no mood to talk, in no mood to prolong this conversation. Her thoughts race from what Marina thinks, to what to do next because the train is approaching Marina's destination.

'We're looking after public services,' Marina says, 'the services for the aged, children, the mentally ill and …'

'There are no mentally ill, there's only bad Karma,' Peter interrupts, and Clara freezes over.

The train is slowing down. Marina picks up her handbag. 'That's my station.'

'I'd better come with you,' Clara says, 'we still have to discuss that document.'

'I thought your briefing note's gone out already.'

'But there's still the report,' Clara's face is begging, don't, don't leave me with him.

'Oh,' Marina slaps her forehead, 'of course, we still have to discuss the report. Let's go.'

Peter jumps up to let them through.

Checking the ground, to avoid stepping on his feet, Clara tries to slip past, but suddenly there on the floor are no longer Peter's blackened toes, but prawns sloshed in tiramisu. Her stomach in her throat. *Oh no, not here,* and she swallows hard.

'Clara, forgive me for being an idiot,' Marina says as they alight from the train. 'Are you OK?'

'I've known less stressful times' And a few paces later. 'Please don't tell anyone what you just witnessed.'

'Who would I tell? Clara, it's only four o'clock, why don't we have a drink over there?' She points to the pub on the other side of the street.

* * *

The pub is sunk in semi-darkness, only the rays of the afternoon sun, slanting through the windows cut the gloom. Marina orders two glasses of wine and they head for the table in the corner.

Clara takes a couple of sips.

'Marina, the man you just met bears little resemblance to the one I married, the man for whom I came to Australia.'

'I've no doubt.'

'He was the smartest man I'd ever met. A physicist. And he was handsome. He had friends, one especially close. Science, politics, history, nothing escaped their sharp minds. His work colleagues looked up to him. Believe me that's how he was, he was not the delusion of my infatuated young mind. I thought I was the luckiest woman in the world. I wanted to be with him forever, I wanted to see him in the faces of my children.'

'So, what happened?'

'We were happy for a while. Our life was nearly perfect. There were some shadows, of course there were. I was homesick, I missed my father, I missed my friends, I missed Amsterdam, but I had Peter for the rest of my life. Him and our future children.'

'And then?'

'And then ...' Clara shrugs. 'It didn't last. Life is not a cruise on peaceful waters; the wind is never far.'

'At first it seemed a physical problem. He was tired all the time. The doctors put him through tests and more tests. They found nothing wrong.

"It's work, he's under too much stress," our family doctor said, and I believed him. Peter changed jobs. Things improved for a year, maybe two …'

'And when did you work out what was happening?' Marina asks.

'Not while we were married. A bad marriage is like a painting, you only understand it when you distance yourself from it. With hindsight, the signs were there for a while. There were issues, small ones. I tried to accept them, adjust.'

'Like the frog in water brought to a boil slowly …'

'Exactly. Things got worse. Every now and then … I won't give you the details, but we made up and we loved each other even more. I didn't realise that he was sick, that our world was about to turn upside down.'

Clara picks up her glass, swirls the wine and finishes it in one short gulp.

'How about a refill?' Marina asks.

'Why not?'

As she sits waiting, Clara's gaze is caught by the man sitting two tables away. *That harsh lined face. Is it from the sun or from a hard life? A hard life, Peter. He used to be so clean and carefully dressed.*

'There you are.' Marina places two glasses of red on the table.

'Medicinal,' Clara says and takes a sip. 'You'd better watch me, I get drunk easily, I'm near enough a teetotaller.'

'So, when did you work out what was happening?'

'The first time his behaviour didn't make sense to me was during my father's visit.' No, she will not go further, silence is safe, words might not be. 'Cheers,' she says and lifts the glass to her lips. Marina's eyes are burrowing into her.

Is it the wine, or Marina's watchful eyes? Suddenly the barbed wire surrounding Clara's life snaps. She has to unburden herself; the urge is unstoppable.

'My father flew into Sydney on a detour from a conference in India. I hadn't seen him since the wedding, nearly six years beforehand. Can you imagine my joy? The next morning we were having breakfast on the veranda. My father squinted into the distance. "What sunshine! What a distant horizon! This sky is higher than anywhere I've ever been."

'"Because the Australian sky is closer to Heaven," I said. The three people I loved most in this world were all sitting there with me. There was nothing more I could have wished for. I was happy, enormously happy. Until … Yes, it was definitely Thursday, I remember it well because it was late night shopping. The door slammed. Peter walked in, a box of vegetables under his arm. I reached to kiss him. His dark sad eyes looked at me a bit too long, strangely … hard to describe … as if … as if they were stuck on something which shouldn't have been there.

'Our daughter, Shosh, was nearly three years old. She adored her father. As soon as she heard him walking through the door she'd come running, "Daddy! Daddy!" And he'd pick her up and kiss her and throw her in the air and she'd scream, "Do it again, Daddy, do it again!" and laugh and chuckle. But that evening he just said, "Hi dear," planted a robotic kiss on her cheek, said hello to my father and disappeared into the bedroom.

'My father and Shosh settled on the sofa to watch television. I unpacked the vegetables, wondering what to cook when Peter appeared, terror in his eyes.

'"What's up, darling?" I asked.

'"My face is changing," he said.'

'What?' Marina stares at Clara. 'His face was changing?'

'That's what he said. I was baffled, of course I was, but I didn't want to be dismissive. He hadn't been himself for days. "Your face is not changing," I said, thinking that nobody in this world would believe that conversation. But my assurance didn't calm him.

'I had no time, I had to prepare dinner. I cut the avocado in half, it was black inside and I threw it in the bin. An argument followed about the avocado, about the shopping, about the household chores … He was enraged. I tried to shush him, I didn't want to upset my father and Shosh next door. He took no notice, so I let him have his say. It seemed to work because he headed for the door. But no, he turned around and veered towards me.

'Then something happened, something my brain couldn't process fast enough, something which defied reality. My feet were no longer in touch with the floor. I was flying, flying towards the wall, my insides smashed against each other. Then he slammed the door and was gone.

'I stumbled to the kitchen table and sat there trying to catch my breath. Stunned.

'Eventually the fog and confusion in my brain began to lift. I cooked the pasta, and was warming up the leftover ratatouille from the day before, when Peter walked back in. We sat down to eat and tried to talk as if nothing had happened …'

'Your father? Didn't he hear any of it?'

'Maybe he did, but I don't know how much …' Clara loses herself in thought.

'And then?' Marina asks.

'A few awkward days passed. The day before his departure, my father and I were sitting in a café when he changed the subject suddenly, "My dear daughter, I don't want to interfere in your marriage, but I'm worried. Is Peter aggressive? Does he abuse you?" The truth was that he never had, but a seed of doubt was sprouting inside me, but I couldn't burden him, and besides, what could he do? "Of course not," I said.

'"You have to tell me. I can't leave knowing you might be in danger."

'"He shouts, he's under a lot of stress at work." That's what I said, because that's what I thought at the time. His job was eating him up, his brilliant mind wasted on mundane work, having to jump like a locust, from one urgent project to the next. But that morning, sitting there, with my father looking at me worriedly, I wondered if what happened that day in the kitchen was not aggression, then what was it?

'The next morning, he flew out.' Clara lifts the glass and takes a mouthful, worry shadows playing on her face.

'And then?' Marina asks, 'What happened afterwards?' But Clara is miles away.

'What happened afterwards?' Marina tries again.

'A great deal.'

'Go on.'

'He was loving and attentive as if nothing had happened. Nothing had gone wrong. One day he came home with a ring, a gold ring with a big black onyx stone. "It's beautiful," I said half-heartedly. "Thank you." I thought that the ring was the sorry he couldn't bring himself to say, and I forgave him, sort of. I never wore the ring, I didn't want to be reminded of what had happened, I wanted to forget, think of it no more.

'A few months went by. At times when my mind strayed, the confusion and fear of that evening returned, I pushed them away quickly. I managed to convince myself that it had been the most unusual misunderstanding. It belonged to another time, another marriage, another life. But then he proved me wrong …

'Marina, I think I'm drunk, I'm talking too much.'

'You have to talk. Talking clears the mind, it lightens the burden. What happened next?'

'Life went on. But I can't explain to you what went on inside our marriage or why. Much of it I can't explain to myself. Me, who was in the middle of it all, for whom the internal conversation doesn't even involve words. Even in a bad marriage there are some good, even happy days. On a bad day I tried to look away, disconnect, tell myself that there is no sky without a cloud, no marriage without problems. You can always find excuses.' Then after a long pause, 'Marina, the less choice you have, the more persuasive your excuses become. You convince yourself that your situation is quite acceptable,' and after a pause, 'but we did have a few happy years together, and I don't want to forget those.' Then looking at her watch, 'Marina, I have to run, I have to pick up my daughter before six.'

* * *

What felt right to Clara minutes ago, doesn't anymore. *I should have kept my private life out of that conversation.* She feels as if she has taken off her clothes and now, she has to walk nude. What if the people in the office find out? She tries to calm herself, Marina is not the sort to blab. Besides, who would she tell? She has no friends in the Department.

Walking home, Clara's mind can't stop replaying the encounter with Peter. After all these years she still finds it hard to accept what happened to him, she finds it hard to reconcile him with the man she met that day nearly ten years ago.

<h1 style="text-align:center">-2-</h1>

Ten years ago, her life couldn't have been more different. Ten years ago, she was living on the other side of the globe, in her native Amsterdam, the city she cycled through most days and knew well enough to be a guide. She knew where the best croquettes and the tastiest herrings were sold. She knew the cheapest cafes where one could sit with friends and talk for hours. She knew where the theatres, the best bookshops and libraries were. At the time, Australia couldn't have been further from her mind. A continent on the map, a country in the Southern Hemisphere, not a country she knew much about, or was interested in. Not until that early April morning in 1988.

She was standing at the window, looking at the grey cloud sagging over the city, over the sticky wet cold. Below, in the narrow street, the breeze churned the puddles between the cobblestones and the reflections of the streetlights still on. The street was waking. Opposite, two shops had thrown their doors open. People, umbrellas, walked past.

It had been a long winter and spring was late to arrive. She stood there thinking that it would be a cold rainy day again, a day of long sleeves and jumper and coat and heavy shoes.

She longed for summer. She longed for sunshine and light clothes and bare arms and trips with her friends cycling through the fields of tulips and green land, and laughter and startled birds whooshing past.

The phone rang.

'Father, are you at work already?'

'Just got here. Clara, make sure to wrap up warm, it's cold out there.'

She smiled. *He's mothering me again.* She was used to him worrying about her, used to his caring words, which like a warm cocoon had enveloped her ever since she could remember.

'By the way, there's been a change in my conference schedule,' he said. 'One of the moderators is in hospital and I've been asked to stand in for him. Sorry, but I'll have to leave next Monday.

'More freedom for me,' she laughed.

'Clara, make a list with all the things you'll have to take to Dafna, so you won't have to rush back and forth like you did last time.'

'I'm not moving to Aunt Dafna's again. I'm staying put.'

'I don't like you being on your own every evening.'

'But father, I'm twenty-two years old. Twenty-two, remember? I don't need babysitting, my nomadic days are over,' she said and held her breath.

The line was silent.

'Ok,' he said at last, 'but promise me that you'll ring her every day and go for dinner every now and then.'

'I will. So have I come of age finally?' She laughed. 'How about a celebration before you go?

'This Friday?'

'It's a date.'

My coming of age. She smiled to herself and began packing her backpack. Coat on, she picked up the umbrella and opened the door; and there it was again, the putrid smell, the smell of witches' brew to entice back the departed. She rarely got angry, but now she was furious and headed to old Mrs Jansen's door across the landing. After the third ring, the door opened and in front of her stood a young man she had never seen before. He looked at her questioningly, Mrs Jansen was out, and he was from Australia, a friend of her friend.

A tourist in shirt and pressed trousers? Well, it takes all sorts.

Could he help with whatever she wanted, which was?

Help? Her expectation of a major confrontation well and truly crushed. 'Ah, the cat, but you can't help me.'

'I like cats …'

'This one is trouble, and your friend can't be bothered to train it.'

'She's not my friend, she's my friend's friend.'

'Whatever. The fact is,' and whether for effect or because the pent-up anger had finally found an outlet, she raised her voice, 'her cat peed in front of our door. Again.'

He looked at her confused.

'Over there, next to the pot plant.'

'I'll tell her when she …' Just then her dog appeared, barking loudly, trying to squeeze past.

'Oh no!' Clara retreated into her doorway.

'Don't worry, he doesn't bite.'

'But he's too friendly.'

'What's wrong with that?'

'Everything.'

He looked at her puzzled.

'Well, you might think that being jumped on by this dog is a privilege, being licked by his sloppy, wet, tongue is pure love. Well, its love and my revulsion don't make for good bedfellows. So, can you tell your friend, sorry your friend's friend, that she either trains this mutt to keep to himself and her stinking cat to pee and shit inside her flat or …' *Or what?* Her mind searched for the threat of all threats. *Kill the cat? But I couldn't kill a mouse.* 'I'll complain, to the authorities,' she said near enough shouting.

He laughed. His shiny, dark eyes narrowed. 'Come in, I'll make you a cup of coffee and we can talk about it.'

She had nothing more to say about the dog, or about the neighbour, but the idea of delaying the library seemed very attractive.

'I have a better idea, I've been inside that flat. Once! Let's go to the cafe around the corner. It's a mutt free place.'

The introductions over, Peter locked the door and they started out towards the cafe.

'Where were you heading before the cat peed on your plans?' he chuckled.

'To the university library.'

'You're a student?'

'Majoring in English and French. My last year. After that, no more essays and exams. None for the rest of my life,' and she had to stop herself doing a celebratory pirouette. She did have ballet lessons when she was young.

As they were sipping the coffee, he told her that he was doing a Ph.D. in Physics.

Ph.D. in Physics? Wow, he must be clever, she thought, looking at the wisps of hair on his hand.

'It's not going well.'

'What's not going well?' she asked.

He looked at her, confused. 'My Ph.D.'

'Oh.'

'I took a month off to cool my brain, move my thoughts away from the same old track. Immerse myself in art and history. There's so much to see here.' He hoped that while he was tripping around, his subconscious would keep churning on his research and when he returned to it, he would see the problem from a new angle. 'New angle, new ideas. At least I hope so.' His eyes on a couple of photographs hanging on the walls.

'Do you like them?' she asked.

'They're very atmospheric.'

She knew it, black and white photographs, of lives long past, would be just the thing for a man dressed like his accountant grandfather. Still, he's definitely handsome.

They talked about Australia, they talked about his week in Paris, the five days he spent in Italy. He was especially impressed by the historic Bologna University library.

University library? 'Oh my God, my friend is waiting!' She picked up her backpack, 'I have to run.'

Nicole had been waiting in the student's cafe for nearly an hour and she was keen to get on with the essay. They discussed the structure, the main points to cover, and then the topic shifted from poetry to love and whatever else crossed their minds. Eventually they had no choice but to retire to the library and work on the essay.

Late afternoon, the next day, Clara was polishing the essay when the doorbell rang. It was Peter Steinberg.

'Would you like to go for a walk?'

'Uhm.'

'Come on.'

'Just give me an hour to finish my essay. You know what? I'll rush it through. Come back in forty-five minutes.'

That evening they walked around the canals and they walked around the cobbled streets. She showed him old buildings, churches, and bridges.

The following days they visited museums and art galleries. Peter knew a great deal about art, but then he seemed to know a great deal about everything. A twin of the encyclopedia, she thought.

'Clara, we've seen art, we've seen history, how about we visit the science museum now,' he said one afternoon.

'Science museum? No way. Science is behind me, thank Heavens.'

'Just one hour. Please.'

'An hour for you will feel a lifetime for me.'

'Don't exaggerate.'

'Peter, my father wanted me to become a scientist. I wasn't greatly attracted by it, but I took his advice and enrolled in a science course. It took me six months of university to realise that I don't care much about the ultimate truth. The relative truth, perceptions, are much more interesting to me. What motivates people, how happiness magnifies beauty, while misery diminishes it. Nowadays I live in the world of the arts and literature and I'm not straying. And poetry, all poetry. As far away from science as possible.'

'C'mon, you'll enjoy it. I promise.'

Instruments, machinery, facts, were not for her. She was a dreamer, her mind comfortable only in the domain of the unmeasurable and unclassifiable. In the fog of beauty, of literature, of intense feelings.

'You know what?' He interrupted her thoughts, 'let's go stargazing instead. We'll have dinner then go to the observatory.'

Darkness had descended on Amsterdam by the time they looked through the telescope.

'Wow!' She cried. 'The sky's studded with stars. Millions of them.'

'Far, far more than millions. Their number is unending. Infinite. Some are dead now, extinguished. What you see is the light they emitted when they were still alive.'

'So, some of these lights are the footprints of the past?'

'Of billions of years ago, isn't that sheer poetry?'

She did not reply, her forehead creased from trying to understand what he just said.

'Maybe the past never vanishes, maybe it never leaves us,' she said pensively.

By the time they left, the streetlights glimmered, their reflections playing on the Amstel River like tiny fires. The church spires pierced the shadow of the sky. That night Amsterdam looked to her a fairy land, people walking past more alive, more beautiful than ever.

A few days later she showed Peter the university and introduced him to Nicole.

'Where did you find him?' Nicole asked later, Clara told her the story.

'I like cats, but I never knew that cat pee could bring you luck.'

'Luck?' She shrugged. 'He's too square, besides he's leaving in a couple of days.'

Not long after Peter left, a letter arrived thanking her for all the sightseeing. More letters followed. Her answers were short, she was busy finishing her degree, and afterwards? She had no idea, but she was not ready to bury herself in a job. She needed a holiday, a long holiday. Amsterdam felt claustrophobic. Maybe it was the sameness of her days, maybe she was bored by her all too familiar surroundings. The grey old buildings looked at her, heavy and tired. She yearned to breathe a different air, see a different sky, absorb the colours of a different world. She had to spread her wings and fly. Peter kept inviting her to Australia. *Australia? Too far. Then where, another European country?* She had tripped around a few, the others she could visit on a short holiday, even on a weekend. Peter wrote to her about the places he would take her, about the miles-long beaches, the rainforests, the snakes and the crocodiles. *Steady on Peter, steady on. I do need a change, but I'm not wild obsessed.* But the sunshine, the beaches and rainforests sounded like Heaven and six weeks after finishing her degree she took off to Australia.

* * *

Two days later she was looking through the taxi window greedily, staring at the Southern Hemisphere. The sky a brilliant blue, the sunshine reflections of diamonds, and in front of her the promise of a real holiday. The taxi was flying past houses and mowed strips of grass. Not a soul on the street. Is this Sydney? she wondered.

Peter squeezed her hand, 'We're going to have a great time together.'

Australia. No tired old buildings, none of the narrow streets of Europe, no history weighing down its people Clara thought as she strolled around Sydney, the next day. The multi-storey buildings, their age measured in decades not centuries, looked uninspiring, but the mere contrast to her home city was so refreshing.

The following Sunday, she and Peter, hands interlinked, walked around Sydney Harbour, past the wharves where ferries took off, past restaurants and cafes. In the distance, yachts sailed drowsily, as a hydrofoil sped past. The Opera House looked on; the sails of its roof flooded with a sunny glare.

'Clara look, look how architecture and nature amplify each other's magnificence. And the result?'

'Is heavenly. And those speckles dancing on the water ...'

'Maybe they're celebrating, celebrating beauty and the joy it brings. As Keats said, "A thing of beauty is a joy forever."'

She looked at him, *Peter, poetry and beauty. I never would've guessed.*

It was past two o'clock by the time they got back to Peter's mother, Eszti, a small woman, quick and opinionated. Cute in a way, Clara thought. Lunch was waiting, the kitchen table set. It was not the sort of kitchen she had at home, but huge; the floor covered by worn vinyl, the room lit by a fluorescent ghostly light. But as they ate and talked and argued about the state of the world, Eszti forever coming and going, serving and contradicting, while Peter, sometimes serious, other times with a smile, winked at Clara as he teased his mother. And Clara could hardly keep a straight face.

The days rolled on; Peter saw to it that each was a new experience. A trip, a visit, a different beach, a concert.

Ever since she arrived the sun had never stopped shining, but one day the weather turned. A strong easterly blew grey clouds towards the land. By evening the rain began to fall. It was Saturday and they were due at Peter's friends for dinner.

Ed, Peter's best friend, was a man of few words and long pauses who took time to venture an opinion. A man older than his age, Clara thought at their first encounter. Toni, his wife, a tall, thin blonde with the boundless enthusiasm of an adolescent, was a refreshing contrast at first, but at times her relentless enthusiasm would grate on Clara like a never-ending high-pitched operatic voice. Theirs was a perfect marriage, he set the rules and she obeyed them. Not a submissive woman, just an indulgent, accepting one.

That night the wine must have untied his tongue because Ed was unrecognisable. He talked and talked. He was telling her what it was like to be the sons of migrants in Australia, in the early seventies.

'We were different from the other boys, and being different was a sin.'

'Different in what way?' Clara asked.

'Well to start with, there was the serious issue of our strange sandwiches.'

'Strange sandwiches?'

'Yes. As they unwrapped their neatly packed white bread slices held together by a thin layer of peanut butter or vegemite, we unwrapped our slices of brown bread, no two the same thickness, loaded with salami and pickled cucumber. You should've seen the disgust on their faces …'

'The pickled cucumber wasn't our only problem,' Peter said, 'Most boys lived for cricket and rugby. We tried to play cricket, tried very hard, we were hopeless. And rugby …?' he shrugged. 'We had as much interest in it as a tree in a dog. So, we were not friendship material. Lucky us, as it turned out.'

'Lucky?' Clara asked.

'Yes. Since we didn't agree with them on most things, we had to think for ourselves, form our own opinions.'

'Clara, we got ourselves two strange boys,' Toni said with a conspiratorial smile.

'Strange?' Peter pondered aloud. 'I guess difference can look strange to some people,' and after a pause, 'Was my mother strange? Because in the seventies no one would have stood out more than my mum. You should have heard her stories every time she came back from a parent and teachers' night. I cringed …'

'Go on,' Toni said.

'Don't think I can. Don't like laughing at my mum.' He winked, his face one mischievous smile. 'Except privately.' But then he turned serious. 'She's been through a lot.'

'Tell us, we won't tell anybody,' Toni said. 'Would we, Clara?'

'Of course not.'

'OK. Some of it she told us, some of it I pieced together. It went like this: My mother, not an inhibited soul as you well know, would always ask a question. "I beg your pardon?" the teacher would say and my mother would repeat the question louder, her accent even heavier. To which the teacher would say, "Sorry Mrs Steinberg, I didn't quite get what you're saying," at which my exasperated mum would repeat the question again. As I listened to her 'w's replaced by 'v's, and 'th's' by 'd's, I could see my teacher's face crumpled from concentration. I wanted to vanish from this world. "These teachers can't even comprehend a simple question," Peter said in a heavy Hungarian accent, then turning towards the corner whispered, "Sorry, mum. No-one'll tell anybody about it."'

Laughter.

'But she wasn't going to worry about anything, because to quote the teacher, "Peter's doing well." She said this again and again.'

'Doing well?' Ed asked in astonishment. 'You were not, "doing well," you were doing brilliantly.'

'Anyway, that's what the teacher said, and my mother would declare that she'd save herself the time and not go to the next meeting. I felt sick with embarrassment. My mother's accent was close to impenetrable. I never told her; I didn't want to hurt her.'

'Peter, you're exaggerating,' Clara said, 'I understand her perfectly well. And you know what? Her English is excellent.'

'It is now, don't forget it's fifteen years since then. And her accent's reasonable, but when she's flustered, or dealing with authorities … But back to me and Ed, it wasn't easy to be the son of migrants, but talking to Ed about it lightened the weight.'

'On both of us,' said Ed. 'We didn't understand our parents. When they told us about their life in Europe, they talked about so much misery and yet there was a longing in their voices. It seemed to us that the youth of our parents had been so much worse and so much better than our own. Now I have some insights why, but at the time …?'

Ed filled their glasses. 'To our friendship,' he toasted and through his heavy lenses his smiling blue eyes diminished to a slit.

'Look at him,' Toni said. 'He looks like a big happy boy.'

Ed objected to being called a boy, and Toni laughed and so did Peter and turning to Clara he looked at her with eyes teary from laughter, or love, she could not work it out. Meanwhile the champagne kept flowing. 'Just one more,' Ed replied to their objections and poured each one a glass. Then another.

'Once we started university, cricket and rugby took the backstage. Science took the foreground. Finally, we were among like-minded people.' Ed paused in contemplation. 'Those were good times. When you're eighteen nothing seems impossible. Deciphering nature, glimpsing the universe was all within our reach. Wasn't it, Peter?'

'It was. But I didn't know how enormously difficult it is to advance the boundaries of human knowledge. I've spent nearly two years on my PhD and what have I got to show for it? Nothing. Maybe it's time for me to pack it in, get a real job.'

'Don't you even think about it. Sometimes it takes many years to get results.'

'Ed, university research is not for me.'

Ed stared at him in incomprehension. 'I find that hard to believe. No, not hard. Impossible.'

The conversation shifted to the next weekend. Should they stay in Sydney and go to a concert, or go away for a day?

'Let's see what the weather'll be like,' said Ed.

On the way to the car Clara wondered whether Peter would give up on his PhD. She understood why he might. She couldn't imagine working for years without a result, without accomplishing something. But Ed didn't think he should, was he right? And the way he looked at Peter ...

She had met Ed twice before, he was so serious, so grave, he would intimidate her into near paralysis. He tried to make her welcome, chat to her. Nothing interesting, nothing to nourish her mind, just trifles. He couldn't keep it up, but he went on trying. Their chat more and more embarrassing, made her shrink into herself. But tonight, she saw another side of Ed. Tonight she saw that he can be good company.

'Penny for your thoughts,' Peter said.

'I didn't realise how close you and Ed are.'

'We're like brothers.'

'More like twins. Identical background, same interests, at times you even complete each other's sentences.'

'Careful, we're not interchangeable.'

'Non-identical twins, silly.'

'That's better.'

Late afternoon, next day, it was raining again. Coming out from the movies, her hand in his, they huddled up under an umbrella and walked back to the car. They walked in perfect step; their bodies close to each other as if it had been one. And she knew that with Peter next to her she would never, ever be alone.

* * *

Her holiday was coming to an end. It had been a dream, but the time to wake up, the time to say goodbye to Peter, to Eszti, to Australia, was approaching fast. She would soon be back in Amsterdam, back with her father and her friends. But what about Peter?

'What is love?' she remembered Nicole asking in one of those aimless, meandering conversations they used to have.

'Love?' She had not been in love with Hans, the young man she spent a few months with, neither had she been in love with Jan, Hans's exact opposite. They were like a few weeks of sunshine after months of rain. But then the rain set in again.

Who would have thought that in Sydney, so far away from her father and her homeland, she would find out what love is? When Peter kissed her, the world seemed filled with goodwill, the birdsong even more enchanting, and when they made love their bodies melted into each other's, lost in the ecstasy and the contentment of one being. And she knew that if he left her, she would grieve for years. But how could she leave her father on the other side of the world? How could she leave Nicole and her other friends? But she couldn't leave Peter either. 'What should I do? I can't go back to live in Amsterdam any more than a baby can go back into its mother's womb.' But she had to, her visa was about to expire.

So, she returned to Amsterdam. To Amsterdam and its winter, got herself a Dutch–English translator's job in a publishing company and tried to settle down to her old life. But Peter's weekly letters unsettled her and a missed letter unsettled her even more.

Spring arrived. The renewal it used to bring fell flat on Clara. And then at the end of May her father departed to a conference just as Nicole and her boyfriend were in Norway. Clara felt as if she had been suspended in the middle of nowhere and abandoned. Abandoned, and ashamed of her thirst for company. She was an extrovert. Loneliness, solitude, made her restless and sad, and that Sunday she felt lonelier than ever. She walked into her father's study, looking for something to read, when she spotted a small globe on the shelf. She could not remember seeing it before. Absentmindedly, she spun it around. And there was Australia and midway in the south was Sydney. She stood there lost in memories. Of sunshine, of togetherness. Of love.

Somewhere a door slammed. The image vanished. *No, I'm not with Peter. I'm thousands of miles away. Thousands!* To her that was not just a number. She had travelled that distance. She had flown over oceans and continents; she had felt the suffocatingly slow passage of time. Sydney forever hiding. Distant, unreachable.

I'm in love with Peter. So why am I still here? Why am I a world away from him?

Two days later her father was back. Next morning, when Clara walked into the kitchen, he was sitting in his dressing gown, busily writing.

'How's the paper going?' she asked and began setting the table.

'It's coming along. It's only in the conceptual phase. Plenty of time, it isn't due for six weeks.

'It's my last for this year,' he added, 'No more papers, no conferences. I'll be staying put.'

'Practicing being a lounge lizard?'

'Why not?' he smiled, not his usual smile, but a thinking, pondering smile.

There was a thick silence. A silence viscous with words, which neither had the courage to utter.

'Clara, what have you decided?' David asked finally.

'Father, I've agonised for months. I don't want to do it, but I have to. I have to emigrate. I miss Peter. Painfully.'

He kept looking into his cup, as a fortune teller looks at coffee grounds.

'I'm very, very sorry,' she added.

He didn't reply. Slowly, he spread the marmalade on his toast then as if he had finally found the words which evaded him, he looked at her.

'My dear daughter, it's the way of the world for the young to adventure away and the old to be left behind, but I wouldn't be doing my duty as a father if I didn't warn you that emigration is a huge step. You might be bewitched by the novelty of Sydney, by Australia, but eventually you will miss your country, your language, your friends. You will even miss me.'

'No, Father! You're the one I will miss most.'

Silence returned to the table; a silence thick with sorrow. She too was sad, sad but relieved. She had told him, she had cleared the air, and she would emigrate.

'I can only say that if you love Peter as I loved your mother, you should go. Apply for a visa and go.'

She knew that his heart wept. But so did hers.

She told herself off. 'You've agonised enough. Can't you see that you've outgrown your old life? You have to do it; you have to emigrate.' And it surprised her how cold and detached she suddenly felt. As if a curtain of ice had dropped between her and her father. That curtain would not melt for months.

A year passed and the much-awaited visa finally arrived and so on a cloudy September day, David loaded her suitcases into the boot of the car. They picked up Aunt Dafna and headed to the airport. The memories of that day stayed with her, the images vivid as if she was still at the airport, standing in front of the departure board, checking for the Bangkok flight, the parting, Dafna crying, her father's tired face and then the flash of an encouraging smile as she crossed into the no return area. Into her future.

Did she cry? If she did, it wouldn't have been for long. Peter was waiting for her on the other side of the world.

-3-

She had been back in Sydney for more than three months, back to Peter's love, the sun and the beach. Life was still a holiday. Even more so on the days when Peter came home early, which he did often. He had lost interest in his PhD research and was looking for 'a real job,' as he put it.

It wasn't quite three o'clock that Friday when Peter opened the door looking happier than he had been for a while.

'Clars, I have some good news,' he said and kissed her, than kissed her again. 'We can finalise the date of the wedding.'

'What are you talking about?'

'I got a job. Look,' he handed her a letter.

She snatched it from his hand.

'It's the computer programmer's position you told me about?'

'That's right, and didn't we say that once I have a permanent position, we can set the date of the wedding. So end of the summer? What do you think?'

She put her arms around his neck. 'I think I love you,' and after a pause, 'I'd better write to my father. But he needs the exact date. He'll have to take a couple of weeks away from his teaching duties.'

'Once I find a rabbi and book the synagogue we'll know the date.'

She looked at him stunned, 'You want a religious wedding?'

'Of course.'

'But you're not religious and neither am I, and what I know of Eszti, neither is she. And my father? He hasn't been in a synagogue in his life.'

'Clars, you don't have to be religious to get married in a synagogue. Many secular people do. It's tradition and I like tradition. One day you will too.'

'Don't be so sure. Religion and me are utterly incompatible.'

'I was talking about tradition.'

'Tradition, religion they fade into each other.'

Her parents were not religious, they did not keep rituals, or celebrate traditions. They belonged to no tribe; they did not seem to need to, and herself? She always felt best dangling in no man's space, unencumbered by loyalties to a claustrophobic, predictable group.

What can I do? She told herself that marriage involves compromise. Wouldn't a traditional wedding be a small price to pay for happiness. Does it really matter how one gets to a destination? Maybe it doesn't, but she was still uneasy.

'Clars,' he interrupted her thoughts, 'it's a hot day, perfect for an afternoon swim. What do you think?'

They packed their swimming costumes and went to catch the bus to the beach.

Why would I let the prospect of a religious wedding spoil my happiness? She thought as she and Peter stood looking at the bay, her body snug against his. The clouds, edges sharpened with gold by the mid-afternoon sun, were floating north. A bird circled above the steely dark waters and vanished into the distance. Below, something wriggled in a cormorant's beak, and then it was no more.

Once that scenery would only remind her that she was thousands of miles away from her native Netherlands, not a distance she could close at a whim. Panic would grip her at the mere thought. All of a sudden, she had to run, run back to her country, to her language, to the familiar. But now with Peter's arms around her, she felt contented and happy.

He kissed her on the back of the head. The tickle of her hair made him sneeze. They laughed.

In two months, you will be my husband, she thought.

'And you'll be my wife,' he whispered.

She didn't think she'd spoken.

A sudden breeze hit the cliffs. A breeze from the distant south where the clouds had gathered grey.

They walked down to the beach.

'Catch me!' he shouted and ran towards the water, but she just lagged behind, savouring the sight of his body. A Greek sculpture, not in the frozen white of marble, but alive and tanned.

He plunged into the water; she followed.

Now and then a wave gave them a ride, the trough pulled them back. Warmth returned to her limbs. She felt refreshed. Energised. Invincible.

The wind picked up. The ocean rose, rumbled, and growled. She was looking the other way when a giant wave grabbed her and pulled her towards the infinite greyness, but then it changed its mind and threw her back, furiously. Her mouth full of water, she coughed and spluttered.

She looked around, 'Peter!' she called, but the ocean stole her scream and ripped it with its roar. Waves and more waves, rolling, breaking. She tried swimming towards the beach, but the booming giant pulled her back. She pushed against it, again and again, past exhaustion and pain.

The wind dropped, the waves less frequent, less savage, she began making headway.

In the shallow water a few youngsters were having fun. A man and a woman hugged for warmth. She looked back, her gaze searching the ocean, there was no sign of Peter. Surely the life savers would have spotted him, would have noticed that he was struggling. *Where are they?* And then it hit her, they had been swimming far outside the flags.

She had to find the lifesavers, she had to find them straight away. She tried to run, but her legs would not obey, the sand moved, shifted, resisted her every step. 'Help!' she shouted. 'Help!' but the wind swallowed her call. *I have to get help. If not* ... The thought of it was more than she could bear. A surge of energy flooded her muscles, and she took off.

In the distance, next to the tall tower, stood a group of young men in their red and yellow uniforms. *The life savers!* She sped up. All the way looking over her shoulder, scanning the ocean. Is someone there? Someone far away? There was no-one, and there was no-one again. *Don't slow down! Run!* But then she spotted something in the water. *What's that? An arm? Is that an arm?* As she tried to work it out, someone staggered out of the water and straightened up. 'It's Peter!' Wheezing and panting she ran towards him.

'I couldn't bear to lose you, I couldn't bear to be parted from you,' she gasped, trying to catch her breath. He did not reply, just put his arms around her and squeezed her until she could barely breathe.

She knew what loss was, but when her mother died the loss was gradual, over many months. She was young then and as the years passed life's distractions softened the pain. The memories of her mother receded, but her eyes, her smile, the shoulder-length auburn hair, the smell of her perfume, were still vivid. She guarded those memories, those snippets of shared life. She guarded the love and the warmth they captured. She was not going to lose them, she was not going to let her mother become just a loss, a concept, an unfilled space. But with the passing years those memories had turned fuzzier and fuzzier. Her mother became her past.

Peter was her future, a future which only an hour ago she had been certain of. Did the ocean laugh at her certitude? At her naivety? Did it want to teach her that you cannot be certain of anything? That life is a blind date?

She was thinking about what happened and how her world could have collapsed in a split second, the cosmic abandonment and pain when Peter said, 'Clars, let's get that frown off your face. We're alive, so let's celebrate.'

'Yes,' she said remembering the other imminent celebration at the end of the summer. Religious wedding or not, she couldn't have cared less.

And they walked on, on towards the setting sun. On the hill, dusk welcomed the lights, and the tatty streets they had walked through many times had never looked more beautiful.

-4-

Mid-January Peter and Ed had hired a cottage in the Blue Mountains for a bushwalking weekend. The cottage stood at the edge of Echo Point. Flame red geraniums and white azaleas trembled in the cool breeze. The blue flowers on the shrubs seemed to have been picked out of the sky, a sky which the clouds had forgotten that day. A whipbird cracked its whip, 'chew-chew,' his mate answered.

Peter was fast asleep, his breathing barely audible, his face serene, peaceful. Clara too was at peace. How beautiful he is, how handsome. She wanted to kiss his lips, his breath, his dark eyebrows, his strong chin, caress his arm, the olive, unblemished skin. But she would not wake him.

She pulled closer to him.

In front of the window, a bush laden with yellow flowers was swaying in the breeze and with it wobbled its guests, a finch and a honeyeater, beak buried inside a flower. The lacy curtain fluttered. On the wall the sunrays danced.

'Breakfast!' Toni called through the door.

Peter opened his eyes.

'We're late.' Clara jumped out of bed and headed for the shower.

Still towelling her hair, she came out of the bathroom.

'My turn,' Peter said.

'Wait a minute, I want to ask you a question.'

'Go on.'

'Do you like your new job? Do you like computing?'

'Well … In an arranged marriage it takes time to fall in love.'

She kissed his cheek, 'I hope you will.'

'So do I. But at least I got out of science. I wasn't meant to be a scientist.'

'That's not what Ed said.'

'What did Ed say?' Peter asked.

'Can't you remember? Last Saturday's lunch?'

'I remember the lunch, how can I not? He told us that he got himself a postdoctoral fellowship at the Sorbonne.'

'He also said that …'

'Where are you two?' Toni called.

Peter opened the door, 'Nearly ready.'

On the veranda, the table was already set. In the middle, a bowl of fresh fruit, yogurts, cereals and a toaster ready for action. Toni had seen to it all.

They were still debating the merits of one walk versus the other, when Ed interrupted:

'We'd better start walking before the sun's too hot.'

The sunshine, the crisp morning air would have energised the dead. At the Three Sisters lookout, a noisy group of young people immortalised each other's smiles, then headed for the bush. Peace enveloped the world again.

Clara was admiring the scenery, the mountains guarding the densely forested valley below, there since the beginning of time. The air was tinged with blue and should have chimed like drops hanging from a crystal chandelier, but there was no chandelier, the crystal did not chime. Instead, a bellbird called.

A large shadow slid over the treetops; the shadow of an eagle gliding silently above.

She stood there mesmerized.

'Every time I see these mountains, I marvel at their beauty as if I'm seeing them the very first time,' she heard Ed behind.

'God's work is perfect,' Peter replied.

She turned around to share her enchantment, but the puzzled look on Ed's face derailed her thoughts. As she was thinking about it, Ed called, 'Let's go!' And they headed for the bush.

The narrow path led through a eucalyptus forest, the silvery trunks gleaming in the sunshine. They walked in single file, Toni in the lead, then Peter followed by Ed, Clara some steps away. Toni's wholehearted laughter echoed through the valley. Clara could not hear what the fun was about. Suddenly there in the middle of the strange forest, homesickness – that tiger which lay in wait wherever she went – pounced on her again and she felt a painful longing for home, for Amsterdam, for her father, for Nicole. Her eyes filled with tears, tears which only the birds could see. She told herself off, 'You've made your choice. The wedding is in a month and your father is coming,' and she sped to catch up with the rest of the party.

After a short break for lunch, they began walking again, and on they walked for hours. By the time they got back to Echo Point clouds were gathering above, but The Three Sisters still basked in the soft yellow of the late afternoon sun.

That evening the four of them were sitting in the lounge room talking about Ed and Toni's departure to France. Peter looked preoccupied. Three whole years, Clara thought uneasily. How would Peter cope with Ed's absence?

'If everything goes to schedule,' said Ed, 'we'll be leaving at the end of September.'

'Three years in Europe,' Toni said with a trill in her voice, face crimson with excitement.

Ed looked at her, worried. 'It won't be a holiday; it'll be hard work.'

'During the week, but what about the weekends? Art galleries, museums, the Alps, Barcelona. Sorry Ed, I think my imagination is ahead of my reason,' then looking at Clara, 'and you'll visit us, won't you? We could all have a holiday in the South of France.'

'And afterwards Peter and I will spend a couple of weeks with my father.' She could see him meeting them at the airport, eyes teared by joy. She is so happy, she could fly. No, she had not given up her father and her friends, she would visit them every year or two. *And the money?* She would find some extra work; she would do whatever it took to see them.

* * *

Later she and Peter returned to the bedroom. He made himself a cup of tea and sat down on the sofa, deep in thought. Clara looked at him, he hasn't been himself most of the day.

'Peter, what are you thinking about?'

He did not answer.

'Tell me,' and after a pause, 'Come on, out with it.'

'I think we should postpone the wedding.'

'What?'

'I think we should postpone the wedding for a year, or two.'

'You're not serious, are you?' She searched his face for the mischievous smile. But all she saw was gloom and sadness. She could barely say, 'Why? Aren't you sure of this marriage any longer?'

'I'm not sure of anything anymore.'

Not sure of his love, she thought, feeling as if she had been punched in her stomach. 'What do you mean?'

'I need to sort out my issues first.'

'What issues?'

'Work, things.'

'We'll sort them out together.'

'I don't think we can.'

'And the wedding? The guests? My father? He's bought his ticket already.'

'I'll look after all that, I'll cancel everything.'

Cancel everything? Cancel all that's beautiful? All that's worth living for? But can he cancel my feelings? Or doesn't he care about what I feel? My love for him? The year I've spent here? He's willed himself into my life and now he wants to walk away. I left my whole world, my father, my friends, my country. For whom? And why would I wait for him? I'm not going to live here alone. Then where? Go back to Amsterdam? Her heart sank. *So, there you are, Clara, you can go back now. No more homesickness.* She imagined herself back in Amsterdam telling her father and her friends that she failed, she had fallen for a muddled-up man. *Oh no, I couldn't live there either. Not anymore.*

'You tell me what issues you need to sort out, then we can decide what's next.'

He didn't reply. She wanted to shake him, beat him until his issues, the issues which were about to turn her life upside down, came out, exploded like the froth of soured wine.

'Peter it's not just cold feet? Not just jitters at the unknown?'

'I don't know.'

She wanted to disappear from this world. She had invested everything in a future with Peter, absolutely everything. Like a novice gambler she had put all she had on one card, and now she had lost it. Her future an empty dark hole. She'd have to start all over again. But where? In which country? In which hemisphere? She needed to think things through, think about what to do next.

She wanted to be on her own, but she was stuck with him in that room, in the mountains and it was past ten o'clock. She lay on the bed fully dressed, boiling with resentment and despair. She did not want to be touched by him, even the sound of his breathing hurt. An hour passed, two. She lay there frozen, staring into the darkness.

As dawn was breaking, the light began to filter through the curtains. He rolled towards her and begged for forgiveness, and love, and togetherness.

'I would never leave you,' he said, 'I love you too much. It's me I doubt, I doubt that I can earn a living enough for you and our children. I don't want to keep you in poverty, I don't want to destroy your life.'

'We can overcome all that. Besides, what about my income?'

'Your income …?'

'Yes, my income.'

He did not answer.

'You don't want to destroy my life? The sure way to destroy my life would be for us to part.'

'I never wanted to give you up, only to postpone the wedding.'

'Wedding jitters?' She ruffled his hair.

'Maybe.'

'Don't worry,' and they curled into each other, relieved.

In the morning Peter was loving and joking and she felt reassured that whatever happened the night before was only an unpleasant spike in their lives. She couldn't wait for their wedding day and her father's coming.

-5-

Dawn. Clara lay wide awake, *my father is coming*! How many times did she fantasise about him coming to visit? How many times did she imagine taking him around Sydney, and later the three of them having dinner, the dinner she would cook. Talking, discussing what they saw. Today her fantasies will turn into reality. What joy!

She tossed and turned. Time seemed to have slowed down. *The wedding is in a week's time, meanwhile I'll make sure that he has a real holiday*, and she began a mental list of places to visit. It was not even six o'clock, but she could not lay there any longer. Carefully as not to wake Peter, she got up, had a cup of coffee and was on her way. Less than an hour later she was standing in the airport, checking the arrivals. Pacing anxiously, then checking the board for updates, again and again. 'At last!' His plane had landed. The time ticked along. The door to the arrival area opened and shut and opened and every time a slight older man walked out, she held her breath.

And then, 'Clara!' the much-loved voice called. It was not a dream; her father was walking towards her. Their faces wet with tears, they hugged and cried, and hugged again. As they walked to the car, David squeezed her arm as if wanting to assure himself that his daughter was there, next to him. For real.

The next day Peter was working, finishing an urgent project and Clara took her father for a stroll around Sydney. They talked and talked.

About Dafna, Nicole and her other friends, about the university, about Amsterdam and about the wedding of course.

'Father, I dragged you to the other side of the world and on Sunday I'll drag you to a synagogue …'

'My darling, you did stretch me a bit, but being stretched is not a bad thing. What did I know about Australia before you dragged me here? Your words not mine. So, no apologies please, besides, do you think I could have missed your wedding, whether in Australia, or Brazil, in a synagogue, or in the Amazon forest? Don't worry everything will fall into place, and you'll be the most beautiful bride.'

That Sunday, the day of the wedding, bright sunshine fell on Sydney as Clara and her father walked from the car to the steps of the Synagogue. He in a grey suit, white shirt, red bow tie, she in her wedding dress, shimmering in the sun.

Two men, overseers of tradition, were waiting at the entrance to the synagogue. Soon the sounds of the wedding march floated into the street.

'Let's go,' David said.

She covered her face with the veil, and they walked down the aisle where Peter was waiting. Next to him stood Ed, his best man.

After a short speech in English the rabbi switched to Hebrew and the ceremony began. Peter understood Hebrew, he taught it to himself while a teenager. He was immersed in the rabbi's every word. Clara had never heard the language before and listening to it's strange, unusual sound she could not help feeling alienated. The rabbi was going on and on. More words flew past her, meaningless, puzzling words. She felt excluded, superfluous. She looked at the goings on, detached. An observer some distance away. She saw two people standing under the *chuppah*, about to be wedded, but that woman …?

Was that dissociation a sort of out of body experience, the culmination of the emotional stress or was it a warning? At the time she did not linger on what happened, because the rabbi slipped back into English and she slipped back to being a bride.

'I Peter Steinberg …' Peter repeated the rabbi's words and the further he got the slower the words emerged as if the meaning of every word had to be considered, weighed, as if every word was far more than a word, far more than a promise, but rather a maze of implications and possibilities.

'I, Clara Housen ...' she said like a robot.

Ed stepped forward with a small velvet box. Peter picked out the wedding ring and slid it on her finger. The sunrays coming through the stained-glass window had lit the gold ring with their fire. Love, marriage, fire it seemed to say.

The rabbi said a few more words at which Peter stomped on a glass, the symbol of a final promise. "This glass might shatter, but our marriage will never break."

The ceremony was over.

She took Peter's arm and to the accompaniment of smiles, waves, and wishes for a long and happy life, they walked back to the iron-bound doors facing the street, and Clara no longer minded the meaningless service which had united them. For a split second she thought she could see Nicole, that she too was smiling.

David stepped forward, shook Peter's hand then embraced her, his eyes blurred by tears. She too broke into tears. Tears of joy and tears of sadness. She missed her mother. She hoped she was somewhere, she hoped she could see her joy.

The religious service might not have been what she had wished for, but at the celebration that evening in the small restaurant there was laughter and there was joy and Clara could not be happier. After dinner she waltzed with Peter. Stiff and self-conscious, he moved as if on stilts. She followed, feet barely touching the ground. Then she danced with her father, while Peter twirled with his mother. Ed and Toni behind.

David bowed to Eszti. She blushed, protested, but joined in. The music, the dance, rolled on till midnight.

* * *

Clara can no longer recall the names of some guests, and what exactly they ate and drank that night, but she remembers vividly her father's departure.

She had been dreading it for days, dreading the moment when they would say goodbye. The evening before, David, Peter and her were sitting with Eszti in her lounge room, trying to keep up some trivial conversation. Outside a storm was raging. A flash of lightning lit the sky. The tree branches weaved and swirled. Then as if released from chains, thunder descended with a crack, a crack which seemed to split the world into now and thereafter. Hail beat the window.

Eszti and Peter left the room to sort out what he would take away.

Clara's thoughts were weighty with parting. When will I see my father again? An uneasy silence settled between them. She could not imagine not seeing him for years. Not seeing his wise, understanding face, not hearing his comforting warm voice. He might look young, but he was not young any longer. A sudden void in her stomach. No, she could not bear thinking about it.

'Clara, my darling,' David said, 'I'm grateful that fate had allowed me to see you married and to get to know your husband. I had a great time here and I thank you and Peter for it. And by the way, the wedding was beautiful,' face covered with a smile of pure delight.

'Treasure its memory, remember the good times when you are down, remember your love for him, don't let disappointments defeat you. And when life throws pain your way, persevere. It will pass, the sun will shine again. Just look after each other. You will look after him, won't you?' he gazed at her with his penetrating green eyes.

Her father's words seemed strange. Anxiously, she rearranged the folds in her dress.

'Of course I will.'

'You have to look after each other.'

'Yes, father.'

Of course she would, she loved Peter with all her being, with her eyes and her hands, her body and her thoughts.

Outside the storm had passed. The gutter, full of leaves, had given birth to a miniature waterfall which gushed past the kitchen window.

Eszti and Peter walked in, Peter holding a suitcase bulging with books, on his arm his late father's favourite jacket.

David stood up to go. Trying to postpone the inevitable, Eszti offered to make tea. 'And I have the best sour cherry strudel there is in the Southern Hemisphere.'

David laughed. 'I'd love to, but I still have a few things to sort out tonight. I have a very eventful day tomorrow.'

Eszti was becoming more and more anxious and as she always did in such moments, she picked up the cat for comfort. 'You beautiful thing,' she purred into its fur.

Peter placed the suitcase into the boot of the car then he and Clara stood under the awning sheltering from the drizzle, waiting. David whispered something to Eszti. As he tried to hug her one last time, the cat jumped out from Eszti's grasp and ran away.

'Let's go,' David said to Peter and they got into the car. Eszti stood wiping her tears. She stood there until the car turned the corner.

Self-indulgence, Clara thought. They were not moving far; they were only moving to the other side of Sydney.

Clara never forgot Eszti's tears. Nowadays, no longer disabled by happiness and youth, she can imagine how Eszti must have felt. Going back inside. The house suddenly strange, uninhabited. The air thin. The cat running in, twirling its tail around her leg. 'It's only you and me now,' she says to her faithful companion, shuts the door and turns the key twice. And she tells herself yet again, 'There is no joy without sadness, life is like a rose, a flower with many thorns.'

Oh memories, they can be so painful, they can make you feel so remorseful. *Why wasn't I more understanding of Eszti? Why didn't I empathise with her?* At the time she could only think of her father. He was leaving, going back to the other side of the world. No-one to share his life with. Yes, there were colleagues and acquaintances and there were the dinners with his sister Dafna, but most of the time he would be on his own. The image of him sitting at the table alone, eating dinner, was too painful to allow in other thoughts.

-6-

Smiling, Clara passed her hand over her tummy. The baby was moving again. Three years had passed since their wedding and she was finally expecting. Peter was right, they didn't have to see a doctor. 'Let's wait, see what God's will is.' God's will? She pondered.

Lately Peter had been invoking God more than she was comfortable with, but otherwise she was happy.

The baby moved again. She could not wait to hold her to her breast, feel her warmth, caress her silky skin, inhale her milky smell. The smell of the new-born, the smell of a promise. She wanted to see her grow and learn and marvel at the world. Her? Yes, she wanted a girl.

She wondered if Peter told Ed about the baby. He and Toni had returned from France last Tuesday and the four of them were to meet tonight to celebrate. She was thinking what to wear when a shudder went through Peter's body and he woke with a shout.

'What's up, Peter?'

'Nothing,' he said, forehead lined by confusion.

'Tell me. What did you dream about?'

'Just another of my nightmares.'

'One of your nightmares?' she stared at him. 'What about?'

Her question hung in the air.

'Please tell me, please. I'm good at interpreting dreams,' she laughed.

'Bollocks, you just want to listen to stories. Don't you?' He smiled a tired smile.

'I do, to your story,' and tried to smooth his brow. 'Tell me what happened?'

'Same old nonsense.'

'You were at university again?'

'Doing my Ph.D.'

'Go on.'

'I don't think I want to.'

'Please.'

'All right, but I can only remember bits.'

'Doesn't matter.'

'It was early morning. I'm in the lab. Alone. The vacuum pump is hissing like a snake, and then …? Oh yes. I have a sample in my hand. I'm going somewhere. Don't know where, all I can recall that I tripped over a mess of electrical cords and hit the wall.'

'That's why you shouted?'

'No, I did manage to balance myself, and hold onto my sample. Then …? Then … yes, I slide the sample into the scanning electron microscope, turn a few knobs, find the fuzzy image, focus it, and there, in front of me is …' he fell silent.

'Is what?'

'My brain.'

'How can that be?'

'It's a dream, Mrs Freud. I thought you're going to interpret it for me.'

'I can't. It's too weird. I'll have to ask Sigmund for help.'

'Best of luck. Anyway, I took the sample out and threw it in the rubbish. I threw my brain into the rubbish bin.'

'Stop it. I'm going to be sick. Is that when you woke up shouting?'

'No. It was something to do with my supervisor. He was standing in front of me, a woman on each arm. Well a naked woman on each arm. Red faced, booming something about being creative. "We'll teach you how! Won't we?" he asked each woman in turn, then turned to me, his face elongated, twisted like an image in a Luna Park mirror. Sinister. That's when I shouted. So, there you are, those were my dreams. Happy?'

'Of course not. You're dreaming about naked women.'

'I'm sexually frustrated, that's why.'

'I know.'

'You know? How come?'

'Insider's knowledge. Joke aside, I don't like you having nightmares. But leaving out the bit about your brain …'

'I can't leave out my brain, can I?' he laughed.

'Stop it. But the rest of your dream is not so far-fetched, is it? Your supervisor, wasn't he always tipsy after lunch? That's what you told me.'

'He was. Not that it stopped him giving advice. No, not about my project, research was the least of his interests. Wheeling and dealing, that's what he liked. A born entrepreneur.'

'Anyway, having made hundreds of samples, taken thousands of measurements, sweated buckets …'

'Sweated?'

'Sweated and held my breath, every time I plotted my results. Will the trend show this time, or will I have to start all over again? Change course of my work? It was nerve wracking, like watching a doctor's face about to tell you whether you're terminally ill or not. My graphs looked like paintings by someone on LSD, not like the tidy results of a physical phenomenon. So after more than two years of such fun, I'd had enough. But I told you some of that already.'

'You did but only bits. I can't believe that you're still having nightmares about your research. Did Ed's return bring back these memories?'

'Maybe, still I can't wait to see them.'

* * *

Evening. They were sitting on the terrace. The Italian song playing in the background left a vague feeling of sadness and loss, but Peter's eyes shone with happiness, his family was whole again. Their return a happy event for Peter, but for Ed the culmination of months of worry.

He was finishing his work at the Sorbonne when he got the news that his father – who had been suffering from cancer for more than a year – had exhausted all treatments. He could either join a trial for a new drug or prepare for the ultimate. 'Trial for a new drug?' his father asked. 'No way. I'm not a rat and to my knowledge you're not a half rat.'

'Dad, the cancer will kill you within months. So, what have you got to lose? Join the trial and see what happens. Please.'

He did join the trial. Meanwhile Ed rushed his work through as fast as he could.

The trial drug was difficult, it tested the limits of his father's resilience and stamina. As he fought to keep on an even keel, feeling sorry for the rats who go through such trials, his health started to improve, and he began gaining weight. By the time Ed and Toni landed in Sydney, he looked and felt much better.

The week before, barely four months into the trial, he had been told that he was in remission. And that evening, in Il Bacio restaurant in Leichhardt, was a celebration of his recovery, of life and hope and family and friendship.

The waiter opened the bottle and poured each one a glass. The champagne crackled and fizzed. As if under a magic spell the whirling bubbles spiralling upwards carried the twinkles of the candlelight.

'Pity you didn't get to visit us,' Toni said looking at Clara.

'We wanted so much to go, but every time we started to plan the trip, something cropped up; Eszti's operation, Peter's deadlines, the renewal of my contract.'

'Life's unpostponable demands,' said Ed.

'But we saved enough for a permanent address,' Peter said. 'Just as well, with the baby on the way…'

'No more landlords, predictability at last,' Clara added.

'Yes,' Peter said and lost himself in some thought.

During their years away, the contact between Ed and Peter had continued unabated. Every few weeks Ed sent him a letter, a detailed account about his work, often about his latest paper soon to be published in some reputable journal. He wrote about their recent weekend trip to the Swiss Alps or the South of France, the cheese and the wine. At times Toni, heavily pregnant by then, added a few lines about an art gallery, or a museum she visited during the week.

Peter was in no rush to answer. He was slaving in the same old job. He tried to immerse himself in his work, but his heart was not in it. Computing did not awake in him the interest and fascination of science; computing was only a means to earning a living. Soon he discovered the advantages of his new situation, not being absorbed by his work meant not thinking about it a minute longer than he had to. Every day, at five-thirty, he switched off his computer and walked out of the office, free to think about what interested him, linguistics.

'To my father's health,' Ed raised his glass.

'To everybody's health,' Toni added.

'Has this drug cured many?' Clara asked.

'I don't know, all I know is that it puts some people in remission for months, even years. According to the doctor my father might be one of those who'll have years. He had a less aggressive form of the disease.' Contemplating how amazing science is, what it had done for his father and their family, Ed picked at the octopus salad then added, 'Science is my God.'

Peter frowned, 'Science can't be your God. Science wouldn't exist if God hadn't created it. God is above science; God is above everything.'

Ed's eyebrows ascended in puzzlement. 'But this is a nonsensical argument.'

'Why? Why is it nonsensical?'

'Because there's no way to prove it. How would you prove that God made science?'

'I might not be able to prove my argument, I don't even want to, but let's face it, Ed, neither can you prove yours.'

'Meaning?'

'Prove that science could exist without God's will.'

'Peter let's look at the facts. He had a tumour. If they hadn't detected it early where would he be now? From scans and X-rays, to operations, from the anaesthetics to the radioactive implant. And the trial drug. It's all science.'

'True, but none of these would exist without the will of God. Just think about the laws of nature, they're all based on maths. Maths is fundamental to nature. Why? Because God built a universe based on maths. Take the Fibonacci series. It describes everything from the arrangement of leaves in plants, to the pattern of sunflower seeds. And what about the movement of the planets, or the shape of the coastline? They can all be described by maths. Simply and elegantly. A testimony to God's omnipotence,' Peter said smiling victoriously.

Ed's face a million thoughts. How could he argue his point, how could he convince Peter of the nonexistence of some unprovable existence?

'Peter, to argue about each one of your examples would take days, so let's take only one. The leaf arrangement makes the best use of light falling on the plant, and that optimisation is described by the Fibonacci series. On that I agree with you. We don't know why nature can often be described by mathematical equations, but that doesn't mean that we should substitute one lack of knowledge with another.'

'Meaning?'

'Substitute our ignorance – which I admit is enormous, but is being decoded bit by little bit – with an axiom. By creating a being whose existence cannot be proved.'

'Or whose existence cannot be discounted,' Peter replied, the smile gone from his face, his eyes zealously sparkling.

Ed looked at him, weariness on his face. Then something happened which stuck in Clara's mind like a bad dream, but too close to reality to be only a dream. Toni's hand disappeared under the table. Ed turned towards her; a meaningful look passed between them.

What did that look mean? Clara wondered. Leave him alone? Don't provoke him, he doesn't make sense anyway? But what just happened was dishonest. Once honesty is gone, what's left of a friendship? The moulted skin of the lizard? Empty and void? Suddenly their friendship felt wrong, nauseating, a spider's web which had stuck to her. She had to scrape it off. She had to escape it. She had to get up and go, but she could not leave Peter there. Neither could she concentrate on what followed. As she sat there thinking about what just happened, she felt that something was slipping away from her. Something undefinable she could not hold on to. God had always been part of Peter's world view but was never at the forefront of his thoughts. Once he kept science and religion separate. Lately his faith seemed to be at the centre of all his thoughts, religion the basis of all his interpretations and judgements. Where would this metamorphosis lead? What would it do to their marriage? Her heart weighed down by disquiet and a sense of foreboding, she could not tell a soul. She was alone, alone with her secrets, alone like she had never been before.

She took a few deep breaths. She had to stay calm for the baby's sake. It occurred to her that she had got into a habit of locking Peter's religious diatribes away. Deep enough not to emerge, deep enough not to disturb her too often.

The conversation shifted to Ed and Toni's life in Paris, but Clara could not concentrate, her mind jumping around from what just happened, to what might happen. Toni confessed that the European holiday had not been what she had imagined back in Sydney. Socially they were isolated, but professionally the trip had been a success. Ed had earned himself enough of an aura to land a senior lecturer's position in Australia, and they were happy to be back.

Distance and time can weaken the strongest bonds, Clara thought as they left the restaurant. She wondered about Nicole, who she had not heard from for months. Was she still the same Nicole or had she too changed beyond recognition? A few days later she sat down to write her a long letter. She was halfway through when Ed rang.

She overheard Peter telling him about Finno-Ugric languages, about how Hungarian and Japanese must be related and in her mind's eye she could see Ed getting more and more bored and impatient. Then Peter said something about God. About destiny.

She cringed. *This friendship is getting thinner and thinner. How long before it snaps?*

The answer came sooner than she anticipated.

* * *

It was a hot Sunday afternoon, one of those days when half of Sydney takes refuge on Bondi Beach. Refreshed from a swim, Clara and Peter were making their way back to the car, carefully avoiding bodies, towels and toys strewn on the sand. They had nearly reached the stairs to the promenade when they heard Ed's call. He and Toni were sitting under a beach umbrella. Clara had not seen them since that dinner in Il Bacio restaurant more than six weeks ago and she was in no mood to renew the contact. Besides she had to prepare for tomorrow's tutorial. She used to know Flaubert's work in detail, but she had to refresh her memory of Madam Bovary and she wanted to discuss his selected letters with her students. They deserve to be stretched; they are an interested group.

But Peter was heading towards Ed already.

Toni looked radiant, Ed worn and tired. They had left their son with his grandmother and were free for the rest of the day. Soon Ed began telling them about his research project.

'I'm only in the setup stage, but finding the right equipment is not trivial, some are not available in Australia. I just ordered a piece from the States, with the freight it added up to a motzer. And it'll take at least six weeks to get here. But enough of my problems. Peter, how's your work going?'

'My linguistics have hit a bit of a dead end.'

'Not linguistics, that's your hobby.'

Peter didn't answer. How could he explain that linguistics was not his hobby, not something he did occasionally, linguistics was an infatuation, an obsession. It had hijacked his mind.

'You know what I'm talking about, your work, your career in the organisation.'

'Work?' Peter shrugged. 'There's too much of it. Now they want me to be on call at night. Be at their disposal twenty-four hours a day. I can't and I won't. I'll find something else, shorter hours, maybe even different work.'

And his career? No, he did not have a career, or care about having one. Invest even more energy in something he had no interest in? Climb the hierarchy? What for? He lived for his family and linguistics. Work was for food and shelter; a functional endeavour.

In the following weeks, whenever the phone rang Peter rushed to pick it up. Did he hope to hear from Ed? Because if he did, he must have been disappointed. Ed had retreated into silence. Has he grown tired of Peter? Wondered Clara. Has he had enough of linguistics and religion? Of Peter's friendship?

She had never rung Ed before, she never felt that close to him and after that dinner in Leichhardt she decided he was just another acquaintance with whom she would only be in contact for Peter's sake. But that evening she needed his help.

Ed was taken aback when he heard her voice and even more by what she said.

'He wants to resign from his job, and the baby is due in a month. How will we pay the bills?'

Silence.

'Please talk to him, you're the only one he listens to,' and the sound of her voice — like a beggar's stranded in a far-off place on a freezing night — made her feel sick. She nearly said, 'used to listen to,' but that would have sounded strange. Besides, appealing to Ed's past emotions would not have worked, you don't get help from someone based on emotional ruins, on what used to be.

'Why, what happened?'

'Too much work. Now he has to be available for night calls in case things go wrong. He's had enough. Ed, you could change his mind. There's still time. He did promise to think about it till next week.'

'Must be hard for you,' Ed said eventually.

'Hard? My contract expires in a month. Just as the baby is due. How are we going to manage? How will we pay the mortgage?'

'He'll find something, I'm sure.'

'Shall I fetch him? Would you talk to him?'

'I can't, Toni is out, and I have to put the little one to bed. But I'll think about it, see what I can do,' and he wished her goodnight.

She sat down on the sofa. She had no-one to turn to. She was alone on this vast continent.

* * *

Peter did leave his job, but soon after Shosh was born he started another. He seemed much happier, a changed man. The money began coming in again. The hard times were over.

Ed and Toni disappeared from their life. Did Peter miss them? Maybe he did, especially on Sundays, but he never said so, never even mentioned Ed's name. They did not make new friends. They had a few acquaintances, they had Shosh and they had each other. They were happy.

-7-

Another three years passed. Clara was still tutoring, and Peter was still working in the same company. He had been promoted but found no joy in his work. Every approaching deadline was like a pack of dogs running at him, about to attack. He lived for his weekends, his outdoor days. But that Sunday he had urgent work to finish and no matter how much he resented it, no matter that he had promised himself not to work after hours anymore, he had to work that day. Work? Struggle through mountains of print, searching for errors in his computer program. He had checked the logic many times. It was internally consistent, which made it even more difficult to work out the problem, because consistency often masquerades as truth. He had been working all morning, but he was still stuck in the same place.

'I don't know what else I can do,' he said to Clara, 'I feel as if I'm fighting an invisible enemy.'

She was at a loss what to say. Her past encouragements never helped, but could she leave him to fester in hopelessness?

'If you can't work it out, nobody can.' She didn't just say it, she believed it. Wasn't he their best programmer?

Peter did not reply, just turned back to his program.

She put Shosh to bed for an afternoon nap. 'She'll be asleep soon,' she said when she returned.

Peter looked up, his eyes on her, but not seeing her, seeing something inside himself, something which demanded his total concentration.

49

'Peter, is something the matter?'

He didn't answer.

She sat down next to him. 'Peter, what's wrong?'

'Nothing.'

She was worried about him. He had been working long hours, but even when he was at home, he was not always there, his mind seemed far away.

'Peter, why don't we go away for a week? Once you finish your project. We could still catch the last of the summer, I heard there're some nice places on the Central Coast.' She kissed him on the cheek, 'Can you take a week off?'

He looked at her absentmindedly, as if he was still wrestling with the problem in front of him. 'A week off?' He asked finally, 'I can try,' and his eyes returned to the paper.

A whole week away! It will help Peter relax, forget about his work. She tried to discard the question marks which had been nagging her; she locked away troublesome thoughts. Weeds, she would concentrate on what is important, find a nice hotel and plan their trip.

On Monday, after her university tutoring, she picked up a few brochures from a travel agent and headed to the nearest café. The coffee took a long time to come, but Clara didn't notice, she was lost in the images in front of her. Blue waters, clean beaches. She could smell the fresh air, she could see Peter playing with Shosh, the two of them laughing. *What happiness!*

She picked up Shosh from the childcare centre. Sitting on the back seat Shosh kept singing, 'This old man he played sticks …'

'Mum can you sing with me?'

Surely Peter's holiday will be approved, Clara thought. It's only for a week. Surely once he finishes the present project, he would be free to go.

'Muum! Please sing with me.'

'OK, OK,' and she joined in.

As Shosh was having her afternoon tea, Clara opened the brochures again, wondering which would be the most suitable hotel for the three of them.

Shosh wanted to know what those pictures were.

'Hotels. Shosh, we're going on holiday.'

'Holiday?'

'Yes, we're going away. We will sleep in a nice hotel like this one,' Clara pointed to one of the photos, 'and from here we'll go every day to another beautiful beach.'

She picked Shosh up, 'Holiday, holiday,' and they did a little waltz. 'Holiday,' Shosh chuckled.

'Now you go and play.'

Clara rang the three most promising motels. They all had vacancies. All they needed now was for Peter's holiday to be approved.

It was nearly midnight when she went to bed. Peter was half asleep, the moonlight coming through the lacy curtains fell on his face. She turned away to face the darkness and pulled the cover over herself. He kissed the back of her head. She felt his lips on her neck, his fingers caressing her spine, sliding down her thighs, circling around her breasts, her nipples swollen with desire, miraculous sensations, him and her. The world vanished.

Later, they lay in each other's arms, drowsing. She had a loving husband, a perfect daughter. Life was wonderful and she fell into a deep sleep.

* * *

The next day, Peter arrived home subdued. His holiday had not been approved. Another project was waiting for him and they needed the results in six-weeks-time, but once that project was finished, he could definitely go. Dispirited, Clara tried to console herself, the holiday was just postponed. But it'll be winter then. Well it would be a different holiday, but a holiday nevertheless, she tried to cheer herself up. Besides tomorrow's Wednesday, my free day.

Wednesdays she took Shosh to the beach, or to a movie, but that day they only went to the playground in the park, ten minutes walk away. When they returned, she sat down to write an application for a public service job. As she read through the job description, she had the feeling that the Heavens must be smiling on her. My skills fit the requirements like a glove. I will get that job, I will, but if not, I will get the next one, or the one after. Soon the short, tutoring contracts will be over.

Her spirits high, she covered the table with her favourite tablecloth, a white linen with silver threads and on it she placed the fine china plates, the silver-plated cutlery and the crystal glasses – their wedding present from her father. She took a step back and looked at her creation. The lights bounced back from the fine china joyously, the silver cutlery shone. *Perfect*.

The roast chicken was nearly ready when Peter walked in, looking freakishly pale. Clara tried to hug him, but he pulled back and headed to the bathroom.

She busied herself in the kitchen, cleaned the sink, wiped down the granite benchtops, put the dry dishes away. *What is he doing?*

'Peter, the dinner's ready!' she called. Then once more.

Finally, he came out and they sat down to eat.

'Yum, yum, chicken,' Shosh said. 'I'm hungry.'

Peter did not question the reason for the festive table, he did not seem to have noticed it. He sat quietly picking at his food. His work again? She wondered. The deadline of his project was three days away.

'Have you managed to solve that problem?' she asked.

'I can't.'

She caressed his hand. 'You will, I'm sure you will.' Only a few weeks ago one of his colleagues told her that Peter was their smartest analyst, he was the one everybody went for advice. If he couldn't solve the problem who could?

He pulled his hand away. 'You're always sure of everything. Don't you understand that I can't? For crying out loud, don't you get it?!'

'Get what?'

'My brain's not working.'

'You're tired.'

'I'm tired. Tired of computing. Tired of it all.'

Tired of it all? The words cut through her heart.

'We have a new girl in the childcare centre,' Shosh interrupted the silence. 'Her name is Rosie. She's really nice,' and she went on describing Rosie, and Peter sort of smiled, and Clara felt a little better.

When they finished eating, Shosh disappeared into her bedroom. Clara picked up the plates, gathered the cutlery and headed to the kitchen.

'Haven't you been out today?' Peter asked when she returned.

'We just went down to the park for half an hour.'

'So, what did you do all day?'

'I wrote an application for a job.'

'But you have a job.'

'A part-time job till the end of the year. Peter, I want to work full-time. I want a real job.'

'And who will look after Shosh?'

'She could go to childcare just as she does now and for the remaining two days, we'll get someone to come here to look after her, maybe even help with some chores.' She picked up the plate with the leftover chicken. 'What do you think?'

'I won't let strangers into this house!'

'Sorry?'

'I won't allow strangers into this house!'

'What strangers? We'll only take someone with good references.'

'I don't trust references.'

'But Peter I need …'

And what followed would stay with her. At the sight of roast chicken on a menu, or a TV advertisement on the topic, what happened next would roll before her eyes with an acuity, a sharpness, as if she was still there in that dining room.

'No strangers in this house! Never!' Peter shouts, his eyes wild with anger.

'I just …' but she does not finish the sentence, because suddenly he is close to her, terrifyingly close. He grabs her shoulders. 'No strangers in this house! Do you understand?!' he screams and throws her against the wall. Bits of roast chicken somersault through the air, the plate lands on the carpet.

He takes a step back, but then he comes at her again, fury and murder on his face. Paralysed with fear, her feet glued to the floor, she stands there, a condemned woman awaiting her executioner.

He slams her against the wall. The plate shatters under his feet. He staggers. Bits of china and roast chicken mix under his strange dance. Bang! A stabbing pain shoots up her neck. Her head has hit the wall. Her heart is pounding. She tries to pull back, but he grips her by the throat, his fingers pressing, tightening around it. The air has left the room. *He's going to kill me. Kill me! Then who will look after Shosh?* 'Nooo!' she screams, a guttural stifled scream. A scream of terror, of an approaching end. 'Nooo!

Shosh comes running, her face contorted with fear.

'Leave my mummy alone! Daddy!' She pulls his trouser leg. 'Leave her alone! Please!'

Peter drops his arms, opens the front door and storms out.

Clara staggers to the sofa.

'I love you mummy,' Shosh says as she sits on her mother's lap, crying. She cries with the misery of the powerless, the misery of a wounded gazelle.

'I love you too,' Clara says holding her tight. She says it because she has to, she says it like a robot, because right now she does not love, she does not feel anything, but fear. Her mind is working feverishly. He could be back any minute. We have to leave. Quickly! But where? Where can we go? Oh, the motel, the motel a few streets away, and tomorrow?

Tomorrow is a lifetime away; I have to survive today first. Leave, get away before he comes back, get away as soon as possible, or I might never see another dawn. Then who will look after Shosh?

She runs to the wardrobe.

'Shosh come here! Here! And don't move!'

Where is the small suitcase? She can't remember. She can't remember anything. She grabs two plastic bags, throws in their nighties, toiletries and they rush to the car. Once inside, she locks the doors, turns the ignition on and they are off. Her mouth suddenly full of an acrid mess. *Oh God, not in front of Shosh.* Leaning over the steering wheel, she takes the left lane and stops the car.

'Mummy, what's wrong?

'I'm tired. Don't worry.'

She starts driving again. *Finally!* The motel is in sight; she pulls into the drive. They made it.

That night she lay awake thinking that she had reached the very pit of her life. Beaten by her husband and running for her life. She always knew that aggressive men exist, but they lived somewhere else, far away, in another world. A world inhabited by drunks and criminals. A world so far away, so distant that it was not worth a second of her thoughts. But Peter? They had argued now and then, at times his shouts frightened her, but then they made up and he was loving and gentle again. Just another loud argument, she told herself, and which couple doesn't argue? And the incident in the kitchen when her father was visiting? Why didn't she acknowledge the obvious? How did she manage to convince herself that what happened was not dangerous? That he would not seriously hurt her one day, that he was not capable of such a thing? She always found some explanation, deceived herself with comforting illusions. Because she cannot face reality? Because she is weak? But weakness leads to debt, and life does not forgive a debt. Now she is paying her dues.

She lay in bed, fearing the daybreak. The inevitable did come, the sun shone again. But not on her world. 'Where can we go? We can't stay here. Then where? Rent a flat? But how can I pay the rent for even the cheapest flat? So where should we go? The street? With Shosh? No, I have no choice. I have only one address, but how can I live under the same roof, eat at the same table, sleep in the same bed with the man who nearly strangled me?'

No answers, no solutions, no way out.

Shosh woke. Clara packed their belongings and drove home. Her heart pounding, she opened the door. There was no sign of Peter and she breathed with relief. But then he walked in. He did not ask where they slept that night or mention what happened the previous evening. He picked up his briefcase and headed to work. Shattered, confused, Clara walked around like a zombie. She could not decide what to do, she had neither the energy, nor the clarity of mind for it. Maybe tomorrow, or the day after, but deep down she knew that she would have to inhabit a nightmare for a long time to come.

That night she lay next to him, watching the dark sky visible through the chink in the curtain, the stars twinkling as if nothing had happened, nothing had changed. The world went on, and Peter slept. While he was asleep, she was safe and she lay there frozen. But then he turned towards her and mumbled something. She didn't say a thing, she couldn't. She could barely breathe. Snorting, he turned away and began snoring. For now, she was safe.

The next days were peaceful, routine returned to their lives. Even the visits to Eszti went on as if nothing had changed. Late afternoon on Saturday, they would walk down to Coogee Beach, Peter holding Shosh's hand, and behind Clara with Eszti talking non-stop — as people who live on their own often do. At times Peter seemed distracted, other times he was his old self. He told Shosh about the sea and the Earth, the waves and the storms.

'Some waves are taller than Grandma's house.'

'Wow, bigger than Grandma's house?'

'Yes, and when they hit a boat, they could turn it upside down.'

He told her that many people came to Australia. They came from the other side of the world and Shosh listened, eyes wide open in amazement. The ships kept bouncing on the waves, but people sat on deck longing for their homes, for dry land, and every time they saw land approaching, they hoped that the end of their journey was close. But Australia was hiding. For weeks and months.

'How long did it take them to get here, daddy?'

'Well around the time when Grandma was a little girl like you, it took months and months, maybe half as much as it took you from your second to your third birthday.'

'That is very, very long'.

'Most people came here because they had to, others were looking for adventure. Like Sinbad the sailor.'

'Who is Sinbad the sailor, daddy?'

'Well, Sinbad was an adventurer in a story. But he did not come to Australia. At the time, the people on the other side of the world did not even know that Australia existed.'

Shosh frowned. How could anyone think that Australia did not exist? But then she changed the subject. She told her father about the little dog next door.

'He came to the kitchen door. Do you think he came because he smelled the roast? Or he just happened to find us?'

'Dogs can smell at long distances. They would be attracted by fresh meat and blood. But cooked meat? Probably not. I think he just wandered in.'

'He was so beautiful. He had dark brown fur and floppy ears and when mum chased him away, he ran and his ears moved back and forth like little wings.'

Nobody would have said that they were not father and daughter. There was a bond between them which no-one would ever break. Seeing Peter walking and talking to his daughter warmed Clara's heart and she refused to think about what was going on in her life, or what the future held.

The following weeks Peter was loving and joking. Now and then the strange look returned, the look which did not see the world around him, but seemed to see a great deal inside himself. As if a secret from deep inside him had managed to escape, something strange, frightening, and he had to push it back. Lock it away.

Having let his guard down once, he found it easier the second and the third time. Shosh no longer implored her father to stop, she just watched in terror and cried. When he did stop, Clara packed their toiletries, took Shosh by the hand and they checked into the same motel for a night. Next day they returned to the fear and the dread.

Nightmares did not frighten Clara, only life did.

One day Peter came home with a present, a stunning ring, white gold with an amethyst stone.

'It's beautiful,' she said. 'But no matter how many rings and jewels you buy me, no matter how many onyxes, amethysts and diamonds, what has been broken cannot be unbroken. Our marriage is over. Peter, I want to move out. Please help me. Help me to pay the rent for a few months until I get some more work. I beg you.'

'I love you more than I love life. If you leave, I'll kill myself.'

So, they plodded along. Him flitting in and out of his world, she thinking how to escape it all. Return to Amsterdam? How? She couldn't take Shosh out of the country without Peter's permission.

Her father was now retired. They spoke by phone every month; the rest was left to letters. He was not taking well to his retirement, his usual energy and optimism gone. In the last letter he said that he had been sick, digestive problems, nothing to worry about, he'd had them all his life. She was worried, she had to go and see him, but only if she could take Shosh along. She had to catch Peter in a reasonable mood, get his official agreement. But Peter's reasonable moods were short lived. How could she risk it? How could she rock such an unstable boat? She plodded on, kept a low profile, and said as little as she could get away with. She was walking among mines, she had to be as careful, as unobtrusive as she possibly could.

One day Peter came home from work unusually early.

'I'm moving out,' he said and began packing.

At last, Clara thought. As soon as he's gone, I'll ring a locksmith to change the lock on the door.

Keeping a discreet eye on his progress, she cleaned the bathroom and just started to clean the kitchen when he put his head in.

'I'm packed. Look after Shosh,' he said and opened the door.

She had been waiting for this moment for so long and yet when the door slammed behind him, she had a gut-wrenching feeling of abandonment. As if she had been thrown down an unending shaft, falling, falling and nothing to grab onto. Like a child separated from his parents in a big city. She had to run somewhere safe and beg for asylum. She had no one in Australia, she didn't even have a real job. The future looked bleak, frightening. An everlasting loneliness, the loneliness of a dead soul.

-8-

Peter moved back to Eszti's house, to the flatette in the attic. Finally, Clara was living the peaceful life she had craved. But some Sunday afternoons when Shosh was away at her friend's place and Clara had time to think, the painful feeling that she was alone in the world took hold of her. A heavy, crushing feeling, fencing her in, paralysing all other thought. On those afternoons she had to remind herself of the life she had escaped from, but her feelings seemed to spring from somewhere deep inside her where logic did not reach. Loneliness followed her around, it weighed her down, it sapped her energy. But then Shosh returned and the house was filled with stories and laughter again.

Shosh was her blessing, but she missed her father. She kept asking about him and every time she did, Clara found some explanation or other. Seven weeks passed and she began running out of excuses. She had no choice, she had to sort out Peter's access to Shosh. Access? The mere thought made her sick.

'When we going to see Grandma?' Shosh asked again one day.

'Soon, very soon,' Clara replied. I have to do it. I'll take Shosh to see Eszti and if Peter is there, we could sort out his access. Still wondering what to say, she rang Eszti the following Friday.

'I won't interfere in your marital problems,' Eszti said, 'except to say that if a marriage involves two people, so must its breakup.'

Clara didn't reply. How could she tell Eszti what had gone on inside their marriage?

59

'When are you coming? Peter hasn't seen Shosh for nearly two months.'

'How about Sunday?'

* * *

The closer Clara got to Eszti's house, the more anxious she was. Will he make a scene? Will he be looking at me with his uninhabited eyes, stare through me as if I'm not there?

Only a few more minutes, she thought, uneasy, her mouth dry. No, I can't, I can't face him. Not him and not Eszti.

'Will daddy be there?'

Clara, go back! Turn around! Turn around and never come back! Not to Eszti's house, not to this street, not even to this suburb.

'Muuum, will daddy be there?'

'I think so,' and she drove on. Minutes later she pulled up in front of Eszti's house.

Peter came to greet them, subdued, but friendly and Clara felt a great sense of relief. The lunch passed in peace. After lunch the four of them went out for a walk.

Eszti and Shosh were out of earshot when suddenly Peter gripped her arm.

'Clara, I have some bad news.'

She pulled away. 'You have no right to inflict more pain on me.'

'But you need to know.'

She looked at him as one looks at an armed intruder. Just shoot and be done with it.

'I know what's wrong with me. I've done the research, I read medical textbooks. I'm a schizophrenic, a clear case.'

'What? Jekyll one minute and Hyde the next?' she asked half mockingly.

'I don't think you know what schizophrenia is, how a schizophrenic brain works.'

'Tell me then.'

'It's infiltrated by strangers. Suddenly my brain is a car driven by reckless drivers and whether they drive me to my destination, or into the wall, or whether they drive me into you, my beautiful wife, it's all the same to them.'

'Just cut out the wife bit. I'm no longer your wife.'

'You'll always be my wife. Until death do us part, remember? Nothing can undo that. Ever.'

They began walking again.

'My brain has been playing up for years. Doctors kept telling me it's stress. Stress? They don't have a clue.'

Self-diagnosis! Nonsense! But she found it hard to carry the thought, because for the first time in years everything which had happened to them started to make sense.

'There's no cure for schizophrenia,' he added, 'but meditation and yoga can help. So I'm already doing them. And the Swami is helping me.'

'The Swami?'

'Yes, my teacher.'

'Where did you find him?'

'I didn't find him, he found me. He's always there with me, always telling me what to do.'

She broke out into a cold sweat. *He's insane, utterly insane.*

Insane? Crazy? He could lose it, he could be violent, but insane? The immensity of their predicament crushed her. She hated him. She hated him for what he put her through, she hated him for all the pain he caused her. Why did he have to involve her in his life? Someone stronger, someone with relatives and friends could have carried this burden better, someone less emotional. A matter-of-fact woman, a woman of action and not of reflection. She might have been better for him anyhow. They might have argued less, they might have enjoyed life more. They might have persevered less. She would have left him sooner; she would have left him as soon as the nightmare started. But then it hit her, no matter how hard it was for her, it was far worse for him. He was the one in Hell. She felt ashamed. And what about Eszti? And Shosh? What does that mean for Shosh? A shiver ran through her. No, she would not think about it, not today, she would sort out Peter's access visits. Access? She could not let Shosh out of her sight. Not now, not ever. But can I deny Peter seeing his daughter?

Just then Peter turned towards her, his eyes dark with sadness. No, she could not deny him access. Shosh would meet up with him, but only in her presence, and she rushed to catch up with her. She had to take Shosh's hand, protect her from whatever was in store for her. Protect her forever.

She did not sleep that night, and the many nights after. Shock and the fear of the future had displaced all her other emotions. In the morning, her mind foggy, she tried to focus, get Shosh ready for kindergarten, but her thoughts kept returning to their new predicament. How should she handle it? What should she do so as not to hurt Shosh? Her worries did not stop in the morning.

'Is anything wrong?' one of her colleagues asked. 'You seem to be out of sorts.'

She was working part-time in a small advertising agency. As part of the creative team she doubled up as editor, writer and whatever else was needed.

'Just a touch of flu.'

She had to finish a piece of work by tomorrow. The agency was struggling, the deadlines were strict, and so was the due date for her rent. She had to keep her job, she had to deliver by late afternoon no matter what.

That night her fear reached a new peak, consuming her, devouring her. She tossed and turned, 'I can't go on like this, I can't,' she screamed inside herself. 'You can't? Clara, get a hold of yourself. You can't live your life in the prison of fear, it will paralyse you. You have to be strong. You have to be strong for Shosh' sake.' As she lay there, she decided to reorganise her life. They would visit Peter, once a month, on the last Sunday. It meant predictability and some control in her life; it meant that after every visit she could look forward to a whole month of peace.

Somewhat relieved, she fell into a thin, fitful sleep.

-9-

The work at the advertising agency was relentless and that Thursday was frantic. One of the team had rung in sick and the deadline for her project was tomorrow. Clara had to step in, but first she had to finish the ad for the dishwashing liquid. 'No more bacteria, only sparkling bubbles,' the jingle went. It needed one more line. What? What would rhyme with it? Couples, cuddles, struggles, troubles, knuckles. Cuddles of course, Clara volunteered, and she finished the ad. She consulted on a possible video, and by the time they finished discussing another, it was one thirty, time for her to go to her cleaning job at the O'Neills.

The O'Neill's house was half an hour drive away in one of the well to do Eastern Suburbs, a big house commensurate with Mr O'Neill's standing in society as a property developer. Georgina, the ten-year-old daughter, opened the door. 'Mrs Steinberg, my mum is having a bath. She said that today you could start on the kitchen.'

Clara emptied the dishwasher, cleaned the stove, washed, and polished the sink until it gleamed, wiped the sideboard. She was washing the floor when Mrs O'Neill wearing a bathrobe, a towel turban on her head, face glowing - emerged from the bathroom, smelling of lavender.

'Hi Clara, all good?'

'Yes, thanks.'

'The bathroom is free now,' Mrs O'Neil said and walked on.

The kitchen floor finished; Clara headed to the bathroom. It was a magnificent bathroom, with high ceilings, marble floor, plants and lights scattered tastefully around. The big glass doors, overlooking the swimming pool and the bushes around it, joined the room with the outside, converging into a big luminous and lush space. But there was nothing luxurious about cleaning it. This time the bathtub had a greasy film left over from Mrs O'Neill's bath oils, which stuck stubbornly to the porcelain. Eventually the detergent and the extra scrubbing did the trick, the bathtub was shining again. Clara moved to the vanity cabinet, one third of its surface loaded with the secrets of Mrs O'Neills beauty, cleansing facial masks, body lotions, Dior moisturisers, makeups, blushers and perfumes. Once the wash basin and the marble top were clean, she returned Mrs O'Neills beauty lotions and potions to their usual place, tidied up the pile of folded fragrant towels and washed the floor. Half of the O'Neils house was done and Clara went to dust and vacuum the rest of the house.

Cleaning her own home, with its two small rooms, tiny bathroom and kitchen induced in her a calm, a contentment, while cleaning that woman's house was a robotic, soulless activity. But it was finally done.

'Thanks dear, I'll see you next Thursday,' Mrs O'Neill said as she gave her the money.

On her way home she picked up Shosh. Shosh kept chatting. Clara listened to her on and off. She was tired.

Her life was a daily climb, a relentless, exhausting climb towards some invisible peak. Surrounded by a dense forest, she could not see past her next few steps. Occasionally a small clearing did appear. She would peer through it. Towards the world? Her future? But whenever she gazed ahead, whenever she tried to imagine the coming years, all she saw was a tunnel where copies of her present days queued one after another. Endlessly.

As soon as they got home, she slipped back into the evening routine. When everything was finished and Shosh had gone to bed, Clara sat down on the sofa. Exhausted, but relieved, another day was over. She tried to watch television, but her thoughts were going around and around. Financially I'm dog paddling and socially I wouldn't be more alone in a cave. I always had friends. Friends, Nicole, I miss you. She had not written to her for years. No, that's not true, she did write to her, but never posted the letters. She could not tell Nicole about her life, so she wrote about her university tutoring and about Shosh. The rest she shrouded in a fog of generalities. When she re-read those letters, she thought they were false, disingenuous. Once she sat down to tell her the truth. She sat staring at the paper for a long time. How could she explain the transformation in Peter when she could not understand it herself? She folded the letter and slipped it into the drawer. Maybe some other time. That other time never eventuated and so Nicole retreated into the past.

I'm lonely, very lonely, but it's my financial situation that is wearing me out. She had only one outstanding job application, for a full-time position in the Department of People's Services. A dream job, it would mean no more advertising, no more tricking people to buy stuff, no more cleaning houses, she would be improving services, for the disadvantaged and the sick.

I'll ring them tomorrow see if I still have a chance.

-10-

The Monday morning train was rolling on. Looking through the window Clara was gazing at the world, not quite taking it in. She was thinking about her new job. Finally, she was doing the work she always wanted. Her life was looking up.

Lately she had even come to accept Peter. Nowadays, whenever she dreamt about him, more often than not, her dreams were of a happier time. I love you more than ever, he whispered in her ear the other night, I'm so lucky to have met you. How happy she was. How enormously happy. But then she woke.

I should not forget what we once had. Violence should not triumph over love. He fell sick and I shouldn't hate a sick man. I should be like Shosh, Shosh never holds a grudge, Shosh always forgives. Suddenly, as if an intense light was pulling her out of darkness, lifting her up, she felt weightless, near enough floating, as if the bitterness she had carried towards Peter, that heavy weight, had been lifted.

Shosh, her smiling dark eyes, her ready laughter. Shosh stayed at her friend's place last night. *She must be fast asleep, long auburn hair spread messily on the pillow, pink cheeks, lips whistling faintly at every breath. I can't wait to pick her up.*

She could see her running towards her, stretching up for a hug, 'I love you mummy.'

'I love you too,' she whispered.

The man sitting next to her looked up from his paper, 'Sorry Madam, what did you say?'

'Oh … nothing. I think I was talking to my daughter.'

The man shrugged, and Clara was back ruminating. Shosh is only five years old, but how would I feel if one day she left Australia? Do I love her as much as my father loved me? Enough to let her go, enough to face old age without her? Hardly a day had passed without her thinking about him. He never tried to talk me out of emigrating, he never said if things don't work out come back. He never mentioned failure. I know why, he wanted me to experience life in all its richness.

He must have known what sort of old age was waiting for him, the years of loneliness, and yet … She was seized by a feeling of shame, of remorse. I left him on the other side of the world, I made him fret and worry for months. The sleepless nights, the black scenarios, all the, 'what ifs.' What if things don't work out? And that night before my departure? Did he wonder whether he had done the right thing by not talking me out of emigrating? Whether he had done right by my late mother? Talking to her would have cleared his thoughts and doubts. He must have missed her more than ever, he must have missed the feel of her body snuggled up to him which once brought him peace, now an empty space which emphasised his loneliness.

The train gathered speed. It was flying past houses and gardens, Clara's gaze brushing over the scenery, more and more details lost. Her cogitations suddenly interrupted by the conductor's announcement. The next station … *It's mine!*

The walk from the station to the office was through a small park, past trees and bushes, rosellas and currawongs. It was ten past nine already and the queue at the café was six long. She hurried past, crossed the street and there was her destination, a five-storey block looking down on the small, family-owned shops in its surroundings. Its name, NSW Department of People's Services, loomed large above the entrance.

'Did you have a good weekend?' Maurice asked as she walked into the lift, then having exchanged a couple of pleasantries, he looked at her intently. 'Clara, about that briefing note, I need to see it before lunch. I have to send it out this afternoon.'

On the second floor she headed to her desk. Maurice continued to his office at the end of the aisle.

She turned the computer on, scanned the document she wrote on Friday, put in the statistician's figures, a few comments, then reread it carefully. 'It's an important document,' Maurice had said to her. 'It's to inform the Minister about the number of children in foster care in the state.' She added three case studies to illustrate the point of the briefing note and at twelve-thirty took a print to Maurice.

'Just leave it there,' he pointed to his in tray. I'll look at it as soon as I get out of the next meeting.'

Mid-afternoon he called her into his office.

'Your briefing note is good, and now it's with Sandy.'

'Sandy?'

'Yes, Sandy Roberts the Deputy Director General. Nothing leaves this Department without Sandy's signature. And every request from the Minister comes down through her.' Seeing the confused look on Clara's face, he added, 'That's how bureaucracy works. I thought you've seen the annual report.'

'I did.'

'Well have another look, and get an organisation chart, familiarise yourself with the structure, it'll come in handy,' Maurice picked up the phone and started dialling.

Clara returned to her desk. She had so much to learn. Only two weeks in the job and she had been hit with an avalanche of facts and terminologies which made her brain hurt. But she was not worried, she would get on top of it soon.

She opened the annual report and started reading.

'The Premier is the head of the government. He distributes the portfolios and appoints the Ministers.' *I knew that much*. She read on. 'The Minister for People's Services, the Hon Ray Manly, sets the policy direction for the Department. The Director General of the Department is responsible for its implementation.'

On the next page was a chart of boxes with the Director General on top and below him the Deputy Director General. *Oh, Sandy Roberts' position*. Below her were numerous directors.

The organisation chart went further; each director sat above boxes of managers. Manager of … the list went on and on. Suspended from each manager was the ladder of their staff, from the highest, down to the lowest position.

'Heavens above, this is huge!' She was about to give up when she spotted Maurice's box, Manager of Communication and Statistics, and above the middle of the ladder, hanging from him, was her own box.

Having got an impression of the organisation, she returned to the annual report, scanned a couple of major projects without retaining much and at five o'clock she ran for the train. She was pleased, her first piece of work went through without a hitch.

-11-

Bathed in the mid-morning sunshine, Ray Manly, the NSW Minister for People's Services, is staring at Clara's briefing note, but all he can think of is the pressure in his stomach. He was out at a function last night, the second one this week. It was a good do; the Treasurer's speech attracted the cream of the true believers. He ate, he drank, and he made some useful contacts. *But what on Earth did they feed me?* His face in a grimace, he opens a drawer, looking for the pills which always give him relief, pops a couple in his mouth then turns back to the briefing note. It is to inform him of yet another increase in the number of children in foster care. But worse follows: 'Due to a shortage of foster homes, some children have been placed in temporary arrangements.' *Bad news! Very bad! Anything to do with children is explosive. Fair game for the Opposition and the tabloids.*

He reads on. On the last page are three case studies, the first is the story of the five-year-old boy sent to his third foster home. He can see the frightened little boy facing another strange family. This boy could have been him. No, he was not brought up by strangers, but neither did he have a family. Nobody knew who his father was, least of all his mother. Too busy with boyfriends and alcohol, she passed her son on — like a parcel delivered to the wrong address — to his grandmother, a tough woman who, having brought up four kids on her own, was not exactly overjoyed at his arrival. To her, parenting was not about loving and cooing and reading bed-time stories, but a duty. A duty she performed with militaristic flexibility. She kept him clean and fed, and made sure he never missed a day's school. Even when he was unwell. When he complained about the two boys in school who picked on him, she said, 'You either beat them to smithereens or put up with it. Life's a battle, you might as well get used to it.'

As it happened, it was the perfect upbringing for a political career.

He scans the briefing note again: More kids need foster care? Of course, marriages aren't what they used to be, nowadays they're as sturdy as hens' eggs. The world has changed, but what is my department doing about it? The same as they've always done, not one new idea in their collective heads. Just as he picks up the phone to ring Sandy Roberts, the Deputy Director General of his department, the door opens with the force of a whirlwind and slams against the wall.

Startled, Ray Manly looks up. *Bugger, what now?*

'There!' The Premier throws a two-page document on his desk.

"Questions on Notice." The title stares at Ray Manly. *Another one?* His gaze rolls down the list. He does not have to look far, the highlighted question is not even halfway down the page, it is question number two.

'How much taxpayers' money has been saved by the restructure of Services?' Ms Helen Pride, the shadow minister, wants to know.

Ray Manly's blood is on the boil. For weeks now, he has been asking exactly that question of the peacock, the Director General of his Department. He might as well have asked what the afterlife has in store for him.

So what now? What should he say to the Premier? No man would go to the police to turn himself in for driving under the influence. Because, when it's all said and done, whichever way he looks at it, he has to acknowledge that he has been under the influence of the Director General. How many times has that master of weaselling and obfuscation managed not to tell him what the restructure is worth? *I should've sacked that bastard long ago.*

'The opposition is after us!' the Premier says, his voice above the polite. 'I need facts. I need to see the savings, or is this another useless restructure? We've had too many of those.'

Ray Manly nods. There have been restructures as far back as he can remember and according to the staff who have been around for years, many before his time. Small departments converged into bigger and bigger departments, in the name of efficiency and cost saving. The super departments were not even embedded when the government, in line with its new philosophy – small means autonomy, small has local flavour – decided to split them up. Those restructures were nothing but a dance where the partners got together, split up, changed partners, danced for a while then coalesced again. And every now and then a star was born.

The star in the latest restructure is the result of a cosmic coalescence, the like of which has never been seen before, the coalescence of all Human Services big and small – into the super Department of People's Services. The stellar restructure promised stellar savings. Now the only thing missing is the proof.

'Ray, this restructure was your idea, but ideas aren't enough. You have to make them work.'

But hadn't he made it work? Doesn't the mere existence of his Department prove that he had? All the hours he put into it, the networking, the wheeling and dealing. Well, it did elevate him from a Minister without Portfolio – the Minister for odds and ends, rats and mice as his wife, Shirley, put it – to the Minister with the biggest portfolio. The highest of the high perches and there is no shortage of ministers trying to push him off. Or journalists eager to make a name for themselves on his account. One has been digging for gossip with the zeal of a missionary for weeks. And now, the Premier is on his back. His perch feels suddenly unsteady.

'Ray, I need a clear picture of the operational costs of your Department, present and future up to two years. When will I get it?'

When will he get it? 'I'll check with them. I'll let you know tomorrow.'

'No time for checking and letting know. Two weeks, and this time you'd better deliver.'

At the threat in the Premier's voice, Ray Manly shrinks back into his chair like a snail into his shell.

'And don't forget that,' the Premier adds, pointing to the Questions on Notice. The door shuts behind him, but the worry of their encounter, like a whiff of burning sulphur, hangs on Ray Manly for the rest of the day. He is in a mess and the man responsible for his predicament is that bloody peacock, the Director General of his Department. In London, while I have to put up with the Premier's rantings. On a study tour? Study tour your arse. And what else? Did he take his extramarital with him? Well, she's a good looker, you have to give it to him; his taste is impeccable.

I'll sort him out when he gets back. The peacock needs to have his tail clipped. Shirley was right, another Minister would've got rid of him long ago. True, and I can too. I can bring in a new Director General any time. In the meantime, I'll deal with his Deputy. I'll send her the Questions on Notice, the Department is an expert in weaselling out of difficult questions, and he picks up the phone to dial Sandy Roberts.

'Sandy, the Premier just dropped another Question on Notice on my desk. In short, the opposition is at it again. They want the savings from the restructure. By next Wednesday, so just broad brush. But, and this is important, the Premier needs the projected savings, for six months up to two years. In detail.'

In detail? Sandy Roberts fidgets, trying to find a comfortable spot. With all the staff changes, it would be like predicting the shape of shifting sands. 'The staff picture is still murky; some are only employed for the transition period. So, it's complicated.'

'And may I ask when the transition period will end?'

Preoccupied by the hopelessness of the task, Sandy Roberts did not notice the sarcasm in the Ray Manly's voice. *End? Do I have to teach the Minister the obvious? Teach him what every public servant knows? A transition period ends when the next restructure begins.*

'The figures are due to the Premier in two weeks. But I need to see the results first, so let's meet next Friday.'

She cannot object, she cannot cause ripples, she is only acting in her position, a wobbly situation from which she cannot throw stones. But Sandy Roberts is not one to agonise about the impossible, she is a practical woman. *So, he wants savings? He'll get them.* She will put the best people on this work. She will ask them to take as many short cuts as they can get away with. Forecasts are never accurate. She can always rely on the imponderable, the unpredictable for an excuse.

* * *

It is close to midnight and Ray Manly is lying in bed wide awake. Thoughts, worries, fragments of conversations with the Premier, with the Director General, are revolving in his head like a merry-go-round. What if there are no savings from the restructure? What then? He has been a worried man for a while, but lately the stress of the office is getting to him. He used to shut the office door in the evening and leave the day behind. He could compartmentalise his life, but nowadays work and family inhabit the same world. His joys, stresses, victories and failures feed on each other.

To minimise stress, he runs five kilometres every day. It takes it out of him because he is heavier now. Networking lunches and dinners, snacks to keep him working late into the night, have turned into more of him. So he runs. And runs. The rest has been left to Shirley. But Shirley is a twice a week woman, and this week nothing has eventuated, and it is nearly Friday. *Friday! And she's already blowing bubbles.* He tries to convince himself that Shirley deserves her sleep, she looks after the children, and that Greg is a handful of a boy, four years old and on the go all the time. A smile comes to Ray's face as he recalls how the boy fought for the ball on Saturday. A born AFL player. And six-year-old Dolly? With her blue eyes and blonde hair, not for nothing she's called Dolly. May God give her luck and a good husband, not that she will need much looking after, she can stand on her own already.

His thoughts turn to the conversation with the Deputy Director General. He has met Sandy Roberts before. Most unimpressive. Will she be able to deliver what that bastard of a Director General did not?

Savings, savings, but what if there are no savings? Cut it, Ray, stop thinking problems, it's past midnight. There will be savings, you'll squeeze it out of them. In the meantime, there can be sweeteners, diversions. Initiatives? That's it, a new initiative! Something to do with …

Shirley stirs. Her hair catches the narrow ray of streetlight cutting through the chink in the curtain. She has nice hair, and Ray Manly caresses the back of her head. His hand slides down to her breast.

Shirley wakes: 'I want to sleep.'

'C'mon darling.'

'Leave me alone.'

The honeymoon, which followed the election, is well and truly over. She is no longer making love to the man who the crowds would one day cheer on Macquarie Street, cheer him for all the wonderful things he has done for them, because she will never be the wife of Ray Manly the Premier. If luck is on her side, she will remain the wife of a Minister, a worried Minister. The wife of his stresses, a slave to the NSW Government.

'But I love you,' Ray whispers, mad with desire.

'I resent being used as a tranquilliser,' she hisses menacingly.

'That's a bit strong, darling. I'm just a healthy male with a healthy appetite. You must know by now.'

'A healthy appetite? More like a nervous tick in the crutch,' she pulls away from him. 'Goodnight.'

Ray Manly is angry. Monogamy is not his choice, it's the choice of our time, and a politician cannot be a philanderer unless he wants to see himself on the front of the tabloids.

He is not going to beg for sex, sex from his own wife. Making as much noise as he can, he jumps out of bed and heads to the kitchen to pour himself a glass of beer. He is about to finish the second glass when his mind strays to his conversation with the Deputy Director General. She will have to come up with the savings. If not, his career will slide past him like an express train through a minor station. He won't allow that. He was not born with a silver spoon in his mouth like some. He got where he got through hard work and a lot of painful elbowing.

He will deal with Sandy forcefully. If there are no savings, the Department will have to cut. Cut staff, cut services. How many? He has no idea. First, they'll have to provide him with a clear picture of the financial situation. They have enough modellers, and the Premier? He'll get his figures. As long as this Sandy Roberts woman delivers. But will she?

-12-

Maurice walks out of the lift with a spring in his step, in his mind's eye images of yesterday's trip to Kiama. The Blowhole, his kids laughing, screaming, and getting wet every time the ocean shot into the sky. He did right by Sue too, she enjoyed browsing the small tourist shops and buying bits and pieces. And that lunch at Dino's restaurant? That lobster! Yes, it was a great weekend, it has reinvigorated him. He can take the world on.

'Hi Maurice. All good?' Sandy Roberts says as she walks past.

'Couldn't be better, and how're you …?' But Sandy is already out of earshot.

Maurice turns on the light in his office, puts his briefcase down, powers the computer and heads out for his morning coffee. On the way to the lift, he says hello to Clara, concludes yet again that she's pretty. Not my sort, but she's an excellent writer. True, she's an English graduate, but she studied English in the Netherlands, yet she writes better than anyone here.

The trees surrounding the oval are still wet from last night's rain. On the leaves, yellow and orange drops of water shine in the sun. The sky is a singing blue. A perfect day, Maurice muses as he sips his coffee. Soon it will be summer and images of him and Sue baking on the beach, the children playing in the sand, fill him with utter joy. My dear Sue, how much you changed me. You have given me confidence and contentment. But secret urges still trouble him. Young Charmaine with her super miniskirts makes him uncomfortable every time she walks past his office.

That girl has everything, body, face, brain. Lucky for the man, if she has one, and judging by the black under her eye, she might have more than one. Pity I can't be that extra.

The coffee finished, he is well and truly ready for the day.

Back in his office, he settles comfortably into his chair when Ping! Sandy Roberts' name flashes on the screen. A smug smile lights up Maurice's face. A request for the Minister. *Oh? Another briefing note?* Maurice reads on. Maurice clicks the forward button. 'Hi Clara, this is important. I'll talk to you about it after lunch.' That solved, he opens his inbox. A long list of emails is queuing for his attention. He accepts the meeting appointments, then looks down the list for the important and the unusual. 'Yes,' he whispers and clicks on the high priority email from Sandy Roberts. 'Upcoming confidential work,' she warns the addressees. 'In the next ten days, nonessential leave should not be approved. Details will follow soon.'

Confidential work? Who else is involved? Maurice scans the 'To' list. His name is not on it. He looks at the, 'Copied in' list and there he is on his own and Maurice's mood hits a low note. *Something is cooking here. Another restructure? The damn things are as frequent as the winter flu. You hardly escape one and the next one gets you.* He scans the email again. The secrecy, the urgency all points to a ministerial of major significance. No doubt Sandy Roberts has discussed it with her inner circle already, no doubt they have chewed over what to give the Minister and what might be best to leave out. But why wasn't I invited? Because I'm only acting in my position, that's why. His stomach is churning, his hands suddenly clammy. Keep your calm, Maurice, keep your calm. Isn't Sandy Roberts acting in the Deputy Director General's position and the Financial Director in hers? And who knows how many other actors are in this Department. Times have changed, Maurice. Times have changed. Nowadays only God has a permanent position.

He takes a deep breath. I might be acting in my position, but I am a permanent public servant, a permanent server of the people in this state, and not sackable! His stress receding a little, he pulls out the IT report. Thirty-five pages of diagrams and jargon. *Torture!* He skims the executive summary, skips the body of the report, scans the top three conclusions at the end. He will find out in the meeting what all this is about, picks up his diary and heads to the IT meeting.

Lunch over, Maurice calls Clara in.

'Have you seen my email?'

'No, I had to …'

'That's OK. I'll tell you what it's about. You might have noticed that Kate is not in today.'

'Is she sick?'

'No, but her mother is. Very sick. It looks like Kate will be away for a while, not clear how long. Her work, in health communication is urgent, so I decided that for the time being, you take over her duties. A development opportunity, you'll learn a great deal.'

'Thank you.'

'And I'll get someone to act in your position until Kate is back.'

'Now your first job. It's a request from the Minister. A briefing note about our services for the mentally ill.'

'For the mentally ill?' She asks, as the blood drains from her face.

'For information only,' Maurice adds, 'just like your previous one. You should include a summary of services, and some stats.' He pauses for thought, then looking back at Clara, 'You'll have to emphasise the importance of our services, their role for a good prognosis. Danny Matheson will give you all the information you need. He's a medic.'

Their role in a good prognosis? she ponders on the way to her desk. But she will talk to Danny Matheson first.

* * *

Clouds are floating across the setting sun as Clara walks to the station, mulling over the briefing note she has to write. *Development opportunity? I would much rather do without it.*

The coffee shop is shut, the chairs piled up against the window. She does not notice the approaching man looking her up and down, evaluating her.

'Emphasise the importance of our services for a good prognosis,' Maurice said. 'Emphasise it, how?' she ponders as she emerges into the street.

'Sorry!' A boy on a bicycle cuts in front of her and disappears around the corner where the Woolworths sign is fluorescing already. It happens again, as if the neon lights of Woolworths unlock the gates to that memory of years ago.

Evening, the city, the tramp, Peter.

She hurries past Woolworths, but the tramp persists, he's taken over her thoughts, eyes following her to the station.

* * *

The Saturday evening train trundled along from one station to the next.

At one of the stops, a group of noisy teenagers invaded the carriage. She snuggled up to Peter.

'Clars, look at me.'

She turned towards him.

'Just as I thought.'

'What? What did you just think?'

'Your face is not just pretty, but very, very beautiful,' and pulled her closer to kiss her.

'So are you, very handsome and this is a perfect evening.'

It was perfect because she had escaped the soulless suburb, its empty streets, its houses enveloped by a dark silent loneliness as if hiding terrible crimes. It was especially lonely on Saturday nights when she was more likely to see a cat, or a possum, than the moving shadow of a human in the barely lit street.

Outside Town Hall Station, the street was teeming with people. Yes, she was in the city, among the crowds and the noise and the energy of it all. Only embarrassment, only the fear of looking weird kept her from skipping and dancing. But then she spotted him. Middle aged, olive skin, face framed by a crop of oily ringlets and finished by a grey beard. He was sitting on the ground, propped up against the wall. Looking at her.

There was something in that look, a connection, a communication she did not want to be part of. An invitation into a world she did not want to enter. She tried to look away, but something drew her back. His gaze, a creepy, invisible thread, had attached itself to her and would not let go. Woolworths, the neon letters above him screamed. The ghostly fluorescence amplified the man's eerie smile. On the corner the traffic light turned green. A noisy crowd crossed the street. Talking, laughing. They walked past the tramp as if he was a lump in the concrete, a flaw which had always been there. How can people walk past him as if he does not exist? How can they be happy in front of such wretchedness? She looked at Peter. He too was staring at the tramp.

'Peter, why doesn't the government look after him?'

'The government? He's not the government's responsibility, he's his family's responsibility.'

'And if he has no family?' she raised her voice, but the hullaballoo of the street drowned her question.

'Christ is your Saviour!' a man with a placard shouted. 'He died for you. He died for your sins.' The tramp smiled an eerie smile. My sins?

A drunk holding a bottle staggered past. Trying to avoid him, a youngster bumped into the tramp's bag. His friends burst out laughing.

'Christ is your Saviour!' Clara heard the call again, this time from behind, not as a promise, more like a statement.

Why? Why did God send his son to Earth? Why doesn't he look after the tramp, and the sick and the deranged? Should I ask Peter? No, he would invoke faith, assumptions she did not believe in. It would turn into another chicken and egg argument. She had learned to live with his beliefs. At times they frustrated her, but for the most part they did not intrude into her life too much. If they tried, she quickly dismissed them, locked them away.

She grabbed his arm. She had to be close to him, she had to be reassured that he was walking by her side, strong and protective. To the end of her days.

Before long they reached Chinatown. The streets were alive with people, and the smells of the Orient. Shops and restaurants, their names inscribed in Asian letters, competed for attention. Roast ducks and spareribs hanging in a window, next door an aquarium of somnolent fish calling for their own demise.

'How about having dinner here?' Peter said and they went in.

It was well past midnight when they got home.

She could not sleep. She kept thinking about the tramp, he had wormed himself into her mind. Peter's gentle touch which used to make her body burn with desire, left her flat.

The next morning, she woke up with a shout, a haunted shout of terror and dread. She had dreamt about the tramp, the homeless man with toes sticking out of his shoes. But there was something disconcerting about him. A vaguely familiar face ...? Eyes? She could not remember.

That tramp had manoeuvred himself into her psyche. Whenever she walks past Woolworths' lit sign, there he is again, looking at her, smiling his eerie smile, and she wonders yet again whether the tramp had echoed something inside her, some connection to Peter.

-13-

Back from his morning coffee, Maurice is going through his in tray when Sandy Roberts walks past. Yesterday's email still irks him. Why was he left out? Hasn't he proved himself over and over again in his ten months here? He is a strategist, the only one. He goes through the email again, slowly. No, he hasn't misunderstood, he has been left out of the management team. His pride hurts. Resentment is boiling, bubbling inside him. Invisible arms are pushing him away, voices are whispering in his ear, 'We'll call on you when needed.'

Come on Maurice, not being included once in Sandy Roberts' inner circle is not a demotion, but he cannot help feeling diminished, he cannot help feeling that on the pecking order he has dropped a rung. I won't let those girls push me aside, turn me into a sideline, into a just-in-case person, because that is the first step to becoming irrelevant.

'Don't let them get to you. They're no better than you,' his mother's words resound in his head.

She was right. I need to look after myself. I can do any management job in the Department and many outside and with another restructure in the offing, unlikely but not entirely improbable, look after myself I will. I will touch base with every high-level contact. I'll ring Bob, talk to him just in case …' As my mother used to say, 'If you mix with those who count, you will start to count too.'

His mother. She taught him many things, she told him to go to university and he did. He studied social science. He wanted to help the homeless, the sick, the disadvantaged, but those sentiments have been diluted somewhat by the realities of life. Nowadays, his position is not safe enough to think of others, nowadays, he has to think of himself.

She would be sixty-five years old this Friday, and a sudden nearness, a loving, calming presence envelops him. He wonders if she can see him. Like the little boy of four decades ago, he wants to show her his achievements. He wants to show her the three rows of four on the other side of the glass wall that partitions him from his subordinates, those twelve people typing away on their computers, are working for him. His gaze pauses above their heads for a while before he turns back to his computer. The next email is from Marina. *Oh, not her again.* But there are others nearly as annoying. He scans them quickly before annihilating them into nothingness. The dross gone, Maurice turns to look at the emails from those who really count, and reads them with the care the sender's position deserves.

'They might be trying to keep me out, but I am still the Manager of Communications and Statistics,' he says to himself, lingering on every syllable and with newly regained self-worth he pushes his foot against the corner of his desk. The chair spins around to face the window.

Outside the air is crystal clear, he can even see the birds circling above the oval and the café where he buys his morning coffee. Behind him, the computer pings. He turns back to his desk. It's an email about computer updates on the coming weekend.

Sandy's secretary walks in and drops a document in his in tray. But just now Maurice has more important tasks to attend to. Ring his contacts, network. There must be some management job on offer somewhere.

He is on the phone to Bob when Charmaine, wearing a mini-mini black skirt and crochet black top, walks past his door. The crochet not quite dense enough to cover the patches of her white skin, or the battle between her black bra and its contents. Bob is telling him about the management course he attended last week, but Maurice is not listening, he is thinking of the animal perfection which just walked past. *That girl knows the art of womanhood.* A bit too well, judging by the reaction on the lower part of his anatomy. But then Charmaine re-appears and walks into his office. *Oh no!*

'Sorry mate, I have to go, something urgent. See you on Sunday,' and Maurice puts the phone down.

Charmaine has brought the final version of the Housing Officers Code of Conduct.

'I'll look at it tomorrow.'

'Thank you,' she smiles seductively.

Charmaine, for goodness sake, I won't be able to get out of the office.

With Charmaine gone the best time of Maurice's day is over, and to make matters worse he has to go to a meeting with Finance. *I should take someone with me, someone financially literate. I can't let those self-important arseholes pull the wool over my eyes with their highfalutin terminology.* He is trying to think of someone when Clara walks in.

'Maurice,' she says as the knot in her stomach is getting tighter, 'I'm sorry but I have to go and pick up my daughter. Her teacher rang. She has a high temperature. I know I've been here less than a month, but ...'

'No buts, just go, you can work from home. As long as the briefing note is ready in time ...'

'Maurice, I don't have a computer.'

'Just fax it through from the Post Office. I'll get someone to type it in.'

She could hug him; she is so grateful. She returns to her desk, packs her bag with the documents she will need for the briefing note. *What else? Oh, the stats,* and she heads to Marina's desk.

Immersed in the world of numbers, she is gazing at her screen.

Clara stops by her desk. Marina looks up, eyes trying to focus.

'Sorry to interrupt, but I have to ask you something. The school just rang that my daughter is sick. I have to go and pick her up.'

'The poor kid. So, you're after the figures for your briefing note?'

'Yes.'

'I don't have them. But I'll finish them by tomorrow afternoon.'

'Could you ring me when you're ready?' Clara hands her a piece of paper with her phone number.

'Of course.'

'The briefing note's due on Thursday,' Clara adds with a sigh. 'What if I can't finish it by then?'

'Just do what you can. Bugger them, you can't be in two places at the same time. You're not a quantum mother.'

'Quantum mother? What's that?'

'In the quantum world, a particle can be in two places at the same time. Sorry, but you're too heavy to qualify,' and seeing the confusion on Clara's face she adds, 'Just a friggin thought, don't listen to me.'

'I'd better run now.'

-14-

Cheeks red with temperature, Shosh is lying on the sofa, her head on her mother's lap. Clara feels at peace. She caresses Shosh's forehead and the sunrays in her hair. I'm lucky, I have her, I have a job and we have this cosy little flat, rented, but peaceful. Its only inhabitants Shosh, me and our love. I'm blessed.

Shosh smiles drowsily and drifts to sleep. Slowly, so as not to wake her up, she places Shosh's head on a pillow and heads to the kitchen to work on the briefing note. Figure out the structure and the main points to cover.

Mid-afternoon Marina calls. 'The stats were easy to get,' and she reads her the results. 'Will you be in tomorrow?'

'I don't think so.'

'Just look after the little one, no rush to come back.'

'She's not that little, but she does need looking after.'

'Clara, if you need anything, and I mean anything, not only stats, just ring. I know how difficult it is to be in two places at once.'

With a warmth in her heart she can hardly contain, Clara puts in the figures. She rewrites a few paragraphs, checks how it all fits together. She is pleased; she will definitely finish it tomorrow.

The next morning Shosh looks much recovered, but she has a mild temperature. After another conversation with Danny Matheson, Clara makes a few changes to the briefing note, 'It should do.' She leaves Shosh in front of the television and hurries to the post office to fax it to Maurice.

Early afternoon, Maurice rings.

'Thanks Clara. It's fine. By the way we had a high priority email from Sandy. The Minister will be visiting the office tomorrow. Don't stress, but it would be good if you could make it in.'

'I will.'

She is preparing dinner that evening when the phone rings. It is Adam, the young man she runs into some mornings when she drops Shosh at school. He walks his five-year-old son to school, the two of them chatting like friends. She noticed them before she fell into the habit of stopping for a short chat. Adam and his ex-wife live in the same street and share the custody of their son.

A few days ago, he invited her for coffee and asked her for her phone number. She was elated, she couldn't have wished to meet a nicer man.

Now Adam has rung to invite her out for dinner, this Friday. He will pick her up at seven o'clock. Yes, I have a date! she thought as she put the phone down. My first since I became single again.

-15-

Ray Manly is lying in bed mulling over his day. Today the answer to the Question on Notice was tabled in Parliament. The Department has done well, they managed to get the Opposition off his back. 'Considerable savings are being made,' their answer said, 'the precise amount will be firmed up once the discussions with non-permanent staff are concluded. In six months' time.'

'Six months?' the Opposition screamed.

'Six months,' Ray Manly argued, 'because we cannot break contracts at a whim, or get rid of temporary staff. We look after families, unlike you over there.'

The arguments went on. The Opposition shouted and mocked, but no matter how nasty they got, they did not get anything to dissect, nothing they could use to compromise and discredit the government.

Ray Manly might have a few months reprieve from the Opposition, but there is no reprieve from the Premier, and tomorrow is judgement day. By mid-afternoon, he will have nailed down the savings to be realised from the restructure in the next six, twelve and eighteen months. He can then decide how to package it for the Premier and how best to sell it to the electorate. If everything looks right, and he ardently hopes so, he will take the proof and stick it in the Premier's face, in his face, or in some other part of his anatomy. No, the gloomy invasion does not seem a good idea, he will drop the document on his desk: 'There you are, there're the savings!' The bully. He and his loyal supporters, Bill Winding the champion schemer and slimy Mike Williams, and the others who would sell their mother to get his ministry. Years ago, he thought that once he got his ministry, his main worry would be those sitting on the opposite side. Not so, his main worry is those sitting on his side and he had better watch his back, and keep crawling to the Premier. 'Well, we all have to crawl to someone.'

Having stopped dreaming revenge, his mind turns to the new initiative. He has thought about it in more detail and he discussed it with the Premier. He is on board: 'Closing down non-acute hospital beds in psychiatric wards means extra beds for general use, and with the waiting lists what they are … It'll be a winner. Let's proceed.'

'A feather in my cap,' Ray Manly says to himself. 'Tomorrow I'll discuss the new initiative with Sandy Roberts. It's time to put some meat on those bones. And after the meeting, if time allows, I'll take half an hour or so to meet the staff, a public relations exercise and a potentially useful one.'

His plan sorted; he can now settle down to sleep. But sleep refuses to embrace him and he lies there for a long while. Shirley twitches. Ray Manly looks at her. She's dreaming already. She barely hits the bed and she's asleep. You'd think that she's been shearing sheep all day. I won't wake her. I don't want an argument; I need to be clear headed for tomorrow's meeting. He tries to relax, again. Think of something pleasant. Uplifting. Oh, yes! Linda, Linda the tall blonde, the Premier's new secretary. Wow! He read somewhere that the result of an interview depends on the first impression. It takes only a few seconds to decide whether the applicant is suitable for a job. In her case it must have been a millisecond. She's a corker.

As he lies there, Shirley's back in his face, he can see Linda undressing, pulling her dress over her head. Slowly. Playing with him, enticing him, her blonde hair falling over her breast. She gets into bed, her hip next to him. She pulls closer. The tall, beautiful Linda. He puts his hand on her buttock.

'Leave me alone!' Shirley screams.

'Sorry, I didn't mean to.'

'Didn't you? So, what did you mean?'

'Oh, let's just drop it,' and he gets out of bed and heads to the kitchen to get himself a beer.

-16-

In the Department of People's Services, lunchtime is coming to an end. The staff, some one by one, others in groups of two or three, are dribbling back into the office. The door of the lift opens again and Ray Manly steps out and heads to his meeting with Sandy Roberts.

'Clara,' Marina whispers, 'the Minister's here.'

Navy suit, blue tie, white shirt, collar touching the pleat in his chin, briefcase in his hand, but what really impresses Clara is his confident stride. He turns right, says hello to Sandy's secretary and disappears into the boardroom. The secretary takes up her gatekeeping role. Whatever is being discussed behind that door, is far too important to allow anybody past.

Greetings over, Ray Manly checks his watch, 'Let's get straight to business.' He does want coffee, but he has to wrap up the meeting by three-thirty. At four o'clock he is due to open the Mums and Babs Community Centre in his electorate.

Sandy has a lot to go through, but she can see the advantages of a shorter meeting, but will she have enough time to explain to him why there will be no savings from the restructure? Well, not in the next six to twelve months, and afterwards? Afterwards anything could happen, afterwards this government might be gone. Trying to predict the long-term future is like wrestling with fog.

The meeting is about to start when the door of the boardroom opens and Lisa, the financial controller, apologises as she walks in. Relieved,

Sandy Roberts clicks the mouse. The graph of the financial projections lights the screen, Ray Manly's face flitting from bored, to confused. Suddenly the meaning of the graph hits him, hits him in the pit of his stomach. His face twists with rage. His temples are throbbing, last week's encounter with the Premier still fresh in his mind. No, he won't allow this woman to play with his future.

'No way! No bloody way! Do you really think I can take this to the Premier? And what about the Opposition?'

He can see the shadow minister waving the graphs, he can hear Helen Pride screeching, 'Savings, ha? Savings for the taxpayer? Where exactly are the savings? It's more than a year since the restructure and not a dollar saved. So much for Ray Manly's brainwave. His super-ministry. He never costed it. He lied to you.' And the whole bench roaring with laughter. Bill Winding chortling and slimy Mike Williams trying to repress a happy grin. *Unless this woman comes up with the savings, I'm finished. The rumours are that the Premier is planning a reshuffle. Slimy Williams is surely lined up for my ministry.*

'Some communication consultants will be gone by the middle of the next year,' Sandy says. 'So, we'll have some savings.'

'Communication consultants? For crying out loud, are you still communicating? The Department has sent out tens of thousands of letters, made thousands of phone calls, stuck posters on every wall. In all languages! You communicated with the deaf and the blind. So, what's left? And as far as the various parts of the Department are concerned, they definitely don't need more communicating, they've had enough emails, meetings, letters. By now even the moles and the morons should be informed. So, it's easy. Streamline the operation. Temporary staff cut; casual staff cut! To minimum!'

'We're up against a strong union. How many positions, even temporary positions, can the Department shed without major union trouble?'

'Far, far more than you have. You haven't closed a single position, have you?'

Sandy Roberts looks at him like a rabbit facing a bulldog.

'No, of course not. About time that both you and that pompous arsehole, the Director General, realise that this restructure is not about organising and reorganising. Not about looking busy. This restructure is for real. "Real,"' he rolls a loud 'r', his face red, apoplectic.

And Sandy Roberts knows that the man in front of her is in no mood to compromise.

'Once the present vacancies are filled, some contractors will go,' Lisa says, 'so there will be more savings.'

The Minister looks from her to Sandy, 'Are you still filling vacancies? Are you two having me on? We can't afford to fill vacancies. And contractors? Some will go you said. Did you mean you intend to renew the others? Get rid. Get rid of as many as possible. How much will that save? Ball park!'

Sandy has no idea. Ray Manly's gaze piercing, the savings noose tightening around her neck, she has to come up with something. Straightaway. *Bugger accuracy, decisiveness is everything*, 'It depends when their contract finishes. In the next year? Maybe five to eight percent.'

'Not enough! We need at least, and I mean at least,' he says, eyes boring into her, 'fifteen percent savings. Would getting rid of vacancies and contractors cover it?'

She looks at Lisa. 'We have to do the modelling,' she says.

'I thought you finished it.'

'Not this scenario.'

'I need fifteen percent. With all the details by mid-morning next Wednesday. The Premier has to have them by next Friday, the latest.'

Sandy Roberts is considering the impossibility of her task when Ray Manly says, 'Can we have some more coffee?'

'Of course.' She opens the door and calls her secretary, 'Some coffee please, percolated will do.'

'Now let's discuss another matter,' Ray Manly says, 'a possible new initiative. I discussed it with the Premier, well bounced it around. We should firm it up and proceed.'

'Yes?'

'In summary, we will reduce the number of non-acute beds allocated to the mentally ill in some hospitals ...'

But we just closed down the mental hospitals, she is about to blurt.

'The short summary of what I'm proposing,' Ray Manly says, shuffling through his papers. 'Bugger, I forgot the folder in my office.'

The secretary walks in with the coffee.

'Anyway, I've tested the waters,' Ray Manly adds and pours Sandy a cup. 'Any sugar? No? I couldn't drink coffee without sugar. I need three heaped teaspoons at least.'

'You tested the waters?'

'Yes. I mentioned it to the Head of the Psychiatrists Association. He said that if it comes to it, he will have to take it to his members. But your staff should do some work on it, only preliminary work for now.'

She takes a sip of coffee. 'I have a medic on staff. He could do some background research and depending on what the research shows … we'll decide what else needs to be done.'

'But wait, I have some good news,' Ray Manly says. 'We will invest in halfway houses … Not yet clear how much. Let's see what the modelling shows.'

Sandy's head is spinning, but one thing she knows that in any announcement there should be some good news to balance the bad. But can you take money from one part of the system and add it to the other and end up better off? You cannot do that in arithmetic. So, can you do it in services for the mentally ill? And what does this initiative really mean for them?

'The Premier wants it implemented by the end of April, beginning of May,' Ray Manly interrupts her thoughts, 'so I'll have to launch it in second week of March the latest, in four-months-time. Three and a half if you exclude the Christmas break. We will launch it under the name Heal in Place.

'All highly confidential of course, no need to give fodder to all those interest groups, not to mention the Opposition. That lot would oppose their own policies if we tried to introduce them. And one more thing, don't forget the bleeding hearts, you need to bring them on board.'

'Of course. They're members of the Integration into the Community working party. We'll discuss the initiative with them the day before the announcement, and they'll be sworn to secrecy.'

'Terrific. Now what else do I need from you?' He pauses for thought. 'Oh, the speech for the launch. A really good one.'

'Of course. My staff will also prepare some fact sheets. Fact sheets are the best way of communicating with the community.'

'Brilliant. By the way, I will announce it on a Friday. By Monday, any opposition will fizzle out and the political fallout will be minimal.' After reflecting for a moment, 'I think that covers it.'

He checks his watch, 'Sandy, I have some time left. On the way out, I'd like to meet a few of your staff. What do you think?'

'What do I think? They will love it.'

Ray Manly picks up his briefcase and the two of them walk into the open plan office. Sandy is relieved, he did ask for cuts, but he didn't ask to close down any suburban branches. It's Friday afternoon and in her mind's eye she can see the overworked clerks trying to find the homeless a weekend roof. She might have agreed to everything the Minister asked for, but closing branches is the red line for her. She would have opposed it with all her might.

* * *

Ministers have visited the Department in the past. They slipped quietly into the Director General's office, as if on a secret mission. Later, when the meeting was over, he — it has never yet been a she — sneaked out just as quietly as he arrived. No Minister ever went to meet those who sat behind the grey partitions.

But here is Ray Manly walking from cubicle to cubicle, shaking the hands of its inhabitant, admiring their photos and postcards. Postcards are an easy starting point for a conversation, they tell him what matters to these people, and what matters to them, matters to him too. He is a Master of Public Relations, and of popular knowledge. From rugby to swimming, from children to holidays, the beach, the bush, skiing and the snow, he chats to them with a smile. He asks questions, he cracks jokes. 'And your role in the Department?' he asks each one in turn, and as they explain he interrupts with, 'That's serious stuff,' or, 'That's very, very important.'

The staff is watching his every move trying to catch his every word.

The Minister, who they have seen once or twice on television, now stands in front of them. The embodiment of power is interested in their work, in their families, their babies, their hobbies. He sympathises, he encourages, he praises. A few are intimidated. 'I'm writing briefing notes,' Clara manages to say. Sandy steps in, 'Clara's been working here less than a month, but she has contributed to a number of areas. She has written some briefing notes, one on foster care and one ...'

'I read the one on foster care,' the Minister says. 'It was clear and concise. I find such briefing notes very useful.'

The cubicle calls over, Ray Manly heads for the lift leaving behind a surge of optimism. People are speculating, maybe his visit heralds a new approach, the beginning of a new era, maybe this Minister understands that the people who do the work are crucial for delivering government policies, improving public services.

Only Maurice is unhappy. He has been left out again, not important enough to be invited to the meeting with the Minister and not low enough in the hierarchy to reside in a cubicle and therefore be introduced to him. Too angry to do any work, he turns the computer off and walks out of the office. He hasn't had a win for weeks and today was a bugger of a day. He is driving along the highway when it hits him, *It's my mother's birthday today.* He had been thinking about her a lot lately and today of all days he nearly forgot her anniversary. She would have been sixty-five years old today. Maybe I too will kick the bucket before my fiftieth, so what's the point in getting mad about the Minister, or Sandy?

His mother. Their last evening still vivid in his mind. The rain drumming the galvanised roof, him washing dishes, she peeling potatoes. He is looking at her fingers and thinking of Helen's. Helen the girl he fancies, but who refuses to fancy him back. Her fingers long and slender, his mother's bony and strong. Ugly, he thought. Stupid me. Those fingers earned a living and looked after the family for more than two decades.

She kept peeling the potatoes, her fingers moving quickly, decisively. She, who could never make a decision, she who always saw too many problems – bigger and bigger problems the closer she got to any one option – was confident in her trade, the trade of cooking, cleaning, washing and ironing. For others.

Eyes gazing blindly at the road, Maurice wonders and not for the first time, what sort of woman she might have become had she married a kind man and not his loud-mouthed, all-knowing father. Would she have been more like a bird soaring high up in the sky than the mouse she turned into? Faced with the thunder of his words, his mother gave in and swallowed her opinions. She swallowed her opinions until she had no opinions.

Maurice never forgot that evening, their last together. She had a stroke the next day and a week later, barely forty-six years old, she was dead. The small woman, who used to look up at him, was no more. Not there to greet him when he got home, not there to look at him with pride. Or love, or anger. Hazel eyes, honest eyes. Wherever he turned he saw her absence. The world is an empty space, Maurice thought, a void, until fate blesses you with someone's love. He missed the clean house, which now looked like a disturbed robbery. The cosy smells of roast and shepherd's pie, which used to meet him in the evening, had been replaced by the smell of pizza, or Indian takeaway.

After her passing, his father, who never worked more than a few hours a week, retired to the sofa full-time, to watch television. Bare chested, barefooted, the eternal can of beer in hand. And there he sat day after day, his gut – a balloon of fat, sprouting a rarefied layer of curly grey hairs – resting on his lap. The smells of beer, sweat, and dirty socks mingled into a faintly nauseating odour. Looking at him, Maurice began wondering whether his father had been drunk when he was conceived. Was his drunken sperm blundering around when accidentally it stumbled into his mother's egg? And if so, what does that mean for him, Maurice? It was a question without answer. It only made him angry.

Why? Why did fate take away the wrong one, Maurice kept asking himself. Fate did not answer, and Maurice went into himself. He thought about life, he thought about death, he thought about the meaning of it all. He pondered, he asked questions. What had been the purpose of his mother's short life? Surely not cleaning, cooking and sharing her life with his father, who loved his beer far more than he ever loved her. Was she on this Earth only to give him birth? Was she just an instrument of reproduction? A broodmare? And what was the purpose of his own life? Or the point of studying when he could be dead in twenty years? He turned to religion. He went to church every Sunday. He thought about right and wrong. He thought about joining the Order. But God had other plans for him, plans which revealed themselves in the shape of Brigid, a tall blonde with a full figure, blue eyes and the round face of a baby.

Gradually, Maurice had emerged from the darkness, finished his studies, graduated, and started working. Brigid is long gone. Nowadays, his thoughts of her are rare, an atavism, a waste of time, but his resolve not to devote himself entirely to anybody is never far from his mind. Not to anybody and definitely not to work, or bosses or causes.

I will not work myself into the grave as mum did. I will look after myself.

<h1 style="text-align:center">-17-</h1>

Dusk. 'Whoooop!' a bird calls. 'Whoooop!' Clara calls back. 'Oh-no,' she looks around, embarrassed. No, no-one heard her. The Minister has read my briefing note. 'Clear and concise,' he said. I should stop fretting every time I get a new task, and she hurries to catch the train. Tonight, she is meeting Adam for dinner.

Two hours later she and Adam are sitting in an Italian restaurant, having pasta and discussing the school, the teachers and the joy of talking to young children. 'Their way of thinking so refreshing.' Adam says and takes a gulp of wine.

'So unpredictable, so imaginative.'

Adam is a mechanical engineer, snowed down with work, currently on some multi-million-dollar project. 'I won't bore you with it.'

'But now that I'm divorced at least my home is stress free. Friday night I go out and have a drink with my mates. I don't have to feel guilty; I don't have to check my watch all the time. No-one is waiting for me only to have a fight when I get home.' He refills his glass. 'Nowadays I take every opportunity to enjoy my freedom. Life can't all be work. There should be some fun, don't you think?'

'Of course.'

Two months ago, he went to Bali with a couple of friends.

'Nightclubs, parties and quite a bit of alcohol,' he says with a "you know the rest" smile, and proceeds to describe some in great detail. Between talking and drinking he hasn't eaten much. She tries to focus on what he is saying, but her attention keeps meandering from the pictures on the wall to the diners. Her gaze falls on the young couple a few tables away, he caressing her hand. Once it was Peter and her. They were sitting on the terrace in Il Bacio restaurant. The candlelight twinkled. 'Motherhood agrees with you,' he whispered. 'You've never been more beautiful.' Blushing, she looked at Toni and Ed sitting opposite. Her blush vanished in the semi-darkness. It was …

'Clara, am I boring you?'

She looks at him. 'Of course not.'

'You seemed miles away. Now tell me about yourself.'

'You know most of it already. I'm from the Netherlands. Came here nearly ten years ago.'

'Have you seen much of Europe?'

'Yes, apart from the Eastern part.'

'I've been to the UK and Italy,' he says, eyes looking at her adoringly.

While they discuss the architecture and the art of Italy, he keeps drinking, chugging down half a glass of wine for her every sip.

Will he be able to drive me home? she wonders as he orders another bottle of wine.

Back in the car he turns the engine on, and they are on the way. Surprisingly, he does not seem to have any problem driving, he is well within his lane.

'Clara you're a very beautiful woman.' As she is thinking where his words are leading, he asks, 'Left or right at this corner?'

She is not sure; she has not been around these streets.

'Left to my place, right to yours,' he adds.

'Right, my babysitter's waiting.'

He drives on and just before he turns into her street, he stops the car.

'I live over there,' she points ahead, 'two blocks from here.'

'Clara I'm mad about you,' and he grabs her by the shoulder and pulls her towards him.

'Leave me alone!' She pushes against him. But his face is already next to hers, tongue trying to part her lips. Her heart in her mouth, she tries to open the door. The door is locked. 'Let me out!' she screams, a muffled scream. 'Let me go!' Her hand scrabbles around pushing down the buttons on the door. Suddenly her window opens. Startled, he recoils. 'Help,' she screams. 'Help!'

'You don't like men, do you?!' he says and unlocks her door.

Shaking, she jumps out of the car and runs home. Her heart pounding as she opens the door. Inside an oasis of calm. The babysitter is watching television, Shosh has gone to bed. She opens Shosh's door and seeing her beautiful face she starts to relax.

The babysitter gone; she heads for the shower. She stands under the running water for a long time, thinking about what had happened, what could have happened, "What is it about me that I attract strange men?" Adam is an alcoholic, and what logic! "You don't like men. But none of this would have happened if I'd taken my car."

She returns to the lounge room. The classical radio station is playing Ravel's Boléro, a favourite of hers and she thanks the Heavens for being single and having a roof above their heads.

It has been a long day, the Minister's visit, the tug of war with Adam, and the memory of that evening in Il Bacio restaurant … Was that evening the turning point of our lives?

-18-

Clara's self-imposed schedule of visiting Peter once a month, while never discussed with Eszti, has become a routine, and on the last Sunday of the month, soon after breakfast Eszti is busily preparing lunch.

By the time Clara and Shosh walk in, three ovenware dishes of food are waiting on the stove. The table is set. After a short chat Eszti is ready to serve lunch and they sit down to eat, and talk, one eye on Peter, who seems to float in and out of their world. At times he answers a question, or voices an opinion, but mostly his sad eyes seem to be looking inside himself, at something only he can see. But when he feels better, they lock up the house and the four of them walk down to Coogee Beach, Shosh holding her father's hand and behind them Clara with Eszti talking non-stop. About Peter, about some friend, talking and laughing, a nervous sort of laughter, and Clara listens. Sort of.

Now and then they catch up with the two in front. Shosh too talks non-stop, about school, about her teacher, about her friends. Peter listens to her, or some other presence, who would know? But Shosh keeps talking and bouncing around happily. Clara looks at them thinking, that is as good as it will ever be, but at least we have reached some middle ground, an equilibrium of sorts.

* * *

After weeks of dry weather, a welcome rain has set in for the day.

Standing in front of the mirror, Shosh is admiring herself in the new dress her grandmother has bought her. She is especially pleased about its

103

colour, a melange of pinks, yellows and purples. Squatting next to her, Eszti is pinning up the hem. Having advised on the length, Clara returns to the kitchen.

Peter looks up, his face gloomy as if he has internalised the grey sky.

'How's your research going?' Clara asks, sitting down opposite him.

'Not well,' he says and clams up in silence. Her other efforts to draw him out are barely answered.

Clara has seen enough of him to know that this is not the silence of the insane listening to some inner voice, this is just a reluctance, a lack of interest to engage in conversation. But didn't Eszti say that Peter has been taking his medication and he is better than he has been for months? And when he is well and has company there is nothing he would rather do than talk about his research in linguistics. As Clara is pondering what's going on, Eszti and Shosh walk in.

'The length is sorted,' Eszti says. 'I'll stitch the hem later. Now let's have coffee.'

She puts a jug of coffee in the middle of the table and a cup of tea in front of Shosh. 'And I bought these at the Hungarian on Wellington Road,' she says smiling mysteriously as she opens a box. She lifts out a cheese pocket, then goes on lifting out the other six and piling them up on the big serving plate. At the sight of the cheese pockets, Peter's eyes throw a momentary sparkle.

'Yummy,' Shosh says, taking her first bite.

'Not yummy, delicious,' Peter says.

'Yummy,' she repeats, munching appreciatively.

'Mouth-watering,' Peter says.

'Whatever. Grandma, can I have the other half?'

Peter smiles, 'A chip off the old block.'

A chip off the old block? Clara's heart misses a beat.

The phone rings and Eszti runs out.

The effect of cheese pockets on Peter's mood is nothing short of miraculous. He is talking and joking, even laughing now and then.

Buoyed by Peter's mood, Clara asks how he divides his time between his various activities. 'My activities? Well … I only have one a day, so it's no problem, but when I get a job … I'll have to cut some out.'

A job? Clara stares at him, stunned. He did apply for two jobs, but that was nearly a year ago. One company called him in for an IQ test. He must have done well because a week later they invited him for an interview. He never heard from them again. Discouraged, he rearranged his life around his volunteering work and his research in linguistics.

'I have to get a job,' Peter says, 'any job, casual, part-time, but paid work. I want to earn some money.' Then looking at Shosh, 'I want to buy you books and musical scores.'

Clara looks at him. *You poor soul, you just want to be a father.*

'But I can't face applying.'

Writing an application, going for an interview overwhelms him. An ocean stands between him and all that, and he only has a canoe to cross it. And then there is his illness, he has to hide it, hide it like a crime.

'Just try, you'll get something,' Clara says. She is about to offer help. To Peter? A far better writer than her.

'Will you, daddy?' Shosh asks, as she sits down on his lap and wraps her arm around his neck. 'Promise?'

'Yes sweetie. I promise,' he says and loses himself in thought.

Was Shosh trying to draw him out when she asked to see his place, or was she just curious?

'Of course, dear. You have to see my castle,' he winks at Clara. 'C'mon sweetie.'

Clara follows them up the stairs.

A musty smell wafts past as the door opens. Inside a tiny windowless room — the only furniture a coffee table and a two-seater sofa, its upholstery a faded miserable brown. From there a door leads into the bedroom, ceiling sloping like the sides of a tent. A double bed and a bedside table facing a window, a big window which looks over the garden wall and beyond.

As if to compensate for all the aspects of his life he has no control over, Peter has imposed a strict order on his flat. No clothes, or shoes to be seen, no knickknacks, no indulgences. The bedcover so precisely laid out; it seems to have been undisturbed for years. There is tidiness, and tidiness, but this place is not just tidy, it carries the imprint of obsession.

Everything is brown. From the third or fourth-hand furniture, to the forty-year-old carpet on which Eszti has spread a few rugs to cover the spots and the holes. But nothing can hide the absence of human warmth, the lack of visitors, of other people's footprints. Loneliness fills the space; it is there in every corner. Not the loneliness of a single man, this loneliness has a different feel to it. Desolation, soullessness? The stamp of insanity?

The tiny kitchen is less forlorn. On the table, like toy soldiers readying for a battle, pens and pencils and next to them, books and notebooks grouped in piles of subject matter: dictionaries, linguistics, history, religion.

'Shosh, see that tree?' Peter points to the pine tree in front of the window. 'It was shorter than you when I planted it, and look at it now.'

'Wow!'

'It shades the kitchen from the afternoon sun, and it has good Karma.'

'Karma? What's Karma, daddy?'

'Something which relaxes me, makes me calm. Allows me to concentrate better.' Confused, Shosh looks at Clara. She signals silence.

'That's it, that's my home now,' he turns around to go. 'Oh, I forgot the bathroom,' and he opens a side-door. Inside a toilet and a shower fed by the smallest of boilers. As Clara looks at it, the image switches. Peter lingering in the shower for as long as he can get away with. Mornings of some years ago. The long showers are gone, just like the rest of his life, his family, his job, the cosy home. Left behind, in the once upon a time.

'Shosh, what did you think of daddy's place?' Eszti asks when they walk back in.

'It's veeery tidy,' and Clara wonders if Shosh is trying to compliment her father, or to cover the uneasiness they both felt upstairs.

'Peter, are you still volunteering?' Clara asks to change the subject.

'Yes.'

'Volunteering? What do you do there, daddy?'

'Martin and I deliver meals for the elderly in this suburb. Martin drives the van and I take the trays in, talk to them.'

'Talk to them?' Clara asks, 'What about?'

Peter shrugs. 'Whatever, the weather, their aches and pains, their families. Many rarely see them.'

'And you?' Eszti asks. 'What do you say to them?'

'Not much,' he falls silent, then, 'I think the family should look after the old and the sick.'

A look, pregnant with meaning, leaps from Eszti to Clara.

'And you volunteer in the conservation shop too,' Eszti says.

'Yes, once a week.'

'He's a busy man,' Eszti says.

'Yes, between the volunteering jobs, my work on linguistics and the doctor's appointments. Not that I want to see him ...'

'But you have to,' Eszti says. 'He has to keep an eye on you, otherwise you'll end up in hospital again. That's what the registrar said, didn't he?'

'He did.'

The registrar? Clara is taken aback. She didn't know Peter had been hospitalised.

'I might not have a choice whether I front up to the doctor or not, but you know what?' He winks at Clara. 'I have a choice in what I tell him. So, I tell him as little as possible.'

'Not a good idea,' Eszti says.

'No? He's not much use. Him and his questions. "How are you? Are you taking your pills?" Yes, I reply, yes to everything which won't complicate things. "And the side effects?" he asks and looks at me for a couple of seconds. The other day I didn't even manage to answer when he said, "You seem to be calmer; you don't rock as much." I agreed with him of course, but my statistics professor didn't. "In order to draw a conclusion," he said, "you need a big sample. Thirty observations at minimum. Tell him, go on. Don't let him get away with nonsense." But I know better than to argue with my doctor. Besides, he doesn't understand statistics, he's only a doctor.'

His statistics professor? Clara looks at Shosh, then Eszti. They don't seem fussed.

'"You must be running out of medication," he says and scribbles something, then hands me a script. The same two or three drugs dosed up or dosed down. What does it matter? They only make me sick.'

'But you're much better now,' Eszti says.

Peter shrugs, 'I'd rather have the nightmares. But I have no choice, the health system is after me. Anyway, when he's finished with me, he says, "You're doing fine, just keep taking the medication," and smiles. A smile straight out of page 133 of the medical textbook.'

Peter could always distinguish formula from authenticity, and since he got sick even more so, as if he has developed another sense, as if he has developed a detector for deceit. The doctor's disingenuous smile is just another given in his life, something to be tolerated, there along with the side effects of his medication.

'I don't like him either,' Eszti says, 'but what can I do? He's just doing a job. He's there to help his patients, not to feel for them. Empathy?' Eszti shrugs, 'Does a bank manager feel for his bankrupt customer?'

Silence.

'Peter, is that all he talks to you about?' Eszti asks.

'Um … he has questioned me about my childhood, about our marriage,' he says looking at Clara. 'He knows my whole life story.'

'And?' Eszti asks.

'And, and nothing. He just made me sad. Your life story is only yours, once you tell it to others, it's not yours anymore. Mine has been dissected and analysed. It's no longer a life story, it's a case study.'

'Doesn't he ask you about the voices in your head? Doesn't he ask about people who are in front of you, and maybe they aren't really?'

Peter shrugs.

Still, quiet, Shosh is fixed on her father's face, eyes magnified by disbelief. Clara looks at her, worried. This conversation is not for a five-year-old, Eszti should not ask such questions in front of her. Besides, how would Peter know who's real and who isn't? Surely for him everyone is real, whoever pops in or pops up, the Swami, the policemen, his statistics professor, the ambulance officers, the butcher. Those who smile at him and those who terrify him. Those who whisper and those who shout. At the first pause in the conversation, Clara makes her excuses and picks up her handbag.

'Mum.' Shosh pulls her hand.

'Yes?'

'My dress!'

But Clara can't stand being there any longer. She has to take Shosh away and go. 'I'll pick it up in a week or two.'

'I want to wear it to Carol's birthday party.'

'You'll have it.'

They are ready to go.

'Peter, don't forget to write that job application,' Clara says to him.

Peter looks at her for a moment too long, then drags his thoughts back. 'I will.'

* * *

A month has passed since Clara and Shosh's last visit to Coogee. Eszti is pottering in the kitchen, Peter and Clara are sitting in the lounge room, he on the armchair in the corner, she on the sofa. Next to her is Shosh, holding the cat on her lap, the two of them wrapped by a calm serenity.

'The magic of a cat,' Peter says smiling.

'She's bewitched by cats, just like Eszti. Peter, did you send that job application?'

'I did, I'll show it to you,' and runs out. Soon he is back with a copy.

Dear Sir/Madam,

I am looking for part-time/casual work.

I am a Physics graduate from your University. I also worked as a computer programmer and later as a systems analyst, but my interests are wide: linguistics, history, science, and philosophy.

I left my job as I developed a medical condition, which does not allow me to sit in one place for extended periods of time.

I love books and have spent years researching various topics. I would appreciate it if you could offer me some part-time or casual work in the University library. Due to my medical condition, sorting and stacking books would be ideal for me.

Yours sincerely,

Peter Steinberg

'It's a good letter,' she says, 'professional.'

He smiles. 'Professional book stacker.'

She smiles back, but her heart weeps. As if a sudden light has reached into the dark corners of his life, she can see it all now: his soulless flat, his loneliness, his lack of choices. How much he has lost, how far he has fallen. How cruel life has been to him.

They are divorced. At times she has the impression that mentally he is still married to her, while she feels well and truly divorced. Divorced, but not immune to his misery. She would like to distance herself from him, to see him as another man, separate, separate but not vulnerable, separate but not rejected, not poor, not at the bottom of humanity. She finds it hard to hold back her tears. She finds it hard not to embrace him, not to comfort him. He is sick and she can do nothing about it. But she wishes he lived in a cosy little flat with the sun streaming into the lounge room, a few bookshelves lining the walls, a decent shower. A doctor who takes more than an obligatory interest in him, the odd phone call, a visit from a friend or two.

'It's three weeks since I sent this letter,' he interrupts her thoughts, 'but I haven't heard from them yet,' and looks at her as if trying to ascertain whether his hope is justified.

'It's too soon for an answer.'

He smiles. Bells of hope are ringing in his thoughts again.

'I will earn money again. Shosh, I will buy you books and chocolates and musical scores.'

'But I don't need anything, daddy.'

'Every girl needs a present now and then.'

'But I don't.'

Clara's eyes clouded over with tears. *Oh, how proud you make me feel, Shosh, how very proud.*

Eszti walks in. Peter jumps up and gives her a kiss on the cheek. Then on the other; Eszti recoils as if she has been kissed by a stranger.

'What's that?' she points to the letter.

'I applied for a job.'

'A job? What sort of job?'

'A part-time job at the university library. Jack of all trades, whatever they can give me. Sorting and stacking books, clerical work, anything that does not involve sitting in one place for hours.'

'Well … let's see what eventuates. Now let's have lunch.'

Eszti places the dishes of food in the middle of the table and serves each one in turn.

Shosh takes a spoonful of creamed spinach, 'My favourite.' Eszti doesn't register the praise. She is lost in thought, chewing her food, as if it's pile of wood shavings.

'He wants a job?' She asks Clara when Peter and Shosh are out of earshot. 'He'll never get a job; he'll only have more disappointments. He might be clever, he might be more knowledgeable than ten of them put together, but no-one wants him around, not even his friends. Our society wants healthy people, it wants people who are predictable. But my son, my brilliant son is often unpredictable. His sickness has set him up for loneliness and loss.'

<h1 style="text-align:center">-19-</h1>

Peter wakes. No, he is not lost in the desert, he is in his bed and there are no jackals around. He hates waking up exhausted and drained, and last night's nightmare was worse than most.

His neck hurts. Is it the pillow? Is it the sagging bed? He turns onto his side, hoping for relief. The medicine bottle on his bedside table is looking at him. Well?

No, not now. He rolls onto his back and tries to stretch, but his muscles won't give, as if they have lost the ability to stretch, as if they are no longer part of his body. No longer under his control. *Damn! Damn these pills*. The doctor did warn him about side effects, but he didn't say that they would turn him into a statue.

The clock ticks and tocks. Seven-twenty, time for him to get up. He was planning to go to the Housing Office and apply for a public housing flat, he nearly forgot that today is Thursday, his volunteering day in the conservation shop. He will go tomorrow. He should have applied for a public housing flat years ago. It's time to distance himself from his mother. It's time for him to be independent, and free.

Come on Peter, get up, but he is not ready for what getting up entails. It is the same every morning. The moment he stands up his body turns into a node, a counterpoint, where opposing forces meet, one contracting his muscles, the other pulling them apart at every move. Caught in the middle, his only role is to hurt. The pain is not sharp, it lingers between mild and medium, between four and six as Dr Stein wants it reported, but its persistence, its relentlessness, saps his energy and fogs his mind.

He has no time for yoga now. He wants to spend a couple of hours in the library, reading and thinking before heading to the conservation shop. He will do his yoga in the afternoon. *And the pills?* He props himself on his elbow, unscrews the top of the bottle, shakes out two pills and with a resigned look pops them in his mouth, takes a gulp of water, before lowering himself back onto the bed. Eyes shut, he tries to relax, divert his thoughts, but he can't help seeing the pills travelling down his oesophagus, down into his stomach. The strong acid whizzing, ripping them apart. Trillions of molecules, poisonous molecules, fighting each other into his blood. The blood gushing, whooshing towards his liver, his kidneys. Bang! The shock of the encounter, the cringing of his organs.

He shudders. *These pills are poison.*

With a supreme effort, he rolls out of bed. He tries to straighten up, but his muscles are fighting the change in angle, 'Damn these pills. Damn!' he curses, his eyes on the medicine bottle. POISON the big bold black letters scream. He shuts his eyes then opens them again. The word is there in even bigger letters. *I knew it, I knew it all along, the doctor is poisoning me.* It's clear to him now, why he feels so bad, why every time he tries to straighten, he feels as if someone has sewn him up tightly, why his tongue moves non-stop, fighting every word he tries to voice. It explains why no matter how tired he is, no matter how exhausted he is, his legs and arms keep moving, when all he wants is to sit and rest. While most people's arms and legs harmonise so the whole can get to its destination with a minimum of effort, the parts of his body oppose each other at every step. He can get where he wants, but not smoothly, not without effort and pain.

These pills will give me cancer. He breaks into a sweat. He has ingested dozens of bottles of that poison, fifty pills in each. *Thousands of pills!* The cancer must have taken hold of him already. The evil cells are multiplying, spreading.

No, he will not take another pill. Ever. Still in his pyjamas, he grabs the bottle with a tissue and runs out. It's rubbish collection day and the bins are out in the street. *Even better.* He crosses the street and drops the bottle into one of the bins.

Back in his flat, he takes his pyjamas off, drops them in the washing basket and walks straight into the shower. Refreshed, and wearing a clean set of clothes, he packs his notebook and the dictionary and heads for the bus.

* * *

Friday. The clock on the wall stands at one fifty when Peter walks into the Eastern Suburbs branch of the Department of People's Services, takes a number from the ticket dispenser and heads to the only free seat. He takes out a book from his bag and begins to read.

'Matey?' the man sitting next to him whispers, 'Are you homeless?'

Peter keeps reading. The man looks at him, looks at his book and with a shrug of his shoulders turns his attention to the old woman sitting on his other side. But she is in no mood to engage and the man turns back to Peter and nudges him with his elbow. Peter jumps.

'Sorry mate, I didn't mean to startle you.'

'What do you want?'

'Just talk, mate, just talk. Make conversation, you know …' he extends his hand. 'John Dexter.'

'Peter Steinberg.'

'Peter what?'

'Steinberg, Peter Steinberg,' he says and looks back at his book.

'Homeless?' John Dexter asks, 'Because if you are, we could keep each other warm tonight. What do you think?'

Peter looks at him dark and angry.

'Hey, I'm only joking, what else can a man in my shoes do? A man with as much shit in his life as me? Don't worry mate, I'm a man of boobs and bottoms and believe it, or not, my girlfriend, well … my ex-girlfriend, has plenty of those. Ex since this morning,' he looks at Peter, weighing, evaluating him. 'So, tell me, do you live on the street?'

'I'm considering it.'

'You mean you have a roof over your head?'

'I do, but not the right sort of roof. It has bad Karma.'

'Bad Karma? Are you crazy?'

Peter's brows knit. 'Maybe I am.'

'Bollocks, anybody who reads big books like that must be pretty smart. So where do you live?'

'In Coogee, with my mum.'

'Ah … Is that why you want to move out?'

'Yes.'

John Dexter silent, Peter looks back at his book.

'Number four,' the client service officer calls.

Two elderly women walk up to the counter. Typing away, eyes on the keyboard, the officer asks something.

'I beg your pardon!' the shorter woman shouts.

'The reason for your visit?!' the officer shouts back.

She lives with her son and daughter-in-law, but now they are expecting a child and they need the room for the baby. The woman speaks fast as if worried that she will not get the time to say everything she has to.

'I have to move out. But how can I? My pension isn't enough for rent, not even for a tiny place. Miss do you think I could get a public housing flat? A bedsitter, perhaps? And …'

'Let's see what your exact circumstances are,' the officer interrupts. 'You fill out this form and come back when you're finished, but if you get stuck …'

'I hate forms.' The woman whispers to her friend as the two of them head to the desk in the corner.

John Dexter looks at the clock, the wait is getting to him. His left leg has acquired a life of its own. His nose suddenly itchy, he takes out a tissue and blows his nose with a thunder.

'My God!' jumps the elderly woman next to him. 'Did you have to shout?'

Immersed in the mysteries of the Japanese language, Peter keeps reading.

'Peter,' John Dexter whispers. 'What's that book?'

Peter looks at him.

'What are you reading?'

'A dictionary, a Japanese-English dictionary.'

'Blimey, isn't that boring?' John Dexter bends down to scratch his shin then straightens up with a sigh. 'I do read a book every now and then, but it has to be good. Lots of action and sex, lots of sex, otherwise I fall asleep.'

'Number five,' the officer calls.

Like a soldier who has been ordered to stand to attention, John Dexter jumps up, grabs his suitcase, and walks to the counter.

'Name?' the officer asks, and the short-bitten nails start tapping the keyboard.

'Address?'

John Dexter shrugs. 'Miss would I be here if I had an address? I need an address; I need a roof above my head. My girlfriend has thrown me out.'

The officer looks up. The man in front of her is a puzzle she has to solve quickly. *Freshly shaven, clean T-shirt. Recent trouble. What if they make up tomorrow?* With the shortage of crisis accommodation in Sydney, the Department has to make absolutely sure that accommodation goes to those most in need.

John Dexter shuffles from foot to foot. He does not like being stared at. 'We had problems for a while, I thought it was her difficult childhood. And childhood doesn't let you be, does it? Sooner or later, it catches up with you. But it wasn't that. We went to a couple counsellor. I thought it was working. Last week, I came out convinced that we'd get back to our old ways. We were happy then.' He swallows, his Adam's apple slides up and down. 'Well, she threw me out. Where am I to go now?'

The clock on the wall stands at two-forty-five. The officer is stressed, the Friday afternoon rush is not over yet.

'Look,' John Dexter points to the scratches on his left arm. 'These are from her long fingernails. "Leave immediately! Leave or …" and she grabbed the kitchen knife. "And take all your stuff, I don't want to see you again!" she shouted. I was so shocked I could hardly walk, let alone start packing. But then she hurt me even more. "By the way, George is moving in on Saturday."'

'Ehhhhum,' the officer clears her throat. 'Do you …'

'"Yes, your friend George," she stabbed my heart the second time.'

'Do you have some proof of identity?!' the officer shouts in exasperation.

'No need to shout, Miss. I'll give you all you need. It's all here,' he bends down, rummages in his suitcase, pulls out a couple of cards and some folded papers. 'Ms, I don't have a place to sleep and tomorrow's Saturday.'

'For you and who knows how many more,' the officer says to herself as another shabbily dressed man walks in.

'John, fill out this form and I'll see what we can do for you.'

'My God! All that?'

'As much as you can. Come back when you're finished.'

Her job is nerve wracking at times. She has been doing it for five years. Five years of sorting, advising and listening to their problems, although listening – the most difficult, the most wearing of it all – is not part of her job description. She tells them what documents they need, which forms they should fill in, and whether to talk to one of the officers behind the glass doors. She decides on the most direct route to solve their problems. At least for the lucky ones whose problems can be solved, but the final decision is not up to her, it is up to the senior officers and their bosses. Restructured, or enticed by more promising careers, they keep coming and going, floating in and out above her head like clouds, managers whom she hardly gets to know and who never get to know her. For five years she has stuck it out in a sea of changing policies, restructures, collapsing walls. She and only she has stood fast, forever reliable, forever helping the little she could.

She looks at the clock, two more hours until the door shuts. The queue, like a magic pudding, keeps renewing itself.

It is Peter's turn.

The officer opens a new enquiry and begins typing: name, address. 'The reason for your application?'

'I need to move out, I cannot live in my mother's house.'

She looks at him; the man is not homeless. Other people are far needier; others do not have a roof over their heads.

'You could get something, but not straightaway. You'll have to join the waiting list. So, there is a wait.'

'How long?'

Eight years, ten? But she cannot say so, waiting times are a government secret and she has to break such news as foggily, as obscurely and as tactfully as she can.

'Can't say, depends on how many vacancies come up.'

A devilish smile lights Peter's face.

Oh, one of those? 'Do you have a disability?' she asks.

'Disability?' Peter wonders aloud.

'Do you see a doctor regularly?' She does not have to ask what for, she has many clients like him.

'Yes,' he says.

'We might be able to house you sooner, but we need a medical certificate from your doctor stating that you can live independently. So …'

'Miss, this form's doing my head in,' John Dexter interrupts. 'These questions are tangled like a plate of spaghetti. I don't even know where to start. Should I apply for housing, or should I apply for temporary accommodation?'

'It's all on the form. Just wait over there,' she points to a chair next to the glass-walled office, 'one of our staff will help you.' But inwardly she curses the form designers, Head Office clerks who sit in meetings designing forms in a language which is a trial even for those who are literate, an intimidating mental climb, and a nightmare for the rest whose brains have been scrambled by years of drug use or heavy drinking. But the prospect of sleeping on the street terrifies them even more, so they sit and wait for help.

The officer turns back to Peter, 'Peter, talk to your doctor and come back as soon as you have the certificate, we'll see what we can do for you.'

He thanks her and heads to the door, the officer's gaze follows him. What if he can't get that certificate? Because many can't. Not able to live independently and not sick enough to be in a hospital, sooner or later they end up on the street.

It is half past three, one more hour until the door shuts. Then at least another half an hour to finish the work. She will go home, have a hot shower, put her feet up, pour herself a Scotch and stare at the television for an hour or two. It is the only way she can put these people out of her mind, distance herself from their misery. But what's the alternative? Stop feeling? No, she would rather be the way she is, besides, every now and then her tribulations do bear fruit, every now and then she manages to help someone. Change their life.

A man on crutches stumbles in.

'Number six!' she calls.

-20-

It's not summer yet, but the sun has been revving up the heat since early morning. Sydney is sweltering, but Eszti's house is a cool oasis and Clara and Shosh are savouring it.

'He hasn't been himself,' Eszti whispers to Clara. Then having decided that Shosh is immersed in the television program, she adds, 'The other evening, he told me that he's given up finding a job, that he had no answer from the university and wasn't expecting one anymore. Then sat quietly at the table, barely picking at his food. It was the sick Peter again, listening to something. Clara, it made me sick at heart. But the next day he seemed much happier, and when he's happy I'm happy. The two of us are yo-yoing together. Anyway, I think he's quite well today and …' The door opens and Peter walks in. 'Talking of the devil … Did you find that book?' she asks.

'No.'

'What book?' Clara asks, her mind still on what Eszti told her. He had no answer from the university. Does he realise that he will never work again, he will never be able to buy presents for Shosh? That he is in a valley from which he will never crawl out?

'A book about yoga and its health benefits.'

'What's yoga, daddy?' Shosh asks.

Having heard Peter talking about it many times before, Eszti can't walk out fast enough.

'Yoga?' Peter says. 'Is a mixture of stretching, balancing, meditation. A bit of everything.'

The explanation is all too abstract for Shosh. 'Daddy, can you show me?'

Peter sizes up the available space, 'No, there isn't enough room.'

'I think there is,' Clara says.

'Look,' he lays down on the carpet. 'I can't even stretch out. And all this furniture! It's closing in on me,' he stands up quickly. 'Yoga needs deep concentration; this is not the place for it.'

'Please daddy, please.'

Thinking, weighing up the place, Peter looks at Shosh. 'OK, I'll try.'

He rams the armchair into the corner, picks up the coffee table and takes it to the kitchen, returns, grabs the big pot plant and takes it out to the hall. 'What else?' He looks around.

'Surely that's enough,' Clara says, worried that any minute now Eszti's love of order and constancy will collide with Peter's intransigence and the walls will shake from their screams. Luckily, Eszti is still in the garden.

Sitting on the carpet, legs crossed, Peter pushes his knees to the floor and holds them there. 'This is only a stretch,' and he starts counting, 'One, two, three, four …' At the count of twenty he removes his hands. His knees bounce up. He is annoyed, he has been doing this exercise for months and cannot master it.

Legs crossed, body bent forward, he extends his arms until he doubles up, touches the floor with his forearms then returns to the sitting position. He repeats the doubling up, and at every return he adds one to his count.

'Daddy, that looks hard.'

'It is, but these will clear the knots in my body. Release the Kundalini, and then the energy can flow freely.'

'Energy?' Shosh asks.

'Yes, the life energy. Sixteen, seventeen …'

'Life energy?' Shosh whispers to Clara.

'I think daddy means the blood in his arteries will flow faster, and when the blood flows the energy flows with it,' she whispers back.

Shosh looks puzzled, 'Arteries?'

'The pipes which carry the blood, like the garden hose carries water.'

'But … Daddy when the garden hose in front of our block is bent over like you, the water stops flowing.'

'Shosh, leave me to it. Will you?!'

Hurt, Shosh looks at her mother and runs out. Clara would like to follow her, but she feels obliged to watch the yoga demonstration to the end.

Hands behind his head, legs crossed, Peter rolls back onto the floor, stays there for a couple of seconds then sits up again. Down again. Up again. Nine, ten, eleven … He has to repeat every movement twenty times, because twenty is two times ten, symmetrical and therefore intrinsically Godly. Sweat is pouring down his brow. Eighteen, nineteen. Twenty! He sits up with a groan, and there he sits, head bent, gazing at the floor.

Suddenly he turns to the corner. 'Not now, not bloody now!' he shouts, then pressing his fingers into his ears and turns back, '*Om namah shivaya, Om namah shivaya,*' he murmurs, again, and again. '*Om namah shivaya,*' his voice louder and louder. '*Om namah shivaya*! I'll kill your bloody orders, if nothing else I'll kill your voice, I'll bloody shut you up one day. Forever!'

Queasy, Clara grips the armrest to steady herself. Never before has she witnessed his madness at such depth. She cannot stay there, she cannot watch this spectacle, not another minute, and summons all her energy to stand up. But just as she does, Peter does too and now is coming towards her. Clara's knees soft, she falls back onto the sofa.

'Where you going?' Peter asks and sits down next to her.

She would like to say anywhere where the world makes sense, as far away from you and the invisible people you're conversing with, as far as possible from your insanity. But even if her goose bumps turn into lumps, she cannot bring herself to be that cruel and before she works out what to say, Peter puts his hand over hers. 'Don't go,' he says.

She pulls her hand away. *I have to get out of here*, but she cannot muster the courage and the strength that would take.

'Clara hold me, please hold me,' and he puts his arms around her.

She pulls back with a shudder. Terrified of his insanity, of him crossing the barrier, the invisible barrier between a man and a woman.

'Can't you hold me for a couple of minutes? Am I that repulsive? Clara, what happened to us?'

She gives him a quick hug. She makes it as official, as matter of fact as she can.

'Thank you,' he says and moves away from her.

Now she is sickened by her own cowardliness, by her lack of compassion. What happened to us? What indeed? A memory flashes through her mind. She and Shosh, visiting him at work. 'What a beautiful family you have,' someone said to him as he introduced them. She dropped in with Shosh so Peter could sign a document for some electrical work they needed for their house. The house with the beautiful garden. The house with the banksia and the cherry blossom, the magpies and the kookaburra. They filled the house with love. There was so much love at first, but then there was so little. So little.

'There's so much pain in me,' Peter interrupts the past. 'Why is this woman smiling? Can't she see my pain? This pain is as big as the universe, it's inescapable, it swallows everything. It's swallowing me. Swami! Help me. I could not have been that terrible.'

Thinking I have to go, I have to get out otherwise ... Otherwise what? She doesn't know, she only knows that she cannot stay here with him. With him and his madness. Her mouth dry, her heart racing, she stands up and staggers out into the garden.

'Heeeelp! Answer, someone! Please!' Peter's voice behind her.

Eszti and Shosh are watering the bushes.

'What's wrong with daddy?' Shosh asks.

'His medication hasn't cut in yet,' Clara says.

'Isn't anybody there? Is the world dead?!' Peter's screams flood the garden.

Clara's skin is covered with goose bumps again.

'I'd better see what's going on,' Eszti says, but just as she turns the water off, the screaming stops. They stand listening. Silence. Eszti turns the water back on, waters the bush, the plants next to the fence and they return to the house.

Peter is in the lounge room, lying on the floor, eyes fixed on the ceiling, murmuring something, something unintelligible. Trying to avert Shosh' attention, Eszti asks her about the holiday care centre. Shosh answers half-heartedly, all the while looking at her father sprawled on the carpet.

'Miaow.' The cat scratches the door and keeps miaowing. Louder and louder, more and more desperate. Shosh makes a move to let it in, but Eszti pulls her back. Eventually Peter gathers himself, stands up slowly, bit by bit, and opens the door. The cat runs in and straight to his bowl. 'Miaow.' It looks at Peter. Peter opens the tin and pours the mess into the bowl. The cat scoffs hungrily.

Clara picks up Shosh's things.

'Why the hurry?' Eszti asks.

'I've lots on, and who knows how the traffic is?'

They say good-bye. A hug to each, Eszti and Peter, and Clara starts the engine as the two stand there waving.

Her weekend is over.

-21-

A gust of wind rattles the windows. Eszti looks up from her book, wondering what the last pages were about. She cannot concentrate. All that shouting this afternoon, has Peter stopped his medication again? He did perk up after Clara and Shosh left. Very strange. She turns the television on, stares at the screen for a while, no, she cannot take any of it in.

The phone? She doesn't trust her hearing. It's worse than last year, and it was far from perfect even then. But just in case, she hurries to pick it up.

'Can I speak to Peter, please?' a manly voice asks.

'Which Peter?'

'Peter Steinberg. Isn't he your son?'

'He is. Who's calling?'

'John Dexter.'

'John who?'

'John Dexter.'

'Can you call back in ten minutes? I have to go and get him.' Odd, nobody ever phones him nowadays. So, who is this man? she wonders as she walks out to call Peter.

Minutes later, Peter picks up the phone.

'I'm John, John Dexter. We met in the housing office on Friday. Remember? I found your mother's number in the phone book.'

Silence.

'Peter, it's John Dexter here.'

'Yes?'

'I'm in trouble, mate, and you seemed a good man. I don't have a place to sleep, well I do, but I can't sleep there. Can you put me up for a night?' And after a pause, 'So what do you think, Peter?'

What does he think? He thinks that he won't be able to put up with his jabbering a whole evening, but can he leave a man out in the street on such a wild night?

'Ok, Take the 373 bus …'

'Who is he?' Eszti asks when Peter puts the phone down.

'Someone I met on Friday. He's going to sleep here tonight.'

'No way, I won't let him in.'

'He will sleep upstairs.'

'And where will you sleep?'

'I'll take a mattress from here.'

'You can't just let a stranger inside that flat.'

'I decide whom I can let in.'

'No, you can't. It's my flat, remember?'

'It's your flat, but I live in it now. But don't worry, not for long.'

'What?' Eszti can hardly utter, 'You want to move out? And how you going to pay the rent?'

'I'll get a public housing flat. To escape you, to escape your eyes. I've had it.'

'Peter, please understand, I'm worried about this fellow. What if he's a criminal?'

'Leave me alone! Alone!' He picks up the mattress from his father's bed and drags it up the stairs. Five minutes later he is back, takes a couple of sheets, a pillow, a blanket and slams the door as he walks out.

Less than an hour later, John Dexter, holding a bulging suitcase, rings Eszti's doorbell. Chain on, she cracks the door open. In front of her a scruffy, dishevelled man.

'Good evening. It's me, John Dexter.'

'Peter's upstairs,' and she slams the door.

'Thank you, Peter, you're a good man,' John Dexter says as he walks in. He looks around. 'Wow! Not a bad place you have here.' He places his suitcase in the corner by the door, 'And you have privacy, your own entrance. Peter, I wouldn't move away if I were you. I'd just keep the old girl at arm's length.'

'Keep my mum at arm's length?'

'She's a spider, is she?'

'Well, I'm in her web.'

They discuss the sleeping arrangements. Peter suggests that John Dexter take the bed.

'No, I'll sleep on the mattress. I'll sleep like a log,' and starts making his bed.

'The Department did promise me a bedsitter. But that won't be for a while. So meanwhile they put me up in a boarding house for single men. Those places claim to have rules. Rules?' he scoffs. 'No doubt some shitty document no-one looks at, somewhere in a drawer. No-one in that place plays by rules.

'Friday night I was buggered. All that worry about ending up on the street, dealing with the chick at the counter, filling in forms. As soon as I hit the bed I was gone. A few more nights like this? Fine by me.

'Last night I was lying in bed, thanking God that I have a roof over my head, when two men began arguing in front of my room. Surely, they'll calm down soon, I thought. Soon?' He sniggers. 'They were still screaming at each other at two in the morning.'

Peter looks at his lips, wishing he could glue them together. Shut the man up, but John Dexter is not about to stop. 'I couldn't take it anymore. I opened the door, asked them to shut their faces. "Clear off!" the scrawny one screamed and blocked my path. You wouldn't have thought that he had it in him to pick a fight. "Go and get your fix," I said and tried to push him aside, and guess what?'

'What?' Peter asks hoping for a quick end to the story.

'He pulled a knife. Like in one of those violent movies. That's exactly where I was, but for real. "One more word and I kill you!" he whispered in my ear. Menacingly. I threw him to the wall and ran back to my room, locked myself in and waited for the dawn. That's why I'm here. Luckily tomorrow's Monday. I'll go and see the chick in the office, ask her for another place,' and with that John Dexter crawls onto his mattress.

Hardly a few minutes pass and John Dexter is snoring.

Downstairs, Eszti is fretting. Who is this man? What if he steals Peter's keys and comes back when I'm not here and robs me?

She is up at dawn. She hopes they're asleep, but she cannot block the scary images rolling in her mind.

Upstairs, Peter too is awake. *Today is my Meals on Wheels day.* He gets out of bed, takes up his yoga position and begins rotating his shoulders, slowly. Backward and forward, backward and forward, left shoulder, right shoulder, increasing the circles gradually. He is stiff, very stiff.

Still asleep, John Dexter snorts.

Fingers interlaced, Peter takes a deep breath, turns his hands outwards and extends his arms. His knuckles crack. John Dexter opens his eyes, 'Good morning,' and he lies there waiting for a break in the counting. 'Peter, can I make myself a coffee?'

'Have a look in the kitchen cupboard,' and Peter is back counting.

Eyes half closed, John Dexter scrambles off his mattress and shuffles to the kitchen. The kettle on, he opens the cupboard above, lifts out the tin of instant coffee, picks up a handful of biscuits from the jar next to it, then hoping for something more substantial, opens the fridge. A lonely carton of milk looks at him from one of the empty shelves.

'You don't have much food, do you Peter?' he asks on his return. But Peter is in no mood for conversation and John Dexter stands there, drinking his coffee and chomping biscuits.

'Blimey Peter, you're good. But what's the point of all this?'

Peter keeps counting.

'OK. I'll leave you in peace. I'll go and have a fag.'

Peter doubles up again and again. The room is moving, seesawing, the ceiling is approaching and lifting and approaching again. His world suddenly black. Suffocating. No, he cannot go on and he sits up and there he stays silently for a long while.

His cigarette finished; John Dexter is back. He looks at Peter sitting head bent as if checking the pattern on the carpet. 'Is your pacemaker about to stop?'

Peter looks up confused.

'You look like you're listening to your pacemaker,' John Dexter says.

'Go to Hell!'

'OK. I'll go, I know when I'm not wanted, but I've one more thing to ask you.'

Despairing, Peter gawks at him. 'What?'

'It's to do with my daughter and all the mess I am in. Remember I told you about my girlfriend. Well, before her, I had a partner who gave birth to my daughter, Belinda. Four years old, she's the apple of my eye. I look after her every second Saturday and yesterday it was my turn. So, I picked her up and took her to McDonalds and then to a movie.'

Peter looks at him impatiently. John Dexter and his blabbing is more than he can cope with.

'When I returned her, her mother decided that the girl is sick. I didn't believe her. But the bitch took her temperature and guess what? Belinda did have a temperature and the bloody woman kept shouting that I didn't look after her properly, and Belinda was now sick. "You take her to the quack, and you buy her the medicine," she shouted. I couldn't find a quack, not on Saturday evening, so I bought some disprin and promised her mother to check on her today. If she still has temperature, I'll have to take her to the quack and buy some medicine. Peter, I have seven dollars left. Seven dollars. Do you think you can lend me some money?'

'Four years old?' Peter says to himself. 'What if Shosh fell sick, and I couldn't afford her medicine?'

'C'mon man, I'll pay you back, I promise. You lend me a hundred dollars, and I'll pay you back in six months or so.'

'A hundred dollars?'

'To survive till the end the week and buy some stuff for my daughter. I have seven dollars and the unemployment benefit is not due till Thursday. The day before my girlfriend threw me out, I gave her all my money. Well, not all, I left myself nearly fifty dollars. Forty dollars of it I spent taking my daughter around.'

Peter walks to the wardrobe and takes out a tin box. Inside all his savings: two hundred and thirty-three dollars. He picks out two fifty-dollar notes and hands them to John Dexter.

'Thank you mate. Thank you. I'll pay you back in six months. I promise,' and John Dexter picks up his suitcase, about to depart.

At the sound of the door slamming above, Eszti pulls the curtain to look out. John Dexter, suitcase in hand is walking away. *Phew!* And she takes a deep breath.

Peter too is relieved; he can finally do his yoga. Standing up, he balances himself on his left foot, his right leg bent, foot resting below his left knee, hands in prayer. Calming, soothing. 'Concentrate on the immense goodness which envelops us all,' the Swami whispers.

'Goodness?' Peter wonders aloud.

'The goodness of mankind, the harmony of the universe.'

But no matter how hard Peter concentrates he can only feel the pain, the pain in his joints, and the stiffness in his muscles. *Where is the harmony of the universe? Where is the goodness of mankind?*

He changes over to his right foot, but cannot stand there for long. Sitting down again, legs crossed, rocking to and fro he murmurs, '*Om Namah Shivaya, Om Namah Shivaya.*'

'Stop moving!' the Swami yells in his ear.

'*Om Namah Shivaya. Om Namah Shivaya!*' Peter screams to drown the Swami. '*Omnamashivaya.*'

The Swami vanishes.

'*Om Namah Shivaya,*' he says softer and softer, '*Om Namah Shivaya.*' He is standing on the beach in a big, big circle. Scores of people, eyes closed, are holding hands, humming a song, in unison, as if the song had been rehearsed hundreds of times already. All swaying with the melody in perfect timing. He opens his eyes. The woman opposite smiles at him, he smiles back at her. The others too have opened their eyes and are smiling at him. Serenely, lovingly. At him. He loves them, he loves all of them. There is enough love in him for the whole of mankind. Once he could only love his family, now he can love the whole of mankind. It's worth suffering for that.

Suffering, but how much? he wonders, remembering that she, his wife, did not want to hold him, she pulled back with a shudder. He wanted to be held by her, not for sex, just a hug. 'Couldn't you hold me for a few moments?'

They are on the beach. The breeze tastes of salt. The back of her neck used to taste like that and so did her breasts. Her curls were always in the way and she laughed, almond-shaped green eyes nearly shut with laughter. Baby Shosh was there too, the three of them playing in the sea. Laughing, carrying on, and now? Where is he now? He is in a black hole of pain. 'Help me God, help me.' Silence. The absolute silence of the Heavens.

His thoughts back, he checks the time. It's just past nine. At eleven sharp he is due to meet Martin in front of the church. He has a shower, puts his jeans on, the shirt he bought the other day from the St Vincent de Paul shop, and the small knitted hat. With his notebook and the Japanese dictionary in his bag, he locks the door and is on the way to Carrington Road for his morning coffee. He works there for a while, then having found two more words which prove the connection between the Japanese and Hungarian languages, he packs his notes and walks out. Down he walks, down towards the church where Martin and his van should be waiting already.

-22-

While Peter is negotiating with John Dexter that Monday morning, Clara is on the way to the office, her mind still on yesterday's visit to Coogee, as she walks through the small park. It has shaken her, has thrown her off balance. The calm she had been trying so hard to achieve, gone again. She has not slept a wink; she lay in bed worrying about Shosh. Even a child twice her age should not have to witness the scenes she did yesterday.

It is five to nine already, but she has to restore herself and joins the queue at the café, then sipping along, she heads to the office, all the while thinking about what happened yesterday, and worried about Shosh, very worried.

Shosh has been coping with her father's sickness; she dealt with it by leading a double life. Her father is a secret, a secret she only shares with her grandmother and her mother. She is alert to every possible intrusion, as if her life hangs on that secret. She did tell her friends that her father lives on the other side of the city, and she visits him regularly. What does he do? He is a physicist. No-one asked her if he works, and no-one asked if he is normal. He is the daddy on the other side of the city, a daddy with birthdays, Christmases and Easters, Hanukkahs, and Passovers. She does not try to stick to accuracy. As far as she is concerned, her friends know enough. She never told them that when he talks, he talks differently from anyone she has ever met, he talks about words, how they connect to each other, how they connect to history, to people who moved across continents thousands of years ago.

He talks about prophets, about Christ, about Muhammad. They are all good men, he always says. She listens.

At times she applies a discount to what he says, not that anyone ever told her to. There is something inside her, a preservation urge, a guard dog which only allows in thoughts and ideas resembling the normal. She sifts information. She cannot tell her friends about his funny hat, how he contorts his body, how he talks to some Swami only he can see. But her father is also the man who holds her hand when they walk down to Coogee Beach – Grandma Eszti and her mother behind – as she recounts to him what happened at school, or tells him about her friends. During those walks she loves him so much. She cannot explain all this to anybody, especially not to her friends, they will only see his funny hat and laugh.

Walking behind them, Clara cannot help noticing how calm Shosh is, how contented. There is a quiet understanding between her and her father, the sort she does not seem to have with anyone else. But when he is agitated, or screams and nobody can calm him down, Shosh is afraid. At times she cries in the car all the way home, and nothing Clara says will cheer her up. At such times, Clara feels utterly helpless, like a one-legged woman facing two flights of stairs and nothing to hold on to.

Shosh has heard irrational arguments, religious mantras before, but yesterday she saw madness. How will that affect her? And if Peter deteriorates? How will she cope with these visits? Visits she, Clara, finds difficult. Tumultuous, mixed feelings overwhelm her. Sometimes as they sit around the table in Eszti's kitchen, or walk down to Coogee Beach, she sees a strange man lost in his world, who looks so much like someone she once loved, but this man is a stranger. What happened to that bright young man? she wants to shout. She wants to blame someone, something. Fate. Destiny. She wants to shout, 'Whoever you are, you who decide who is healthy and who is sick, you had no right to take his mind, you had no right to inflict on him such a dreadful sickness. And you had no right to punish Shosh, or Eszti, or me.' If only she could shout it, it would lighten her soul.

And then there are the questions, tormenting questions, because no matter how much she struggles, she cannot find answers. Why do I take Shosh to see her father? Guilt? Pity? Shouldn't I go on my own? But what if not seeing her father will damage her even more? And what about Peter? Life has robbed him of so much, can I rob him of his young daughter? The answer is different after every visit. But after yesterday's events it is, 'No'. No, until the New Year. She will reassess the situation after the Christmas break.

* * *

Clara looks up. She has read the summary of the report a few times, but she is still unclear what exactly the policy is about. She can't concentrate. Scenes from yesterday's visit parade in front of her eyes; Peter shouting at the corner of the room, Peter begging for a hug. Her fear. Fear? No terror. Shosh asking what's wrong with daddy, Shosh looking at her father sprawled on the carpet. *It's always the same, I'm wrecked by every visit, and this time more than ever.*

The light coming from the window dims suddenly. Marina is standing in front of her.

'Clara, are you alright? You look so pale.'

'I'm OK, but I wouldn't mind going out for lunch, and clear my head.'

'Great idea.'

They agree to leave at twelve.

The café is nearly full, but there is a table next to the window and Marina hurries to it.

'Clara, are you sick?'

'I feel a bit off, nothing which a nice lunch won't fix,' then looking around, 'Marina, nearly all these people are from the Department.'

'Early lunch for all.' Marina laughs.

The service is quick and soon the coffee arrives, followed by the toasted vegetarian on Turkish bread.

'Delicious,' Clara says.

'Not bad,' Marina replies and takes a sip of coffee. Her face twists in a grimace. 'Horse piss. Instead of stressing in that office I should've opened a café. But I like my work too much. I'm a born detective and analysis is detective work. The rest ...?' She shrugs, 'and then it's him,' she points to the door where Maurice has just walked in with a man.

'What about him?' Clara says, but the background noise amplified by the gurgling, and whistling of the coffee machine drown her words.

133

'What about Maurice?' she says, this time louder.

'I can't deal with him. I get knotted every time he says something to me. Then you should hear me stumbling. My accent becomes impenetrable even to me. We barely tolerate each other. Haven't you noticed?'

'I can't say I have. He's been nice to me, but I don't know the man. I can't work him out.'

'Work him out?' she laughs. 'There's nothing to work out. The only difference between him and the Sahara Desert is a thirst to climb. Climb the hierarchy and climb Charmaine. Haven't you noticed how he looks at her?'

'At her bust?'

'And the bits below. Clara, I have to get away from him, from him and the whole friggin Department. Their idiotic rules, their hierarchy, their gobbledygook.'

'So why don't you?'

'I tried, but there's a catch. I need a reference from my manager. Ask Maurice for a reference?' Marina says with a dismissive wave of the hand. 'I break out in a sweat just thinking about it. Can a deer ask the hunter for a better patch of grass? It's Kafkaesque, don't you think?'

'Try him. If he wants to get rid of you …'

'I'll ask him, if I muster the courage,' and after a pause. 'Maybe after my trip.'

'Trip?'

'We're going overseas. Leaving in February. We'll celebrate the beginning of the New Year two months late, but at home.'

'Wow.'

'It's a while away, but I'm counting the days. It's so long since I've seen my friends. Since I felt warmth and an easy acceptance.'

'It's tough. I missed Europe for years. At times I still do.'

'Clara, I miss home, especially now. That time of the year it's winter in Transylvania. As I lie in bed at night, listening to the fan stirring the friggin heat around, I think of home; the cool air, the snow falling, and the pain of homesickness makes me want to howl,' she picks up her handbag, looking for something. 'Look, that's where I want to be,' she holds up a photo of her much younger self in the snow.

'You look so happy.'

'I didn't know how happy I was … Anyway, this year we'll miss out on a white Christmas, but there'll still be plenty of snow,' she smiles from ear to ear.

'Is the whole family going?'

'Yes. All three of us. My son Alex, and my husband of course. I wouldn't travel without him. The two of us are totally devoted to each other. Emigration brought us together. We speak the same language; we laugh at the same jokes, we share a past, we share memories, we share nostalgia.'

'And reinforce it?'

'Yeah. No good if you want to forget your native land, but I doubt many migrants do,' she falls silent. 'Migration, emigration, dislocation. Clara, back home I couldn't have imagined a hot Christmas. I knew it's hot in Australia, mentally I did, but not viscerally, and this obsession with presents … Over there, Christmas was simple. The shops were empty, no Father Christmas, nothing to buy. Nobody gave presents and yet it was magic. I'd pull the curtains in the morning and look out. The road, the trees, the roofs, would all be covered with thick snow. Polka dots of sparrows, the odd car driving past, otherwise silence. The thought of spending a whole month there …' her face lights up from the anticipation of it all, 'not to mention the bonus …'

'Bonus?'

'I'll be away from Maurice. Yes, I'm obsessed. And you? What're you doing for Christmas? Any plans?'

'I'll take my daughter to Tasmania. Leave the week before, get away from the shopping madness.'

'And what about your duty to this friggin capitalism? Isn't that why God sent his son to Earth two thousand years ago?'

'Just one more sin to add to my many,' Clara says smiling wickedly.

Marina's eyes twinkle with enjoyment, 'Clara this lunch has revived you. Your colour is much improved and you're smiling. Sorry, but we'll have to go back.'

-23-

Peter opens his eyes. On the patch of sky visible through the window, a puffy white cloud is floating westwards. Calm, self-assured, as if it knows where it is heading and why. 'Oh, that beauty, that tranquillity, that calm,' he whispers wistfully. 'Thank you, God, thank you for the privilege.'

He is lying there at peace with the world when the Swami whispers in his ear, 'Go downstairs. Go and help your mother with the Christmas shopping!'

'I will. Now go to Hell!' Anger wells up in him again, against the Swami, against the people playing their cruel hide and seek game, against all those who order him around. Manipulate him. Not letting him be.

As he walks to the bathroom, it strikes him that his body is free of stiffness. It moves with an ease he has long forgotten; it moves like a well-oiled machine. He did well to throw those pills away, he should have done it long ago.

He is passing the shaver up and down his face, when behind him someone lets out a peal of mocking, taunting laughter. He looks back. There is no-one. He turns towards the mirror. As if it has been restrained for too long, the laughter erupts with a new-found energy. Loud. Spooky. Sinister. Covered with goose bumps, Peter stands there frozen. The shadow in the mirror laughs at him again. He tries to turn around, but his feet wouldn't move, they have become one with the floor. 'Peter!' The voice behind him yells. Shivering, he breaks out in a cold sweat.

Below the window a truck sounds its horn. The voice vanishes. Sweating profusely, Peter walks out and slams the bathroom door.

He towels himself, puts on a clean T-shirt and jeans and heads to his mother's place.

He has not been downstairs for a couple of days and Eszti is pleased to see him. Standing on her tiptoes, hands on his shoulders, she reaches to kiss him. Peter's body shakes, like a leaf in the breeze.

'I'm so glad you came,' Eszti says as Peter moves a chair next to the open door and sits down. And there he sits silently.

She looks at him: just a physical presence. No, he's not himself today. She cleans the table, washes the breakfast dishes, then begins polishing the sink. Clutching the steel wool with her arthritic fingers, she rubs the stainless surface, with desperate energy. Round and round her small hand goes, faster and faster.

Suddenly, Peter jumps up, puts the kettle on and returns to his chair. The Swami is telling him something, something about loving and his mother, something about being nice to her because she is seventy-two years old.

The kettle is whistling. Louder and louder, then a shriek loud enough to wake the dead.

'Peter dear, can't you hear?'

Peter shudders at something.

'Peter, the kettle!'

He pulls the kettle off the stove. He is about to put a teaspoon of coffee in his cup, but changes his mind and returns the coffee to the jar.

'Aren't you going to make yourself a coffee?' Eszti asks. 'You don't need to sit alone; I'll have one too.'

'I don't want coffee,' he says, eyes gazing at the rays zapping his mother's face. They stop on her zig zag nose, then move down and seal her lips. The anger in his eyes stabs at Eszti's heart. *It's going to be a bad day*, and she turns to the sink again. The sink is gleaming, but Eszti keeps polishing. Partly to distract him, partly to break the uneasy silence, she starts talking about her friend, but then she gets carried away and tells him about her friend's husband.

'He's sick. He cannot do things for himself. The son doesn't help. He's always busy, only God knows with what. Remember him? He studied law. No, not law … Oh, I remember, he studied architecture.

Even then he was always busy. Nowadays, everybody boasts how hard they work. You'd think this country has reinstated slavery. They should try working in a factory, like I did. I had a degree in literature. Hungarian literature. In Australia? As useful as a sack of devalued currency. Devalued to nothing.

'I was happy to land a job in a clothes factory, overlocking trousers, hemming skirts. Hundreds, thousands. Only God knows how many. I was paid by the garment. Twenty cents, fifty cents, I didn't care how much, I just finished as many as I could. But did I ever complain? Nowadays they're all whinging. It's a fashion. Well, the daughter-in-law does work hard, in her case it's probably true, she works full-time and they have two children. Remember the little one we saw a few years ago? Before they moved away? He's a big boy now, he's going to school. And she had another baby, a beautiful girl, well she's on the photo. It's easier with the little one. But the other one, the son? He doesn't like his teacher. Small kids, small problems, big kids, big problems. When she tried to talk to …'

'Shut up, will you?'

'I thought you might be interested.'

'Stop gossiping. For crying out loud. Stop it.'

'I can't open my mouth anymore.'

'No, you can't bad-mouth everybody.'

'I wasn't …'

'You were! You're vile!' he shouts and jumps up to go.

'Come on dear, we have to do the shopping. I need you to …' but Peter is gone.

Eszti has stopped polishing. Helplessness is creeping up on her. She rubs the back of her head; it is hurting even more than it did in the morning. She puts the plates away, takes the tablecloth to the porch and shakes the crumbs off. In the garden, Peter is pacing.

'Peter. Come on dear. I'll change, I'll put something light on and we can go.'

'Come on,' she pleads with him, and again.

Peter returns to the kitchen.

'Oh, I nearly forgot. I have a Christmas present for you. And since Christmas is only four days away, and we're not too fussed about celebrations, I might as well give it to you now,' and she hurries out. Soon she is back holding up a jumper.

The jumper, its dark green and brown pattern, reminds Peter of something. It reminds him of … But just as he is about to work it out, Eszti interrupts:

'It's warm and you need a warm jumper.'

'I don't need anything.'

'You lost your only jumper, you need something for the cold days.'

The jumper looks at him, the repulsive colour of a dead crocodile. Bent back on itself the label: Size M.

'Don't you like it?'

'I do,' but the resentment on Peter's face does not escape Eszti.

'Shall I exchange it for a different colour?'

'I don't want a different colour.'

'Look,' she puts the jumper against his face, 'this colour suits you. And the medium size should be perfect on you.'

The Swami's head pops up behind Eszti's right shoulder. 'Large!'

'I only wear large.'

'Large would hang on you. You would look like a walking coat hanger.'

'Large!' Peter shouts.

'Shall I exchange it?'

'No, I don't want you to exchange it, or do anything else for me.'

'So, you won't wear it?'

'NO!'

'Would you like something else instead?'

'No! Nothing! Do you understand? I don't want anything from you. Nothing!'

'I cannot put a foot right,' Eszti says in a thin, barely audible voice of someone in her last hour on this Earth.

'Leave me alone! Leave me alone! Forever!' Peter howls and storms out onto the street. Down he runs, down towards the beach, past the cafe where he has his morning coffee, past the swimwear boutique shop, past the fish and chip shop. A dog comes running from around the corner. They narrowly avoid each other. The dog barks at him, hoarse, loud, furious. Just out of the Thai restaurant, a couple look at the dog, look at Peter. The woman grabs the man's arm, and they hurry past.

Without looking left or right, Peter runs across the street. Horns honk. He keeps running. He speeds across the beach, stops for a moment to catch his breath, then plunges into the water. *My mother, bad Karma, her house, bad Karma. I have to leave. I have to move out.* The sea drags him in. Suddenly a dark mass of water rises in front of him. Higher and higher, closer and closer. Life, or death, he does not care any longer. The wave grabs him, lifts him up and throws him onto the shore.

Dripping, he crosses the beach and heads to the small park opposite, where a few children are playing. *Shosh?* It is Sunday afternoon. Clara is at home preparing dinner. Shosh is on the swing. 'Faster daddy, faster,' Shosh cries out and looks back at him, big brown eyes, smiling from ear to ear. Peter hurries past the children, as far as possible from the Shosh-lookalike girl.

In the corner of the park is a bench, from there he cannot see the children, or Shosh, and there he sits, lost in his world, for a long, long time. Families walk past, but Peter does not register. He does not feel thirst, or hunger, or the chill of his wet clothes. His thoughts are conversing with the Swami.

'What do you need a flat for?' the Swami asks. 'You can sleep under the stars. You can live on the street; you can live in the park. Meditate. Connect with the consciousness of the world, connect with the poor, the sick and the old. Then you'll be happy.'

The sun is setting. The wind from the south-east is gaining strength, pushing dark clouds over the land, blowing sand from the playground, where the big, navy-blue merry-go-round and the seagulls are, onto the grass and onto Peter's feet. The bush is whistling furiously. The sea roars as if all the anger in the world had come together in that endless and menacing grey vastness. It contains Peter's anger against his mother, against the doctors, against the Swami who got him into trouble so many times, against the images which have conspired to project him to the fringes of humanity. Anger against his body, against his existence.

The sky lights up. Thunder breaks with a bang, reverberates for a moment or two then loses itself in the roar of the ocean. Violent rain descends on the sea and the land. Soaked to the skin, Peter is sitting on the bench, water running down his face. He will not return to his flat, he will not return to be under his mother's gaze. Not ever.

At home Eszti is sitting waiting. Meaningless television images roll in front of her eyes. She cannot remember if she has taken her blood pressure medication. She cannot afford to be sick; she cannot afford to die. She cannot leave him alone on this Earth.

'He won't be your problem anymore, Mrs Steinberg,' the doctor said to her matter-of-factly. Words she has not forgotten.

It's ten o'clock, 'Where is he? He will come back. He will, but she finds it hard to chase away the black thoughts. She makes herself a cup of tea and returns to watch television. On the screen, people are coming and going, shouting at each other. She has no idea what the story is about, she cannot concentrate. The Heavens crack with thunder again, then all is quiet. She should switch off the TV, but she cannot bear to be alone. Not now.

She returns to the kitchen, makes herself a sandwich and another cup of tea. She eats slowly, absentmindedly.

Looking down on her from the opposite wall are two of her late husband's paintings. In one, two peasant women walking side by side in a Hungarian village, the other … the other reminds her of his last months. She should take it down, but that is his last and best painting. A self-portrait, his hands towards the viewer, the palms facing the sky. Why? the man asks. Why me? He was dying at the time. Now she would also like to ask the Heavens why? Why did it inflict on Peter such a horrific sickness? Peter, her only son? And why was Europe such a pathetic place, why couldn't the Europeans live together peacefully? She would still be there. There the doctors might have talked to her differently. They would not say, 'He won't be your problem anymore.' The heartless man.

The clock strikes eleven. Peter bought her that grandfather clock and how happy it made her, how very happy. Now she wishes he hadn't, she does not want to listen to its chimes, she does not want to be reminded how late it is.

-24-

Tasmania, two days before Christmas, a week to the start of the New Year, the last of the millennium.

The hills of Launceston descend towards the Tamar River as Clara speeds along the deserted road. Life has taken me from the Netherlands to the end of the world. But was it life, or my own restlessness? The road veers to the left and there in the distance is the sign she has been looking for, 'Longford,' and her thoughts shift from the introspective to the practical.

Sitting quietly on the back seat, Shosh yawns. It has been a long day.

Having nearly missed the village centre, Clara slows the car to a crawl. They pass a couple of B&B places, turn right, and there is their destination.

The Tame Bull is a sprawled out single-story building, a splash of poppies in front. Above the door a bell chimes in the breeze. Standing on her tippy toes, Shosh pulls the bell cord with far more zest than it is intended for. The sound of hurried steps, and as the door opens, a smell of wood smoke wafts past, the smell of a mountain cabin where the fire burns all year round. In front of them a tall, solidly built, middle-aged man with grey hair and an honest face. He is Brian, the man who took her booking.

They follow him along the dim corridor and shelves loaded with blacksmith and hunting knickknacks. Clara is trying to recall how many nights she has committed to spend in this strange place, when a buxom woman who seems to have walked straight out of a seventeenth-century Dutch painting, appears. Round pink cheeks, blue eyes and short curly honey-blonde hair. She leads them to their, "renovated, superior room," while she makes girly conversation with Shosh.

It is a big room, with pretensions of old English glamour: plush carpet, heavy velvet drapes, floral upholstered chairs, a dark brown wardrobe and a chest of drawers.

'By the way, we offer home cooked dinners, but only at eight hours' notice,' Mary says, one foot outside the door. But she is not going yet, because she has to tell them about tonight's menu and its health benefits. Clara's patience is wearing thin, and Mary, being a perceptive woman, and alert to her guest's every wish, changes the subject, 'Breakfast between eight and nine, and the parking,' she pauses for breath, 'only parallel to the fence.'

The humidity which met them in Launceston has given way to a cool late afternoon. The sun is drifting in and out of the clouds, the horizon far, far away, maybe at the edge of the Earth, and Clara's emotions are swinging between hope for a new life and a painful loneliness, the sort of loneliness that overwhelms one in a strange, foreign land.

By nine o'clock, Longford has descended into a silent darkness. Exhausted after the long journey Shosh has fallen asleep. A light breeze is swaying the curtains, playing with the leaves in front of the window. In the king-sized bed, wrapped by a sense of security, of home, of being looked after, Clara drifts into a peaceful, deep sleep.

When they enter the dining room the next morning, the breakfast tables are set. On the sideboard, lined up like marching soldiers, jars of jam and fresh crusty bread. But nothing is complete without Mary's commentary.

'The jams are homemade, every one of them. The cherries are from our garden, that's the one over there.' She points to the jar at the end of the line. 'The others from fruit from nearby farms. And the eggs? You have never tasted fresher eggs. Laid this morning, by our chooks. We have fourteen chooks in the backyard. Have a look at them sometime.'

Lecture finished, she picks up the used crockery from the next table and heads to the kitchen. Clara's eyes follow her through the wide-open door. Soon Mary is fully immersed in cooking, but Brian is not interested in food just now. He pinches her sizable bottom. Mary jumps. Clara bursts out laughing.

'Mum, what's so funny?'

'I'll tell you later.'

'You always say that when you don't want to tell me something,' Shosh says sulking. Soon Mary, holding two plates, comes out of the kitchen and heads to their table, and Shosh's attention shifts to her breakfast. The poached eggs are cooked to perfection, the cherry jam is divine. Shosh is enjoying it too much to hold a grudge for the earlier offence.

On Mary's advice, and acknowledging her deficiency in Australian history, especially convict history, after breakfast Clara and Shosh set out for Woolmer's estate. It is one of those mornings when the sun is shining, but the cool breeze and the crisp air would invigorate a wilted soul. High hedges of berries wall the side of the road. Further along, in the valley, under the bridge, a river makes its way sluggishly between the banks, bushes and weeping willows hanging over it. Every now and then a car goes past, but soon the birds and the bees reign over Longford again.

The estate is high on a hill. The next tour is about to start, the visitors already assembled in front of the souvenir shop which overlooks squares and circles of pansies, each bed one colour. Their uniformity, their sameness, heralds the practical.

Having given an overview of the place, the guide, a middle-aged woman, related to the family "by marriage," she is quick to emphasise, takes them to the old family quarters, ceilings so low they threaten decapitation, peeling wallpaper, worn carpets, worn even in places where visitors are not allowed to walk. The first room is where the old Woolmer ailed for twelve months before he gave up the ghost.

Bored, Shosh tugs at Clara's arm, wanting to go. But just then the group is ushered to the newer part of the building and the ceiling lifts. They are now in a big ceremonial dining room, the table set with exquisite china. The most treasured piece of furniture turns out to be the chair where some royal has placed his posterior on his only visit.

'Shosh, at the head of the table, over there, sat a Prince once.'

'A Prince?'

'Yes, a famous royal.'

'Ah!'

The meeting with fame, or with its long-ago imprint, must have pleased Shosh because she is no longer complaining.

By the time they finish the tour, clouds are gathering. A warm summer rain begins to fall.

After dinner Clara and Shosh return to their room. Clara tries to read but Shosh is restless. She begs to go somewhere, anywhere, for just even a walk.

The streets are deserted, only the odd car parked under a dim light. The mellow sound of a flute playing, *Silent Night* wafts past for a while, but then it stops. Utter silence. Not the silence ahead of a great coming, but a silence to end another day of an unassuming simple life.

* * *

Too busy organising the trip, Clara had not given much thought to the Christmas celebration and when the dozen or so grey heads sitting around the long rectangular table turn to look at the two of them as they enter the room, her first thought is I must be in the wrong place. She is about to turn around, but Brian is already pointing to her seat, and there on the table is her name tag, next to it is Shosh's. There is no mistake, this is the Christmas party.

Brian fills her glass and pours Shosh an orange juice.

Margaret, the woman sitting opposite Clara, seems to be the youngest in the gathering. Next to her is her friend, Dotty. Each wearing a pink tissue hat.

'And who is this young lady?' Dotty asks.

'Shosh,' she says, smiling from ear to ear.

Dotty and Margaret are widows and bursting to talk. Within moments Clara has learnt more about them and their families than she has in a year about her neighbours in Sydney.

'I don't see them as often as I'd like,' Margaret says. 'My son is overseas a lot, work, holiday, whatnot. Now the whole family is in the UK.' She falls silent, then, 'I miss them, of course I do, but this one,' she puts her arm around Dotty's shoulders, 'is like a sister to me.'

'Yes, we have each other,' Dotty says, 'and Jeff . . .'

'Dotty's son,' Margaret adds.

'Yes, he's wonderful to me, but he has his own life. Today he's at his in-laws. Well . . . ex-in-laws,' and after a pause, 'He couldn't bear spending Christmas without his daughter,' then looking at Clara. 'And you? What is a young soul like you doing here?'

'Um … I'm divorced.'

Shosh has left the table and is now the centre of attention. Talking to one woman, then another, talking and laughing.

'I'd better not,' Dotty says when Brian is about to refill her glass.

'Go on, there's only one Christmas a year.'

'Maybe later. Wow! Look at that …'

Mary has just walked in pushing a loaded trolley, on it a roast turkey, a big ham, salads and cooked vegetables.

The ham, the turkey, the wine. The main course over, the company is getting merry. Paper horns are booing. Crackers are popping, exploding. The party is loud enough for the New Year to hear. Dotty pulls one cracker with Margaret and one with Clara. Shosh is going around pulling with whoever she can, banging and laughing.

'Clara, I don't want to intrude,' Margaret says when the noise has died down, 'are you trying to find someone? Rebuild your life?'

'I've rebuilt my life. I've found a full-time job. The rest?' she shrugs, 'The rest, who knows?'

'The rest will come. Just make sure that you don't miss the opportunity when it presents itself,' and after a pause, 'You need someone to share your life with.'

'And you, Margaret? Are you following your own advice? Are you doing what you're preaching to me?' Clara asks, smiling impishly.

'Me?' Margaret shrugs, 'There aren't many men left at my age. Besides, I'm too set in my ways,' she falls silent. 'To tell you the truth, I'm comfortable with my habits and peculiarities. Getting used to someone at my age …? For that you have to be young, more flexible than I am.'

'Maybe you just have to try and see. Be open to opportunities,' Clara says, a playful smile on her face.

Shosh is back, her eyes shining from all the fun, and Clara no longer minds being there, she is glad she came.

The Christmas lunch is nearly over. The delicious plum pudding is gone too. The gathering has settled down to a cup of coffee when the doorbell rings. It is Jeff, Dotty's son, a youngish man, medium build, with a pleasant face. After a short chat he helps his mother up from the sofa and the two of them depart.

'Jeff's a high school teacher,' Margaret says, 'and a farmer, he has a hobby farm.'

'He seems a nice man,' Clara says.

'It broke Dotty's heart when his marriage ended. She was worried about Olly, her granddaughter. Three years old she was at the time. A bit of a tomboy, but with the self-reliance of a child much older. Still, children need both their parents, don't you think?'

Clara nods.

'I said to her, "At least he has joint custody, that's more than most fathers do." Does your ex-husband have joint custody of Shosh?'

'No, but he sees her on weekends,' Clara says, intimating the end of the topic.

They sit in silence. Three women have left, another is taking her leave. Margaret looks at her watch, 'My neighbour will be picking me up any minute.'

'And tomorrow? Why don't I take you for a drive tomorrow?' Clara asks.

'I don't know dear; I don't know if I'll be up to it, but give me a call. She scours her handbag for a pen, writes down her phone number just as the neighbour walks in.

With most people gone, Clara and Shosh return to their room.

The sun is about to set as they walk out of the hotel. Further up, next to the road leading out of Longford, a field of poppies is swaying in the breeze. Christmas Day is coming to an end.

* * *

In the backyard the next morning, Mary is getting ready to feed the chooks. Two hens have noticed the preparation and are running towards her, flapping their wings as if about to take off. Now the others are on the move. The more the commotion, the more Shosh is enjoying it.

'Mum, the brown one! Look at it! Look how she gobbles up everything.'

Mary throws more grains around. The yard, the hens, the fruit trees; a heart-warming scene, a cosy domesticity.

'They're good egg layers, all except this one.' Mary points to the smallest in the brood. 'Not much of an egg layer, more like a …'

'Mrs Steinberg,' Brian calls from the house, 'someone wants to talk to you.'

'To me?'

'Yes.'

It's Jeff.

'I have a suggestion. The weather's beautiful, why don't I take the two of you to Dove Lake? We could walk around the lake, have lunch, watch the birds and the jumping fish.'

It's a very enticing proposition. She wouldn't mind meeting him for an hour or two, but a whole day? Her dinner with Adam never far from her mind. Is Jeff a trustworthy fellow? Margaret had only good things to say about him.

'Well, what do you think? It's an easy walk. Even for a Sydneysider,' he laughs.

'I was going to take Margaret for a drive. I'll talk to her and ring you back.'

Margaret is about to go to the cemetery, to be with her husband.

Well Clara? Should you or shouldn't you go?

'Shosh, would you like to go for a trip?'

'A trip, where to?'

'To a big lake, to see fish.'

Shosh's eyes sparkle, 'I do, I do!'

So, its decided, and with Jeff at the wheel, Clara and Shosh set out for Dove Lake. Jeff turns out to be a talker. He tells them about his farm, about teaching modern history and everything Clara has already heard from Margaret.

'How come you chose to stay in Longford?' he asks.

'Because it's famous. Didn't its bakery win a meat pie competition?'

'Um ... we have to boast of what we've got,' he says with a half-smile. 'Have you seen much of Tasmania?'

'Not much, not yet. We visited Launceston a couple of times.'

'And the park with the beautiful peacocks,' comes Shosh's voice from the back, 'And we visited that place ... mum what's its name? With the room where the Prince sat.'

'Yes, we visited Woolmers.'

'And what did you think of Woolmers?'

Clara shrugs, 'What did I think ...? We were shown everything from the old Woolmer's bed to his worn bedspread and his potty. Call me unpatriotic, but is the potty of a sick old farmer history? True, he was one of the first white residents in the area, and everything connected to him must be of interest to some people. But me? I've never been interested in local history, not here, and not in the Netherlands. I'm interested in the big events, and I'm interested in social history,' and after a pause, 'I guess, there was some of that. The woolshed, the blacksmith's shed, but I would have liked to find out more about the convicts. How they lived.'

'Big events? You speak like a European. I spent five years in the UK … and I tripped around Europe a lot. I've seen the footprints of war; I've seen what humans are capable of. When it comes to history, we cannot compete with Europe. This is a young country. Still, it did manage a genocide in its short life.'

'Five years in the UK?' Clara asks. 'People return to their homeland after a year, or two, but after five?'

'After a year or two it's an impulse, after five years it's a well thought through decision. I missed Tasmania. I missed the sky, the beaches, the fresh air, but more than anything I missed the simple life and a sense of belonging. By the time I came back, I knew exactly how I wanted to live. That's how the idea of a hobby farm was born.'

Silence, except the barely audible car engine and the odd car whooshing past.

'Oh, I forgot to mention the most depressing part of that tour at Woolmers,' Clara says, 'The story of the last Woolmer, the lifeless bachelor, who spent his time watching television, playing with guns and passing his lonely evenings in a corridor-like room. What an utterly dismal existence. I couldn't get him out of my mind for days.'

'Some people don't miss companionship; others can't live without it.'

Cheeks burning with embarrassment, tongue-tied, Clara's gaze is fixed stubbornly on the road.

'You're single, aren't you?' Jeff asks after a while.

'I'm divorced.'

'Does Shosh's father takes an interest in her?"

'He loves her.'

'Remarried?'

'No.'

'What does he do?'

'He's a physicist.'

'Clever man.'

'Are we there yet?' Shosh calls from the back seat.

Oh, how grateful Clara is for her interjection, how grateful she is for not blabbing about their secret. She is in no mood to tell Jeff about Peter, or about their cursed marriage.

'Another twenty minutes,' Jeff says, 'and if you're patient, I will show you a magic place.'

'Yes, magic. Magic exists only in stories.'

'You'll see.'

'Promise?'

'I do.'

'Do you see your daughter often?' Clara asks.

'Two or three times a week.'

Wondering if Shosh heard, Clara turns to look at her. Shosh is staring ahead, eyes wide open. A perceptive child, she knows how to keep a secret. Not that anybody has ever asked her to. How does she know what to say and what not to say? How does she know where the boundaries are? A child, not quite six years old, carrying an adult weight on her shoulders.

The car is swallowing the miles. Clara is savouring the luxury of being driven. From the corner of her eye she looks at Jeff. His profile, well defined, strong, attractive.

The last empty space in Dove Lake car park is waiting for them. By the time they start walking the sun is high in the sky. The lake is still, its surface a perfect mirror. Shosh looks at the reflections of the gumtrees, marvelling how they were formed and why they are upside down when the trees point to the sky, and how come the branches tremble in the water at the slightest puff of wind.

'I don't know,' Jeff replies to her questions.

'It's something to do with physics,' Clara says.

'I bet my daddy knows. Mum, are we going to see him next weekend?'

'Do you want to?'

'Yes, I do, and I want to give Grandma her Christmas present.'

'We'll visit them if not next weekend, then the weekend after.'

They have been walking for nearly two hours, when below the path a wooden table with three benches appears.

'Just the place for a pleasant lunch, don't you think?' Jeff says.

Shosh can't be happier, she is hungry. Jeff takes out the sandwiches he prepared that morning and they sit down to eat.

Now and then a few people walk past. Then only the sound of water coming and going, lapping the tree trunks with a soothing regularity. In the distance, a fish jumps out of the water and lands with a splash.

After lunch, Shosh scrambles down to examine some weed washed out of the water.

Jeff puts his arm around Clara. She has not felt a man's touch for a long, long time. Sensations she has long forgotten resurface in her, their intensity frightening. Is it attraction, or years of depriving her body of its demands? Because it is not love, she knows how love feels. Besides, she and Jeff are so unlike.

Shosh turns around. She looks at them, her eyes sad, menacing.

Jeff pulls his arm away. The magic moment is gone.

-25-

The plane has broken through the clouds. Looking through the window, Clara is lost in thought. Images of her holiday keep popping up against the luminous blue sky. It was a good break, I feel healthier, more alive than I have for years. But how long can this feeling survive my everyday life. Life? No, just an existence. I can't fall into that rut again. I can't and I won't. I've been plodding through life because I thought that's all I could do. I stuck to a strict routine, with as much optimism and ability to see past the next step as a robot. I can do far more than I think I can. I was even worried about this trip. Why? Because I worry about everything, because I've given up expecting anything pleasant from life. I've been wrong. Life's shutters are far more open than I thought. Out there the sun is shining. I should enjoy that sunshine. I won't allow Peter's sickness to take over my life again and I will protect Shosh, I will shield her, far, far more than I have. We will visit Peter less often, and after each visit I will take her to a movie, or invite one of her friends to sleep over. To brush away the day's events, end it on a happier note.

Back in the office, a few days later, she is telling Marina about her trip when Maurice walks past: 'Have you had a good holiday?'

'Yes, an excellent one.'

'Clara, we need to discuss your next project … when you finish.' The reproach in his voice unmistakable.

'Go on, you can't let the boss wait,' Marina says with a derisive, contemptuous smile.

'Unfortunately,' and she picks up her notebook.

'Clara, I have a beaut one for you,' Maurice says leaning back in his chair, hands clasped behind his head. 'The Minister will be launching a new initiative. Very sensitive stuff, top secret at this stage. Absolutely top secret.' He pauses to let the gravity of what he just said sink in. 'An initiative to help the mentally ill to heal in their own surroundings. It will be launched under the name, Heal in Place.'

Heal in Place? she wonders.

'Confused? Just hear me out.' Maurice straightens up in his chair. 'We will reduce the number of non-acute beds dedicated to the mentally ill in some hospitals. This will free up nurses and social workers for home visits, to check how they are, what they need. Simply put, support them in whatever way is necessary to heal in their own surroundings. The sick will have more freedom, the staff will have more responsibility and variety in their work.' He slaps his thighs, 'A win-win situation if ever I've seen one.' Then, convinced that he has impressed on Clara the sheer brilliance and importance of the initiative, he leans towards her, 'And your part in all this?'

'My part?' she asks uneasily.

'Yes, and it's a crucial one. You write well, so Sandy and I decided that you should write the Minister's speech.'

'The Minister's speech?' she echoes with a sinking feeling.

'Yes. Only a draft at this stage. Have a look at some previous speeches. All speeches have the same format. And don't worry about the greetings, introduction, the easy stuff. The Minister's staff will put all that in.

'Now, while we're waiting for the results of the analysis …' he taps his fingers on the desk, 'Oh, I'd better talk to them,' and Maurice walks to the door. 'Simon!'

Simon comes rushing.

'Simon, we have an important request from the Minister.'

'A ministerial?' Simon asks with the expression of a dog who just got an adoring pat.

Maurice starts telling him what is needed and the further he goes the more worried Simon looks. 'By when?'

'By mid-February. We'll firm up the date at next management meeting. Meanwhile you should start working on it, Clara has to include the figures in an important document.'

A shadow crosses Simon's face.

'The best figures you can come up with,' Maurice says and turns his gaze to the document on his desk.

Crestfallen, Simon stands up to go. He is barely past the door when Maurice calls after him, 'Simon, ask Marina to help.'

Simon's face lights up in a smile.

Maurice turns to Clara, 'Now back to the speech. Think about what to include and how best to emphasise the importance of self-reliance. Try to find a few human-interest stories, stories of people who with support, managed to rebuild their life after a short stay in hospital. Have a chat to Danny Matheson. You met him, didn't you?'

'The medic? Yes, I did talk to him a couple of times.'

'He knows a lot about the mentally ill.'

So, do I, a great deal. Not something she can share with the man in front of her.

'That's it for now, but I'm sure there'll be more work on this topic.'

She does not want more work on this topic, she does not want any work on this topic. To her, the mentally ill are not an abstract group of people, their suffering is not something she heard about in passing, or read somewhere, she has seen it with her own eyes. How many times did her insides churn when she saw Peter staring into the abyss? How many times did his insanity terrify her? Nauseate her? How many times did she lie awake at night thinking about his future? When someone's mind snaps, the family follows into its cracks.

Walking back to her desk, thinking, Heal in Place? What does it actually mean? I should have asked Maurice if this initiative is intended to improve life, or to save money. No, I wouldn't have got an answer, Maurice is a public servant; he has to do what the Minister wants and I have no choice but to write the speech. She picks up the phone to dial Danny Matheson.

'With professional support, some of the non-acute patients could do well outside,' he says.

'Which ones?'

'Hard to tell. Each case is different.'

Those who are not far gone? But since she does not expect a definitive answer from the Department's medic, she thanks him and puts the phone down. Shouldn't the system look after all of them? Surely they need more hospital beds, not less; both acute and non-acute. But it is not her job to hold the Minister to account, or to formulate policies, her job is to write the Minister's speech. Justify the new initiative. Justify it? How? She has no idea. She will first work out the format.

She opens the folder with the previous speeches, scans a few, reads a couple, all the while thinking about their relevance to the speech she has to write. When she next looks at her watch it is five-twenty. She cannot stay late; she has to pick up Shosh by six o'clock. Later times are for emergencies only.

It has been raining all afternoon. Avoiding the puddles, fighting the southerly wind that tries to turn her umbrella inside out, Clara jostles her way through the crowds heading to the station.

The train is running late. Town Hall Station, a beehive in the peak hour, is now a vertical pencil case packed to its last. A train has been cancelled and the next one is running late. A woman is grumbling something about trains, about developed countries. The announcer apologises for any inconvenience.

Inconvenience? Clara checks her watch.

Finally, the train pulls in, she will just make the six o'clock deadline. Relieved, she leans against the window. *The Minister's speech, the mentally ill, Peter.* He is in front of her eyes, wearing the sloppy joe his mother bought in a sale in some cheap shop, the perennial beanie on his head, vacant eyes fixed into the distance, a St Vincent de Paul bag in his hand. Non-acute. What about him? And what about all the others who don't even have a roof over their heads? What should I write in that speech? Praise the new initiative? Promise that it will change their lives? They will be supported to, 'Heal in Place.' Which place? On the street? Or in the park? Or hunting for a cool spot when the heat of Sydney's summer becomes unbearable.

She has seen them in libraries, she has seen them in air-conditioned trains, riding endlessly between Sydney and the Central Coast, Sydney and Wollongong. Sydney and anywhere. They were in no rush to get to a destination, because they had no destination. Their whole life had no destination. As far as they were concerned, the longer the journey took the better.

At least Peter has a roof over his head, but what will happen when Eszti is no more? Will he end up on the street? Walking with his St Vincent de Paul bag, rummaging for food in rubbish bins. Shosh's father? What will I do then? Because no matter how sorry I'll feel for him, I won't take him on, I can't. His unpredictability terrifies me. Why?

At times, when she walks in the city, her mind miles away, there he is, coming towards her, and every time he does, her heart skips a beat. Why do so many people look like him? Because it has never been him, never except once. He was walking towards her, bag in hand, a beanie on his head, the same sloppy joe and worn jeans, worn not by design, but by time. She quickly turned into the first narrow street, a few paces later she looked back in terror. He wasn't there, and the feeling of terror gave way to shame, an intense shame which stayed with her for hours. Why wasn't she brave enough to stop? Why wasn't she brave enough to talk to him? But she knows that if he crosses her path again, she will do the same, turn into the first side street and vanish.

She dreads being hugged by him, yet she does want to hold his cold hand, she wants to comfort him. But she is afraid that he might think that she will be there for him again, because she won't. She has learnt her limitations, she has learnt that love is not infinitely enduring, that no relationship is infinitely enduring. She keeps telling herself that she is no worse than most people, but deep down she detests herself. I'm weak, I'm pathetic.

The trip to Tasmania brought her hope, but Maurice has changed all that in ten short minutes. Now she has no choice but to get involved in the new initiative, and not superficially, not only on the margins, she has to write the Minister's speech. But first she will find out about Peter's social worker. Is he of any help? After dinner, she dials Eszti's number.

Having told her about their Tasmanian holiday, Clara asks, 'And how was your Christmas?'

'My Christmas?' Eszti says. 'It came and went.'

'And Peter? How is he?'

'Sorry, can you speak up please?'

'How's Peter?'

'He's very well, in fact better than he's been for a while.'

Clara couldn't have expected a more beautiful Christmas present. 'So, the two of you had a nice Christmas lunch?'

'Um … no, not really.'

'Why not?'

'He hasn't been well for days. Then on Christmas Eve we had a big argument, about that charlatan … What's his name? My God I'm becoming more and more decrepit. That cheat … Oh yes, John Dexter. Peter gave him another fifty dollars. Clara, I'm not poor, but I have to be careful with money. And Peter? He's on a disability pension for goodness sake. I said to him, how could you give away your savings to a stranger? He was furious. "Don't tell me what to do! It's my money!" he screamed and ran out.

'He didn't come down for Christmas. I didn't want more arguments, so I let him be. I read, watched TV and tried to preserve my peace.'

'But you said he's better than he's been for a long time.'

'Yes dear, he is now.'

'He was worse and now he's better, how come?'

'My dear, a lot has happened since Christmas, a great deal.' Eszti sounds remote, tired.

A lot? Whatever that "lot" implies; Clara knows that it can't be good. Does she want to listen to the whole story? No, she just rang to find out about the social worker. But can she not enquire about what happened? And when she does, Eszti starts crying.

'Like a criminal,' she says between sobs, 'like a criminal.'

'Sorry?'

'The police marched him out of the house.'

'Why? What happened?' Clara asks. Anxiety is welling up in her, she can guess what must have happened, but she has to listen to Eszti, show interest.

'The morning after Boxing Day. The festive season was finally over. It's lonely when you have no company. Finally, I could go to the city and walk around the shops.

'I was making myself breakfast when I heard a strange noise at the back of the house, and just as I walked to the window to see what's going on, it stopped. So, I sat down to eat. The noise started again, louder and louder, like … like an approaching train. It's my neighbour, the old Wood, I thought. You know the one?'

'The busy one?'

'Yes, the one who's always sawing, or mowing, or chopping wood, or building something. But just to make sure, I ran to the window to check. Clara, not in my life …'

'What? What happened?'

'It wasn't the old Wood, it was Peter. Peter, pushing a wheelie bin, running into the street. Nearly nude.'

'Nearly nude?'

'In nothing, well … not nothing, in the skimpiest of underpants. I shouted after him. He looked back in terror. "He wants to kill me," he screamed pointing his finger at some presence, and stepped onto the road. He stepped out just as a car came blasting its horn. Well, he did make it, but my heart nearly didn't.

'I dialled his doctor, in utter panic. The phone rang out. Just then the front doorbell rang, and guess what? It was the old Wood. He came to tell me that his granddaughter saw Peter and she is terrified. He's a very sick man, I said, as if he didn't know. I'm about to call the doctor.

'"They'd better do something about him soon. Who knows what he might do next," the old pisspot said and walked away. I dialled the doctor again. Do you think I could talk to him? "Hold on please," and I waited, one ear on the phone, the other listening for Peter.

'Finally, the receptionist got back to me, only to tell me that the doctor was not in. "But if it's urgent, call the ambulance," and I did. Straightaway.

'Meantime Peter had returned to the garden and was banging the back door. His screams cut through me. I didn't want to lock him out, but Clara, I'm only a small woman …

'The front doorbell rang again. I ran to the door. And guess what?'

'What?' Clara asks uneasily.

'It wasn't the ambulance, it was the police. The old pisspot must have called them. I told them what happened, I told them that Peter is a schizophrenic. They wanted to know if he stopped his medication. How would I know? He's an adult, he's not going to tell me.

'They opened the back door. At the sight of the police Peter froze. "I'm not going with them," he whispered to me, but the policeman took him by his arm. "Leave me alone!" he shouted, looking like a cornered animal. Clara, do you know how it felt? I kept telling myself that we're not in Hungary, the police in this country are decent. Still, I couldn't stop shaking. I've reached the limits of whatever was keeping me together. My internal scaffolding was finally collapsing.

'The police were still here when the ambulance arrived. "He probably stopped taking his tablets," the ambulance officer said, took Peter and drove off.'

'Heavens above, you must have been utterly drained.'

'I was. Peter, the old Wood, the police, the ambulance, all in one hour. I was bursting to talk to someone, anyone. You were not here, so I rang Lilla. She's not a good listener, but at least she has an ear. I didn't tell her what happened, except that Peter was getting worse and had stopped taking his medicine.

'Anyway, his medication has been adjusted, now he's back doing his volunteering jobs and working on linguistics. I think he's much better. You'll see when you come to visit. When will you?'

'How about Sunday?'

'All right, but don't let on that I told you what happened.'

'Don't worry,' and after a pause, 'Eszti, I admire you. I don't know how you can take all that.'

'Well, he's my son, isn't he?'

'He is. Still … Eszti, I meant to ask you something.'

'Yes?'

'His social worker, is he of any help?'

'He is. Clive visits him once in six weeks or so. He takes him for a walk, sometimes for a cup of coffee. It's only for an hour, but for a whole hour Peter has a visitor, he has someone to talk to. And as I look at them, I feel as if the weight I carry is suddenly lifted from my shoulders.'

'I can imagine,' Clara says, pondering whether a few extra visits a year would improve Peter's life, or Eszti's. 'Some people might do well,' Matheson had said. But would Peter?

* * *

Clara is tossing and turning, but sleep evades her. The image of Peter running across the street, frightened by someone who isn't there, intrudes again. She tries to redirect her thoughts, think of something pleasant. Tasmania. Jeff, Shosh and her having lunch. The lake, the jumping fish, Jeff. Jeff? Peter, the police.

No, she can't sleep.

She checks the clock. It's 4:35. *It's nearly morning.* She is too tired to face the day, if only sleep would come, calm her, bless her with peace and tranquillity for a couple of hours. But Peter is back again, and so is the sorrow, and the pity she feels for him.

'Pity is my greatest peril,' she recalls some writer saying, someone whose name escapes her. Pity is my peril too, and if I don't change it will become Shosh's peril. A few days ago, I felt so good, so energetic. Now I'm back to being my old self. Back to indecisiveness, to feeling down again, festering in misery and gloom.

This is self-indulgence! I have to change, I have to change for Shosh's sake, I have to change for my own sake, for our survival. Another woman would have shrugged her shoulders at Peter's misfortune, she would not want to know about him, or about Eszti. Another woman would be in another man's bed by now. She would not visit Peter, and she would not allow Shosh near him.

I should be like this other woman and I should start right now. I will give the Minister everything he needs, everything he wants to do his dirty job. I will do what I am asked, so I can make a living and bring up Shosh. And if I contribute to the pain of the world, so be it.

-26-

The sun is blasting down on Sydney, and it is not even eight o'clock. The city is in for another hot and humid day.

'Mum, look!' Shosh points at the opposite wall.

The two of them are having breakfast, Clara's thoughts miles away. She has to catch an earlier train, so she can work on the Minister's speech. She has done the background work, written a few paragraphs, and provided nothing urgent comes up, today she will put it all together.

'Muuum?!'

'Yes?'

'Look at it, isn't it beautiful? It's like a movie.'

The eucalyptus tree in front of the window is throwing shadows on the wall, live shadows of leaves dancing in the breeze. Waiting for their daily feed, the rosellas on the balcony rail are making a racket.

Having finished breakfast, Shosh hurries to feed the rosellas. Clara is midway through the morning chores, when Shosh runs into the kitchen, gets a rag, and runs out.

'Shosh, what's up?!'

No answer. Clara runs to investigate.

On the balcony, squatting in a puddle of milk, Shosh is trying to wipe away the accident, while fighting a dozen guzzling rosellas. At the sight of Clara's mop, the choice between survival and a feast is clear, and they whoosh off. She wipes the floor, 'All clean again.'

'Mum, I'm worried about the maths test.'

'You'll be right, you're a very clever girl.'

'You always say that,' Shosh grumbles gratefully.

'Only because it's true,' and Clara plants a kiss on Shosh's forehead.

Shosh's face lights up in a smile. Clara smiles in response, with a sense of delight at Shosh's sparkling eyes. *Her eyes? His eyes.* A thought which overwhelms her, crushes her, a thought which keeps her awake at night. A secret thought which she would keep from herself if she could.

They are ready to go. Shosh picks up her lunch box.

'Not salad sandwiches again,' she grumbles with the look of the condemned.

'No, it's Vegemite, the salad is in the box. Let's go.'

The closer they are to the school, the more apprehensive Shosh is about the maths test. But Clara is grateful, she is grateful for all tests. To worry about a test is natural, harmless. To worry about her insane father can injure her for life.

Today there are only two children in the schoolyard, and Clara is uneasy about leaving Shosh there so early, but she has to get to work without delay and draft the Minister's speech. She will follow the standard practice, write some text around the format — which she has from the previous speeches — and put in the figures later. Marina has been working on them for days.

The cubicles are still uninhabited as Clara walks into the office. Maurice's room sunk in darkness. She makes herself a cup of coffee and begins typing. *Heal in Place*, the NSW Government's new initiative for the mentally ill. A paragraph on the background follows. 'Following the previous reform, XXX mentally ill patients were released from hospitals, to be integrated into the community.'

Integrate into the community? In front of her eyes is the chimney sweep lookalike tramp, barefoot, blackened skin peeping out through the tears of his frayed dirty trousers. Does he feel integrated into the community?

He is downstairs every lunchtime, coming and going, smiling to himself. Suited business men and women walk past him, talking shop, wheeling and dealing, dollars, the boss, their careers. Young men and women, with meetings to attend, decisions to make. They have learnt to look away, learnt how not to see. The tramp is of no consequence to them, his life plays out far away, in a parallel world.

How come those young men and women in their business suits cannot see the relevance of the tramp's life to theirs? Does the ego clip the imagination? Then she is back to writing again. 'The Government has set up the new Department of People's Services, so each person's needs, whether health or housing, can be looked after by the same organisation. Under this structure, mental health consumers get the best services available.'

A consumer of mental health services conjures in her someone trying to eat his own head so he can swallow his insane mind. Is Peter a mental health consumer? A machine, an automaton there to gobble up whatever is put in front of it? No, he is a sick man, a man riddled by nightmares, a man suffering intensely. A man who once loved his wife, and fathered a daughter. *Loved his wife? No-one could have loved me more.*

Looking at the computer screen but seeing Peter and her on the cliffs at Wattamolla. They were there hoping to spot whales. Above, a cloud floated westwards the sun re-entered the stage of the sky. Below, a wave smashed against the rocks and exploded into thousands of rainbow drops. The ocean hummed.

'Stunning,' Peter whispered, 'it makes me want to live forever,' and after a pause, 'But only if you're next to me,' and he took her face in his hands and smothered it with kisses.

'Clars.'

'Yes.'

'We're one forever, aren't we?'

She agreed, they were one as far as she could see then, they were one forever.

'Clara, how's it going?' Maurice is standing by her desk.

Startled, she looks at him. 'OK,' then she is back to writing the speech. The underlying philosophy of the new initiative is developing self-reliance in the mentally ill. Therefore, after a short stay in the hospital, non-acute patients will be free to live in the community. They will be visited by professional staff who will support them in whatever way is needed. XXX such patients are anticipated to benefit from this initiative.

By lunchtime she has a raw draft. She takes the print to Maurice, but he is not in his office.

As she walks out of the building to buy lunch, there is the chimney sweep lookalike tramp again. He is wandering aimlessly, two dark yellow teeth protruding above the bottom lip, laughing at her as if only he can see the absurdity of his situation. She has a weird feeling that he can read her mind, that he has a way of knowing who she is and what she does. It makes no sense. She does not believe in the supernatural, but she has a strong sense that he can read her thoughts, that he can see her hypocrisy. Her legs heavy, she can barely walk past him.

'You're a joke,' he seems to say. 'I don't need your pity. I don't even need a bed, or nurses, or social workers. How would they find me? I'm a floater, I'm of no fixed address, I live on the street. Heal in Place? What place? On the park bench? Put it in the Minister's speech, because that's your only worry. Get it over and done with. I don't need handouts, I can eat leftovers from rubbish bins, I can sleep in the park. I'm self-reliant. I'm happy. Can't you see? He bursts out laughing. An eerie, unearthly laughter. His laughter chills her to the bone. She is no longer hungry. Nearly running, she turns back and heads to the office.

Back at her desk she opens her draft, deletes a paragraph, corrects two others. It reads better now, she is close to finishing it when Maurice rings, 'Clara, let's have a look at what you've done so far.'

'I still need the numbers and I have to include some personal stories,' she says handing him the print.

'You can do that tomorrow,' Maurice says, his eyes on the document, but the further he reads the more furrowed his brow.

What now? wonders Clara, sitting on the edge of the chair.

Maurice looks up.

'Clara, this is not a speech. Where is the enthusiasm? Where is the conviction? Where is the emotion?'

'I followed the format of the previous speeches. They're mainly about facts.'

'Not all. Besides, I'm not saying you shouldn't include data. You have to, of course you do, but this speech has to be convincing and cold figures will convince no-one. For that you need emotion; you need to mention families, carers.

'And you have to emphasise the benefits of integration. You have to point out that long hospital stays are detrimental for the mentally ill, while self-reliance and integration into the community can improve their lives. Spectacularly.'

Clara is no longer listening. If she doesn't tell him she will choke, tell him that Peter has a social worker, that his six-weekly visits make bugger all difference to his life. And there is something else she has to get off her chest. She has to tell him what sort of person Peter was once, and who he has become. She wants to tell him that it can happen to anyone, even to him, even to his children, it can happen in any family, that … But Maurice's smooth, vacuous face does not invite confessions. Nothing she could say would affect him, besides if she's hidden her situation from him all this time, why open up now? To change government policy? Her story would not make the slightest difference. Then why? To ease her soul?

'Maurice, do you really think that this initiative will improve their life?'

'It will. For many. Clara, we're changing their lives, improving them, we are.'

Clara looks at him. *Make believe?*

'Now you'd better finish that speech.'

'But I still need Marina's figures.'

'Don't worry about them, just finish the rest. I'll send you the figures tomorrow.'

She returns to her desk, has an apple to quench her hunger and is back to writing. An hour and a half later she still hasn't found the words which would light up the speech with conviction and emotion. She will think about it tonight. She puts in the other changes Maurice asked for, turns off her computer and heads home.

-27-

Marina is sweating on a new analysis, the figures for Clara's ministerial. 'Bugger!' She curses again. She scrolls down the screen, down the next one, then a few more. Dots here, dots there, missing figures. *No, I cannot use this file,* and she dials IT to ask for a new file. She is describing what she needs, when the high-pitched voice of a twelve-year-old interrupts:

'Marina, who's your manager?'

Who's my manager? Um … who isn't? Do you want to go through the whole ladder?

'Maurice Fry asked for the analysis,' she says with a sinking feeling. 'It's for an urgent ministerial.'

'Then Maurice should ring me. Best of luck with this work.'

Marina is about to say *it's not luck I need, I need a bloody file,* but the phone clicks.

The dictatorship of the hierarchy is weighing her down again. She has to get a new file somehow. But how? she ponders, staring at the wall. *That's it, I will use their friggin hierarchy in reverse. I'll ask Simon to get a new file, let him sort it out with Maurice. Let him work the hierarchy, the ladder and the fishing net.* But Simon is not at his desk, he is nowhere to be seen. Simon loves walking around the office, 'Thinking,' he said to her the other day. She looked at him. *You, thinking? More like wearing out the carpet.*

She has no choice; she has to talk to Maurice. She gives herself a pep talk – Maurice is the last man she wants to face today, or ever – and

169

holding a document summarising the problems with the data, she knocks on his half-open door.

Maurice is on the phone, and she stands there waiting for him to finish. She waits, and she waits. *Bugger! This man does not have phone conversations, he only has phone interruptions,* and she walks in.

'Great, just great, and you?' Maurice looks up, 'Just a minute.' He covers the phone with his hand and pointing to the document in Marina's hand. 'Just put it in the in tray, thanks.'

'About the analysis Simon asked me to do …'

'Not now. I'll get to you later,' and Maurice lifts his palm from the receiver, 'I was about to congratulate you …'

Marina walks out.

* * *

Back from another meeting that afternoon, Maurice pulls out a document from his in tray just as Marina's slim tall body walks past his door. *Too masculine.* He did promise to talk to her, but he is in no mood for it. Not in a mood to deal with her and her strange accent.

'It's not my fault that oil and water don't mix,' he complained to his wife, Sue, the other evening. They were having a slap-up meal in their favourite Chinese restaurant.

"Three Dousands?" she asks and looks at me for an answer. "I sink …"

I look at her, sink? Why don't you? or the equivalent in her strange language. Of which she's very proud of course, and as I look at her utterly confused, the silly cow smiles at me defiantly.'

'Don't say,' shock and disbelief on Sue's face, 'you mean the number cruncher?'

'Yep. She looks at me, her face painted with, "Do you think you can humiliate me?" Well I have neither the time, nor the interest in playing power games. So, I ask, "Sorry?" She gawks at me, her face painted all over with, "No way am I going to repeat what I said." The cheek of it. So, I ask again, "I beg your pardon, Marina? I don't quite get it." To which she bursts out in her mutilated accent, explaining what she meant, and I've no choice, but to listen to her again. I'm entitled to be resentful; don't you think?'

'Of course, work is not about power games. Besides, you have bigger fish to fry.'

Yes, Maurice has bigger fish to fry and now he has to read Charmaine's report.

Generally speaking, Maurice does not mind migrants. Nobody can accuse him of intolerance, or narrow-mindedness. He does not mind Clara; Clara is easy on his eye and Clara barely has an accent.

Maurice welcomes what migrants have done for his country. He is a big picture man and when he looks at the big picture it is clear to him. They brought variety to this country, and he loves variety. He loves yum cha, and pizza, and he loves all sorts of curries and Thai. They brought Charmaine, or more accurately the bits which later made Charmaine. Yes, migrants are great for this country, as long as they are at least second generation. As long as they have learnt how to speak, as long as they have learnt the unwritten rules and demeanour of this land. If only this country could import second generation migrants, he would not have to waste his time. He is a busy man, he doesn't have time to teach them English, they should learn it before they start working. If he were a migrant, he would spend all his time learning the language, he would take elocution lessons, and if nothing worked? If nothing worked … Yeah! That's it. These days anything can be solved with technology. All first-generation migrants of non-English speaking background should walk around with subtitles. He wouldn't have to spend his time trying to work out what Marina and the likes of her are saying. Why hasn't anybody thought of it? And as he is sitting there, Marina's image walks past, a screen with flashing subtitles hanging from her neck. *Exactly.* Maurice smiles to himself.

There we go, she's wasting my time again, and Maurice looks back to the document in front of him. That, and his next meeting take up the afternoon.

* * *

Having spent the whole day trying to get some sensible figures for Clara's ministerial, fretting, then telling herself off for fretting, Marina takes one more look at her results. *As they say, garbage in, garbage out, but if Maurice is not worried about it, why should I be?* And she sends him the results with the caveat: 'Based on the latest data available. It's my day off tomorrow, but if you could get a new file from IT, I could redo the numbers the day after.'

Pleased to have extricated herself from an utterly futile job, she turns off her computer, picks up her handbag and she is on her way. As she walks into the lobby, who should be there waiting but Maurice. *The arsehole promised to talk to me, but did he?*

The doors of the lift open and she follows Maurice inside. Standing in the corner is Kelly-Anne, black dress, deep red lips delineating a permanent smile.

'Early night for us,' she giggles, and looking at Maurice. 'Can't let work take over your life, can you?'

'Of course not. You need balance.'

'You sure do. And how will you balance today, Maurice?'

'I have three kids, you know.'

'Yes, but do they still need your undivided attention?'

'Do they ever.'

'How old is the youngest?'

'Two years, already.'

'A handful I bet.'

'Three handfuls.'

The lift has reached the ground floor. 'Good Night,' Marina says and walks out.

'Good night,' Kelly-Anne mutters. The doors close and the lift continues its descent to the managers' car park.

By the time Marina has reached her car, the drizzle has turned into heavy rain. The traffic is crawling, the monotonous sounds of the windscreen wipers, like deep breathing during meditation, reinforce her calm. Now and then an impatient driver squeezes in front of her. She doesn't care. *After my day in the office … Oh, I have to ring Clara.*

Marina parks her car and runs up the stairs. Inside the flat, dead silence. A note on the table says, 'We are out helping a man from dad's work to shift some furniture. We guarantee you two hours of peace and exclusive use of the TV. Enjoy.'

Marina smiles. *The cheeky boy*.

After dinner she dials Clara's number to warn her about the figures. 'They're rubbish, because the file I used had lots of missing data. Any policy based on those figures will only cause trouble. Clara, I won't be in tomorrow, but could you remind Maurice to get a new file from IT? I could redo the analysis the day after tomorrow.'

And with that her working day is over. She does not have to answer to anyone, she doesn't have to do anything for anyone. She takes her violin out, tunes the strings and plays a few scales. Then a few more. Six weeks ago, she decided to audition for a violinist position in an amateur orchestra. She has been practicing ever since.

She opens the exercise scores, plays a few bars, stumbles. She tries again. She cannot play virtuoso, she cannot play fireworks. Her coordination was never perfect, but once she could play this exercise. Now her left-hand fingers are not quick enough. She tries some slower ones then reverts to the virtuoso, and keeps going. She can hear the improvement, but is it enough to play Vivaldi? A movement or two?

She adjusts the strings and begins to play. She trips. It doesn't matter, she is thousands of miles away, back in Transylvania. It is Sunday afternoon. A warm lazy sun shines over the hills. In the grass, yellow, pink and blue flowers sway with the breeze in perfect timing, birds are singing the most delicate of tunes. Further up, in the forest, in the cool of the trees, she and Radu are picking tiny strawberries and blueberries, their taste — the result of all good things, a fertile soil, the mellow sun, the birds' love songs — is exquisite. That taste has eluded her ever since they left.

Autumn. Outside a cold, remorseless wind. She and Radu are standing at the window watching the departing flocks of swallows and dreaming about travelling. About the faraway sea, about a better life. What is a good life? she wonders now as the music of autumn comes to an end. Peace, food on the table and the warmth of people she craves so much.

She packs the violin away. Tomorrow she will pick up the tickets for their overseas trip, and the thought of being home within days makes her want to scream with happiness, and tell the whole world about it.

-28-

The next morning, Marina, buoyed by the plane tickets in her handbag, is walking out of the travel agency, just as Peter is about to go in.

'Peter,' she says, inadvertently, but it is too late now.

He looks at her, confused.

'We met on the train, remember? I was with Clara.'

'Ah.'

'Are you going travelling?'

'I'm going to India.'

'Interesting country. I might make it there one day.'

'I'm going to an ashram to improve my yoga and meditation techniques.'

'Well, have a good trip,' Marina says and walks on.

Having picked up his ticket to India, Peter heads home. Eszti is in the lounge room knitting a jumper when Peter walks in, smiling.

'Is everything OK?'

'Fine. Mum, I'm going to India ...'

'What? What did you say?'

'I'm going to India.'

'Have you lost your ...' but she stops mid-sentence.

'I'm going there to improve my yoga and meditation techniques.'

'What's wrong with your techniques?'

'They don't work. They don't help me calm down. But there is an ashram in India, where they could correct them.'

She looks at him aghast. 'An ashram in India?'

'Yes. They guarantee that after two months spent there one can master them. And attain total bliss.'

Eszti's eyes bulging, 'Total bliss?' she asks. 'Total bliss?' her voice boiling with exasperation. 'And how much do those cheats charge for bliss? Because I could do with some.' But before Peter can answer, 'No, don't tell me, I won't give you money, not for total bliss, or for half a bliss.'

'I don't need money; I bought my ticket already.'

'What? What did you say?'

'I bought my ticket already.'

'How? Have you robbed a bank?'

'I sold my violin.'

'You sold your violin?'

'I had no use for it. It only sat on the top of my wardrobe gathering dust.'

Eszti has to summon all her willpower not to argue with him. That violin was bought when they could least afford it. How many hours of hemming and overlocking went into that violin? Well, what's done is done. But she is beyond herself with worry about his trip to India.

'What can I do?' she asks Clara, that evening.

'I don't know,' she doesn't know or wants to know. She has enough problems. The speech is weighing on her mind. It's due in a couple of days and she hasn't got the figures yet.

It is past seven and she still has to cook dinner and help Shosh with the bath.

-29-

An hour on the road already and Maurice is still crawling along, ahead of him a line of cars as far as he can see. As if he wasn't fed up enough already, the traffic stops suddenly. He waits, and waits, but the tension between the passage of time, of his time, and the lack of movement in front, is getting to him. Radio National is getting to him too. *Same old, same old.* On the next station a man is singing to an African beat. Maurice joins in. Humming and jigging. Heaven! In the privacy of his car, he can let his hair down. Metaphorically speaking. Well, at the age of forty-four a balding head is not that unusual.

Maurice loves a good tune, a good tune with a good beat. Not to dance, dancing is hard work. Counting his steps, while trying to mirror his wife's movements and listening to the music at the same time, how can anyone do that?

'Lots of men can,' she told him. 'To dance well all you have to do is let go, immerse yourself in the sounds and the rhythm. Let the subconscious takeover. And trust your partner. It's simple. Like sex. She fixed him with her intense blue eyes, 'Do you count when we have sex?' But then she decided that on that topic she was better off being left in the dark and added quickly, 'Same with dancing, just let go and move with the rhythm. Harmony is everything.'

Dancing never gave him pleasure, but jigging does, jigging comes naturally to him.

The next song is a whining monotony, but now the cars are moving. Overflowing with pent up energy, and determined not to waste another second, the drivers are pushing from all sides. Maurice's blood pressure hits the danger zone. 'Go to Hell!' he shouts through the open window. 'Go to Hell!' And for the sake of even-handedness, he curses the Road Transport Authority for the poor phasing of the traffic lights and he curses the Planning Department for designing roads modelled on a lazy human gut. 'The bloody …!' he screams, about to curse the NSW Government, but stops in mid-sentence, remembering that he is one of its cogs, as the Department of People's Services materialises in the distance. Maurice turns the corner, drives down to the basement and parks his car. By the time he walks into his office it's nearly ten o'clock. He will have to get his coffee later.

Ping! Kelly-Anne's email lights his screen. Kelly-Anne, his nominal manager, his manager according to the organisation chart – she inhabits the box above him – but to Maurice she is only an overlay, a blanket a couple of sizes too small, and he pokes out from underneath as often as he can to deal with Sandy.

The other day she told him that according to her astrological chart – and Maurice is a great believer in everybody's right to their own delusions – him and her are one hundred percent compatible. Work compatible, she hastened to add. Just as well, Maurice thought, I've no interest in any other sort of compatibility with you. But since Kelly-Anne's astrology chart shows that they are work compatible, no doubt his acting job will soon be converted into a permanent one. Because if he, Maurice Fry, knows anything, he knows that all managers prefer to work with people who they like. The rest is secondary.

If only he didn't have to deal with her emails. Kelly-Anne's emails are like her speech, beating around the bush, circling around the issue, a fox playing with a chicken before pouncing. Eventually the circles become smaller and the reason for the email is finally unveiled. This time she is unusually short. Freedom of information request from the Minister's office. *Another one?* He had a couple of requests already this week. *Bugger! Nowadays, any nonentity can ask questions of the Minister.*

The nonentity this time is Di Smith. *Bugger her! Bugger the Freedom of Information Act!* He reads on. What is the recidivism rate among drug-using prisoners and how much do their coming and goings in and out of prison cost? she wants to know.

Wants to know? Oh no, she wants to cause trouble. Tread carefully, Maurice. Di Smith's a mortar shell.

Based on past performance, her outrage is contagious. It goes from the shock jocks to the tabloids and the current affairs television programs. The battler versus the NSW Government, the tabloids scream. She is front page material, and no murder is gruesome enough to displace her. Wasting taxpayers' hard-earned money on drug addicted criminals could start a chain reaction of indignation which could keep the media busy for days.

A housewife, Di Smith spends her time gathering facts which support her convictions. NSW has a weak government; NSW is going to the dogs, and if the opposition leader cannot do his job, she will. Her questions are a common occurrence, her letters spell trouble for the government.

She is a woman of passion. She hates the Greens, the do-gooders, she hates Labor, she hates anybody who relies on government assistance. Dole bludgers, daylight robbers, most of them. But most importantly she hates union officials, 'Working class? No class and definitely not working. They wouldn't know what work is.'

Her husband is a middle manager somewhere in the prison system. He keeps the criminals off the street while she holds the wasters and the thieves of public money to account. As far as she is concerned, she and her husband work in the justice system.

And now Di Smith has another bone to gnaw on.

Maurice is about to forward the email to Clara. *No, she's new and she's politically naive. Charmaine, you sexy thing, you're my safe bet.* 'I leave this to your professionalism …' and he hits the send button.

The phone rings, it's the Minister's office. 'We need a draft of the speech.'

'I'll send it through straightaway,' and Maurice calls Clara.

'The Minister's office is on my back. They want a draft of the speech.'

'But I still need the figures. Marina said that her data file was incomplete. She said that if you can get a new file from IT …'

'We can't mess around with new files. Her figures are based on the latest available data and that should do.'

-30-

The next day, having included Marina's shonky figures, Clara scans the speech once more and consoling herself that her name is not on it, since all documents go out in Sandy's name, she emails it to Maurice.

Mid-afternoon, she is sorting out her files when Maurice stops by her desk.

'They're happy with it. Excellent work and quick turnaround. Take the rest of the day off.'

Too tired to pick up Shosh, she drives straight home. The speech is behind her and the thought of an imminent hot bath is cheering her along. The afternoon traffic jam has not started yet and half an hour later she is parking her car.

The mailbox is overflowing with advertising brochures, but among them there are a couple of envelopes which she will have to look at.

Lying in the bath, staring at the ceiling, she is grateful for the silence, for not having anything urgent to do. Suddenly the speech cuts into her thoughts, 'You've argued for the closure of hospital beds. You've justified the initiative when you knew it was wrong.'

'I had no choice. I was a pawn.' But another voice says, 'You were a pawn, and you will remain a pawn. You will keep propping up more policies which will hurt vulnerable people, or at the very best, help them as much as a few drops of rain help to break a drought.'

Guilt is weighing her down. She will ask for a transfer, but if she can't get one, she will look for another job. She will not have her hands dirtied again, she will not have her soul blackened. There must be another way and she will find it. Feeling somewhat more hopeful, she gets out of the bath, ready for the rest of the day's chores.

* * *

Shosh has gone to bed.

Silence at last. Clara sits down on the sofa and turns on the reading light.

The lounge room is in semi-darkness, the book on the coffee table is still open on the same page as yesterday, and the day before, and the day before that. She is in no mood for reading. In no mood to immerse herself in some imaginary story.

The lounge room is a mess, the clothes she wore to work today still on the sofa, Shosh's toys and books spread on the carpet, but Clara just sits there, her eyes resting on the shadow of the small stone sculpture standing on the wall unit, an African couple with a child. The three of them are holding hands. Their togetherness sharpens her feeling of loneliness. Suddenly the silence of the lounge room is no longer the quiet she appreciated so much when she got home this afternoon. This silence hurts. It is a pain akin to loss, the pain of an absence. Absence of another voice, of a hand to hold, the warmth of another body. Her awareness acute, her surroundings suffocating. To pull out of its grip she turns on the television. On one of the channels is an American movie, on the other some commentary on the news, then sport and more sport. She turns the television off and walks to the window to pull in the curtains. The sky is dark. The full moon looks at her, cold, indifferent. Her loneliness unbearable, she heads to the kitchen.

As she is waiting for the water to boil, she picks up the mail laying on the table, unopened. Annoyed at all those people who keep fit by polluting other people's mailboxes, she throws the advertising leaflets in the bin then opens one of the envelopes. It's a card from Peter. A few lines only. 'I'm well. Working hard on my techniques ...' Instead of a signature, he has drawn a snake with a diamond in its head. Has he found peace? He doesn't say.

The second envelope is a bank statement. She looks at it, and looks at it. Her bank account has gone up by nearly one hundred thousand dollars. An international money transfer from the Netherlands. *Oh, it's my inheritance. My father's money has come through.*

She has a deposit for a flat. She will not have to deal with landlords anymore. 'Thank you, father,' she whispers, 'thank you.'

Her father! He has been her guide, the light which illuminated her path in life. She misses him, at times unbearably. Oddly, it was his death which marked the turning point in her life.

* * *

It was around eight o'clock, a time when Peter should have been on the way to the office, but he stood in front of the mirror examining his face as if he was seeing it for the first time, as if he needed to be introduced to himself.

The phone rang. Who could be ringing at such an early hour? she wondered, her heart heavy with a sense of foreboding.

It was Aunt Dafna. She wanted to know how everybody was and then,

'Clara, your father is in hospital.'

'Hospital? Why?'

'He has pancreatic cancer. He is in a bad way.'

Her knees went soft, she had to sit down. 'Cancer?'

'Yes.'

'And why didn't you tell me?'

'He didn't want to tell you over the phone. He thought he'd tell you when you came to visit. Besides, the treatment seemed to work, two months ago he was still in remission.'

She had promised her father that she would visit him, but she couldn't leave Shosh with Peter, neither could she take her overseas without his permission. Aunt Dafna muttered something, but Clara was no longer listening. *He didn't tell me because he thought that I'm not strong enough to bear it, that's why.*

'But surely they can treat him,' she said.

'He has had all the available treatments already.'

'I'll be on the way as soon as I can.' The possibility that he might not be alive by the time she got there grabbed at Clara's heart.

Two days later, she left Shosh with Eszti and flew out.

She had been homesick for years. For years she had missed her native city, the canals, the old buildings, the museums, the flower shops, the cafes. She thought that if she could have Peter, her father and her Dutch friends, she would be in Heaven. But in time Peter's transformation, his nonsensical behaviour became a far greater misery to her than her homesickness, and like a sharp pain obliterates discomfort, the greatest misery won out. Her troubled marriage took over her thoughts. She ceased to be homesick. Amsterdam receded into the past. By the time the plane landed, her native land did not arouse in her more than a vague curiosity. That's all it was. She gazed through the window of the taxi. Amsterdam looked like a long-lost relative, remote and strange, a relative she would need time to know again, but in whom she was no longer interested.

She picked up Dafna and sometime later their taxi stopped in front of the hospital.

'He's on the second floor. Don't tire him out,' Dafna said wobbling forward on her walking frame, her fingers knotty with arthritis. Every step seemed a conquest. Standing upright, balancing and still progressing was nothing short of a triumph over an invisible enemy.

Her father was lying in bed, eyes closed, his face as white as the wall behind him. A thin tube led oxygen into his nose. His breath laboured; his forehead covered with droplets of perspiration.

'Father,' she whispered and wiped his face with a wet tissue. 'Father, it's me, Clara,' and kissed his forehead.

He opened his eyes and looked at her. Reassured? Comforted? They sat in silence, her hand resting on his. Behind, the sound of Aunt Dafna's frame faded away.

Words evaded her. Now the most powerful language was the language of silence. His life was draining away. She wanted to cry, but she had no tears. Death, which was about to rob him of his life, robbed her of what it could now, before her own time came. She had become a character in a play, she and her father on the edge of existence. Surrounded by the infinite emptiness and absolute silence.

She sat watching him. Was he asleep? Was he conscious? It was time to tell him what she had wanted to say to him so many times, but never did for fear of sounding too sentimental.

'I love you,' she whispered. 'I thank you for being my father, and I thank you for being my mother. You could not have been a better parent and you couldn't have loved me more.' A tear rolled down his cheek, and as if that opened the gates to her tears, she too started to cry.

She sat there in the shadow of his passing. She had no idea what went on in his mind, if anything, whether his life was rewound and replayed. But images of her life rolled before her eyes. She saw herself, a twelve-year-old child, crying for her mother as he stroked her hair and told her that at least she was not suffering any more. Later as a teenager, walking with him, talking about history, about the good and the bad in the world. His first meeting with Peter, and later him standing in front of the departures board in Amsterdam Airport, the day she left him for Peter, the love of her life. But it was his tired and reassuring smile, as she headed to Customs, the no return area, she would remember till her last day on this Earth.

He gave me so much love and I? What have I done for him? She consoled herself that at least he never found out what was going on in her life, at least she had protected him from that. She began crying again. She cried for her father who would never again talk to her, share his thoughts, who would never again guide and encourage her. She cried for Shosh who would never know a father like hers, and now had lost her much loved grandfather. The grandfather who came to visit and brought her presents and read her stories and listened to her as if she was the centre of his universe.

David did not open his eyes again. A few hours later he found eternal peace.

She rang Dafna: 'It's over.'

'*Baruch Hashem.*'

It was strange to hear Dafna invoke the Hebrew Heavens. She had never been religious and yet in the face of death, of its finality, she had returned to her ancient roots.

After the funeral, Dafna handed her a letter. 'It's from your father,' she said and walked out of the room.

Clara sat down on the sofa and opened it.

My dear daughter,

If you are reading this letter I am no longer of this world.

When your mother passed away, I prayed that I would live long enough to see you married to a good man and see my grandchildren. It looked to me that life had granted me both my wishes. But now I suspect, with great sorrow, that Peter is not the blessing I first thought. He has drawn one of the most unfortunate cards in life. He is no longer the person you married. I worry that your life will be a difficult one. To see the man you love metamorphose into a stranger must be the greatest pain imaginable.

Remember that on your wedding day I asked you to look after each other? You promised you would, but the puzzlement on your face did not escape me. I wanted you to look after him if he fell sick, or if he got in trouble of some kind. And I hoped that he would look after you if Heaven forbid you were struck by misfortune. Not in my blackest nightmare could I have imagined that he would end up the man he has.

I worry that he will hurt you. I worry that your life together will damage Shosh. You are under no obligation to persevere with that marriage. You cannot possibly look after him. You will have to look after yourself and Shosh. You are young and you have a future. It will take time, but you will make a life for yourself again. I hope you will, otherwise your mother and I have failed.

I am sorry that I cannot leave you a secure future. Academics are not millionaires, but I did have a good salary. I also had lots of expenses. First it was your mother's sickness, later I had to help Dafna regularly, but I have savings in the bank, probably enough for a deposit on a flat in Sydney. I left my will with your aunt.

I pray for a bright future for you and Shosh. Just have faith in yourself.

My eternal love,

Father

The sun had set. Night was falling on Amsterdam as she sat on the edge of the sofa and cried, and prayed and begged: God give me strength to bring up Shosh, to love her like my father loved me. Enough for two people. She did not pray to a specific God, she prayed to any God who would listen to her pleading.

She sat there contemplating her future. Future? Living with Peter? For how long? And why am I still with him? Because it seems easier. I'm weak. Pathetic. This marriage is destroying Shosh, and it's destroying me. I used to stand up for myself, but now I am constantly pleasing, I am always on the other side of myself. I should stop deceiving myself. It's time to change, it's time to be honest and strong. It's time for me to start a new life. I'll get a full-time job and move out.

A week later she caught the plane to Sydney.

Her father's words never faded. They picked her up when she was down, they gave her strength to persevere.

* * *

It is past midnight, but she is in no mood to go to bed. The inheritance, remembering her father's passing, has stirred up memories, and emotions which she still finds hard to bear. She should stop recalling the past, stop worrying about the future, or the speech. She has to switch off. Listen to some music?

She puts on one of her favourite records, Mendelssohn's Violin Concerto in E minor and lies down on the sofa, eyes shut. Slowly, the beauty, the magic of the music, takes over her whole being. It elevates her high above her struggles, into a world without words. A world of honest feelings. A world without lies.

Both her parents were musical. Her father had a beautiful warm voice. Her mother played the piano, and her father sang. Other times they all sang; opera marches and at Christmas they sang Christmas Carols.

The other day, on the radio, Pavarotti was singing, 'O Sole Mio'. Suddenly it was not the famous singer, but her father. She sang along, her eyes closed. She wanted to hold that image, but the song finished, and her father vanished.

Charles Aznavour singing, 'The Old-Fashioned Way' was her mother's favourite. One evening, they were listening to his singing when her father bowed to her mother and they began to dance. How beautiful they looked. It was not them dancing to the song, it was Charles Aznavour singing to their movements.

Once there was beauty in her life.

She turns the record player off. She has to go to bed and get some sleep, she has a meeting with Kelly-Anne and Maurice in the morning.

-31-

'As you know, the Integration into the Community working party will get together on Wednesday. It could turn out a difficult meeting,' Kelly-Anne says, looking at Maurice, 'so it will need our full attention.' Then turning to Clara, 'Now, while Maurice and I are cajoling and persuading, I want you to take the minutes. A great development opportunity for you.'

Set up nine months ago, the working party had been Maurice's idea. 'All organisations which could object to our policies, which could stir up the media, should be invited,' he reasoned at the time, 'let them vent their opposition in the meeting.' He was about to say let them piss from inside the tent out, rather than the other way, but since he did not want to offend Kelly-Anne — who holds one of the keys to his permanency and whose overdeveloped visual imagination makes her averse to blokey jokes — he just said, 'Better the devil you know,' another of his favourite clichés.

'And the best person to chair it,' he added, 'is Kelly-Anne,' who could hardly supress an 'of course' smile.

Well done, Maurice! he congratulated himself. *You loyal subordinate, you. Brilliant! You double scored, one with Sandy as an ideas man, and one with your boss, Kelly-Anne. You're a strategist to the tips of your fingers.*

It was Maurice's philosophy that you build up your boss's career, and when she climbs another step, she will take you along. But Maurice's proposal was not all self-interest, at least not one hundred percent self-interest. Kelly-Anne has talents, talents which have benefited the

Department a great deal. She has that pacifying modus operandi, a genius for bringing consensus. She listens, she picks up nuances and she is alert to political implications. Kelly-Anne knows how to steer a boat away from danger.

Public Service is written in Kelly-Anne's every cell, and the Department provides a cosy home for her likes and ambitions. She loves the status quo. She loves meetings and protocols, and she loves hierarchy. It gives her clarity of purpose. The pecking order tells her where she fits and how many promotions she needs to become Deputy Director General. That is as far as she wants to go. For now. Chairing committees and working parties is great CV material and an opportunity to make a name for herself across a number of organisations, and to have a day away from Sandy's control.

Having explained to Maurice and Clara their roles, and warned them about the possible pitfalls, Kelly-Anne closes the meeting, switches her phone to her secretary and asks not to be disturbed. She has to think about the details, how best to steer the discussions, and about the practicalities. Maurice's role is to add a manly weight to any argument which might arise, but she has misgivings about him. He likes to take over, he likes to big note himself. She will make it clear at the very start of the meeting, that he works for her, that he is her report.

She is proud of how much the working party has achieved in its nine months of existence. She has managed to steer its members — an uneasy mixture of people who behaved like a herd of goats out of control — in the right direction. All the Department's policies have been accepted. Yes, she achieved a lot last year. She did work hard, but she is smart enough to know that hard work never gets you far. You need luck, and last year luck was on her side. Close to her birthday, Pluto, the planet of renewal, entered the orbit of her ruling planet, Neptune, the planet of harmony and power in one's life.

Their configuration has not changed much since, so she is hopeful about Thursday's meeting. She'll only have to convince the gathering of the merits of the new initiative. It won't be easy, but she will prevail.

The secretary puts her head around the door, 'I sent out the reminder email. Do you need anything else?'

'That'll do for now.' But Kelly-Anne knows better than to leave the invitation to the impersonal electrons and she picks up the phone to call the crucial people. Suss out the scene, touch base with the important members, find out whether they are coming. She clinches every call with, 'We meet at nine for nine-thirty. We can chat more over coffee and pastries.'

She shouldn't have worried; they are all coming.

* * *

Wednesday, nine-thirty. The hubbub of old acquaintances has died away. Sitting at the head of the long rectangular table is Kelly-Anne. Not yesterday's Kelly-Anne. Overnight her rusty red hair has turned blonde, her lips, usually a deep red, are now a light pink. Her top half packaged in a dark green jacket, a hint of a black satin camisole peeping between the lapels. The ensemble finished with a chunky silver art nouveau necklace, a perfect counterpoint to her long neck.

Smiling, she thanks people for coming, and for the benefit of the new member and those who might have forgotten, she points out that Maurice is one of her staff – 'He's managing the statistics and communications for me.'

As Clara is marvelling at Kelly-Anne's new look, the effort which goes into preparing to chair a meeting, Kelly-Anne begins her report.

'As you know, when it comes to the services for the mentally ill, there is always room for improvement and speeding up their recovery is this government's highest priority. To that end it has decided on a new approach, an approach grounded on solid evidence.

'We know that long hospital stays are detrimental to the confidence of the mentally ill, their self-reliance. Plenty of evidence for that. Clearly, it's far better to support the mentally ill, help them heal in their own surroundings than keeping them in hospital for long spells.'

The woman sitting at the opposite side of the table looks at her worried, 'What do you consider a long spell?'

'I'll take questions at the end. Now, where was I? Oh, yes, I was about to clarify what this initiative consists of. To put it simply, adjustments. Only adjustments. We will close down a proportion of non-acute psychiatric beds in some hospitals and …' she looks around the table, 'and like all changes, these too can be translated into great opportunities.'

'No more closures,' the woman sitting in the front row explodes through her adenoids. 'They …'

'Let me finish.'

'But you just closed down …'

'Will you let me finish?!' Kelly-Anne raises her voice and the look in her eyes would zap the woman into extinction if it were physically possible. Kelly-Anne hates being interrupted, and being interrupted by a nobody from a small non-government organisation is an affront to her. It is not only a lack of manners, it is a lack of rights. Interrupt her in the middle of an important announcement? How dare she?

'We want to encourage self-reliance in the mentally ill,' Kelly-Anne says defiantly. 'And the best way to do that is to help them integrate into the community.'

'Bollocks!' the woman bellows. 'Integrate into the community? Which community? Why don't you just say you're going to throw them out of hospitals?'

The people in the room look on impatiently. They do not want to listen to a squabble, they want to know exactly what the Department is cooking up this time.

Clara notes, 'The support for the closures is not unanimous …'

'Some nurses and social workers will be transferred to the field,' Kelly-Anne raises her voice. 'They will visit the mentally ill, support them, encourage self-reliance and help them to heal in their own surroundings. Therefore, the name of the initiative, Heal in Place. And there is more,' she pauses for effect, 'the Minister will allocate three million dollars for halfway houses.'

'Three million dollars?' a woman sighs in astonishment.

But Jenny Scott from the Humanists for the Rights of the Mentally Ill organisation is not impressed. 'Three million dollars?' she scoffs. 'You'll do well to get six houses for that. Or don't you know how much a house costs in Sydney these days? And assuming that you can convert each house into four small bedrooms, you'll accommodate a total of twenty-four people. Twenty-four people at most.'

Clara is jubilant, someone is standing up for the mentally ill. 'According to Jenny Scott …' she writes.

A long discussion ensues. With house prices being what they are, the Department will not be able to buy anything close to transport and hospitals.

'Halfway house, or full-way house, you can't put insane people in the middle of residential areas,' the man from the Concerned Citizens Group says, his gruff voice bouncing around the room. 'The people I represent will never agree to it. Never!' he repeats just in case anyone has missed the emphasis. 'The houses will have to be next to industrial estates.'

'And call it the insanity estate?' Jenny Scott asks. 'Not in my backyard, eh …? But leaving this aside, six half-way houses? A blessing for a handful of people, but what about the other thousands?'

'Which thousands?' Maurice asks, derision in his voice.

'Which thousands?' she echoes. 'For your information, there are about 30,000 homeless in this State, and a significant percentage of these people are mentally ill.'

'Where are all these homeless you're talking about?' he asks. 'You can see a few around Central Station, around Surry Hills. Surrounded by beer bottles. Alcoholics. And alcoholics do have a problem, I'll give you that, but you know what?' His gaze scans the people around the table, 'Alcoholics are not mentally ill. I've met a few pisspots who can't stop drinking. But they're in touch with reality. Well … when they're sober.'

Jenny Scott is fidgeting, face distorted by frustration. 'But many homeless are mentally ill, and they don't all congregate in the city. Some are in the suburbs, some in the country. If they're lucky, they might sleep at their friends', or relatives' place. I know someone who sleeps in a laundry.'

'So, he's not on the street, he doesn't sleep in the rain, or in the cold.' Maurice says.

'But in a laundry,' she retorts, a murderous look on her face. 'Don't you know the definition of homelessness?'

'Of course I do. Theoretically speaking he is homeless but …' Kelly-Anne clears her throat, her warning look stops Maurice in mid-sentence. He was about to say, that as far as he is concerned anyone with a roof over his head is not homeless. Besides, whose fault is it that the man sleeps in a laundry? Is that the Government's fault? Or is it his relatives' fault? But Kelly-Anne reminded him that he is stepping into politically unacceptable territory.

Clara has stopped taking notes. The dialogue between Maurice and the people in the meeting has to be witnessed to be believed and Maurice's condescension cannot and should not be reproduced. She has learnt the rules, the assumptions, the controls imposed on her work. She is a public servant, a small cog in that big organisation, her role to justify government policies, not to question them. She should be working for the other side then she could be uncompromising, like Jenny Scott.

'I'd like to get on with the agenda,' Kelly-Anne says. 'We're running out of time and …'

'But first tell us,' Jenny Scott interrupts, 'would six half-way houses, house all of them? Some of them? Or bugger all?' she looks from Kelly-Anne to Maurice, 'Can't you see we need those numbers?'

Maurice signals impatience. Jenny Scott is a pain, and she has taken over the meeting.

'You're wasting our time. Those numbers depend on who considers himself homeless.'

'Or herself!' A woman shouts. 'Or herself. Women are homeless too.'

'It was a manner of speech, Ms … A manner of speech. Do I have to spell out men and women every time I speak of people?'

'Just don't make women invisible.'

'If you're living in the park,' Maurice says, 'you might be there because you want to be there. Does that make you homeless? There're many reasons why you might want to live there. You might be claustrophobic, or you don't want to live in a suburb where you're more likely to win the lottery than to talk to another human. So, you join the other homeless. At least you have company. Besides if you want to live in the park nobody can shift you'.

Kelly-Anne's face is covered by a broad smile and as usual when she agrees with someone, she nods her head up and down like a walking pigeon. Still, she wishes Maurice would talk less, stick to the Public Service rules and the phrasebook of permissible sentences. 'Can we get to the next item, everyone!'

'No, not until we have the facts,' Jenny Scott says. 'Why don't we invite someone who knows to our next meeting?'

A worry cloud slides over Kelly-Anne's smile. She does not like this woman, not a bit, but she needs to handle her carefully, she is from a very vocal organisation. *If I oppose her suggestion, she will cause problems, and if I agree …? Hmm …* She looks at her, *Oh, that's an idea. There's no guarantee that the statisticians can get that data, besides it takes them years to do their surveys.*

Smiling again she says, 'OK, I'll ring the Manager of the Statistics and Interpretation Department, maybe someone can join us after lunch. They're only a few blocks away.'

Jenny Scott's face lights up as if she has just won a round-the-world trip. 'I'm not just being difficult; we do need that data.'

'You? You not just being difficult?' Maurice asks, smiling with as much condescension as he can muster.

Gales of laughter, Jenny Scott's cheeks a glowing pink.

Kelly-Anne proposes a short break so she can ring the Manager of the Statistics and Interpretation Department. She is in luck, one of the senior statisticians is free to join them after lunch. That sorted, she heads to the bathroom. She needs to touch up her face. The meeting room was stuffy, she could feel her face becoming shinier and shinier. She hates having a shiny face, and she has to have a break because Jenny Scott is wearing her out.

Her husband is wearing her out too. He wants a child. They have postponed it for years and she is thirty-seven years old already. There is no time to waste and Larry keeps insisting that they try as often as possible. Increase opportunities, increase probabilities. Kelly-Anne feels like a broodmare. A trapped broodmare.

She is ambivalent about children in general, and about one of her own in particular. The maternal instinct is not pulsing in her veins, but Larry wants a child, and she has stopped taking the pill.

What if I fall pregnant? she thought last night, as Larry was approaching his glorious release – the release which would have produced a large number of children if it were biologically possible, but definitely at least one – she froze. In her mind's eye she was already pregnant, her belly a big balloon, her ankles swollen, and as Larry screamed, 'Yes!' she screamed 'No!' Inwardly. No to childbirth, no to breastfeeding, no to getting up at night, and no to part-time, meaningless work. Let the world reproduce. Let people who want children have them, if that makes them happy, if that gives meaning to their life. The meaning in her life comes from work. Like chairing this working party. It can be tiring, but it makes her feel good, and in the process, she does some good for the world.

* * *

Lunch over, the gathering is back in the meeting room. The Senior Statistician is there too, he has made it just in time.

Having done the introductions, Kelly-Anne describes the problem: what is needed and why. The Statistician asks a few questions to clarify the details and is now in deep thought, lips moving from side to side.

In the room, steely silence. Finally, the lips stop, the Statistician rubs his chin and looks up:

'It depends, are we talking about the proportion of homeless who are mentally ill, or the proportion of mentally ill who are homeless?'

'Just give us everything,' Jenny Scott says.

The meeting holds its collective breath. The Statistician's face metamorphosises into a frown from thought exertion.

'We don't have that data,' he says finally.

'So how can we get it?' Jenny Scott asks. 'Can you run a survey?'

'A survey?' he pauses for thought, 'Of course we can run a new survey. But there is a cost.'

'How much?' Kelly-Anne asks.

'Can't say. I have to scope the work first,' and after pausing for thought, 'but …' His lips move side to side as if the taste of the wine is not to his liking. 'No survey can ask the homeless whether they are mentally ill. It's a privacy issue and we have to comply with the privacy laws.'

An, 'I told you so' look passes from Kelly-Anne to Maurice. With all the goodwill, homelessness information on the mentally ill remains a problem without a solution. Kelly- Anne feels vindicated.

'What about linking the names with some other government records? Medicare? Couldn't you get the information that way?' Jenny Scott says.

The expert is 'pretty sure' that it cannot be done.

'Can't we get an exemption?' Jenny Scott pleads.

'Impossible. It's a matter of privacy laws.'

'We have to try every avenue,' Jenny Scott keeps on.

The members are getting impatient, the topic has been explored long enough. The expert cannot agree more, and he pulls up a short presentation about the other statistical information available from his department. For a fee of course.

Kelly-Anne keeps nodding.

Jenny Scott is fidgeting: why is the Statistician talking about the frequency of marriage breakdowns in the metropolitan area, when all they need to know is the number of the homeless mentally ill?

The presentation over, the expert is ready to depart. Kelly-Anne thanks him profusely for his contribution.

The next item on the agenda is activities for mentally ill outpatients. Basket weaving, scone making, water colour painting and their relaxing effects. A lively discussion follows on how often patients should participate in such activities and which hospitals are best equipped to offer them, or at least some of them.

'Things are improving for the mentally ill,' Kelly-Anne says, happy to finish on a positive note. 'Not as fast as we'd like, but things are going in the right direction.'

And with that the meeting is closed.

'Clara, send me the notes tomorrow,' Kelly-Anne says and hurries to report to Sandy.

Sandy's door is shut. She is in a meeting.

Bugger!

Back in her office Kelly-Anne opens a new email. 'Sandy, the working party went well, the usual disgruntled organisations have been pacified. The initiative has received the seal of approval,' she clicks the send button.

-32-

Maurice is cogitating, the working party is over. Tomorrow is the announcement and next week, once the media has lost interest in the topic, which given its subject matter should not be more than a day or so, he will take a couple of days off. Visions of a long weekend with Sue and the kids, brings a smile to his face. The five of them cruising along the Central Coast. A dip in the ocean then a meal in their favourite restaurant. Their seafood is tops.

Sandy's secretary bursts in.

'Sorry, but this is urgent. Sandy wants you to look after this,' she points to the front-page article in *The Daily*.

'Consider it done,' and Maurice starts reading. The piece is about a tramp who met his maker on a park bench yesterday.

Three years on the same park bench, the article says. The regulars who walked through the park knew him. They often stopped to talk to him. On his good days he was a cheerful fellow. He told them not to wash. 'Water's bad for you, it damages your skin,' and true to his belief, he did not shower for weeks at a time.

Three years on the same bench, three whole years, the article says again and again … 'But he was happy,' Maurice whispers to himself. 'Happy! This is not the Soviet Union. People are not locked up for sleeping in the street. This is a free country,' he says to himself with the pride of the owner. 'A free country!'

The tramp got wet during last week's thunderstorm, got pneumonia and died. 'Tragic. Very tragic. But don't we all have to die eventually? I'll ask Clara to write a briefing note on this one, feed the Minister some ammunition. Just in case this story blows up into a scandal.'

Phew! This is not good timing. But almost immediately he has a flash of logic. Let's not get paranoid, this isn't about hospital beds. The man was in the park, not in hospital.

The phone cuts in. It is Wayne Goodfellow, the Director of the Sydney area, 'About the newspaper article …'

'Yes. I've seen it, just some wet behind his ears journo stirring. I wouldn't worry about it.'

But Wayne Goodfellow is worried, he needs to clarify what really happened. 'Our officers talked to him just a week ago. He was perfectly OK. Well not perfectly, you know what I mean … The rain didn't help, and the unusually low temperature must have sealed his fate. The point is, you couldn't have shifted him from his bench unless you brought in the Forces.'

'He was a free agent, and this is a free country. I wouldn't agonise about it. We're about to write a briefing note on this one.'

Having reassured Wayne Goodfellow, Maurice waves to Clara. But she is on the phone, talking to Eszti.

'Clara, sorry to disturb you at work, but I thought I'd better tell you, Peter arrived back last night.'

'Back from India?' she asks trying to overcome the sinking feeling inside her. *That's it, my emotional holiday is over.*

'Yes, a month before he was due. My dear, it looks like bliss is no easier to find in India than in Coogee.'

Eszti is saying something, but Clara is no longer listening.

While he was away, there were hours, sometimes whole days, when she did not think of him, calmer days and she tried to stay there. It involved willpower, it involved conscious redirection of thoughts. But when she was not successful, she consoled herself that he would be in India for a few more weeks. False hope, wishful thinking. Even sane people find Indian ashrams difficult. I should have known he wouldn't last two months there.

'Eszti, I have to go, my manager wants me,' Clara says seeing Maurice heading towards her desk. 'I'll ring you later.'

'An urgent request,' Maurice says as she walks into his office. 'Have you seen the papers today?'

She has and she has seen the story about the tramp.

'The Minister will need a briefing note about what happened. I just talked to Wayne Goodfellow, the Sydney Area Director. They did everything in their power to shift him from the bench,' and seeing Clara's grave look he adds, 'His staff will tell you more. It's a tight case, it should be easy. And don't forget the usual emphasis.'

They did everything? She no longer trusts Maurice. Her blinkers have come off, now she understands how he works, she understands his demands for the right emphasis. She will check, see if there was a real effort to save this man's life. But if there wasn't, she will plead headache, flu, whatever and go home. She has never done that, but she will this time.

* * *

Meanwhile, on the other side of the city, in his ministerial office, Ray Manly is sitting at his desk, worried. 'Damn!' Things looked so smooth and easy. 'Damn, couldn't he have kicked the bucket in a month or two? Now Ms Helen Pride, the smooth talker of the Opposition, that smiling sewer rat, will have something to gnaw on. The bloody woman won't let go.' A sudden pang of anxiety inside him. *Calm down Ray. The Department will sort it out. They're brilliant at arguing their way out of trouble.*

A knock and his secretary's blonde frizz comes through the half open door, 'Sandy's on the phone. Would you like to take it?'

'Would I ever. And no interruptions please.'

The frizz retreats.

Sandy assures him that the tramp was offered accommodation. He refused it, 'I don't want handouts,' he said.

'Brilliant, brilliant, a tramp after my own heart.'

'Our officers spoke to him last week,' Sandy adds. 'He shook hands with them and exchanged a few jokes.'

'Phew!' Like a newborn baby whose lungs have just opened up, Ray Manly takes his deepest, longest breath. 'Excellent, send me a briefing note with all the ammunition.'

'It's on the way.'

201

'Terrific.'

The whole affair couldn't have turned out better, but he is not celebrating, not yet. Articles in the tabloids have a strong impact. For that dollar fifty, they draw all the tears they can. They could put a dent in the initiative, give it a bad odour. Even kill it. Then the Premier would be justified in sidelining him. He is thinking about possible disasters when it hits him: he could turn the episode to his advantage. Under the new initiative, that tramp would have been visited by a social worker, by a psychologist, professional people, masters of communication. People who know how to convince the inconvincible, the hard-headed and obdurate. They would have picked it that he was in danger. This tragedy just proves that looking after the mentally ill is not about hospitals, not about beds, but about professional communication. *That's it.* The death of this tramp is a real opportunity. It will prove how important the new initiative is. A long overdue intervention.

* * *

Clara has tracked down the social worker from the Homelessness group.

'One of our staff talked to him only last week, he was in his usual spot, on the third bench from the main street. He made sense, he was logical, well, the logic of the mentally ill. You know what I mean … Internally consistent but based on strange assumptions. We tried everything, but you know how it is, you can't force them to move away.'

'No, I guess not.'

'As long as they're not a danger to others, or themselves,' the social worker adds.

'But wasn't he a danger to himself? Isn't his death good enough proof that he was?'

'Imminent danger. Only imminent danger. Surely you're familiar with the rules,' and the social worker's voice hits the lower pitch of an official.

'Yes. Imminent danger,' Clara says more to herself than in agreement. If sleeping on a park bench for years is not living in imminent danger, what is? But she is in no mood to debate with this woman what, 'imminent danger' means. It would be as futile as arguing about a colour with the colour blind.

She says goodbye and puts the phone down. What should she write? She scans the article again. The man was barely older than Peter. She shudders.

'Oh, not again, I won't go back to all that.'

She has been working on herself, trying to push Peter to the periphery of her life, give him the status of ex, of was, of past perfect, but when she wasn't successful, she consoled herself that he wasn't due back yet. At least we don't have to visit him for a week or two, meanwhile I'll try not to let his return spoil my peace.

Last Saturday, Jeff rang to tell her that he got his divorce.

'And how are you and Shosh?'

'She's fine. Growing up, and me? No change.'

'Just as beautiful?'

'Flatter, flatter.'

'No, just an impression. Are you planning to come to Tasmania in the near future?'

'I can't.'

'Clara, I don't often go away. Because of the farm, because of my daughter,' he paused. 'My mother, my dogs, the sheep,' he laughed, 'but I could take a weekend off to visit you in Sydney.'

'That would be nice.'

'What sort of things would you like to do?'

She could not think of anything, she just wanted him to come.

'Well how about we walk around the Harbour, have a nice lunch, maybe go to a movie. Will Shosh be staying at her father's? How is he, by the way?'

'I'll tell you more when I see you,' she replied thinking: I will one day, one day when the time is right. Meanwhile, you'll have to trust me.

'I'll try to be in Sydney next month, maybe sooner. I'll let you know in time.'

On Saturday she and Jeff were planning a pleasant weekend, and now …? She is back to the newspaper article. The tramp had been lying on the same bench, on and off, for three years. Three years? More than one thousand nights? She can see him. Vividly. Having lined the bench with piles of paper, he lies down, to sleep. But he cannot let himself go, he cannot let drowsiness take over, because if he does, someone could rob him. He has only a few dollars in his wallet, but for him every cent counts. Then there are the hooligans who for the sake of a joke would rob him of his peace, even beat him up, and who knows, do him in? Dawn breaks. He rubs his eyes open. People walk past, on the way to work. He is lying there, skin grey from not having washed for weeks. It's eight o'clock. Does he buy himself a coffee? A sandwich? Or does he walk around? Is he talking to himself? Or to the passers-by? No, he is lying down on his pile of paper again, newspapers and documents. Briefing notes? Briefing notes with the Department's logo. Familiar briefing notes she can recite with closed eyes.

The shock of it jolts her back. *This job is destroying me.* She has been trying to get another job. She has sent in two applications. One she could do standing on her head. She has not heard from either of them. *As soon as I finish this briefing note I'll ring them, see if I still have a chance.*

Maurice is on the phone, 'Clara, how's the briefing note going?'

Ring whom?

'Clara. Is the briefing note coming along?'

'Yes, but I do need another hour.'

'OK, but not more.'

'That'll do.'

She starts writing again. *He had been visited by …*

Her briefing note is passed from Maurice to Sandy and from Sandy to the Minister.

* * *

Fresh from his lunchtime run, Ray Manly is climbing the stairs of Parliament House when two young journalists block his way.

'Minister, what are you going to do about the homeless mentally ill?'

'We are offering them accommodation.'

'So how come they're dying in the park?'

'They are not dying in the park. Let's not exaggerate. It was one, very unfortunate, but he was offered help.'

'What sort of help, Minister?'

'He was offered accommodation. But he was a proud man, he did not want to accept it.'

Having done the communication bit, Ray Manly looks at his watch.

'Now will you excuse me, gentlemen, I have some urgent matters to attend to.' He makes his way past the journos, who retreat from the steps of power.

-33-

Back from his morning coffee, Maurice is collecting his thoughts. Today is the announcement. If the Minister pulls off the initiative without a hitch, and the chances are that he will, that's another feather in my cap and my permanency is inevitable. It's time to start thinking higher and broader.

He has no desire to spend more than a year in his current position. The next step has to be Kelly-Anne's position, or a directorship in a different department. Once he gets his permanency, he can take Sue and the kids for an extended holiday. With a month of annual leave and more than two months of long service leave, he could easily take three months off. That's the beauty of being a Public Servant, long service leave depends only on the length of the service, no matter if his positions were acting or not.

The group is working well. Charmaine could stand in for him, and in his mind's eye she is already sitting in his chair, black crochet top, skirt barely covering her buttocks, her delicate pubic warmth flowing into him … *Oh no!* He can hardly breathe.

As he descends from the dizzying heights, it occurs to him that Charmaine has already acted in his position twice — one month when he had the accident, and three weeks when he was on exchange with that woman in Brisbane — and since acting jobs have to be rotated among his subordinates, it is Clara's turn now. *No way!* He has to find an excuse for picking Charmaine over Clara. A few moments later he has the solution. *That's it!* Acting jobs under three months are not scrutinised.

If he goes away for a couple of days short of three months, he will not have to advertise the position, he can appoint Charmaine directly. Clara is politically naive, and his job demands political astuteness. A perfect excuse! He'll have no problem convincing Kelly-Anne and Sandy that Charmaine is the right woman to warm his chair while he's away.

* * *

As Maurice is working on his succession, Peter is on his way to the State Library. He buys himself a takeaway coffee and sipping along, strolls down Macquarie Street. As he walks past the NSW Parliament, he is overcome by a sinister feeling. Fear, the fear of power, something his parents acquired in Europe. They rarely talked about it, but they said enough to imbue him with it from an early age. It is in his blood, in his every cell, and today that fear is stronger than ever.

He walks past the Parliament just as Ray Manly is announcing the government's new initiative.

'Heal in Place, the government's new initiative, is a new dawn for the most vulnerable in our community, the mentally ill. A much overdue intervention after years of inaction from the opposite side.

'Research shows that the mentally ill do not want to be kept in hospital for extended periods of time. They want to live the sort of life the rest of us do, and so they should. They want to be able to go to places, spend time with their friends, with their family, and this government is committed to supporting them,' he looks at the speech in front of him, 'therefore the government, in consultation with the relevant parties, has decided that after a few days in hospital, after their medication has been adjusted, non-acute patients will be able to go home. Not to be abandoned to their carers, but to start phase two of their recovery. Now what will this consist of?' he asks looking at the Speaker, 'Support, support by professional health workers to heal in their own surroundings. I should add that our health workers are some of the best in the world.

'So, we will close down a proportion of non-acute beds in a number of hospitals and transfer some of the nurses, social workers and some psychologists, to the field. They will visit the mentally ill regularly and support them in whatever way they need in order to negotiate life. Build up their self-reliance. Because self-reliance is the key to independent living.

'Ladies and gentlemen, this initiative is not only a new dawn for the mentally ill, but for their families and their carers.' His gaze returns to the speech again.

'We have also thought of those who don't have a home to go to. We will increase the number of half-way houses. In the next financial year, we will spend three million dollars on additional half-way housing.'

'Window dressing!' Helen Pride the Shadow Minister shouts, but Ray Manly is not fazed. He reminds her that in their three years in power her party did nothing for the mentally ill. The other questions and criticisms he handles with just as much aplomb.

His interview on local radio is a success.

'From now on, after a short stay in the hospital, non-acute patients will be free to live in the community. They will be visited regularly and given professional support. Their wellbeing will be looked after by my Department.'

A few people ring in to tell their sad stories, elderly parents looking after psychotic relatives.

'But that's exactly it,' Ray Manly intercedes, 'the previous government neglected the mentally ill, but our government understands their plight. Under our initiative such terrible things will not happen. I promise you.'

Heal in Place will not solve all their problems, he admits a few calls later, but it will improve their situation a great deal.

And so, the new initiative is launched without a hitch. A cause for celebration and Ray Manly begins to plan a big night out with Shirley. On the way home, he stops at a garage to buy a bunch of flowers. Shirley loves flowers, she is a romantic.

* * *

Monday. Feeling on top of the world, Ray Manly picks up *The Daily*. 'Drunk Knifed A Passer-by', the title on the first page screams. He scans the next two pages, then one more and there is what he is looking for, 'Closures of Hospital Beds.' Well not exactly what he is looking for. '… closures, but not in the rich Eastern Suburbs … The battlers have to carry the burden for the rich.'

Bugger! This is not over yet.

Meanwhile the talkback radio switchboards are running hot. People are outraged. You can't trust the government, our politicians don't care about the battlers. Ray Manly is only there for himself. The shock jocks keep fanning the flames. The media monitors cannot type fast enough.

By lunchtime, the ministerial office is flooded with emails, information requests, from hospitals, from community organisations, from private citizens. The numbers of non-acute beds to be closed down are a sham.

Maurice's computer is pinging non-stop. Emails from Sandy forwarding requests from the ministerial office are drowning his inbox. Journalists and citizens questioning the facts. Maurice forwards the requests to Simon who forwards them to Niu. She is now acting in Marina's position.

'Niu, how's it going?' Maurice asks every time he walks past her desk. He does often because he is worried, if those figures aren't rectified soon, he can say goodbye to his permanent position. The more Maurice enquires about progress, the more stressed Niu is. How can she work out what went wrong? She cannot even find Marina's file. She keeps checking her watch. She can't wait to turn off the computer and go home, but time has never been slower.

* * *

Tuesday. Niu has rung in sick. Simon is nowhere to be seen and Maurice is fuming.

'Has anybody seen Simon?' Nobody has and no-one knows where he is. Maurice is seething. *There goes my permanent position, I shouldn't have let that horsy woman go on holiday until this was settled.*

It is past eleven o'clock when a sheepish Simon slinks in trying not to be noticed, but Maurice has seen him. 'Where on Earth have you been?' he asks through gritted teeth. 'It's nearly midday.'

'I had to take my daughter to …'

'Today? For crying out loud couldn't you make other arrangements? One is on holiday, the other has private engagements. You'd think this office is only to be used when you've nothing better to do.'

F____ yourself, Simon shouts. Inwardly. He could not help being late today. He had to take his daughter to the dentist, and the public service is a family-friendly employer. Besides, he was only away a couple of hours.

'Simon why so few closures in the Eastern Suburbs? And all only in one hospital?' Maurice bellows. Simon looks at him perplexed.

'You don't know, do you? Well, you'll have to work it out. The Minister needs an answer urgently.'

An hour later, Simon is still sweating. *Where is that bloody file?* He scrolls from folder to folder, from file to file. 'At last!'

Clara has heard enough to know what Simon is wrestling with. Those numbers Marina has warned her about, and she in turn warned Maurice, that bad data file has given them nonsensical results. There you are, Maurice, it's revenge time. The revenge of sloppiness and apathy, she says to herself with some glee.

Simon goes through Marina's numbers. Once, twice. The East lost … *Nonsense!* He tries to find out how Marina arrived at those numbers. He cannot. *Damn her! Did she have to go on holiday now, now when the Minister is on the boil?* He is still immersed in the maze of Marina's numbers when the phone rings. It's Maurice. He has stormed out from a meeting to check on his progress.

'Simon, you have no time to fart around. For God's sake, just do a quick and simple. The Minister needs the answers, in an hour!'

'You'll have them.'

Don't you worry, I won't fart around. He makes some quick assumptions, does a few back of the envelope calculations, and before the hour is up, he emails the results to Maurice. Maurice looks at the new numbers, *they'll do,* and he forwards the email to Sandy who sends it to the Minister. Less than an hour later Ray Manly's Public Relations Officer is onto the press with the new numbers and an apology.

The Daily does not publish the letters from the objecting Eastern Suburbs citizens. The complaints to the Minister are answered with a promise of acquiring more halfway houses to service the Eastern Suburbs, after consultation with the relevant parties of course.

Two days later the tabloids have moved on to a gruesome murder, taking the outrage of the electorate with them. Apart from those whose lives will be directly affected, few will remember the Minister's new initiative.

Having declared it a success, Ray Manly instructs his Department to implement the initiative without delay.

-34-

Ten days have passed since the launch of the Heal in Place initiative, and today Marina, looking ten years younger than her former self, is back at work. Having answered Simon's, 'How was your holiday?' with 'Wonderful,' she turns the computer on. Her inbox is full. She deletes the dross, answers the others. *What else?* She doesn't feel like working, her thoughts are still on the overseas trip.

'Clara, how about a cup of coffee?'

'The best proposal I had for days,' and the two of them slip out quietly.

'You look astonishingly well,' Clara says as they are waiting to be served.

'A proof that being away from this place does miracles. Now tell me, are the mentally ill healing in place already?'

'No, not yet. But the announcement has gone through, the policy has been accepted ...'

'And how did it go?'

'Well, how do you think it went?'

'I hope I wasn't missed.'

'You were for a couple of days. The figures for the Eastern Suburbs were, to quote the tabloids, "a sham".'

'I could've predicted it. I had no reliable data to work with.'

'And Maurice wouldn't get you a new data file.'

'Yeah.'

'Well, they got what they deserved,' Clara says.

Marina looks at her, 'Which is?'

'If you think the tabloids are bad, you should've heard the shock jocks. The Minister was in trouble. He must have put pressure on Sandy who must have dished it to Maurice, because he was in utter panic. He screamed at Simon; Simon lost it with Niu. The poor woman was close to tears. Next day she rang in sick.'

'But they sorted it out, didn't they?'

'Simon revised the numbers.'

'The moron revised the numbers? You're kidding me.'

'He did. In a couple of hours.'

Marina looks at her stunned. 'In a couple of hours?' she asks, brow approaching her hairline, 'No-one could have been that fast, let alone that moron.'

'He must have done one of those quick and dirties Maurice asks for.'

'Hate to think what he came up with.'

'Well, they've been accepted. The tabloids published a few revised numbers and an apology from the Minister.'

'And surprise, surprise, he declared it a success.' Marina's eyes narrowed by a mocking smile.

'Yes. So, there you are, the Minister's planning and Maurice's brilliant support,' Clara says, eyes sparkling with mischief, 'coupled with the sheer disinterest of the electorate in matters concerning the seriously mentally ill, ended in another reform of their services. Now tell me about your holiday.'

Marina takes a sip of her coffee. 'The truth, or the official version?'

'What do you mean? The truth of course.'

'You know what?' she says after a long pause, 'Distance distorts. My country did not match the country of my memory. My town looked grey, and my relatives? Well … I don't know if I told you, but my only family there is my husband's. His mother and his sister. They showered him with love. It was nice, but their warmth didn't extend to me. I was his wife, a bit of … how shall I put it …? A useless necessity?'

'They haven't seen him for years.'

'Clara, I think I no longer invite warmth. Perhaps that's why I feel so lonely here.'

'Don't exaggerate. They just couldn't relate to you.'

'Um … don't think they even tried. Truth be known, we had bugger all in common.'

'You have such different lives.'

'We do, in their imagination. They think that in the West people are rich and no-one's life is as hard as theirs. "Count your lucky stars," my mother-in-law said to me. I was lost for an answer. I should've told her, yeah, I have a friggin ball in Sydney. Humiliations, put-downs, people scrunching their faces as I speak. I've done it all, I was even lectured about my bad manners …

'What bad manners?'

'Didn't you notice?'

'Don't be ridiculous. What happened?'

'I must've been … Ah, I was still studying for my Masters, so I must have been two years in the country by then. My overseas qualifications were worthless, I had to get an Australian degree. So, I was studying and working. Working at *Sue's Wholesome Food!*'

'A cafe?'

'A takeaway sandwich shop. I worked there for three years. Three whole years making sandwiches. Long story, but back to my manners. I just finished work one afternoon and was on the way to university. Dog tired from standing on my feet all day, I needed a pick me up. So, I walked into this shop to buy a drink. "Can I have an orange juice?" I asked. "Please," the twenty-year-old slob said, "We say please in this country." "Please," I said, obediently like a half-wit. Now I'd tell that friggin slob where to go, I'd give her a demonstration of bad manners. I've acquired plenty since. I'm nearly assimilated.'

Clara smiles, 'And the rest of the trip?'

'The rest of the trip …?' Marina shrugs. 'I felt like an impostor. I couldn't wait for the visit to end. So much for all those days and nights longing to see them.'

'But what about your friends?'

'I did meet up with two. At first, we couldn't stop talking, by our third encounter the conversation slid down parallel lines.' Marina falls silent. 'Clara, there's no going back, there's no rekindling old feelings. Once I accepted that, I started to enjoy myself. Shall we have another coffee?'

'Not for me.'

'Then let's have a cold drink,' and she waves to the waitress.

'Once we went up in the mountains, I found what I was dreaming about all along. I even found my young happy self. The mountains were exactly as I remembered them. The three of us took the chairlift to the top. The sun was shining, the air was crisp, the snow sparkled.' Marina's face covered with pure delight. 'Clara, if there is a Heaven, I know its address.

'As I stood there looking at the beauty around me, I remembered a childhood fairy tale, about a place where there is, "youth without old age and life without death." That day in the mountains made my trip worthwhile.'

'And your son? Did he enjoy the old country?'

'He did every minute of it. His grandmother introduced him to the youngster next door and for the rest of the holiday I hardly saw him. The two of them skied every day. Now he's paying for it, he has to catch up on weeks of missed school. But I'm sure he'll keep going back.'

'And you?'

'Me?' Marina shrugs. 'I don't know. I don't want to see the family ever again, or my old friends, but I can't see myself resisting the call of those mountains,' and after a pause, 'Clara, the hold of my native land will stay with me as long as I live. The rest is a mirage.'

'Sad to lose the love for your people.'

'It is. Clara, maybe it's a migrant's fate to exchange belonging for insight,' a shadow of sadness swooping over Marina's face, 'but you know what? It's more painful to be an outsider among your own people than among strangers. I came back thinking that I don't belong there, and I don't belong here, but seeing you today it occurred to me that maybe I do belong with you, and with all the other non-belongers in this country. If you don't mind me calling you that.'

'You summed us up perfectly. Now let's head back. It's nearly lunchtime.'

'What else is new in the Department?' Marina asks as they enter the office.

'The Director General is away on holiday. The rumours are that he will soon be leaving for the Federal Public Service. Anything else? … Oh! As you can see, we have a new manager,' Clara gestures towards Maurice's office where Charmaine is now talking on the phone. 'Maurice got his permanency and has gone on holiday. With a spring in his step. He's due back in two months.'

'May he win the lottery beforehand.'

'Amen.'

Clara is unusually happy, Jeff rang her last night. He cannot come next weekend, because his mother is having an operation on Friday, a relatively minor one, but he wants to look after her when she comes out of hospital, on Saturday.

'But I'm coming for sure. I'll ring you when I know more. I can't wait to see you.'

On the other end of the line Clara blushed, her face lit by a sudden happiness.

-35-

Autumn is on the way, the leaves on the deciduous tree at the end of the street have started to yellow. The nights are cooler now, and for the first time in weeks, Clara woke up feeling refreshed.

It is the fourth Friday of the month, her day off. Shosh is at school. The shackles of routine off, Clara is free. The city beckons. Yes, that's what she'll do, she will mingle with the crowds, the people rushing past, feel life pulsating around her. She might browse in a few shops. The clothes, the colours, the strong lights, the loud music will energise her.

An hour later she is strolling through the Strand Arcade, so different from the functional, soulless shopping centres sprinkled around Sydney, admiring the window displays. She never ventures into the small boutique shops; she cannot even dream of shopping there. To her, the clothes in those shops are to be admired, worn in imagination, not bought.

As she stands in front of a shop window marvelling at a dress, the shopkeeper, a fragile woman, long past middle age, steps out, 'Would you like to try it?'

'No thanks,' Clara says. *It's too expensive, it's out of my reach.* 'Not now,' she adds. But she stands there for a while wondering how it would look on her.

No, I won't try it, I'll sleep on it first.

* * *

Saturday. Eyes narrowly open, Clara looks at the clock. Quarter past six. 'There's still time,' and she pulls the light doona to her chin and descends into a sweet state of semiconsciousness. *Jeff. What about Jeff? Oh, he's coming to visit*, she smiles to herself. The fog of loneliness, which has surrounded her for years, is lifting, vanishing in the sunlight and she snuggles up in the doona, at peace with the world. But what am I going to wear when Jeff comes? And there is the dress again, as irresistible as it was in the shop window. Its sinuous folds, its colour, a deep dark red, have wormed themselves into her mind. She has not seen anything so beautiful and elegant for years. No, I can't afford it.

But the image of the dress is stronger than her resolve. I have to try it. If it doesn't fit, I will regain my peace of mind, and if it does? If it does, I'll work something out.

After breakfast, having dropped Shosh at her friend Fiona's place, Clara heads to the city, all the way thinking about Jeff's visit. Will we get on? Two people who hardly know each other thrown together for two whole days? In her mind's eye recollections of their trip to Dove Lake, his profile, his strong arms. 'He's good-looking and I like good-looking men. Like? Love.' She smiles to herself. She has not been with a man for years. I should have offered to put him up in the lounge room. But wouldn't that be too suggestive. Suggestive of what? Oh, for goodness sake, Clara, you're a woman, aren't you? It's not friendship you want, you want physical connection. Isn't it time to revive those blunted senses, feel that oneness with a man. Do you still remember how good that feels? I do, with the right man, but is Jeff the right man? Because that trip in Tasmania doesn't count, we didn't have a minute to ourselves.'

It is nearly lunchtime. The sun is high in the sky, but the city's tall buildings shade the streets into near dusk. She turns into the Strand Arcade and walks on, looking at the window displays. *That's the one!* She has not deceived herself; the dress is as beautiful as she remembered it.

The shopkeeper has seen her, 'I knew you'd be back. So would you like to try it?'

'Yes, please.'

The shopkeeper rummages through the coat hangers and pulls out the dress. It's even more beautiful than it was in the window. Clara takes the dress and disappears into the fitting room, slips it over her head, zips up the back and looks at the mirror. *Heavens above, this is perfect!* Against the dark red, her complexion is less pale, more sensual. The top a snug fit, below the waist, flowing waves. Afford it or not, she has to buy it, and not only for Jeff. Probably not for Jeff at all. *He cannot move to Sydney, and we have to stay in Sydney so Shosh can visit her father.*

'Well?' the shopkeeper calls.

Clara pulls back the curtain.

'Wow! This dress is made for you. The cut, the colour. Absolutely perfect.'

'My first indulgence in years,' Clara says as she hands her the money.

The woman wraps the dress in tissue paper, with the care one would award to a fragile work of art, ties it with white ribbon and slides it into a purple bag. Clara walks out smiling.

The sun, the dress, and Jeff is coming. What happiness! We will click, we will.

But if they don't, she will start going out, she will go to singles dinners. She will meet someone eventually, someone who will be a father to Shosh, someone to share her life with, the good and the bad, the happy times and the dramas. Someone gentle, someone kind-hearted. Peter was kind-hearted too, once. And her father? She never met a more generous and gentle man. She was lucky that way.

Bag in hand, she strides up Elizabeth Street. Opposite, the path leading into Hyde Park is bathed in sunshine. Further up, below a line of trees, a few people are sitting on the grass. 'Why not?' She crosses the street; she will sit a few minutes in the sun and celebrate her purchase.

Couples with children walk past. She longs to be one of them, she longs to be holding Shosh's hand and a father holding the other. 'It will happen, it will.' She is walking up the path, dangling the bag with the red dress, dreaming about a new life, about a family.

Next to the fountain, the path widens into the shade of the tall trees. Here and there a ray of sun filters through the leaves. What joy! She walks on, looking for a bench. There are only a few, all occupied, all except one at the very end of the alley and she hurries towards it. But the bench is not free, a man is lying on it. She drops her gaze to the ground. *I don't want to know. This isn't my problem* and at the nearest clearing she cuts across to the lawn. She walks a few paces, the trees are fewer now, and then whether from curiosity, or the guilt she feels whenever she sees a homeless person, she looks across. *No, it can't be.* But there he is, the familiar hat, the hand which she knows so well, the fingers which once explored her body, hanging lifeless. *Why is he lying here?* Her knees weak. *What shall I do? If I talk to him, he will make a scene. But can I walk past him? Past the man I shared my bed with? Can I walk past Sosh's father?* But she does. Fast, nearly running, straight to the closest bus stop.

She climbs the steps of the first bus and collapses on the seat. What shall I do now? Who can I contact? His doctor? On Saturday? No chance. Then what shall I do? Leave him in the park for two days? And two nights? No, I will ring Eszti, find out what happened. Has Peter left home? But shall I tell her where he is?

'Town Hall!' The driver calls out.

Clara walks to the door.

'Lady!' A woman pulls her arm. 'You forgot your bag.'

She turns back, picks up the bag with the red dress, gets off the bus and heads to the train station, wondering what to do next. She will not pick up Shosh, she will go straight home and phone Eszti.

She still doesn't know what to say to her as she dials her number. Eszti is not home and Clara takes a deep breath of relief. I'll pick up Shosh, do some cleaning then ring Eszti again. But when she does there is no answer. She rings her at four, at five and at six. Eszti has vanished.

It's nearly seven o'clock when she tracks Eszti down. She has been to Lilla's place. It was her birthday; her whole family was there. 'Some people are lucky,' she says.

Yes, some people are lucky. 'And how's Peter?'

'He has been very tight-lipped about that Indian ashram. They promised him bliss. Bliss? Organised thieves, making money from the gullible.'

'At least he's back now.'

'He was, but then he disappeared again. It's been unusually quiet upstairs and I was wondering whether to go up and check on him. In the end I didn't, but he's definitely home now. Making a lot of noise. As if …'

Clara is no longer listening. Should she tell her that he was lying on a park bench. No, I won't. He's home now.

'Eszti, does he have a good doctor?'

'Dr Stein? Well, you know how it is. They're good if they can help. But I doubt he helps many. That's a dreadful illness.'

'Yes, it's a dreadful disease, but he's coping. With your help …'

'Thank Heavens I still have the strength to help him. But I won't always be here.'

'Not always, but for a long, long time.'

'Is that Grandma?' Shosh calls from the hall. 'Can I talk to her?' And Shosh tells her about her day. She has been at Fiona's place and her mother took them out for lunch. 'Is daddy all right? Can I talk to him?'

Eszti's voice swells with delight. 'I'll go and get him.'

'Thank you, Grandma,' and Shosh sits down on the sofa waiting. Finally, Eszti rings. 'He can't talk to you now. He'll ring you tomorrow.'

Shosh's face falls in disappointment. 'Is he well?'

'He's very well dear. He'll ring you tomorrow.'

* * *

Sunday. Sandwiches and straw mat packed; Clara is ready to take Shosh to the beach.

'What if daddy rings?'

'If he rings, he can leave a message and you will ring Grandma and ask her to call him. I think he'll go out first and ring you in the evening.'

But Peter didn't ring that evening.

'Shosh, I'm sure he's all right.'

'When we going to visit him?'

'Not next weekend, next weekend is Fiona's birthday, but the weekend after.'

'Promise?'

'I do.'

-36-

Sitting at her desk, Clara is reviewing the job interview she just had, what she said and what she should have said. *I should have done better, but those long-winded questions? By the time ...*

Her phone rings. It's Jeff.

'I sorted things out. I'll come to Sydney the Saturday after next. But if that day is inconvenient ...'

'It's perfect.'

There is no joy without some lurking shadow, and this time the shadow is Eszti. She has to talk to her, tell her that the next two weekends she has commitments she cannot change, they will visit the weekend after. It will be difficult, but she will stand her ground. And with these conditions firm in her mind, she dials Eszti.

After the usual pleasantries, Clara asks, 'And how's Peter?'

'Same. No better, no worse. Are you coming this weekend?'

'We can't, it's Fiona's birthday party. I promised her mother to help with the preparations. I owe it to her, she minds Shosh after school.'

'And the weekend after? Don't tell me you can't. Peter wants to see Shosh.'

'I've got something on. But we'll definitely come the following weekend,' she can feel the reproach in Eszti's silence. The hurt and the blame. She is not wrong.

Eszti is mulling over this latest let-down. Shosh's visits are up to Clara, up to her goodwill, and if they are becoming less frequent, what

223

can I do? A healthy man would stand on his dignity, would take it to the Family Court, but Peter? In a court Peter wouldn't count as much as a fly.

'Ok, I'll see you then,' Eszti says finally. Clara puts the phone down, relieved. *Two free weekends! And Jeff is coming!*

* * *

Sunday. 'Mum look, this one shines and this,' Shosh holds up another shell, 'doesn't shine at all. Why?'

'Maybe it's due to the chemicals on their surface. Maybe one is smoother than the other. I don't really know.'

They are walking on the far end of Balmoral Beach to keep away from crowds. Shosh is jumping from rock to rock looking for shells for her collection. Occasionally someone walks past, but most of the time there is no-one around. Nothing, but silence and the hiss of the waves rolling in. Every now and then, Splash! And Shosh shrieks and laughs and complains, but on she goes jumping and getting wet. Further in, in the small rock pools, the water is crystal clear. From time to time a small wave laps the rocks and breaks the rays of the sun shining on the pebbles below.

It's past midday. Shosh's enthusiasm for shells is petering out. She is hungry. The sun warmed boulder, a few steps away, is inviting them to sit down. Clara spreads a napkin on her lap, unpacks the sandwiches she made that morning and the two of them eat watching the bay, the windsurfers and the two lonely yachts in the distance. The silence only broken by Shosh's questions. Far too many questions which Clara cannot answer. Frustrated, Shosh stops the, 'whys' and begins wondering whether Fiona will like her birthday present. The party is in the afternoon, and Shosh can hardly contain her excitement.

Clara too is happy. Jeff bought his ticket already; he will be here in a week.

* * *

Leafing through a report which has been sitting on her desk for days, Clara's thoughts keep meandering. Jeff will land in Sydney in a couple of days. In forty-eight hours! These numbers in the second column, what do they actually mean?

The phone rings.

'Eszti?'

'Clara, sorry to disturb, but I had to ring you. Peter is in hospital. In the acute ward.'

A chill runs through Clara. *In the acute ward? He wouldn't have gone in voluntarily.* The rest, the details of what exactly happened, she does not want to know. One always pays for knowledge. Besides, she has had enough of dramas.

'He's much better, now that he's taking his medication again,' Eszti adds.

'Then he'll probably be home soon,' Clara says with as much optimism as she can muster.

'Maybe,' and after a pause, 'Clara, I know you had something on this weekend, but do you think you could make some alternative arrangement and visit him on Saturday? It would cheer him up to see Shosh.'

And what about Jeff? He's bought his plane ticket already. What shall I tell him?

Because I won't tell him that Peter is insane.

The weekend with Jeff which has sustained her for days, the hope that her life might turn the corner, that there are still pleasures in store for her, is slipping away. *So, what shall I do? Not visit Peter? But can I leave Eszti to cope on her own?*

She has no choice; she has to ring Jeff. She will tell him that Peter is in hospital and they have to visit him. He does not need to know why he is in hospital. But if he insists? She can blame it on some complaint which needs further investigation. Maybe they can meet up on Friday night and then on Saturday after the visit to the hospital. *After the hospital? No, the visits to Peter always shatter me.*

'Eszti, I'll see what I can do. I'll let you know on Friday.'

The conversation with Eszti over, she dials Jeff.

Jeff can't help wondering whether she is genuine, or whether this story is an excuse for something she is hiding from him. She has been very tight-lipped about herself, about her marriage, about her life. It occurs to him that he barely knows her.

'I'll talk to them, I might be able to use the ticket some other time, but I don't know when I can take a weekend off again. The next few weeks the farm will need a lot of work … Maybe in a month?'

'A month?'

'Yes.'

'Not more, I hope.'

'I hope not.'

Desolate, she puts the phone down. My life postponed again. But what can I do? I have to visit Peter; I owe it to him. I owe it to him for how long? Will this debt hang over me for the rest of my days? Is this a life sentence?

'What do you owe him?! You can't pay back love with pity; you can't pay back good times with resented duty. Or guilt. This visit might cheer him up for a few hours, but no matter how often you visit him, no matter how many days, weeks, or months you give up for him – these visits might be a few hours, but their effect lingers for days – you can't provide him with the support, the warmth, the companionship he needs. Or doctors and nurses who take more than a passing interest in him, look after him before he's too far gone.

Where is Ed? Doesn't Peter deserve an occasional hour of his time? In memory of their friendship? In memory of their shared youth? Of what Peter once was. Of his love for him, of his amazing knowledge. What is friendship if it can be extinguished so easily? Shouldn't its embers smoulder for years? It's all I would expect. Smouldering, only smouldering, not burning eternal. But if friendship is no longer possible, surely some form of a relationship is. Of giving, of not forgetting. Of not abandoning him entirely, of not letting him sink into the deepest human misery. And she wonders if Ed too walks past tramps as if they do not exist. Will he walk past Peter one day? In her mind's eye a recent television program about consciousness, the expert saying: few animals are capable of empathy, but most people are. And if they are not, what are they?'

I have to visit Peter. I have to visit him because nobody else will and I have to go to support Eszti. She shouldn't have to cope with such a burden at her age. I will pick her up and take her to the hospital. But deep-down Clara knows that she will go for herself, she will go so she can look at herself in the mirror. She will go so Shosh will not judge her one day.

She can't bear seeing him behind locked doors, and she is afraid of him, afraid of his insanity, of how he might act, of what he might say. But she has to go.

<h1 style="text-align:center">-37-</h1>

Eszti has been ready since eight o'clock. Peter's T-shirts, pyjamas and the fresh fruit have been packed and repacked. She has fed the cat, closed all the windows, pulled the curtains in and set the radio on full blast, because what robber would break into a house full of people? She has watered the garden and pulled the weeds out, the ones which survived her weeding of the last few days. Clara is not due to arrive for another twenty minutes or so, and she looks around for something to do, anything which needs her energy.

Peter has been in the hospital a few times before, every time he stopped taking his pills, and whenever he did, he slid down the same road, a road paved with extreme delusions, from where only a couple of weeks in hospital could bring him back. But this time … no, Eszti does not want to recall what happened.

He has been in the hospital for a week now and the daily visits – more than an hour of buses and walking each way – are wearing her out. But at least she is among people, all travelling in the same direction, sharing in each other's lives if only for a short while. Distracted by their conversations, accents, clothes, she ceases to think about Peter, now and then. But deep inside her, emptiness reigns, her body is hollow, uninhabited. It is the best she can hope for.

Looking after Peter for two long years would have taken a toll on anybody, but it has taken a greater toll on her, because she has no family. She is alone. It's not that people don't talk to her, the opposite, they keep asking, 'How are you, Mrs Steinberg?' And just as she is about to crack the door to her world open, only a crack, not open fully, she sees the fake smile and feels its indifference. Tell indifference how she really feels? What would be the point? And the distance between her and them turns into a chasm.

A family would have empathised, they might have persuaded Peter to take his medication, they might have tried to talk some sense into him, they would have told him that the Swami is not real, that God does not talk to humans. They might have shared the visits to the hospital, they might have …, they might have …, but what's the point in thinking what might have happened? Because there is no family, not in Australia and not in Europe. Half went during the war, and the rest passed on since.

She has an occasional catch-up session with Dr Stein. A catch-up when she talks and he listens, well, sort of listens, but he never reassures, never has a sympathetic word to say. Some say he has a good reputation, and every time they do, Eszti feels her blood pressure rising. Good reputation? He hasn't done much good for Peter. And he is a cold man. He is made to a different recipe from any doctor she has ever known. Of this she is convinced.

No, there is no-one to encourage her, no-one to talk her out of her dark thoughts.

And no-one to defend her. Her head still hurts from that knock. She keeps telling herself that he lost it, that he is a sick man, and she shouldn't blame a sick man. Still, my own son? I'm on my own. There's Clara, but she has her life. Clara was wrong for Peter; he should not have married her. But they had Shosh, and Shosh is the light of my life, and one day she'll be old enough to visit me on her own.

She checks the lock on the back door once more and walks out to the front of the house to wait for Clara. Some cat has been at it again, the beast has shat over the path. Hers wouldn't have done such a thing. She grabs the hose, turns the water on and sprays the concrete. Over and over again. Bits of cat shit are flying around like a pack of swarming wasps.

The familiar honk, Clara's car pulls up, and there is Shosh, her ray of sunshine, loving and hugging.

Half an hour later the three of them are standing in front of the door of the acute ward, waiting. A nurse opens the door, locks it behind them and leads them to the courtyard – a rectangular enclosure surrounded by high walls and finished off by an L shaped building. To their left, through the half-open door to the, 'Nurses Room', a man is keeping a discreet eye on the goings on.

'Daddy!' Shosh calls.

Peter, or more accurately a gaunt, subdued version of him, is coming towards them. He thanks them for coming, pecks each one's face in turn, and pointing to a small table, invites them to sit down. He assures them that he is all right, that the food is good and all in all his stay is not too bad, then asks Shosh about her school. Her usual ebullience absent, her answers half-hearted, her attention on her strange surroundings.

Eszti's cat stories are a Godsend. Small talk, trivia is all they can manage as they nurse their feelings of uneasiness, pity, and pain. Voiceless, mute feelings drowned by what is acceptable to all. Honesty has no seat at their table. Honesty would hurt them, but most of all it would hurt Peter and Shosh.

Every now and then a patient walks past and Peter, like a well-mannered host, does the introductions.

Leanne, a late thirties, early forties thin woman, stops by them, takes out a photo and hands it to Clara.

'My daughter,' she says, her face covered by utter delight.

'She's beautiful!' Clara says, then turning to Eszti and Shosh, 'She's like a doll, look,' and hands them the photograph of a smiling blonde baby with pink cheeks.

'She's very beautiful,' Eszti says, 'you're a very lucky woman.'

'She's so cute,' Shosh adds.

Leanne's eyes light up.

'Who's looking after her now?' Clara asks.

Leanne starts crying.

'I'm sorry, I shouldn't have asked.'

Leanne walks away.

'She doesn't have a baby,' Peter says.

'What? What do you mean, daddy?' Shosh's eyes magnified by the incredulity of it all.

'She does not have a baby,' he repeats staccato, emphasising every syllable.

Clara looks at Eszti and Eszti looks at Clara. No-one says a word. This is a psychiatric ward and being shocked at someone's story is no more rational than being insane.

'Does it really matter if she has a baby or not?' Peter asks looking at Clara. 'Isn't her reality her only reality? And isn't that reality more important to her than yours? Or the world's?'

'I don't know, maybe they're all important.'

'Well, for me, God's reality is the only reality.'

Shosh is sitting quietly, her big brown eyes following Leanne, then the tall emaciated older woman who walks in and out of the room in a hurry as if she is about to miss an important appointment; first with the tall grey wall, and then with the television. She talks incessantly to some presence.

'That's Julie,' Peter says, 'She's from a royal family. Well, that's what she thinks.'

'What if she really is?' Shosh asks.

'There might be some other reason why she's here,' Clara whispers.

'Like what?'

'Some behaviour which doesn't square with reality,' she replies looking at Peter with unease, but Peter's mind is somewhere else, his eyes pointing inward again, towards his private world.

'What's reality?' Shosh insists.

'Can we talk about this later? Let's talk to daddy now.'

'Peter!' Clara calls out to overcome the sudden distance which has inserted itself between them, 'Can we have some coffee?'

'Of course, dear. Come on, Shosh, let's make coffee,' and the two disappear into the kitchen.

A barefooted man, smoking relentlessly, walks past, then past the three men sitting at the next table. One of them says something. The other two sit in silence. The first one tries again. Is he a nurse? Nurses do not wear uniforms.

The tall, scrawny older woman walks in and out of the courtyard talking to herself. Looking at her, Clara is overwhelmed with questions: What will happen to her when she leaves the hospital? And to Leanne? Who will care for them? How often will social workers visit these people? And will those visits change their thinking enough so they can cope with life, even with a rudimentary sort of life? Will Leanne abandon her phantom daughter? Pay rent? Cook a meal? Will someone say hello to her, talk to her from time to time, or will she have to go through life like a ghost? Feared and rejected by everybody. *Heal in Place? I shouldn't have written that speech, I shouldn't have justified that cruel policy.*

Guilt is weighing her down, the guilt of her role in their lives, of her role in Peter's life. Guilt for not visiting Peter more often, for trying to disconnect herself. There will be no life for her while he is so lonely, while he is so sick. In sickness and in health, she vowed at her wedding. She thought that she could get out of it, forget her promise, but every time she is about to free herself something happens. She is on the seesaw again, the seesaw which never stops. Up and down it goes, up to some bright future and down into her past, layer by layer, into the memories of their love, his early sickness, his violent outbursts. *There's no way to disconnect. This is for life.*

Peter and Shosh are back. Peter seems to have come alive through the coffee making process. His cheerfulness must have rubbed on Shosh, the two of them are chatting happily.

Peter places the tray with the four mugs – all different colours and sizes – in the middle of the table and sits down.

'This place can drive you mad,' he whispers between slurps. 'There's nothing to do. People smoke themselves to death.'

'Nice to get visitors, isn't it, Peter?' a nurse says as she walks past.

'Yeah, but I'm afraid I can't entertain them.'

'They're just happy to see you. Aren't you?' she asks Clara.

Happy is not what she would call the way she feels, but she nods in agreement.

Julie, the emaciated grey woman medicated against her royal descent, is approaching again. She stops by Clara.

'Peter's a good man, you're lucky to have a husband like him. Always talks to me. Not like the male nurse. He just gives me pills.' She draws on her cigarette. 'They're going to kill me. These walls …' a rasping loud cough reeking of nicotine, 'It's a prison in here. The days are a street long. At night, they zonk you out.'

'Don't worry dear. We will survive,' Peter says smiling.

'You think so?'

'I do.'

'Thanks for that. You're a good man,' she looks at Clara, 'the best,' and walks away, leaving behind an awkward silence.

Eszti caresses Peter's face, 'And how are you, dear?'

'Never better,' he says winking at Clara, takes another mouthful of coffee then departs into his world.

'Peter, what do you do all day?' Clara tries to draw him back. She would like to put her hand on his sunburnt arm, caress him, heal him. Instead, she nudges him as she repeats the question.

'Breakfast, pills, evaluation, walk from one wall to the next, lunch, pills, sleep, walk, watch TV, walk, dinner, watch TV, pills, knock out. I do manage a few miles every day. At least four of us are pacing and smoking at any one time. I don't smoke, not yet, but they all do. All except that fellow over there. He doesn't smoke and he doesn't walk, he lies in bed all day.'

'All day?' Shosh asks.

'Yes, he just got up. One of his parents must be due to visit. They visit him in turns, carefully avoiding each other. They've recently separated.'

Eszti puts a reassuring hand over Peter's back, 'You will get out soon. Just try to get better.'

Heavy silence, heavy enough to collapse under its own weight. But there is Leanne again, coming to show her baby. She is missing her painfully. Clara nods with understanding. More difficult moments, more silences. Eszti is restless, a kettle of water about to boil. Eventually she can't control it any longer and departs to talk to a nurse. Barely a few moments pass, and she is back. 'Nobody wants to tell me anything. In Europe, the doctors are not like that. They have more compassion.'

'What is she on about?' Peter revisits this world.

Eszti explains.

'She doesn't know. Leave her alone,' and he tells them that all the nurses are nice, but there is a special nice one in the afternoon.

Eszti is no longer listening. Too worried about Peter's progress, and still boiling that no-one wants to tell her anything, she stands up and begins pacing. She has caught up with Lianne and is now walking behind her. To and fro they walk. To and fro. All of a sudden, she turns around and returns to the table. She brought all this fruit and she forgot to give it to Peter.

Peter does not feel like eating, and at Eszti's third attempt, he takes the bag of fruit and offers it around. The patients are not interested, but some of the nurses oblige. At Peter's prodding some take two pieces. He returns with one plum. 'That's for you,' he says to Shosh and hands her the plum. Shosh does not want to take it. The fruit is for daddy. He should have at least one piece.

'Come on Shosh, just think of all the vitamins in it. Plums are healthy, they're good for you'.

'Daddy, I shouldn't, it's for you.'

At Peter's insistence, Shosh takes the plum. She is not hungry, she does not like plums, but she does not want to anger her father. She bites into the plum, her eyes teared over. She does not want to be there, and she does not want her father to be there. These people are nice, but weird. She wants to be somewhere else, somewhere where there are different people, people whose words she can believe, predictable people. She wants to be in an open space, not shut behind high walls.

Eszti leans over to kiss her forehead, 'You shouldn't have forced her.'

'It's OK, Grandma, it's OK,' Shosh says, voice shaking.

'I think we should be going,' Eszti says, 'Shosh and Clara will visit you soon. Won't you?'

'Of course,' Clara says, looking worriedly at Shosh.

'And I'll be here tomorrow.'

In the car, on the way back, heavy silence. Eszti is thinking of her husband, he was lucky not to see his son in a mental asylum, not to see him behind locked doors. She is worried. What will happen when Peter gets out of hospital? As much as it hurts her, she has to admit that she is too scared to live with him in the same house. As if aware of her pain, Shosh leans against her and caresses her hand.

'Shosh, how about we drop Grandma home, and we go for a walk on Coogee Beach?' Clara says.

'I'm not going to Coogee Beach.'

'OK, not Coogee Beach, perhaps to another beach. Better still, let's go to the movies.' Shosh's eyes light up. She would like that.

-38-

Five days have passed since Peter left the acute ward. He is no longer behind closed doors; he is allowed to go out, and he has been out every day since.

It is mid-morning, and Peter is sitting in the autumn sunshine, savouring his coffee and trying to decide which bookshop he should head for next. Somewhere he has not been for a while, that is not too far from a bus stop so he can be back in the hospital in time for lunch. Meanwhile, back in his ward, the phone is running hot.

'One of our patients is well enough to be transferred to your ward,' the nurse from the acute says to her opposite number in Peter's ward. 'Can we start the process?'

'Straight away? But we have no vacant beds.'

'Sorry, but you'll have to find one. We need that bed. We're an emergency ward.'

'I'll talk to the registrar, see what we can do. I'll get back to you asap.'

The registrar is stressed. Even before the introduction of the new initiative, every bed counted, and so did every nurse. Now he is six beds less and has lost one of his nurses. She has been transferred out to the field, "To support and encourage self-reliance," the woman bureaucrat said. Nonsense, drivel, he thought. The bureaucrats are in charge and I'm powerless. Powerless to do the best for my patients, powerless to change the system. A man locked in a room and ordered to run a marathon.

Nowadays he spends his time juggling his patients, deciding who goes and who stays. The woman he discharged the other day was not fit to live on her own, and he lay awake that night wondering how she would manage. 'She will be visited by a social worker,' the bureaucrat said, but how often exactly, she could not say, and the rest of the time?

He scans the files of his patients. They are all sick, different degrees of delusion, but unfit to face the world. So, whom can he release? Peter Steinberg has been in his ward for nearly a week. But Peter Steinberg has a history of relapses. Then whom? He goes through the files of the other patients again. They are bad cases, worse than Peter Steinberg. He really should release two, to have a free bed available for whoever else might turn up. He cannot find two and he cannot find one. He looks at Peter Steinberg's file again. He is progressing well, the notes say. He has been out every day. 'If he's reliable enough to be let out every day, he might be well enough to go home.' He goes to check him out.

Peter is lively and makes sense. The registrar is relieved.

'Peter, you're much improved. You don't need to stay here much longer. As long as you take your pills, you'll be all right out there. So, all the best,' the doctor shakes his hand and is gone.

Less than an hour later, the social worker drops in.

'Peter, I heard you're doing really well. We'd like to discharge you.'

But he is happy here. Happy with his bed, happy with the nurses and even happy to take his medication. The latest pills are easier to take.

'I'm not moving back to my mother's house.'

'Not to your mother's house, but what about a halfway house?'

Peter's thoughts are miles away.

'Peter,' she raises her voice, 'there's a halfway house in Botany. I might be able to get you in.'

'Botany?'

'Yes, one of the residents is moving out. What do you think?'

Worry lines crease Peter's forehead, whatever he thinks he is in no mood to share.

'Why don't we go and have a look? You've nothing to lose.'

Peter looks at her, crushed and defeated. 'OK,' he whispers.

'I'll pick you up at two-thirty tomorrow.'

The social worker gone; Peter begins to rock. To and fro he rocks, to and fro,

It's only God and me now.

It's only God and me.

* * *

The next day at the agreed time of two-thirty, the social worker is back to pick Peter up.

'You must be looking forward to getting out of hospital. Aren't you?'

'Sorry?'

'You must be looking forward to getting out of hospital.'

'I guess so.'

'Freedom at last, spend more time with your friends.'

Freedom? He has plenty of freedom where he is. And friends? He does not need friends, he has God.

It's raining. The windscreen wipers are shooing fast. Relentlessly. The car travels down the road for a while, turns left, then right into a narrow street. '18, 20, 22,' the social worker reads out the numbers. 'That's the one,' and she stops the car in front of a fibro cottage, a tiny patch of garden in front.

'They're expecting us,' she says unlatching the small iron gate.

A thirty-something, solidly built man, a volunteer as it turns out, opens the door. Inside, the smell of cigarettes mingles with the smell of old carpet and like an entitled resident it persists even in the lounge room where the window is wide open. On the frayed sofa, two men are watching television. While the volunteer does the introductions, Clive keeps staring at the screen, puffing on his cigarette insatiably. Chris is focused exclusively on the flies buzzing around his coffee. He has to chase them away, but one persists. Its persistence is aggravating and Chris waves his hands more and more vigorously. The fly escapes again. This is a fight he has to win, and he pulls out the saucer from under his cup and brandishes it around, barely missing his cup. Finally, the fly is gone. With a satisfied smile, Chris looks at his visitors.

The room which would be Peter's is locked, its occupant is out, but Clive's room is its mirror image, and he agrees to show it to them. The room reeks of cigarette smoke like a disco bar. On the bed, a war of pillows, blankets and magazines, while on the floor is the rest of Clive's life: an open packet of cigarettes, underpants, socks, and a half full mug of coffee.

'It's a big room,' says the volunteer, 'with less stuff on the floor.'

The clean and tidy kitchen is a nice surprise. In the middle, a table with six chairs and a pace away, a big fridge with a padlock on the door. The sight of it stops Peter in his tracks.

'We open it at mealtimes,' the volunteer says, 'in between, you'll just have to ask for the key. I promise you; you'll never be hungry here.'

The visit over, they return to the car.

'Think about it,' the social worker says, 'and let me know tomorrow.'

Peter cannot think about anything else. He can still smell the cigarette smoke, see the padlock on the fridge door and his future flatmates. But what's the alternative? His mother's flat?

Outside the rain has picked up. Sheets of water are sliding down the car window, obscuring the road ahead.

-39-

'I saw Peter two days ago. The two of us had lunch in the little café, you know the one, the one opposite the hospital. I think the new medication is working.' There is a high note in Eszti's voice. On the other end of the line, Clara is wondering whether she looks as cheerful as she sounds.

'Yesterday I didn't visit him. By the time I finished with the dentist it was quite late and I decided that I might as well squeeze in a haircut. At my age you can't let your hair grow long, can you?'

'You need to look after yourself, whatever your age.'

'But I did ring the hospital, "he's well," the nurse said, "in fact, well enough to go home within a couple of days." Great news, but where will he live? I asked,' and after a pause, 'Clara, don't judge me. But I can't bear him living upstairs, not after what happened.'

'Why? What happened?' Clara asks, thinking that Eszti was always too attached to Peter, and since he fell sick she wouldn't let him out of her sight. Has the umbilical cord become a burden all of a sudden? Why? And the more scenarios her imagination invents, the more she shrivels. *Surely, he didn't, not his old mother.* She wants to disappear inside herself. She cannot cope with Peter hurting his old mum.

'Apparently, they're trying to get him into a half-way house.'

'A half-way house? But that's great, it might be just what he needs. He will have some company.' Clara tries to inject some optimism in their conversation. 'This hospitalisation could be a blessing in disguise. It might turn his life around.'

'Maybe,' Eszti says, sniffling.

'Maybe both your lives are about to turn the corner.'

'Well … I'll visit him tomorrow. I'll find out what exactly they have in mind for him.'

'Eszti, I have a proposal. I have a day off tomorrow, in lieu of some overtime I worked last month. Why don't I take you out for a light lunch? I know a good place not far from the hospital. Afterwards, I'll take you to the hospital. I won't go in, because I have lots on and I have to pick up Shosh early, but it should make your day easier.'

* * *

Eszti checks herself in the mirror once more. She believes in looking respectable, that all people should try to look respectable, 'You don't dress for yourself; you dress so you don't offend the people around you. They have rights too. They're entitled to pleasant surroundings.' She puts on a touch of lipstick, 'So I don't look like the walking dead,' picks up the two bills she will pay at the post office next to the hospital, then checks her purse for money. Everything is in order; she is ready for the outing.

A few blocks away, Clara gets out of the car to stretch her legs and savour a few quiet moments. It is the end of autumn, and quite cool, but the sun is shining. There is an uplifting feeling in the air and she wants to breathe it in, fill herself with its energy. The camellia bush is in flower. She walks on, past a bush covered with the tiny yellow flowers, past the patches of white and violet pansies soaking up the sunshine. It's a privilege to be alive. She has not felt this good, this energetic, since her holiday. She also feels good because Peter is better, and because she is taking Eszti out for lunch. It should lift her spirits, especially on such a beautiful day. She returns to her car, and not long after she rings Eszti's doorbell. A policeman opens the door. 'Mrs Steinberg?'

'Yes. But what's going on?'

'It's about Peter.'

What now? she is about to ask, but the policeman is leading her to the lounge room and through the open door she can see a crushed Eszti sitting on the sofa, a policewoman by her side.

'Mrs Steinberg,' the policeman says as they walk into the loungeroom, 'I'm afraid we have some bad news …'

240

'Bad news?' *The worst?*

'They found him dead this morning.'

In her mind's eye, Peter is saying goodbye to her and Shosh just a week ago.

'What happened?'

'They found him below a fifth-floor window of the hospital. I am very, very sorry.'

'But, I saw him two days ago,' Eszti tries to bargain, 'he was so well. Even the nurse said that he was well enough to move out.'

'Mrs Steinberg, the mentally ill can be unpredictable,' the policewoman says and puts her hand on Eszti's. She pulls it away like someone not used to being touched. Shoulders stooped; she is staring at the carpet. 'He's dead, he's dead,' she whispers as if trying to convince herself.

Shocked into silence, with Peter's death hanging around the room, Clara's only thought is Shosh. What am I going to tell her? She's not quite six years old and she has to learn about her father's death. No child should be told such news. But I have to, I have to tell her. How? How can I tell her that her father killed himself?

'Can I make you a cup of tea?' the policewoman asks.

Eszti does not want tea, she does not want anything.

'The social worker could tell you more,' the policewoman says and offers to take her to the hospital. Eszti does not want to go to the hospital, not yet, she wants to be on her own. 'Please understand,' she pleads.

A questioning look from the woman officer to her colleague. The man nods, 'OK, we'll come back in an hour, or so, and take you to the hospital.'

Eszti locks the door behind them and returns to the lounge room, and there she sits in silence, lost and confused. Clara looks at her with an odd remoteness. No matter how much she wants to identify with her sorrow, she can't. Eszti's pain is not hers. Hers is Shosh's pain. Shosh's future. Shosh's future?

Clara has grieved for Peter already. She has grieved for the sane Peter, for years. Lately, his absence no longer troubled her, his physical presence did. Still, she would like to comfort Eszti. If only she could tell her the way she sees it: that Peter is better off dead, that he is finally at peace. *Can't Eszti see that?*

A flock of cockatoos is shrieking above the house. Above the sea of Eszti's disbelief. Disbelief at Peter's demise, at his cruel destiny. Disbelief at the futility of the months and years in front of her, the pointlessness of a future. Bent forward, as if she is about to take off and run, she keeps looking at something in front of her. A void, an abyss? A giant black hole? It is pulling her in, ripping her apart. She sits there motionless, frozen in incomprehension.

The cat is scratching at the door, and keeps scratching. Eszti shuffles to the door, slowly, as if with the death of her son, part of her has died too. The cat looks at her questioningly. Is it the smell? The smell of tragedy?

'My beautiful boy, my beautiful boy …' she whispers as she sits down again. 'I have to tell Lilla, I have to tell the others,' but she just sits there moaning.

'Everybody abandoned him. First his friends, and then the rest of the world. Even I abandoned him at the end. I didn't want him to live here. I was afraid of him.'

'He was sick,' Clara says.

'Yes, he was sick,' Eszti says, eyes gazing at something. Memories? Peter? Her son, her only child. The child with the sparkling brown eyes, asking questions, questions which she was not smart enough to answer. The child for whose future she emigrated, for whom she had done every menial job she could get, and later had hemmed and overlocked thousands of dresses and trousers. The grind and the slog. How pointless it has all been. But in front of Clara, there is a different Peter. Walking the street alone, skin sallow, eyes staring in terror at something only he can see. Other times he is talking to her, the erudite conversation, a tirade of religious mantra.

He suffered so much. How long did he suffer? It occurs to her that calendar times are meaningless, felt times, times etched in the psyche are the real times. Happiness is always short, but years of sickness, hallucinations and loneliness must feel much, much longer. How many years did he actually suffer? Five times, ten times, twenty-five times as many years? *But that is Hell itself. No-one deserves such a life. Should I tell Eszti? No, she will work it out eventually.*

The grandfather clock chimes once.

'Eszti, I'll have to go soon, to pick up Shosh. Let's have some lunch first.'

Clara makes a couple of sandwiches and a cup of tea each. Eszti takes a few sips of tea, but she does not touch the food.

'Clara, you'd better go. I'll ring the policewoman not to come. I'll take a taxi to the hospital. I'll be back by the time you and Shosh get here.'

* * *

Sitting on the sofa, her arm wrapped tight around Shosh, Clara is telling her that her father had an accident.

'A very big accident,' she adds after a long pause. 'And he is …' The word's stuck inside her, 'he's …'

'He's what, mum?'

'He's no longer … he's dead,' she says, watching for Shosh's reaction, checking how far she can go, how much she should tell her.

Shosh does not flinch. She just sits in silence. Older than her years, but not old enough to understand what death means. Death and its finality. Not old enough to imagine how her father's death will impact on her and her grandmother. How their world will change.

Later, much later, as if her mother's words have finally reached something inside her, as if she has just become aware of what Clara said, she starts asking questions. She wants to know what happened.

'Shosh, they found him dead this morning.'

'This morning?'

'Yes, early morning.'

'Where?'

Clara's thoughts are racing. Should I tell her?

'Mum, where did they find daddy? In bed?'

'Yes, Shosh.'

'What happened to him?'

'He died in his sleep. The doctors think he had a heart attack. That's all I know. Now let's go and help Grandma.'

Driving along, on the way to Coogee, Clara is mulling over her conversation with Shosh. I will tell her the truth when she's older, when she's sixteen, seventeen. Then she'll be able to deal with what really happened, and as soon as I get to Coogee, I'll talk to Eszti. Swear her to secrecy.

-40-

The maggot of guilt is burrowing into Eszti, devouring her. She used to visit Peter every day, then she visited him every second day. Yesterday, she could have visited him after the dental appointment, but she went to have a haircut. By the time she finished she was too tired to drag herself to the hospital.

Clara tries to calm her. He was under professional care; he was in safe hands. No-one would have visited him every day, those trips to the hospital would have been too exhausting, even for someone much younger. No-one would have done for Peter as much as she did.

Shosh looks at her grandmother confused; she cannot understand what Grandma has done wrong. Could she have stopped the heart attack? Seeing her big questioning eyes, the pain in Eszti's soul is more than she can bear, because Shosh has Peter's eyes, and because Shosh is fatherless now.

'Eszti shouldn't you arrange the funeral?'

'Sorry, what did you say?'

'Shouldn't you arrange the funeral?' Clara says louder this time.

'Yes, the funeral …' and Eszti begins pacing around the kitchen, deep in thought. 'If he's to be buried in the Jewish tradition, because I'm sure that's what he would have wanted when he was still …' She cannot say it, she cannot utter the word, 'he has to be buried within twenty-four hours. Oh my God, I have to find a rabbi straight away.' But there is a complication. The coroner has to confirm that the fall was indeed suicide, and has submitted Peter's body to forensics.

Eszti has been to the hospital. 'I saw him. His face was so tranquil, so beautiful.' She is not religious, or superstitious, but the thought of cutting her son up fills her with terror. She cannot bear its finality, more final than death itself. Nobody is going to cut her son's body up; she will fight it with all her might. She is seventy-two years old and nearly deaf, but she knows how to fight. She has survived the Second World War, emigration, factory work, widowhood, seeing her son disintegrate. She is no shrinking violet.

She dials the coroner's office. She tells them that they can scan, X-ray, measure and photograph, but not cut, unless they want to cut her. The man on the end of the line reassures her that they don't intend to cut, her son will go to his grave with his body whole. Uncut and unblemished.

Relieved, she can now organise the funeral and she wonders out loud whom she should invite, and what else to arrange when the phone rings. It's Cantor Fuchs. He heard of the terrible news and wants to express his condolences. He remembers Peter well, 'What a tragedy, what an enormous pain for you.'

'Thankyou Cantor, thank you so much for ringing,' Eszti manages between the sobs.

She has hardly put down the phone when it hits her, how come she didn't think of it? She should have asked the Cantor to do the service. He speaks her language, and there is something else, the Cantor is not Orthodox. He will speak to her heart, to her loss. Cantor Fuchs knew Peter, he said such nice things about him.

'Clara, I'm in no mood to listen to the mumbo jumbo of an Orthodox rabbi. I'll ring the Cantor, see if he can do the service.'

'Of course, I'll be honoured,' the Cantor says, 'enormously honoured. He was such a remarkable fellow, such a good man, what a loss.' He will give a wonderful service, he assures her. A heartfelt service. He can barely imagine what she is going through. 'Such a loss.'

Tears roll down Eszti's face.

'Thank you, thank you so much.'

But the time of the funeral is entirely up to the coroner, and they wait for his call.

Finally, the call arrives. 'The body will be released tomorrow morning.'

Now she can firm up the time and she dials the Cantor. Once, twice, three times. The Cantor has vanished.

Sometime later the phone rings, but it's not the Cantor, it's John Dexter. Eszti is about to slam down the receiver, but not before she gives him a piece of her mind. Tell the charlatan that he will not extort money from Peter again, no matter how convincing his stories are.

'Not unless you follow him to the after world.'

'What?'

'He's dead. Dead! Do you understand? You swindler. You fraud!'

'Mrs Steinberg! …'

'Don't Mrs Steinberg me, just leave me in peace.'

'I rang to say that I have the money. I want to pay him my debt. He helped me when I was in big trouble, he was a good man.'

'Oh, leave me alone,' she says, tears flooding her eyes.

'When did it happen?'

'Yesterday. Goodbye.'

'When is the funeral?!'

'Tomorrow.'

'I'll be there,' John Dexter manages to squeeze in.

'Don't you dare!' and Eszti slams the receiver down.

'Who was it?' Clara asks.

'John Dexter. I don't know where they met, all I know is that he slept upstairs one night. And Peter gave him money, I suspect he gave him all his savings.'

'He was a generous man.'

'Too much so.'

'He always gave to charities' Clara says. 'Not peanuts, but serious sums.'

It is nearly five o'clock. Eszti has finally tracked down the Cantor.

'Tomorrow's fine,' the Cantor says. 'Two-thirty tomorrow. I'm booked out the rest of the day.'

'OK, two-thirty. Can we talk about the speech?'

'Not now, I'm late for an urgent appointment. I'll ring you later.'

Six o'clock, seven o'clock. No word from the Cantor. Eszti is beside herself.

'Don't worry,' Clara tries to calm her, 'he'll ring tomorrow.'

'What if something happened to him?'

'Nothing happened to him, he's just busy. Eszti, have a shower and try to get some sleep. We'll have to go now.'

* * *

It's long past midnight, but Eszti can't sleep. She is thinking about Peter's last hours. Could she have prevented it? She might have, but for how long? This sickness often ends in suicide. Poor Shosh, only six years old and now fatherless. Clara was right not to tell her how he died.

Shosh. How will she remember her father? Will she remember him as he once was, or only the recent him? Only the insane man? Is that what she will take with her into the future? Will she live with an image of her mad father for the rest of her life? The pain is too much for Eszti to bear. Her thoughts shift to the funeral. Has she invited everybody? She goes through the list of names again.

The next morning, soon after nine o'clock, the Cantor is on the phone.

'I'll meet you at the Chevra Kadisha, and we'll talk about the speech. Don't worry, everything will be fine. What a terrible day for you.'

As she puts the phone down, it occurs to her that he has no set fees, he gets what people give him. Charity. *How much shall I give him? I should talk it over with Clara,* and Eszti begins getting ready. She will look presentable for Peter's farewell, and she puts on her best suit. She looks around, *what else? Oh, my hearing aid.*

The doorbell rings. It's Clara and Shosh.

Midday, Clara sets the table, and they sit down to eat. Eszti takes a couple of spoonfuls of soup and starts crying, 'Today is my son's funeral.'

Shosh strokes her hand, 'Gran, please don't cry.'

* * *

Two dozen or so people are waiting in the hall of the Chevra Kadisha, but all Eszti can see is the coffin. On the pedestal, inside that wooden box, covered with a navy velvet drape, with the sparkling golden Star of David, is Peter's body. *This is a nightmare. A grotesque nightmare.* But the wreath of irises and white carnations leaning against the coffin is the one she ordered yesterday, and the man in a dark suit talking to a small group of people is Cantor Fuchs, and in the corner is the hospital registrar, Peter's doctor. *No, this is not a dream, this is for real.*

A man walks up to Cantor Fuchs, and taps him on the shoulder. He looks back at the people in the hall and seeing Eszti, he rushes to kiss her hand. 'I've prepared the speech. I just need a few details. Your only son?'

'Yes,' Eszti whispers.

'If I remember, he was a scientist?'

'Yes.'

'Good man, educated man,' mutters the Cantor as he scribbles in his small notebook.

In the hall a sudden silence. People are taking their seats. The Cantor looks up from his notes, 'I have to go. Don't worry, everything will be fine. It will be the most beautiful goodbye.'

Eszti looks at him baffled, but the Cantor has no time for questions. He has to start the service. The congregation stands, Eszti the shortest among them. Next to her Clara, her arm around Shosh. The sound of an ancient prayer resounds in the hall. The Cantor's baritone voice leads the way. Some people murmur along. Eszti stands in silence, she does not understand Hebrew, not a word. From time to time, she turns to the woman next to her to ask where the congregation is up to in the prayer book, then tries to follow the English translation on the left page of the book.

The prayer finished; the Cantor climbs the stage.

'We mourn the passing of a good man, a proud father, and a gentle and loving husband.'

A gentle and loving husband? ponders Clara. Yes, he was gentle and loving once, but that was years ago. Why doesn't he mention his suffering? Why doesn't he say that life is unfair, that you the people before me, you can have the strongest faith, you can obey the religious laws, it will not help you. It won't help you any more than it did those ancient people bribing their Gods with their offerings. Why doesn't he say that some people end up living a nightmare, no matter how strong their faith is? The man in that coffin happens to be one of them. A loving husband? Images of their last year of marriage play before her eyes. She feels like screaming, Nooo!! No, you lazy bastard! You can say anything, anything, but not lies which deny human suffering, lies which deny the fear of a young child. Such lies should never be said, not even at a funeral.

'An educated man. An honest man, a loving son and father, an educated man.' He coughs.

'A good husband, a father for whom nothing was too much when it came to his child, an educated man.'

Eszti is crying silently, Clara's left arm around her. The two of them stand together, one nursing her pain, the other thinking of years ago and what might have been. Seeing him alive had been more painful to Clara than looking at his coffin. She is worried about Shosh. Very worried. Right arm around her, Clara squeezes her tight. Shosh does not respond. She is silent. Vacant?

The service over, the coffin is loaded into the black limousine, and Peter's last journey begins. The autumn sun follows him. Weak and sad, it too seems to be saying goodbye.

Later, in the cemetery, as they are standing around the freshly dug grave, 'Oh my God!' Eszti cries out as if she has seen a ghost. 'That charlatan,' she points to a man hurrying towards them, 'that charlatan has to disturb my peace, even here.'

John Dexter nods to Eszti and stops at the left of the group.

Standing close to her mother, trying to become one with her, Shosh's gaze follows the coffin as it is lowered into the grave. 'Goodbye,' Clara whispers and throws in a red rose. The men start shovelling. The sound of earth landing on Peter Steinberg's coffin, more and more remote, drums in a symphony petering out. Then silence.

Cantor Fuchs looks at the small group. Four men and eight women. Four men? Five with the new arrival. Without the obligatory ten men, he cannot recite the prayer for the dead.

'Don't worry, we'll do it anyway. Everybody join in,' and he begins … The men whisper along, followed by the women's illegitimate utterings and John Dexter's embarrassed mutters.

'I don't want to intrude,' John Dexter says as they are about to leave, 'I don't know your tradition, but can I say a few words please?'

The Cantor looks at him puzzled. 'Go on then.'

'I met Peter when I was in trouble. I was unemployed, I had been cheated by the very people I trusted. They robbed me of my money. I lost trust in people, and I was homeless. I was homeless and Peter offered me his bed. I was penniless and Peter gave me money. He gave me money to buy a Christmas present for my young daughter. I knew he was not well, but he had a good heart, a better heart than anybody I know. I will never forget him, not till my dying day.

'I rang him yesterday to thank him for what he's done for me. And to repay my debt. I was too late. Mrs Steinberg, here's the money I owed him.'

'You don't have to, John, your debt doesn't count any more, nothing counts anymore.'

'Please, use it for his daughter. May God bless her.' He puts an envelope in Eszti's hand and departs.

'It was a good funeral,' Eszti says in the car, on the way back. Her face white, tired. 'And John Dexter? Who would have thought he is such a decent fellow?'

<h1 style="text-align:center">-41-</h1>

Emotionally and physically exhausted, Clara can't stop thinking, can't stop her mind rerunning the events of the last two days. Over and over again, the police, the funeral, Eszti. But the conversations with Shosh nag at her most. Could she have done it better? How? She has no idea. Suddenly her thoughts are back to the same question, why did he do it? The nurse said they were about to release him, that he was quite well. 'He was well enough to move to a half-way house. Maybe he didn't want to go there, maybe he was too frightened of change. Long term sickness kills confidence. It diminishes flexibility, the ability to adapt. But I'm only speculating. How would anyone know what made him do it?'

What if the nurse is right, what if moving to the half-way house had been the last straw? Did they force him out? Did they force him out because they had no beds? Because of a shortage of non-acute beds? Because of the Heal in Place initiative? Her insides twist in horror. *No, I am not going to assume this guilt. The new initiative was not my idea, I only wrote the speech.*

Maybe he was well enough to realise that his life was not worth the struggle, the struggle to tame his nightmares, the struggle to avoid getting in trouble, causing mayhem. Maybe he'd had enough of doctors, pills, hospitals, ambulances, police. Maybe he took his life because to him, it was the only rational thing to do. For years now, his life had been a lonely and frightening existence in a nonsensical world. A beautiful day, just another day of suffering. Music only a noise. He had the right, and he had the courage to do it.

Heavens above! One day I'll have to explain all this to Shosh.

Dawn is breaking, a whole hour before she'll have to get up and start her chores. But she is too anxious to lie there, too anxious to be indoors. She has to get out of the house, she has to clear her mind. She jumps out of bed. Shorts and T-shirt on, she checks on Shosh. Shosh is peacefully asleep, and Clara heads out for a walk.

The street is deserted. The sun is on its way to the summit. A bird calls. A car drives past, its pungent, ugly exhaust hangs around long after the murmur of the engine has died. A loud whoosh. A man on a bicycle rides past and disappears over the hill. The birds chorus bursts forth again. She walks on. Past houses, neat gardens, carefully cut hedges.

Over the road, two crested pigeons are pecking at the ground. 'They are bound for life,' Peter said to her once, 'just like us.' She had been bonded to him ever since she met him. First as a lover and a wife, and later … Later as what? What was her status when the worry and fear for him took over her thoughts? It turned her into an insomniac, it made her pray for his future, when she had never prayed before. Because she loved him, in spite of what happened in the past. She loved him, but not as a woman loves a man, more as a mother loves her sick son, or as an older sister loves a troubled younger brother. She treasured the good days they had together, those distant memories. She guarded them so as not to be drowned by what followed.

Suddenly it hits her. She no longer has to worry whether he is all right, she no longer has to worry what will happen to him in the years to come. She will never again freeze in terror at the sight of a tramp picking leftovers from a rubbish bin, because that tramp will not be Peter. He will be some miserable being, but at least not Peter. *It's over and I am free. Free!* She wants to scream, *Freee!* She feels so light, she can near enough fly. If the world is the sum total of all the joy and pain on this Earth, today's world is better than yesterday's, because Peter's pain and demons are no longer part of it. That's why the sun is shining, that's why the sky is so brilliant, that's why the birds are chirping so joyously. It's a celebration.

She too is celebrating. She walks past a house, then another. Next to the fence, a eucalyptus tree has shed its bark and on its trunk the insect scribe has written something. She caresses the unintelligible inscription. What does it say? How many years, how long before these scribblings will vanish? Scribblings. Writings. Briefing notes, Minister's speeches.

Did I contribute to Peter's death?

-42-

Many sunsets have caressed Peter's grave by the time Eszti has rid herself of guilt, and grown to accept Peter's fate. The battle has aged her far more than the passage of time could have.

She shrank into herself, her hair turned white. Nowadays, she lives only for Shosh, she lives for their walks on Coogee Beach, their long conversations. Shosh has always shown an understanding beyond her age, and now that she is eleven years old, she is especially good company. They meet some weekends and during school holidays. Today she is in Coogee again. It's Good Friday, and one of her friends is coming to visit.

Eight hundred miles away, in Tasmania, Clara and Jeff are walking around Coles Bay.

It is a crystal-clear morning. The bay is silent. Every now and then the sound of a gentle slap against a moored boat, then it is back to its previous calm.

'What beauty, what tranquillity. Jeff, let's sit down for a while. Take it all in.'

She has come to love him. He is sane, their love is sane, so different from the mad intensity of alternating happiness and desperation in her last years of marriage to Peter. It is even, calm, profound. She and Jeff are different, but different like two pieces of a jigsaw complementing each other.

Whoosh! A bird flaps above, almost skimming their heads. Startled, Clara pulls closer to Jeff. He puts his arms around her. Oh, those strong arms, she could stay in their embrace forever.

'Clara, we've known each other for five years. Don't you think it's time to make a decision about our future?'

She has been thinking of nothing else for months, but the endless dialogues for and against moving to Tasmania have only paralysed her into indecision.

'I'd like you and Shosh to move here, I want us to live as a family. I want that more than anything. But forget what I want, what do you want?'

'But what about Shosh? What if she doesn't settle here? Some plants wither when transplanted.'

'In a year she'll start high school. She'll have to change schools anyway. Some of her friends will move on. Didn't you say that one of them has already moved to the other side of Sydney?'

'And Eszti? What about Eszti?'

'And what about you? Don't you have a right to a life?'

'Yeeeee,' a bird calls.

'You heard it. You have no choice now.'

She laughs.

'Oh Jeff. It's so hard,' she says looking at him. That face has become so dear to her.

'Shosh will adjust, she'll make friends, she gets on well with Olly.'

'I'll think about it. Give me one more week, please.'

Back in Sydney she goes through the for and against list again.

Her new job is excruciatingly boring. Marina has moved back to Europe, to Germany, 'for a more interesting job, the snow, the mountains, and to be half a planet away from Maurice.'

If not for Jeff's nightly calls, if not for my trips to Tasmania, I'd drown in loneliness. The only reason for living in Sydney is Shosh. But isn't Jeff right? In a year Shosh will start high school. She will have to change schools anyway.

The alternative to her current life is Jeff, love, family, fresh air, beautiful beaches. It will do wonders for Shosh. Every Tasmanian holiday has given her a blush of health. But will she get used to living there? Why wouldn't she? Families do move, children change schools. They adapt.

The night before she is due to give Jeff an answer, her choice is clear. They will move, but not before the end of the school year. She is about to pull in the curtains, when her gaze stops on the star-studded sky. 'Some are dead now,' Peter whispers in her ear. 'Yes, some are dead,' and she pulls the curtains in. On the world and her past life.

And so, a few months later, Clara and Shosh move to Tasmania. Shosh starts the last year of primary school and Clara settles down to a simple life, tutoring French and English Year 12 private students, and helping Jeff with the farm.

* * *

It is the first Sunday of the fruit picking season. Clara and Jeff have been up since dawn. Looking at the blue sky, the distant horizon, the trees laden with apples rosy as a baby's cheeks, Clara thanks nature for crafting such perfection, and life for giving her a second chance at happiness.

By the time they are back from the field, Shosh, a late morning riser, is up. Jeff's daughter, Olly, is there too, having arrived on Friday night for a weekend visit. She is bursting with news. She came second in the cross-country running competition, but only by four seconds. 'I'll bet you, I'll come first next year.'

Clara looks at her new family, comforted and happy. A few weeks ago, she and Jeff spent a weekend in Sydney, but how relieved she was on Monday when they caught the flight back to Tasmania. Has she become a country girl? Or is Sydney just an album of bad memories, a city of loneliness among all those people rushing around? Of meaningless work? Or does she need to be away from Sydney so she can bury her memories under layers of a different life?

She has achieved contentment with the most unlikely man. As a history teacher, he reminds her of her father, but while her father had two left hands, Jeff is a fixer of things, he can fix his car just as easily as he can install an electric switch or repair the fence around the farm. But he is also the man who astounds her with his original interpretations every time they see a movie, or a play in Hobart.

The past is receding, is losing sharpness, and yet, whenever she walks past a homeless man there is Peter again, starring at something only he can see. Sorrow sets into her soul, a painful, dark sorrow which at times lingers into the night. A shadow of sadness follows her dreams, and the next morning she wakes up depressed.

Given time, a river can polish pebbles, can wash away weeds, shouldn't time wash away her troubled memories?

<h1 style="text-align:center">-43-</h1>

One year passed since they moved to Tasmania and Clara is getting ready for tonight's celebration. Standing in front of the mirror, she is combing back her unruly hair, when Jeff walks in. He stops behind her. Their faces reflect back from the mirror, two faces one body.

'Darling, wasn't the move to Tasmania the best decision of your life? You look so healthy, so beautiful.'

'It was because you're handsome. And I love handsome men.'

'I don't like that plural of yours.'

'A generalisation from the particular,' and she turns around to kiss him. Smiling eyes shining with happiness. But then her face turns pensive.

'If only Shosh would smile more often, if only she would laugh the way she used to … Remember that loud, wholehearted laughter?'

'Worth bottling.'

'If only she was her old self, my life would be perfect.'

'She will be, you'll see.'

Clara is not convinced. Shosh has not made any friends, not even with Olly. On weekends, when Olly comes to stay, the two girls barely talk to each other. Shosh's retiring character and quiet interests cannot match Olly's boundless energy and zest for life.

Olly is a year younger than Shosh, but there is much more to their difference. She is a tomboy; her life takes place outdoors. On hot afternoons, when they go out for a dip in the ocean, Olly, a top swimmer, runs into the water and off she goes riding the waves, while Shosh sits on a mat reading a book. From time to time, she interrupts her reading to go for a short swim. Although a good swimmer, Shosh never strays far from the beach and before long she is back reading.

Olly is a child of the ocean, but also of the forest. She likes climbing trees, catching fish in the creek, observing the birds. She picks flowers and leaves just to feel their texture. In the evening, she pleads with Jeff to go and watch the possums or follow the sounds of the night, and no matter how tired he is, Jeff has to give in.

Shosh too likes the outdoors, but for her the trees are not there for climbing, not for proving physical prowess, but to sit in their shade and read. Or dream. She looks at plants and animals from a distance, she has no need to pick a flower to feel its petals, or stroke an animal, any more than she has to stroke a curtain, or a carpet. Nature is her home, a background to her life.

So, the much-hoped-for friendship with Olly – a cheerful girl, earthy and confident – never took off. Mediocre at school, but very popular, she has never met anyone like Shosh, withdrawn and aloof. She looks at Shosh with a sort of quiet intolerance and avoids her whenever she can.

Shosh might not have adjusted socially, but she is doing outstandingly well at school and Clara tries not to worry. But the sad look which takes hold of Shosh's eyes at times, fills Clara with unease.

* * *

It's autumn. In the garden, the leaves of the Pin Oak tree, a multitude of colours from yellow to red, are spiralling to the ground at the slightest breeze. Jeff and Clara are outside, cleaning the path. The cool, crisp air, the smell of the dry leaves, is so invigorating that given the time she would spend the whole day outdoors. 'Why doesn't Shosh help? Or go out? Why is she always inside? Even on Sunday?' And Clara returns to the lounge room to check on her.

'Shosh aren't you going out? It's so beautiful out there.'

Shosh looks up from her book. 'What did you say?'

'Aren't you going out?'

'Where would I go?'

'You could meet up with one of the girls who dropped in the other day.'

'I don't think they like me, and I don't especially like them.'

'Pity.'

Shosh looks back at her book and Clara turns around to go.

'Mum!'

'Yes.'

'Mum, why did you take me away from Sydney? I was happy there.'

This is hardly news to Clara, but she is pleased that Shosh has finally opened up, that she wants to talk about it.

'Shosh, you can go back to Sydney once you finish high school. You can go to a university in Sydney.'

Shock, and disbelief on Shosh's face, 'But that's years away.'

'Yes, it is,' and even Clara is surprised how uncompromising she sounds. Her heart aches at Shosh's unhappiness, but can she let a teenager rule her life? Rule their lives?'

'I can't wait that long. This place is killing me!'

'Shosh, don't be a drama queen. I know it's hard to be without a close friend, but you have classmates, and you have us.'

'I don't have anything here. Nothing! I'm going back to Sydney to live with Grandma.'

'Don't even think of it. You can't disturb her peace. She's not young and she suffers from high blood pressure.'

'Then I'll live on the street. Anywhere, anywhere is better than here.'

'And how will you study for the exams? Or you want to drop out of high school?'

'I can't stand it here!' Shosh screams and runs out of the room sobbing uncontrollably.

Shosh does not mention the topic again. During school holidays, she flies to Sydney for a week to catch up with friends and spend time with her grandmother – under strict instructions to obey and help her. She returns looking withdrawn, hardly ever volunteering what she did in Sydney. Clara doesn't want arguments, she doesn't probe, she lets her be. Chances are that Shosh had a good time, but she can hardly bear Shosh's remoteness. It fills Clara with disquiet, angst.

'Changing cities, it's hard for anyone, let alone a teenager,' Jeff said to her after Shosh's latest trip. 'Still, families do move, and teenagers adjust. Shosh might take longer than most, but she will settle down eventually. At least I hope she will.'

-44-

It is the end of February; the fruit picking season starts in a couple of weeks. This year the farm has yielded an unusually big crop and Jeff is wondering whether Olly and Shosh could help out or should he hire someone? Clara does not want to involve the girls. 'They are busy with schoolwork, especially Shosh, now that she's in year eleven.'

Tall and slim, she is a budding beauty. Every now and then a school mate drops in. Boys come once or twice then disappear, girls turn up on occasions. There is a dissonance between Shosh and them, like instruments playing the same tune, but not synchronising, not quite in time. And with every passing day Clara can't escape the growing realisation that Shosh is too different to ever find a soulmate among them.

The heatwave, which began two days ago, shows no signs of abating. As she often does these days, Shosh has locked herself in her room. Clara, holding a plate of berries in her hand, knocks on her door.

There is no answer. She knocks again.

'Shosh, please open the door.'

'Shosh!'

Shosh opens the door, tears running down her face.

'Oh my God! What's wrong?' Clara tries to hug her.

Shosh pulls away.

'What's wrong, Shosh?'

'I can't take this place; I can't live here.'

'What happened?'

'Nothing happened. Nothing!!! That's the problem. Can't you see that I'm lonely? Are you blind? You have Jeff, but what do I have here?'

'A family!'

'What family?'

'Shosh, Jeff is not your father, but he cares about you a great deal. And this family, with all its limitations, is better for you than having no-one, but me. Three opinions at the dinner table are more interesting, merrier than two. In Sydney you depended on me too much, on my moods, on what happened to me at work. We reinforced each other too much.'

'Mum, I tried to get used to this place, only the Heavens know how much I tried. Now I know for sure that Jeff will never be my father, no matter how hard he tries. He'll never be my father, because no-one can replace my father. And Olly? It's no-one's fault that we're so different. We avoid each other. I'm a rock in her path, and she's no more than a piece of noisy furniture to me. I miss Grandma and I miss Sydney. There's no life here for me. I want to be where there's life, I want to be close to Grandma, she has no-one. She's so lonely. And I want to be close to my father's grave. It's strange, but visiting his grave calms me, it gives me peace, a sort of peace I don't find anywhere else.'

'I understand, Shosh.'

'No, you don't. And you never will.' The anger on her face stabs at Clara's heart.

'Don't worry, I haven't turned him into a saint. I haven't forgotten his violent outbursts, the packing, the running, the hotel rooms. But there was another side to him,' Shosh says sobbing, 'when he was alright, when he told me stories, explained things to me. I remember how he listened to me as I chattered about school. About my friends. I miss him. You don't miss him, you never even mention him, you want to condemn him to oblivion. It doesn't work, mum.'

'I only want us to forget the violence and the fear. I want us to remember him as he once was, before he got sick. Remember the real Peter.'

'You can't dictate to me what I should or shouldn't remember. Not to me, not even to yourself. You cannot heal when you can't talk about it.'

'I never forbade you to talk about him.'

'I don't want to talk to you about him. You only want me to be happy, happy as if nothing ever happened, nothing ever broke, nobody ever died. We had one family, now we have another family. Is that what you think?

'You want my pain to disappear? Well, I can't make it happen. OK?! And don't ever say to me that we moved here to have a family. We moved here so you can be with Jeff. You moved here out of your selfish motives.'

'Yes, I moved here to be with Jeff, and to get out of Sydney. I had to get away from everything which happened to us there. I had to get away from my old life and I thought it would also help you. Shosh, we talked about it already, you're not imprisoned here, you can move back to Sydney when you finish high school.'

'Don't worry I will. I've been thinking of nothing else. That's why I'm studying so hard. That's why I'm doing so well at school, because I know that my life depends on getting into a university in Sydney. And as soon as I do, I am out of here. Now I'd better get back to my studies.'

Clara walks out of the room, crushed. Crushed by Shosh's unhappiness, crushed by not being able to see a way out of their situation. Leave Jeff? Move back to Sydney? Start all over again? Destroy Jeff? Jeff, who removed the web of loneliness which surrounded me for years, Jeff who brought light and joy back into my life when I thought it no longer possible? How could I live without him?

'You moved here out of your selfish motives,' Shosh said. Is this true? Be honest, is this true? It is, but only partly. I wanted to bring Shosh up in a family, give her, if not a father, someone who would love her and care for her, someone she would one day love back, appreciate. 'You moved here out of your selfish motives.' Shosh's words jolted her and not only the words but the resentment, the hate on her face. How did Shosh get to that? Shosh, the most loving daughter she could have hoped for? What have I done? Maybe I don't deserve Shosh's love, but I deserve some recognition for my struggles. The struggles to protect her, to give her a good childhood in spite of all the hurdles. A bright girl, how come she can't see any of that? Why is she trying to rob me of the only thing I put all my energy into, the only thing I never compromised on, motherhood.

She tells herself off, 'Shosh is unhappy and unhappy people are not rational.' But Clara cannot help the cold bitterness inside her.

After that argument Shosh retreats into herself. She has a lot to think about: life, death, her father, her grandmother, family. 'Family what family?' she keeps asking herself, feeling painfully alone.

Nowadays, the light in her bedroom is on into the small hours. Night after night Shosh sits at the desk studying, refusing to give in to tiredness, urging herself on. Soon you'll be out of here, soon you will cease to be a reminder of what happened to your father. You will cease to be a ghost of the past.

-45-

The exams are only two weeks away and for Shosh they cannot come soon enough.

It is past ten o'clock. Jeff and Clara have gone to Hobart. Still feverish from the flu, Shosh packs her books away and heads to the lounge room to watch television. On the commercial channel a policeman is setting up a crime scene, as a body is taken away. *Cops and murders!* and Shosh flicks across to the ABC. *Jackpot!* On the screen awe-inspiring pictures of stars and the planets. It is a program about the cosmos and Shosh keeps watching it, transfixed.

'The universe is infinite,' the astronomer says.

'Infinity,' Shosh whispers. Infinity fascinates her. How can one divided by zero be infinity? The question has intrigued her for a while. One divided by one is one, one divided by a tenth is ten, by a thousandth is one thousand. As that number becomes smaller, the result of one divided by it becomes big, bigger, immense. And if the number is zero, the result is infinity. The infinity which overlaps the stars, the sun, and the living. The infinity which engulfs all life, from the grass to the cherry blossom, from the laughter of children to the misery of the lonely. All the pain in the universe, all the weeping and crying. the happy anticipations, the dark disappointments, aging, starvation, friendships, great ideas, brilliant conversations, the dance and the music. How can that be?

It occurs to her that no-one she knows asks such questions. Why? *I must have inherited this interest in maths and the cosmos from my father. But what else did I inherit from him?* She breaks into a cold sweat.

It is not the first time that she has asked this question. It is not the first time that the horror movie of her possible future rolls before her eyes. Then follow the sweat, the stiffening of the muscles, the dread, the difficult breathing. She tries to calm herself. *So, what if I did inherit it? What can I do about it? Pray? What did praying do for my father?*

She turns the TV off and crawls into bed, and there she lies in the darkness, alone with her fear. No, she cannot see a way out. *So, what should I do? Kill myself?*

She keeps tossing and turning, but the fear and the pain inside her will not abate.

It is well past midnight when an idea comes to her. I can do something! Something more useful. I can fight for the rights of the mentally ill, I can fight for justice. That's it! That's what I'm going to do. I will not study science; I will study law, and I will do some good in this world. Calm settles over her. In the garden the chorus of cicadas has reached the high register. *Could the laughter of a little girl fill the universe with hope, could it make the stars twinkle? Are there infinities within infinities?*

And Shosh falls into a deep slumber.

<h1 align="center">-46-</h1>

True to her word, Shosh moved to Sydney as soon as she finished high school. She enrolled in a law degree. Her studies were not taxing, she had time to socialise, make new friends, even earn some money from casual waitressing. When she arrived home for the Easter weekend, Clara could not be more pleased, Shosh had turned into a beautiful happy young woman.

But now in her second year, the parties are over, her course much more demanding and Shosh feels pressed for time, her visits home are rarer and rarer, shorter and shorter.

Clara can't help noticing that Shosh is growing away from her. Is life always a trade? You can have happiness, but only if you pay for it, only if you trade something in, only through loss? She has given up her father and her native land for Peter. Has she given up Shosh for Jeff?

Shosh rings home occasionally and when she does there is no warmth in her words, just cold duty. But even her sense of duty seems to be waning. So, Clara rings her, always apologising for disturbing her. She does not want to tell her how much she misses her. Shosh does not seem to be in a receptive mood for motherly love.

Clara can't stop worrying about her. Every time there is a big storm in Sydney, or in the summer when the temperature climbs into the high thirties, every time the radio reports a major accident in Sydney, Clara panics, 'I hope Shosh's all right.'

* * *

Three weeks have passed since their last phone conversation.

'Shosh? It's so nice to hear your voice. How are you, darling?'

'I'm fine. Grandma's less so.'

'Why? What happened?'

'She had a stroke. She's alive, but her memory is gone. So, it's not all bad,' she laughs.

'Is she in hospital?'

'No, not anymore.'

'She's at home?'

'No, she's not well enough to live on her own. I had to put her in a nursing home. Just as well she gave me power of attorney, otherwise I don't know what I would have done.'

'You never told me.'

'I never told you what?'

'That she gave you power of attorney.'

'Why would I? That's wholly between her and me.'

Silence.

'When was the stroke?'

'Two weeks ago.'

'And why didn't you ring me?!' Clara erupts. Then adds in a whisper, 'I just want to help.'

'There was no need.'

'I'll come and visit.'

'Why don't you come at Christmas? Then I won't have to come to Tasmania.'

'I didn't know that it was such an imposition.'

'Well, it is. Nowadays the Christmas holiday is my only time off.'

Her only time off? Even so, most people spend those days with their family, but Shosh does not believe in our family.

Clara is still pondering her conversation with Shosh as she recounts it to Jeff in the evening.

'At times I have the impression that she wants to detach herself from us completely. Why?'

Jeff rubs his forehead. His face, old and weary, stabs at Clara's heart.

'I think there's more to her resentment than growing up, she's no longer a teenager,' and after pausing for thought, 'I don't want to persuade you one way or another, but in my opinion, you should visit her when it suits you.'

A few days later, holding her breath, Clara dials Shosh's number.

They agree to meet mid-January.

-47-

The cheap café was Shosh's choice, 'It's all I can afford,' she said.

It's full of young people, mostly students. Why was she so adamant that I should not buy her dinner? wonders Clara as she sits waiting for her. Erect another fence between us? And why do Shosh's words can cut through my heart? She is still searching for answers when Shosh, wearing a T-shirt and jeans split at the knees, walks in. A couple of heads turn towards the beautiful young woman, then to Clara, who gets the prize: a hug.

While they are waiting for the food, Shosh volunteers that her studies are demanding, but not very interesting. She looks a little detached, even sad, but every now and then glimmers of good company shine through. The conversation moves to Eszti, 'She's in a reasonably good place. All she needs is some clothes.'

Early afternoon, the next day, armed with a shopping bag of clothes, Clara rings the intercom of the nursing home, dread inside her at what and whom she will find. The intercom voice is annoyingly cheerful, but it does the trick, the door opens then snaps shut behind her.

Inside, a corridor of silence sandwiched between two rows of equally spaced grey doors, all shut. She turns the corner and there is Eszti, wearing clothes which would fit a much bigger woman, holding the handrail. Alone, lost. Upon hearing steps, she looks up, vacant eyes sparking suddenly. 'Oh Shosh! I'm so glad you came.'

'Eszti, I'm not Shosh. I'm Clara. Remember me? Clara, Shosh's mother.'

'Clara?' Eszti looks at her stunned, then bursts out laughing. 'Shosh, Clara, I'm glad you're here.'

Behind them a door opens. 'Ester love, your room is the third on the right, isn't it? Now be a good girl and take your guest there,' the nurse says as she walks past.

Arm in arm, they head down the corridor towards Eszti's door. She stops suddenly and looks at Clara:

'They left me here. All of them. Even he left me. Without one word.'

'Who left you?'

'My husband.'

'He died, Grandma, he was very sick.' Grandma rolls off her tongue naturally. The Eszti in her mind is still the feisty, energetic woman of once.

'Died?' Eszti stares at her in shock.

'Many, many years ago,'

Disbelief on Eszti's face, 'Died?' she asks again.

'Yes Grandma. Now let's go.' And the two of them take the remaining steps to her room.

It is clean and tidy. Soulless.

Trying not to look at her nappies, Clara helps her undress.

'I like it,' Eszti says about the skirt. 'But why don't you wear it?'

'I don't need it Grandma, you do.'

'But it would look good on you. Everything looks good on you.'

'I have plenty of clothes. You don't.'

The jacket is too long, perhaps too loud and Eszti does not care for it. Neither does she seem to care for the blouse. But she promises to wear it, then with her old dress back on, she hurries to the bathroom to put lipstick on. Clara shakes her head, *Life, it never ceases to be funny.*

Eszti returns, smiling an orange smile. They pick up the conversation, but nothing Eszti says is a response, a follow up, a reaction to what Clara has said. By the end of the visit, she is utterly drained. Physically, but more so emotionally. Somehow, a world without the real Eszti does not make sense.

'I didn't realise how difficult a visit like that is,' Clara says that evening. She and Shosh are having dinner, sharing a steamy pizza and a salad. 'Shosh, I want to help you, take some weight off your shoulders. From now on I'll come to Sydney once a month and visit Eszti.'

'Thank you, but I don't need help. I'm coping.'

Gazing at the floor, Shosh falls silent. A short while later, she looks up, her face troubled.

'Mum, do you think I should have a heart check?'

The slice of pizza in Clara's hand, stops in mid-air. 'Why? Is something wrong?'

'Just a precaution. In case I inherited dad's weak heart,' Shosh says, staring at her mother. Clara cannot hold her gaze. Her mouth suddenly dry, she returns the pizza to her plate. 'You're too young to have heart problems,' she manages to say.

'So, I shouldn't worry?'

'No, I don't think you should.'

'I shouldn't worry because he didn't die of a heart attack. He killed himself. Didn't he?'

Barely able to breathe. 'He did, Shosh. He did,' she mutters. 'I'm very, very sorry.'

'I thought so. For years.'

'Then why didn't you tell me?'

Shosh shrugs, her face hardened. 'It wouldn't have brought him back, would it? Not that I would have wished on him more suffering.'

Clara wants to hug her, hug her tight like she used to when Shosh was a small child and hurt herself. But there is no seat next to her, and judging by her face, there is no room for her love in Shosh's heart.

'Shosh, the day he died I promised myself to tell you at the end of high school. But you were so unhappy at the time, so Jeff and I decided to tell you once you were in a stable relationship, once you had someone to help you through. Help you more than we can.'

Shosh is sitting pensively. In the middle of the table the pizza is no longer steaming, and neither of them is hungry anymore.

Shosh smiles a sad smile, 'At least it's all cleared now.'

'Yes, it's all cleared.'

Silence. Clara's guilt mixing with Shosh's pain.

'Mum, about tomorrow. I'll be waitressing, but we could meet on Sunday and take Grandma out for lunch.'

It turns out a difficult lunch, Eszti eating, dribbling, laughing loudly for no reason, and with that, Clara's visit to Sydney has come to an end.

On the plane back to Tasmania, she tries to convince herself that it was a good visit. At least we cleared the facts about Peter's death. Shosh seemed to have taken it better than I would have predicted, but one never knows with Shosh. She hasn't been the most affectionate daughter, maybe she will be even less so in the future. But she is studying and working. It could have been worse. Much worse.

After the visit to Sydney, Shosh's phone calls dwindle away again and with every week that passes without hearing from her, Clara is more depressed. Her unhappiness seeps into everything she does, the lessons she gives her pupils, the conversations with Jeff. Sometimes they argue. She always finds excuses for Shosh's behaviour, which more often than not she does not voice, in case Jeff thinks differently. She can't have Jeff saying anything bad about Shosh, judging her. As if Jeff knows, he does not even mention her name, and that upsets Clara too. Is he tired of Shosh, or is it self-preservation?

-48-

Now in her third-year of university, Shosh seems to have mellowed, she rings more often and Clara hopes that the grit in their relationship is settling, the bad times will soon be over.

It is nine-thirty. Jeff has gone to work, and Clara is about to go out shopping when the phone rings.

'Mum …'

'Shosh?!'

'Mum, Grandma had another stroke last night. A final one.'

Ever since she visited Eszti in the nursing home, Clara knew that Eszti wouldn't last years, that she could be gone any time. Yet, she is shaken.

'Shosh, I'm very, very sorry. I know the two of you were very close.'

'Yes. But I wouldn't have wished on her a longer life. Lately, she didn't even recognise me.'

'Oh, Shosh.'

'Well, she's at peace now. Mum, the funeral is tomorrow. If you want to say goodbye …'

'Of course I do. I'll catch the first flight.'

'As long as you're here before twelve.'

* * *

After the funeral Clara remained in Sydney three more days to spend the evenings with Shosh.

277

It is their last evening.

'Mum, I'm doing my third-year project,' Shosh sounds unusually lively and Clara is overjoyed.

'On the government policies for the mentally ill.'

'Oh.'

'Fascinating stuff. The Richmond Report, and the various policies after that,' and after a pause, 'Mum, you worked in the Department of People's Services, didn't you?'

'Yes, long after the recommendations of the Richmond Report were implemented.'

'But there were policy changes during your time, weren't they?'

'There were.'

'Around the time when my father became very sick, I mean in his last year of life?'

'Yes,' Clara says barely audibly.

'Interesting. You told me that you wrote reports, briefing notes and on occasions minister's speeches.'

'Yes, including some about the mentally ill. What services were available and … I can't remember what else.'

'Whatever. Maybe we can chat about it after I finish the research.'

Finish the research? Shosh has been difficult enough and now she is raking up the past. Raking up the past when I've managed to distance myself from it. I even started to hope that luck had finally found us, that we are on the track to a real mother-daughter relationship, to harmony, maybe even love. How wrong I was. My life is only an extension of my old life. A new building on old ruins, on shaky ground.

Back in Tasmania, Clara is preparing dinner, frying pancakes, her thoughts still on her latest meeting with Shosh, when the doorbell rings. She runs to investigate. Two young men in black suits, each with a bible in his hand, are selling after-life happiness. She tells them that she is only interested in earthly happiness and shuts the door.

Is that smoke? She runs into the kitchen. Oh no!

The frying pan is on fire, the flames are about to reach the cupboards.

'Jeeeff! Help!'

Jeff comes running. He turns off the stove, throws the tea towels onto the flames. Not contained, the flames are now poking out around the edges of the towels. 'Clara, a blanket. Quickly!'

Jeff grabs the blanket and throws it onto the stove. The flames are soon smothered but now the blanket is smouldering.

'I nearly burnt down the kitchen,' Clara says, tears running down her face as she sweeps the burnt bits from the floor.

'It's not Eszti's passing, is it? It's Shosh. What happened?'

Clara tells him about her project.

'When Shosh starts on something which interests her, she never gives up. Will she let me be one day?'

'She has to deal with a very difficult past, and make peace with the world. But why shouldn't she work on that project? Any reason?'

'She can work on it, but I deserve some peace.'

'Why don't I talk to her, ask her not to bother you with that topic?'

'I might lose her completely.'

In the coming days while Clara is trying to regain her peace of mind, Shosh is buried in her research. She has to read every government policy relating to the mentally ill, all Hansard transcripts of every discussion which took place in the NSW Parliament in the last twenty years. The more she reads, the more convinced she is that no government cares about the mentally ill. She has no interest or the time to ring her mother, and every time Clara rings her, her phone is either engaged or switched off.

Clara is more and more worried. Worried about Shosh, worried about her research. Where will it all end?

<h1 style="text-align:center">-49-</h1>

As Clara sits down for breakfast, pale, dark circles under her eyes, picking at her food, Jeff's heart sinks again. *It's Shosh, the conflict with her is devouring Clara. Her energy gone, rarely a smile on her lips.* He has thought about that relationship a great deal. He doesn't understand why Shosh rejects her mother so uncompromisingly. She rejects her mother like a body rejects a transplant. Shosh did have a difficult childhood, but that was because of her father's sickness, and she can't blame Clara for that. No, he cannot understand what went wrong between these two women. From now on he would not even try, he would concentrate in helping Clara. She needs to step back, let Shosh cool down. But how? Should I take her for that overseas trip we've been talking about on and off for a couple of years? She could renew her connection with her native land, and I would learn about her roots. Afterwards the two of us could travel around Europe for a couple of weeks. It would be a real holiday and some relief from the unending conflict with Shosh.

Clara is overjoyed at the suggestion, 'Let's think about it and make a detailed plan.'

Evening. They finished dinner and are discussing how to organise three weeks away from the farm, when the phone cuts through.

Shosh has finished her research.

'Mum, I won't beat around the bush. I know why my father killed himself. Grandma told me that the day before he died, they wanted to move him out of the hospital and he didn't want to go. Why? I don't know, maybe he felt sheltered there, or his choices were too dismal.

'Now I know why they wanted to move him out. Because of a shortage of non-acute beds, the result of the government's initiative introduced only weeks before his death. I also know that you worked in the Department of People's Services around the time. That you wrote various documents, including speeches for the Minister. I did the research, I read the transcript of the Minister's speech announcing the initiative. A new dawn for the mentally ill, the Speech said. Well, there was no new dawn for my father. Did you or didn't you write that speech?'

Clara is about to choke. How can she explain to Shosh how it happened? And why? How can she explain to Shosh the struggle between what she had to write and the reality of her life? But in the end, she did write it, she did justify the Minister's proposal.

'I did, Shosh.'

'You didn't tell me. You never mentioned a thing about all that. I know why. You never told me because you have blood on your hands. And not just anybody's blood, you have my father's blood.'

'How dare you say that to me! That policy was not my idea. I only wrote the speech.'

'You only obeyed orders, didn't you? Have I heard that excuse before?'

'Shosh! Shame on you!'

'You gave ammunition to the Minister, you helped him justify his rotten policy, you helped him push helpless people into even deeper misery.'

'But how could I have changed anything? I was only a small cog in that system.'

'A small cog, but without it, the system wouldn't have worked.'

'And you think they wouldn't have found someone else to write it?'

'They would've. That's why the mentally ill are on the street, that's why so many commit suicide, because there are always people like you who are prepared to do the dirty work.'

'Don't be a prima donna, Shosh, or are you that naive? Have you any idea of what it was like to be a single parent in those days? How hard it was to get a job? Especially as a migrant?'

'You should've cleaned houses; you should've cleaned toilets. I would have been proud of you. As it is I'm not only ashamed of you, you disgust me!'

'Have you gone …' Clara shouts.

'Say it, mum. Say it. Ask me. Shosh, have you gone mad?! Ask me!' she screams. 'You can't, can you?! You weak woman. No courage to look reality in the face. Forever pleasing, forever accommodating, forever compromising. Muddling through life.'

'Sorry, it was just a figure of speech. I am very, very sorry.'

'Your sorry is worthless. Your sorry doesn't remove the axe of madness hanging over my head. Do you know what it's like to be afraid? Being afraid every hour of every day? Asking yourself what if? Imagining it constantly. Yes, I fear it. I fear being weird, I fear being alone, I fear being abandoned by the world. If your liver or kidney rots, everybody feels sorry for you, but when your brain goes awry, people mock you. Avoid you as if you're possessed by the devil.'

Clara is silent, she cannot say that she too feared the same thing. For years. That she had many sleepless nights thinking about it. But she knows that she cannot come close to what Shosh feels.

'Shosh, nobody's a perfect copy of one parent.'

'Not a perfect copy, but what about having a perfect copy of a few genes. A few evil genes? Then you're done for, because the world doesn't care, the world wants you to disappear. All those people in government offices, making policies which throw the insane onto the street, don't care. They just keep writing their irresponsible bullshit. They don't know what it's like to be schizo. But you knew, and in spite of it, you joined their ilk. I'll never be able to look at you without remembering your role in my father's death. Never!'

'Shosh, I worked there because I had to make a living. You will understand one day, one day when you have your own kids.'

'I won't have kids. I won't give life the satisfaction of torturing more people, and as far as I am concerned the topic is closed. I've been thinking about it a lot lately. I need time off, off you and Jeff. Off my current life. I want no contact with either of you.'

'Shosh don't ...' But the phone clicks.

The following evening, her heart in her mouth, Clara dials Shosh's number. There is no answer. She rings her the evening after, and the one after. She rings her for two weeks. One day a message says that the number is no longer connected.

Shosh has vanished.

* * *

It is late afternoon. Long strips of clouds are cutting across the fire of the setting sun. Shosh's birthday is coming to an end. Today Clara is missing her more than ever. She will never be whole without her, without her love.

'Let's go,' Jeff says.

They cross the road and walk down the few steps leading to the beach. The sea is one vast darkness. Jeff's arm around her, they stand in silence watching the water. A few metres away, on a rock is a lone seagull, standing erect as if it owns the ocean. The waves come and go. The seagull does not flinch.

Oh, how she would like to be like that seagull. A stone statue. Impervious, unaffected.

'I can't believe Shosh is twenty-two years old today.'

'Clara, you have to go to Sydney, you have to talk to her.'

'Don't you think I would if I thought that she'd talk to me.'

'Try it, see what happens. A bit more hurt? You're hurting anyway.'

'And how will I find her?'

'Try her friends, someone must know where she is.'

'But I don't know her friends, let alone their phone numbers. Besides, the academic year is finished.'

'I'll find you something, let's go home.'

As soon as they are back, Jeff heads to Shosh's room. A few minutes later he is back holding an old notebook. In it, a list of a few names with phone numbers. Phone numbers of her friends from school, friends from years ago, from before they moved away from Sydney.

'And I found this,' he hands her a legal textbook. On the back cover a phone number, and next to it the name Cindy.

'Cindy?' Clara tries to recall. 'I think Shosh mentioned that name to me a couple of times. I'll ring her.'

She is in luck, Cindy picks up the phone. She too has lost contact with Shosh, but she will ask around. She will track her down.

-50-

Clara is barely through Sydney Airport when her phone rings. It's Cindy. She has spoken to a few of her colleagues, they too have lost contact with Shosh, but one promised to make some enquiries straightaway.

'She knows lots of people. There's a good chance she'll find some leads.'

'Thank you. Cindy, please ring me as soon as you hear from her. I'm so worried …'

'Mrs Steinberg, I'm sure Shosh is OK. I'll ring you this afternoon. I might know something by then.'

It is two-thirty. She has a couple of hours to kill, 'Now or never,' Clara says to herself, and calls a taxi.

Half an hour later the taxi turns the corner. She shuffles closer to the window and sits staring at the houses passing by, with the intensity of someone who cannot miss the unusual scenery. But it is not scenery she is looking for, but a house.

Suddenly she leans forward, 'Here! Can you stop here please?'

'Madam, didn't you say number eighty-four?'

'I was mistaken, this looks to be the place.'

The driver shrugs his shoulders, 'As you wish.'

The suburb lies in stupor. There is no-one around, no-one but the summer heat. Heavy, still. It hangs over houses and the silent street. A dog walks past her, tail between his legs.

She could have sworn that Peter lived further up, in number eighty-four, but number sixty-six looks just the place. The same detached, dark-brick building, a hint of a second floor, the same porch, a window on each side. But something does not look right, and she stands there, trying to work out what it is. *It's the front garden!* The house she is looking for was set further back from the street.

She walks on.

Eighty, eighty-two, eighty-four, she reads out the numbers. Eighty-four? But eighty-four is a three-storey block, the only three-storey building for as far as she can see. She walks past it, then past eighty-six, but the next house, the fibro cottage, with a small porch, where a cat is snoozing on a frayed armchair, she remembers well. Suddenly it all makes sense, the house was where the three storey block now stands. It has been demolished, erased. Time has moved on, and a pleased sad smile lights her face. The proof isn't only the building in front of her, but the carefully paired socks pegged on the line, on one of the balconies, the tidily hung shirts, the children's T-shirts. New people, different lives. So very different.

She has been in Sydney many times, but never back to this street, never to this suburb. So why now? Curiosity, a wish to test herself. Could she look back on those years, detached, as a dying man looks at his body? With the calm of an out-of-body experience? She had to see the house; it was a thirst she had to quench eventually. She had to walk down that Coogee street where she and Peter walked so many times. No, it wasn't yesterday that she came here that first time, it was more than two decades ago.

The scorching sun is burning her neck, burrowing into her head. She is tired. She flew into Sydney, dropped her luggage at the hotel and came straight here. She came here to face the past and found nothing but new bricks. *The past's address is only in one's head*, and she turns back.

Walking towards the beach, searching for a place to cool down and have something to eat. Three quarters of the way down the road is exactly what she is looking for. She takes the seat by the window and orders a coffee and a sandwich. From there she can see the cliffs where she and Peter stood all those years ago.

Her thoughts return to Shosh. She cannot imagine not seeing her, not putting her arms around her. Not sharing her life, not getting to know her husband, seeing her children. Shosh's children? 'No, I will not have children,' Shosh has said, 'I won't give life the satisfaction of torturing more people.' Clara didn't know what to say. How could she disagree when deep down she knew that Shosh was right.

She has to find her; she has to talk to her. Shosh might listen this time, she might understand. She is older now; she must be wiser.

It is nearly four o'clock; she has not heard from Cindy. How long should I wait? She sits there for a while longer. More and more worried, she dials her number.

'I was about to ring you,' Cindy says.

'You've got news?'

'I haven't found out much, except that she dropped out of university last year. Pity, she was about to finish her third year.'

'Dropped out? Shosh dropped out of university, why?' Clara asks with a sinking feeling as a memory spirals up inside her.

'I don't know.'

'Do you know what she does now? Where she lives?'

'No.'

'Something must have happened,' Clara says with a sense of foreboding.

'Mrs Steinberg, it's not rare for students to drop out of university.'

But Clara is worried. Why would she abandon her studies? And only one year before graduation? Her mind is nagging her; Peter too dropped out of university.

Suddenly an image. She and Peter stargazing in Amsterdam. They are looking through a telescope, at the night sky. Looking at the stars. 'Some are dead now,' Peter says, 'what you see is the light they emitted billions of years ago.'

'Maybe the past never vanishes, never lets go,' she replied, but now her whole being revolts against those words. It has to vanish; it has to let go.

Has Shosh fallen in with the wrong crowd? Is she taking drugs? No, surely not Shosh. Not Shosh? How many parents can say that they have not been surprised by how their adult children turned out. The baby in the pram with rosy cheeks and a big smile, will never look to his mother a potential emaciated drug addict. Or a robber, or a Nobel prize winner, or a breaker of world records. Imagination does not extend that far. No, she could not be sure of anything, there is no guarantee that Shosh is not in some sort of trouble.

'Mrs Steinberg?

'Mrs Steinberg, can you hear me?'

'Yes. Thank you, Cindy. Thank you very much. If you find out anything else …'

'I'll ring you straight away.'

She has been worried before, but now she is close to panic.

'Would you like another coffee?' the waitress asks.

'Yes please, a strong one.'

Why did she drop out of university? She was a brilliant student. But no matter how much Clara does not want to think about it, memories, associations are hammering her brain. 'No, Shosh is not a carbon copy of her father,' she tells herself again.

And she sits there drinking her coffee, plunged in worry. For a long, long time.

The waitress is stacking the chairs, the café is about to close. What can I do now? Clara wonders, as she pays her bill. The only thing left to do is to ring the phone numbers from Shosh's little notebook. I will track Shosh down, maybe not today, or tomorrow, maybe not even this week, but I will eventually. I won't argue with her. It does not matter that she dropped out of university, as long as she has not fallen into bad company, as long as she is not a junkie. As long as she is not in some sort of trouble, nothing matters.

Back in the hotel, refreshed by a shower, she dials the first number from the notebook. 'Please check the number and dial again.' The answers from the next three numbers are no different. People have moved on; the phone numbers are no longer valid. At the fourth attempt someone picks up the receiver. 'Sorry, I never heard of her,' a man says. The next call is answered by a young woman. 'I think, I knew someone by that name. A couple of years ago?' The other two phone calls are just as inconsequential.

So, what now? But no matter how much she racks her brain she cannot see a way forward. Maybe this is a job for a detective. No, she's not going to hire a detective, she will not spy on her own daughter. She will find her eventually, but if she doesn't … No, this is not an option. She will not give up. Ever.

'Parenthood is a road paved with pain and sorrow,' she says to herself, looking at the fading light. But then a memory. Shosh, a small child, playing, talking, laughing. She and Peter joining in. How happy they all were.

Her gaze shifts back to the room. *Isn't that desk lamp strange? A modern lamp shade on a classic stand.* Its yellow light is falling on a notepad. Next to it a black pen with a golden tip. Absentmindedly, she picks up the pen and starts doodling. The ball point slides on the paper with unusual ease. Shosh, I want to talk to you, she writes. *But would Shosh be any more receptive than she has been in the past?* She keeps scribbling, scribbling and wondering. *Should I write her a letter? No point, I don't have her address.*

She sits there lost in thought. The urge to write to her is egging her on. *You will find out where she lives. You will.* And she pulls out her notebook.

My dear Shosh,

Whether you want to talk to me or not, I will always love you. I did from the moment you were born. The moment I saw you. You were a beautiful child, clever and curious. You brought me and Peter enormous joy. Can you remember how you tormented your father with your endless questions? And the more questions you asked, the more he dug himself into a ditch he could not get out of.

Do you remember our trip to the Royal National Park? You probably can't, you were three years old. Not quite three years old.

It was early summer, the sun bathed the trees. On the branches, tiny blue fairy wrens skipped from branch to branch, jiggled their tails hurriedly for a moment and took off. A lonely dark-blue bird with the tallest thin pair of legs emerged from somewhere. It walked as if on stilts, spindly feet stepped tentatively, bright red beak pecking the mud.

The smell of barbequed meat tinged the air, its smoke spiralling into the sky. We were sitting on a blanket watching a raft of ducks gliding on the water. Oh, we were so happy, all three of us.

'Look daddy, look,' you pointed to the lyrebird walking out of the bush next to you.

'It's a boy lyrebird,' your father whispered.

'How do you know it's a boy?' you whispered back.

'Because of the tail, only the boys have such long beautiful tails.'

'Why don't the girls have a beautiful tail?'

'I don't know, sweetie, that's how nature made them.'

'What's nature, daddy?''

'Everything around you, this forest and its birds, and the animals.'

'Animals? I can't see any.'

'Some are asleep, some only come out when we're not here.'

Two ducks floated down the river. The lyrebird called out then disappeared into the bush.

I unpacked the sandwiches and as we ate, we talked about the birds and the trees, the sky and the clouds, and you kept asking questions and more questions. After lunch, you played with your three faces rag doll. Jenny, Jo, and Louise, remember them? Three children with one body. You would impersonate each one in a different voice while Peter and I couldn't keep a straight face.

Jenny screamed as she fought with Louise:

'Shut up, Louise,' you, pretending to be Jenny, shouted, 'that's not what the teacher said.'

'She did, she did, isn't it, Jo?' you answered, metamorphosed into Louise.

'I don't know,' you answered shyly, for Jo.

The argument was escalating, someone had to intervene. So, you — embodied as Sally, your teacher from the childcare centre, the pretty young woman with a diamond in her nose who wore long skirts, believed in reincarnation and in Gandhi's methods of de-escalation of tension – said:

'Stop fighting, darlings.'

And as if by magic, the fight stopped, replaced by monologues about who loved her teacher more. Eventually, slowed down by your endless yawns, the competition lost its intensity. Still murmuring the three-doll act, you put your head in my lap and drifted to sleep. But there is another part to this story, something you wouldn't remember, even if you'd been awake. Your father took out a report and began to read. I was still caressing your forehead and watching him reading when he raised his head from the report and looked at me absentmindedly. Frowning from intense concentration. It was the second time I'd noticed it. Remember that look? That gaze which would return every now and then?

'Peter!' I called to him, 'Peter, is something the matter?'

He did not answer. His work, I thought, and I thought so, so many times over the years. I did not know that even while we were in the same room, he saw people I did not, he heard conversations I was deaf to. I kept being part of his world as well as I could, a world which turned out to have different rules, a world which sneaked up on me gradually, imperceptibly. A world which eventually violated my sense of reality. I did not understand what was happening to us, not at the time. Not until he turned violent. Then nothing made sense anymore.

Dear Shosh, what happened to our family is not my fault. Sometimes what happens to families is no-one's fault, it is life's fault. But as you well know, that was not the end.

The story of what followed had many players, background players I was not aware of at the time. Players who kept throwing stones into the lake of our life. By the time I understood what was going on, I couldn't see a way out. It was around this time that I was asked to write the Minister's speech. Don't think that I did it willingly. I searched my soul, I agonised, but it is *true I did write it. As soon as I sent it, sorrow and guilt came over me and stayed with me for years. You blamed me for not being strong enough. You were right, someone else might have done things differently, but only with a great deal of help. I was alone. Alone clinging to a rock, trying to hold on, trying with all my might, as the wind blew furiously, the waves rolled towards me, the water pushing, pulling, sloshing over me, and I felt if I let go, I would sink and you, my dear Shosh, you would sink with me. Rightly or wrongly, that's how I felt.*

Shosh I miss you terribly …

The shrill of the phone. It is Jeff. He wants to know if there is any news.

'Only that Shosh dropped out of university, and no-one knows where she is.'

'I was afraid of that. Clara, we have to find her.'

They talk a while longer, then she returns to finish the letter. She will send it as soon as she finds out where Shosh lives.

* * *

With no further news about Shosh, five days later, Clara checks herself out of the hotel and heads to the airport. Just before she boards the plane, she rings Cindy once more.

'Cindy, I'm going home. If you happen to speak to Shosh, tell her that I miss her. That I've thought a great deal about the two of us and I'm sure that we can sort things out.'

'I will, Mrs Steinberg. I will.'

Back in Tasmania she keeps asking herself, 'Is Shosh all right? Did she disappear only to get away from me?'

Jeff has no answers, 'The one thing I can say for sure is that Shosh is not the only young woman in this world who doesn't want contact with her mother. I used to know a girl like that at university.'

Whatever that girl's reasons were, Clara is sure that Shosh's motivations to cut all ties are far, far more complex.

<h1 style="text-align:center">-51-</h1>

The summer has given way to autumn. The days are cooler now. The rays of sun languid, but the sky is a brilliant blue. Tasmania in autumn is especially beautiful.

Tonight, there is a chill in the air, and Jeff has set the fire. Sitting on the sofa, watching the frolicking flames, he is wondering whether Olly's boyfriend could help with some work on the farm, when Clara walks in with a dish of roast chicken and vegetables.

They sit down to eat. This is Shosh's favourite dinner, but to remark on it would be to acknowledge her absence. They have talked about her often enough, speculated where she might be, what she might be doing. It only led them down dead ends.

The fire is crackling and sputtering.

'Clara,' Jeff breaks the silence, 'I'll have to get someone to help out with the repairs on the farm, do you think – Is that the phone?'

It's Cindy. She has news.

'I spoke to Shosh.'

'You did?' Clara asks, barely able to breathe.

'Yes. She's in the UK. She met someone and she's sort of settled there. The two of them are working for some organisation fighting for the rights of the mentally ill.'

'In the UK?'

'Yes. Mrs Steinberg, I told her that you're missing her, that you need to talk to her. She said she does not want contact,' then hesitating, 'She asked me to tell you: "Not now, or ever."'

'Mrs Steinberg, I'm very, very sorry.'

'Cindy, it doesn't matter. The main thing is that she's all right. She has a life and she's found a calling. I always knew that she would surface, that she would do something useful on this Earth.'

'We all thought so. She's outstanding in every way.'

'Cindy, I cannot thank you enough. If you're in Tasmania come and visit us.'

'I will Mrs Steinberg.'

Clara puts the phone down. 'Shosh is all right! Shosh is all right!' her thoughts scream. And suddenly there is nothing more she wishes for. She will learn to live without seeing her, without hearing her laughter. The price of love is the pain of its loss.

Acknowledgements

My thanks to Laurel Cohn and Helen Williams from Laurel Cohn Editing and Manuscript Development Services, for their advice and editing through the entire process of bringing this book to fruition.

My gratitude and heartfelt thanks to Des Berry, whose feedback assured me that this story is an important one and convinced me to persevere.

With our world noisier than it has ever been, the Sydney Customs House library reading room offered me the quiet shelter I needed to think and write.

I thank my husband Alex, who never tired of reading my revisions, for his questions and his advice, for spotting mistakes and inconsistencies and more than anything for encouraging me to keep writing.